BEHIND ENEMY LINES

A SPECIAL OPERATIONS EXECUTIVE MISSION

ANGUS MCLEAN

Published 2021 by Smoking Gun Publications

ISBN 978-0-473-57926-5

MORE TITLES BY ANGUS MCLEAN

Early Warning Series:
Martial Law
Getting Home
Stand Fast

The Division Series:
Smoke and Mirrors
Call to Arms
The Shadow Dancers
The Berlin Conspiracy
No Second Chance

Chase Investigations Series:
Old Friends
Honey Trap
Sleeping Dogs
Tangled Webs
Dirty Deeds
Red Mist
Fallen Angel
Holy Orders
Deal Breaker

The Service Series:
The Service: Warlock

Nicki Cooper Mystery Series:
The Country Club Caper

BEHIND ENEMY LINES

BY ANGUS MCLEAN

1

Tuesday morning

The ceiling fan did little more than shift the hot air around. Even first thing in the morning, Jensen's clothing stuck to him. He wiped a handkerchief across his brow and took a sip of iced tea.

Winter was almost done but still it was horribly sticky. Cairo was a stinking hole of a place at the best of times, full of beggars and tramps and sly locals who'd steal your wallet with one hand but knife you with the other.

Not to mention it was a hotbed of spies and traitors on both sides, everyone out to see what everyone else was up to. He loved it and loathed it in equal measure. On paper, Jensen was a Captain in the Royal Navy. Any image of a seafaring man couldn't have been further from the truth.

The office itself was barren, a hodge-podge of standard hotel furniture in bland colours and military-issue filing cabinets, dominated by the wide oak desk Jensen used. It was arranged so that his back was always to the wall, and rumour was that he had a long-barrelled Colt Navy concealed under the desk for any unwanted visitors. On the wall behind the desk was pinned a massive map of the Middle East, smaller ones around it showing Europe and its various constituent countries.

He replaced the glass of iced tea on the side table and crossed his legs. At least the threadbare pastel armchair was comfortable. The man in the matching chair opposite him waited patiently. He wore sharply pressed khakis and the pips of a subaltern. He had a soft chin and sandy curls that bounced when he moved his head.

'So where are they, then?' Jensen eventually asked.

Lieutenant Littlewood took a breath, let it out carefully, and looked his superior in the eye. 'They're in prison, sir.'

Jensen's thick eyebrows shot up his lined forehead. 'Pardon me?'

'They were both arrested for brawling last night, sir.' Littlewood cleared his throat delicately. 'In The Crooked Cat, sir.'

Jensen's eyebrows dropped back into place and he licked his lips. His eyes narrowed. 'I hope you're not having me on, Bert. This is not the time for schoolboy gags.'

Littlewood gave a firm shake of the head. 'Absolutely not, sir. It seems there was a brawl between a few of our lads, a bit of Army-Air Force banter got out of hand, you might say. These two happened to be there and got themselves involved, the Redcaps were called and these two were the only ones unlucky enough to get arrested.'

Jensen inhaled slowly through his nose, his lips tight. 'And what sort of condition are they in this morning?'

'A little the worse for wear from the drink, I'd suggest. Not too bad otherwise. Apparently the Kiwi did knock out one of the MPs, so he was dealt with a little more...err, robustly.' Littlewood allowed himself a twitch of a smile. 'I doubt it did him any harm though, sir. Tough sods, those New Zealanders.'

'No, I doubt it did either.' Jensen rubbed a hand across his sticky face, pressing his fingers into his eye sockets. He could feel a headache coming on. 'Good Lord, Bert, I'm of a good mind to send the bloody fools back where they came from.' He shook his head in frustration. 'Too bloody late though, isn't it?'

'We need them in the air in two days' time, sir.' Littlewood waited again, watching his boss work through it. He knew the plan and he knew the immense pressure it brought. Operations like this were usually weeks, if not months, in the making. This one was a fastball from London, and had been thrown together within a week.

Two specific men were needed – or rather, one specific man and one specific *type* of man. Getting his hands on those two had been surprisingly easy. It was the rest that had turned to hell in a handbag in a single evening in a sleazy Cairo bar.

'They're waiting downstairs, sir,' Littlewood said. 'Shall I have them brought up?'

Jensen gave a curt nod. He grabbed the cane that was leaning against his chair and used it to get to his feet. It was a heavy, thick piece of hickory with a solid handle, sturdy enough to support his full weight. 'Yes, bring them up. Let's get on with it.' He caught Littlewood's eye and gave a wry smile. 'At least we know they're fighters.'

'Very good, sir.' Littlewood opened the door and spoke to his man in the corridor outside. While he waited there, one of the local staff hurried down the hallway to him.

'Colonel-sir, you like tea? Coffee?' Ahmed was a small man with a pointy beard and an eager-to-please smile. To him everyone was a Colonel, and Littlewood always took the time to have a chat when he could.

This time he shook his head, wary of letting outsiders into the office at such a time. 'Thank you Ahmed, maybe later.'

'No problem, Colonel-sir.' Ahmed bowed and backed away. 'Just call me, Colonel-sir.'

Five minutes later the two men stepped through the door into the office.

One was tall and lean with a neatly trimmed moustache, blonde like the hair that fell rakishly across his smooth forehead. He wore the crisp uniform of a Flight Lieutenant in the RAF, although Jensen noted the ripped pocket and a stain that may have been blood upon one sleeve. He strode into the office and snapped to attention in front of the desk Jensen now sat behind.

The other man was almost the complete opposite. Shorter and stockier, he had dark hair and dark eyes in a sunburned, unshaven face. His battledress bore a Sergeant's stripes but no other insignia aside from parachute wings on the right shoulder. The sand coloured beret he wore had the distinct flaming Excalibur badge of the Special Air Service.

The second man brought himself to attention and stared at the wall above Jensen's head. His knuckles were scraped and he had noticeable swelling around his face.

Jensen stood slowly and eyed them. Littlewood closed the door and waited. This was the boss' show. The wait dragged on as Jensen eyed the two men. Neither man moved, although he had the distinct impression the pilot was gagging to speak.

'Do you know who I am?' Jensen said quietly.

'No, sir.' Not surprisingly, it was the pilot who spoke, his cultured tones clipped and nervous. 'Sorry, sir.'

'No apology needed, Flight Lieutenant Balfour-Napier,' Jensen said. He glanced to the soldier. 'And you, Sergeant?'

'Not a clue,' the man said, before adding a belated, 'Sir.'

'Do you know why you're here?'

The pilot shook his head. 'No, sir.'

The soldier's dark eyes shifted from the wall to meet Jensen's gaze. 'If it's about last night, sir, I've got nothing to say.'

Jensen almost smiled. The man had the strong accent often found Down Under, which Jensen had always found rather pleasant despite the roughnecks it usually came from.

'I don't expect you would, Sergeant Hastings.' He took his seat and waved them down. 'Sit, gentlemen.' He cocked an eyebrow as they took the chairs opposite him. 'Although, given your behaviour last night, I use that term loosely.'

As soon as they sat, the pilot spoke again.

'If it's all the same, sir,' he said, 'Napier is fine with me. Just Napier.'

Jensen gave the briefest of nods. 'Certainly,' he said.

Sergeant Jack Hastings

Hastings ran an appraising eye over the man before him. Cream suit, knotted tie despite the heat, weathered complexion but soft hands. Interesting.

The fly boy beside him was a different story altogether. A poncey git with a double-barrelled name and girly eyes. Fat lot of use he'd been to his aircrew mates in the scrap last night; he'd stayed right out of it. Only got arrested because he'd given one of the MPs a bit of lip for roughing up another RAF tosser. It hadn't even been Hastings' scrap; just having a couple of quiet brews while he stewed on an earlier run-in and waited to get his next set of orders when it all kicked off. He couldn't stand by and miss the opportunity to give the RAF lads some, not when the army boys were into it.

The Redcaps had turned up, truncheons swinging, and one of the lads had gone down with a brutal crack across the head. Hastings had dropped the MP that did it, knocked him out cold, but he'd copped it worse from the other rozzers. It'd been worth it, though, even if he had spent the night in the klink.

The first set of orders had dragged him off operations to Cairo, supposedly to uplift some kit for the blokes. He'd been surprised to be called in to see one of the 20th Battalion commanders, his original unit, who told him he was required at a ceremony the next day. There was a Military Medal with his name on it for actions on Crete. That conversation hadn't gone well when Hastings refused, and he'd been given a night to think about it.

Then he was supposed to meet some Captain in the Joint Technical Board, whatever the hell that was.

The Colonel had been most insistent that he do it, so here he was.

2

Jensen caught Hastings sizing him up.

'I'm Captain Jensen,' he said. 'I'm who you're here to see. What is said in this room is completely confidential. Top Secret. Is that understood?' He looked from one to the other until both had nodded. 'If that confidentiality is breached, lives will be lost. Not least of all your own.'

Something about his manner told the two men he was deadly serious. Both wisely stayed quiet.

'You have been assigned to me for a short-notice, short-term operation of the utmost importance,' Jensen continued. 'Operation Fusilier has already commenced, and you are here for the sharp end of it. Have either of you heard the name before?'

'No sir,' they both said.

'Well, that's something.' Jensen's eyes glittered. 'Thursday night, gentlemen, two days from now. You will be parachuting behind enemy lines, just the two of you.'

Hastings raised an eyebrow. 'So we're going behind enemy lines, then?'

'About as far behind them as it's possible to go,' Jensen said.

The Kiwi gave a slow nod but said nothing. Napier opened his mouth to speak but Jensen cut him off.

'Never jumped operationally before? I know.' Jensen tossed his chin at Hastings. 'He has; that's why he's here. You have other uses, Napier.'

'Very good, sir,' Napier murmured.

'Your mission is to infiltrate a German stronghold, and locate and recover a stolen prototype plane. You will bring it back to England in one piece. Got it?'

Napier's cheeks glowed pink with excited curiosity. 'Yes, sir.'

'I thought you'd like the sound of that, Mr Napier.' Jensen wasn't smiling. 'And if you can't get it out of there, you are to destroy it.'

Napier gave a slight nod, and Jensen could see the cogs turning in his head.

'The plane we are talking about is the latest de Havilland Mosquito. We know that the Luftwaffe are desperate to get their hands on anything that will give them some advantage in the air. Right now, and for the last several months, we've had it all over them up there.'

'Very kind, sir,' Napier said with a self-deprecating smile.

'There's a new model of the Mosquito, the XJ2. It's made a great machine even better.'

Jensen noticed Napier nodding his agreement.

'Faster and larger than the Spitfire, two-man crew, it's more agile than anything else we've got. Fairly standard armament, but it's biggest plus is just how easy it is to both fly and manufacture. The RAF boffins reckon it'll reduce training times and get more planes in the air faster. For that alone it's a major asset to our air force. It's a crucial factor in our air superiority. If we lose the air war, we've lost the lot.'

He paused and shifted his gaze between the two men. Hastings was giving nothing away, but Jensen knew what he would be thinking.

'You have a thought on that, Sergeant Hastings?'

The dark eyes met his and Jensen saw the hint of a curl to the man's lip.

'It seems an awful lot of effort for just one plane, sir,' he said.

Jensen shrugged. 'It does seem that way, doesn't it? But it's a bloody great machine, better than anything the Jerries have got. If they can replicate it, well, we've lost an advantage haven't we?'

'Surely they kept the plans though, sir?' Napier sounded dubious now. 'Can't they just build more of them?'

Jensen gave him a withering glare and Napier visibly wilted. 'Of course they kept the plans, Mr Napier. These boffins aren't entirely stupid, fortunately.'

'Very good, sir.' Napier shifted uncomfortably and mentally kicked himself for thinking out loud.

'But we have spent months developing the new prototype. If the Germans replicate it, then they're not months behind, they're right on our jacksie, so to speak.' He let out a slow sigh and clasped his hands together, looking carefully from one man to the other.

'The other part of the problem is, the plane was stolen by one of our own. A traitor.' He paused and took a sip of tepid iced tea. 'We cannot allow that to happen. If we let the Germans get away with that once, we invite them to do it again. Understand?'

'Sir.' Hastings' face betrayed his thoughts on traitors.

'The chances of you making it in are slim. The chances of making it out alive...' Jensen hiked his shoulders. 'Almost zero.'

Napier opened his mouth to speak then thought better of it and shut up again.

'But the consequence of not at least trying, is to condemn any number of our men and women to certain death.' Jensen steepled his fingers and looked each of them in the eye. 'That's the hard truth of it, gentlemen.'

He let that sit for a few moments.

'You'll notice I said men and *women*. Not just soldiers or sailors or airmen. Agents. *Spies*. This is about more than a stolen fighter-bomber, although that's bad enough in itself. As of this moment, you two men are seconded to the Special Operations Executive. Heard of it before?'

Napier nodded. He'd spent time recently with the military intelligence bods after his escape; of course he had. Hastings gave a slight nod.

'Mr Churchill calls us the Department of Ungentlemanly Warfare,' Jensen told them. 'Others call us The Circus. I don't give a damn what they call us; I just want the job done, and you're the men to do it.'

'Sir, just one question, if I may?' It was Napier, his tentative tones undercut by the upper-class confidence he carried.

Jensen raised an eyebrow, said nothing. The young man – God, they were both so young, barely in their early twenties – cleared his throat before speaking.

'The plan you mentioned just now...errr...' He seemed to struggle to put his thoughts into words, and shifted uncomfortably in his chair. He turned and looked at Hastings for a long moment, as if hoping the Kiwi might jump in and save him. When that didn't happen, the pilot turned back to Jensen, who was still waiting.

At the door, Littlewood rolled his eyes to himself and sighed loudly. Napier glanced in his direction then back to Jensen again, tapping his lips with one thoughtful finger.

'The plan, sir...ahhh, how exactly....ahhh...'

'Spit it out, boy.' Jensen's tone was terse, and Napier nodded, getting the message.

Flight-Lieutenant Frederick Balfour-Napier

'How exactly do we do that, sir?' he blurted. 'I mean, two men, behind enemy lines...an enemy stronghold...err, it all sounds rather, err...you know...if you know what I mean, sir...'

He finished lamely and his cheeks flushed as he sat back again. The room was silent for a moment. Littlewood may have smiled.

'All sounds a little insane, doesn't it?' Jensen said. His eyes twinkled mischievously. 'That's because it is, Mr Napier. It is bloody insane.' His face darkened, all sign of merriment gone. 'But it's also bloody important, and there are no ifs, buts or maybes about it. It needs to be done, and you two are the lucky ones chosen to do it.'

Napier had regained some composure and decided to press on. It felt like he was being railroaded into something he had absolutely no desire to do at all, so it was now or never.

'And why is that, sir?' He glanced at the silent Hastings again, getting nothing but a blank stare back. Fat lot of help he was. 'Why us?'

Jensen plucked a Woodbine from a packet and lit it, pushing the pack across the desk. Both men took one and shared a match. Jensen took a long draw and blew a perfect smoke ring towards the ceiling.

'Frederick Balfour-Napier,' he said. 'First class fighter pilot, involved in the Battle of Britain, awarded the Distinguished Flying Cross. Six confirmed kills to your name. You recently trained on the Mosquito with a view to moving to changing squadrons.'

Napier sat and listened, his brow still furrowed. He knew all this, and it didn't answer his question. He smoked with the casual arrogance of someone who was bored, although he was far from it. The talk of a traitor had him interested, but the rest of it was complete madness.

'You speak excellent German, having spent holidays abroad and attended boarding school in Switzerland. You are also an accomplished skier and enjoy mountaineering, at least in a civilian setting.'

Napier noticed that Hastings raised an eyebrow in surprise, and smiled inwardly as the Captain turned his attention to the soldier.

'Jack Hastings,' Jensen said. 'An original member of L Detachment, Special Air Service. Volunteered for it, no less. Previously with 20 Battalion in Crete. Expert with vehicles of all sorts. Parachute trained, expert with explosives and all manner of weaponry.'

Napier looked at his companion with a new curiosity. It explained a lot. Hastings looked back at him coolly. Jensen indicated Hastings with his cigarette, ash drooping from the tip.

'He'll get you two in there,' he told Napier, 'and you'll get you both out.'

'I see, sir.' Napier sat back and crossed his legs at the knee. 'Very good, sir.' He nodded as if he got it, which he wasn't sure he did, and took a drag on his cigarette. He glanced to Hastings again. 'So you're the heavy, then?'

Hastings gave a cold grin that exposed white teeth against his tanned face.

'Guess so,' he said laconically. 'I like to kill fuckin' Germans.'

Captain Jensen

Jensen chuckled to himself. 'That's about the size of it,' he said. 'Now, any further questions?'

There were none, so he gestured Littlewood forward. 'Lieutenant Littlewood will run through some administrative matters with you first, then I'll give you the full briefing.'

He pushed himself up on his cane and came around the desk. 'Where's that little man with the coffee, Littlewood?'

'Oh, I can...'

Jensen waved him off. 'No no, I'll do it. You sort these two out.'

He lumbered to the door and opened it, almost bumping into Ahmed, who was there with a tray of refreshments. Jensen caught his balance on the cane, his gammy left leg almost giving out on him.

'Ah, there you are. Just pop that on the table, will you?'

Ahmed bowed and carried the tray into the office, carefully placing it on the low table by the armchairs.

'There you go, Colonel-sir. I have brought you the finest coffee, the one you like, and there is sugar there and milk for you.' He grinned broadly, clasping his hands to his chest. 'Also the iced tea, Colonel-sir – I know how hot you feel it, sir.'

Jensen grunted. 'Well you have that right. Thank you, leave that with us.'

'Thank you, Colonel-sir.' Ahmed bowed to Jensen then turned and bowed to the other three men as he backed up to the door. 'Thank you, sirs, thank you.'

Jensen closed the door behind him and helped himself to an iced tea. Too blasted hot for a coffee just now. He sipped the sweet drink, noting how the ice had melted already. The locals were a pain in the behind, but they did cater well.

3

Clutching the blankets up around her neck, Carla lay in the grey morning light and watched condensation trickle down the window.

The blackout curtain was too short for the window, allowing a crack of light to creep in like a ghoul's hand every morning. Not even the steady draught around the rickety frame was enough to keep the window dry.

The dormitory assigned to the Imperial Hotel's domestic staff was a house commandeered for the purpose, three rooms that each housed three basic cot beds and three small dressers made by nailing together packing crates.

There was little privacy, but the girls did the best they could. Carla had been lucky enough to be put in with Trudy and Martha, both of whom worked in the kitchen. They were cousins and were not only good at cards – many games had been played by candlelight late into the night – but they were occasionally able to smuggle back food left over after one of the officers' banquets.

Carla never entered into political talk with them, but neither of the girls was a vocal supporter of the Third Reich. She suspected that, like her, they were just doing what they needed to do to get through.

As usual the cousins were up before dawn to prepare breakfast for the men. Before opening the door, Trudy gave Carla a gentle shake of the shoulder.

'Wake up, sleepyhead,' she whispered. 'Time to get up.'

Carla was awake but feigned stirring, which wasn't hard considering she felt like death. The bedframe squeaked as she rolled over on the lumpy mattress and looked blearily up at her roommate.

'Thanks,' Carla muttered, and Trudy smiled.

'Don't be late and make your friend even grumpier,' Martha added, peering past her cousin's shoulder with a mischievous grin.

'Huh.' Carla grunted.

'She already has a face like a dropped meat pie,' Martha continued, bringing chuckles from both the girls. 'Don't make it worse.'

Carla pushed herself up to a sitting position, pulling the thin blankets around her. She rubbed her eyes and yawned. The girls had lit a lamp to give the small room a warm yellow glow.

'See if you can save me an egg, would you?' she asked, and Trudy gave her a mock pout.

'What are we, your personal chefs?'

Carla yawned again. 'Yes, exactly.'

Martha yanked the covers off her and laughed. 'Maybe,' she said. 'Come on, cousin, we need to get a move on.'

Carla threw her a good-natured curse as she scrabbled to get the covers back, but the girls were gone and the door closed. She heard them clattering down the stairs then the front door banged, no doubt waking up the girls in the other rooms. It was the same every morning.

She threw the covers back and put her feet on the cold wooden floor, shivering as she got up. There was no heating in the rooms and her breath misted when she exhaled. It was always a race to get dressed as quickly as possible. Carla saw that the girls had left a large bowl of hot water for her as they usually did, bless them. She raced through a wash as fast as she could, breaking records as she then dressed in her maid's uniform.

As she buttoned her warm coat and reached for the hair brush, she wondered if today would be the day. The day something happened.

She could only hope.

4

While Littlewood ran through a basic admin briefing with the two men, Ahmed made his way downstairs to the ground floor of the Paradise Hotel. The whole hotel had been commandeered by the British but a number of local staff had been retained as cooks and cleaners.

Ahmed was a junior manager, a position he valued highly as it not only paid well and carried some social standing, but it also gave him full access around the hotel. Ahmed had never worked in the hospitality industry before the war – back then he'd been a con man, a thief. The war had brought many wonderful things for him. A new name, new identity, a new job.

And the opportunity to make even more money on the side.

He had laid eyes on all four men in the office upstairs, and had them committed to memory. The brusque Captain Jensen, who was clearly the boss, and his wet-behind-the-ears subaltern, Lieutenant Littlewood. That one liked to chat, liked it far too much for his own good – almost as much as he liked the girls Ahmed found for him. Ahmed took it all in, sorting out the useful from the nonsense.

He knew a lot of people in this city, on both sides of the line, people that were more than happy to pay for any tid-bits of information they could glean.

Ahmed had never seen the other two men before, but the fact they were there at all was interesting. Jensen was an important man, which meant they must be important too. A soldier and an airman together; now that was something.

Ahmed skirted past the kitchen to the rear entrance of the hotel. Letting himself out into the back alley, Ahmed made a beeline for a man he knew.

A man who would be very interested indeed in his news.

———

'It's a very small town, a village really,' Jensen said. 'A place called Alpenbad.'

'Alpine bath,' Napier noted. 'A spa town?'

Jensen nodded. 'Right in the heart of Bavaria, near Alpspitze.'

Napier nodded, having a reasonable idea where it would be. He'd been to Bavaria before as a child.

'Well behind enemy lines, sir,' he said.

'Yes, and that's the point. In this little spa town is a hotel being used as a debriefing centre by the Nazis.' He paused for a second. 'Not just the Germans,' he said, *'Nazis*. Hitler himself has been there recently, as have many of his top echelon. Right now they have a very special guest, and they're about to get another.'

Hastings nodded silently, all ears. He saw no point in interrupting, but Napier couldn't help himself.

'Who is it, sir? Who is this wretched traitor?'

Jensen looked across the desk at him, a shrewd look in his eye. 'This is another reason why you're involved, Mr Napier,' he said. 'You happen to know the man.'

Napier frowned, thinking hard but coming up empty.

'A Pole you flew with in the Battle of Britain, a renowned Squadron Leader.' Jensen saw the realisation dawning, and looked the younger man in the eye. 'Karol Jankowski.'

'You can't be serious, sir...'

'I'm deadly serious,' Jensen said firmly. 'Two days ago he stole the prototype Mosquito from an airbase in Norfolk and flew direct to Alpenbad.'

'How do you know where it went, sir?' Hastings enquired. 'Did you have a tracker of some sort on it?'

'We did actually,' Jensen said, 'although he was smart enough to disable it before taking off. We have a source, though, someone working for us in Alpenbad itself. An agent, codenamed White Rabbit. We knew from this source that something was about to happen, but we didn't know exactly what. As a precaution, we placed tracking devices on various projects being worked on, including the new Mosquito.' He pursed his lips, his eyes glinting. 'Unfortunately we couldn't stop him. He killed a sentry and stole the plane, flew straight to his masters in Alpenbad.'

There was an edge of bitterness in Jensen's voice as he spat out the last few words.

Hastings sucked in a slow breath, his heart thumping in his chest. So this was it. They'd been given the what, and now they had the why behind it. His fists clenched involuntarily and he caught Jensen's eye. He scowled.

'The dirty bastard,' he grated. 'Wait until I get my hands on him; I'll break his bloody neck.'

'No.' Napier shook his head, anguish rolling over him like a surprise storm cloud. 'No!'

He burst to his feet, the chair scraping hard on the floor as he shoved it away. The room was silent aside from his breathing and the pacing of his polished shoes on the floor.

The Captain regarded Hastings first, his gaze boring into his skull, before turning back to the pilot.

Hastings looked at him too. The handsome face was visibly distressed, but at least he wasn't crying. Hastings didn't like a crying man, so he had to give him that.

'The intelligence we have is A-grade,' Jensen said. 'Karol Jankowski is being debriefed by the SS, and has been interrogated at length already. We suspect that is what is behind a number of other attacks. He was a Squadron Leader; he knew a lot. But worst of all…' Jensen waited until Napier stopped pacing and looked at him. 'Jankowski is politically connected in Poland. Most of his family is involved in local or national politics there, as well as in business. Not only that, but he was attached to Intelligence before he went rogue.'

'Oh God,' Napier muttered. He straightened his chair and flopped into it again. This was all news to him, and he could see why the Nazis would be glad to have such a man.

'Several members of his family have now been killed or captured, as well as a number of other people of influence in Poland. Added to that, we know for a fact that the top SS interrogator is coming to see him. A Major Heinrich Wolf.' Jensen's lip curled as if the very name gave him a foul taste. 'He is a stone-cold psychopath, brilliant at what he does.'

Hastings listened in silence. He understood Napier's shock, but he figured that was the difference between them. While Napier had been buzzing around the skies playing at war, he'd been down in the trenches getting his hands dirty. He'd seen up close the brutality of the Germans.

They were murdering bastards and that was that.

———

Napier felt his head spinning and he forced himself to take a breath. It was incomprehensible that a colleague, a brother-in-arms, could commit such an act. A traitor, a man he'd spent time with. The bloody bastard.

He took another breath and let it out slowly. By God this changed things for him, right here and now. He became aware of the eyes on him and checked himself. The briefing wasn't over yet.

Hastings finally spoke. 'Sounds like this Major Wolf needs a bullet in the head, sir.'

Jensen looked at him and nodded abruptly. 'Exactly. If he's there, he's not to walk away.'

'And Jankowski, sir?' Napier's lips were tight and a nerve twitched in his cheek. 'We get him out? Bring him back for interrogation?'

Jensen nodded again. 'That's right. That's the plan. But gentlemen, I don't need to tell you that operations don't always go according to plan.'

'So if things go south?' It was Hastings again, his laconic twang so distinctive. Jensen noticed the absence of a "sir" in his question, and brushed it aside.

'That's what you're there for, Sergeant,' he said coldly. 'You kill him.'

Napier physically flinched. He opened his mouth to speak but Jensen cut him off with a warning finger.

'You make sure he can't give up any more names. We're in serious trouble in Europe right now, and the last thing we need is any more of our secret allies being taken to the stake. The war is hanging in the balance. Do you understand?'

Hastings nodded curtly, as Jensen had known he would. The man was a ruthless killer himself, ideal for such a task.

'Mr Napier?'

Napier had been staring at the floor, dumbstruck by the events of the last few minutes. Eventually he raised his head and looked at the Captain. He bobbed his head slowly.

'Yes sir.'

'Right.' Jensen sat back in his chair and gave Littlewood a glance. 'That's enough for now. Go and get yourselves cleaned up, have something to eat. You'll be back here after lunch so we can iron out some last details.'

The two men stood and crossed the floor. Jensen stopped them before Littlewood opened the door.

'Gentlemen,' he said. They stopped and turned. 'Make no mistake, gentlemen. This is a very dirty business. But it needs to be done, and I make no apologies for that.'

Littlewood opened the door and ushered them out. Jensen watched them go. He had never been a great believer in any deity, but he hoped to God this operation went as planned. Europe was awash with German soldiers and the threat to cross the Channel was imminent. At such a crucial juncture in the war, they couldn't afford to have their legs taken out by their own.

He reached for his cigarettes and shook one loose. He sparked it and sat back, blowing a neat smoke ring that shimmied towards the ceiling. Jensen watched it without seeing. He was sending two young men to rescue or kill one of their own, and the weight of the decision sat heavily on his shoulders.

He'd been right, Jensen reflected as he took another drag. It was a very dirty business indeed.

5

T he Imperial Hotel was the centrepiece of Alpenbad.

An imposing building in the centre of the town with wide pillars to the roof and a low set of steps from the roadside to the entranceway, its dark Gothic style reflected the lives of those it was home to.

Once a health resort revered by the wealthy and envied by the working class, it was now home to a detachment of SS soldiers and intelligence agents. High level meetings were held there, and top brass from all arms of the military and security service were sent there to rest and recuperate. Not only that, but interrogations were often carried out there too. Suspected spies, troublemakers, dissidents of any sort.

Men with black souls and venom in their veins came and went, and murderous deeds were plotted and executed.

As she scrubbed the tiled floor on her hands and knees, one thought was uppermost in Carla's mind – men always thought it was longer. No matter how often she cleaned the toilets, no matter how sparkling she would leave them, she knew with utmost certainty that they would be filthy again the next day. How they managed to piss on the floor, the wall and the seat, she did not know. But they did. Sometimes they hadn't flushed, no matter what they'd done in there.

It was one more reason to hate them.

She paused and sat back on her feet, taking a breath. The smell of bleach and hot water overrode the stench they had left, and she was almost done. She was due for a break after the toilets, but that meant spending time with Magda. She would rather work through. Or stick needles in her eyes.

The door behind her opened and heeled boots clacked on the tiles. She heard them stop behind the stall she was in, a grunt, then they moved to the next stall. The rustle of clothing followed by the splash of a stream into the bowl and a sigh of contentment.

Carla leaned forward again to finish around the side of the toilet, her head low enough to see the shiny black boots in the next cubicle. The flow eased and she saw a dribble hit the floor between the polished boots and the bowl.

It's never as long as you think it is, she thought to herself, and it made her smile. Just another Nazi who overrated himself.

He moved away and she heard the water run in the wash basin. She finished around the side of the toilet and got to her feet. She turned to find the SS man standing at the door, watching her. Not smiling, just watching, a predator's eyes running over her as she emerged from the cubicle. Even in her maid's uniform it was impossible to hide her slim figure. Nineteen years old and with pretty green eyes and wavy, dark hair, Carla did well to avoid most of the wandering hands at the hotel.

But there were times it was impossible, and she had the feeling this was going to be one of those times. She didn't know this man's name, but had seen him before. He was a type, the standard issue SS man – hard, arrogant, brutal. Some of the girls got a hard time from them, and she knew of a few who had been raped by these men.

Pausing there with the bucket of dirty water in her hand, Carla assessed the situation in a split second. The SS man had his foot against the door, blocking the only exit. She was alone. He had a pistol on his hip, but it was his hands that concerned her more. She knew what these men could do – *liked* to do – with their hands.

She could scream for help, but that would also carry consequences. Speaking out against these men did no one any good, and she needed the job – she needed to be in this hotel.

Things were not looking good right now.

The SS man leaned his shoulder against the door and ran his eyes over her again. Carla took a breath and forced herself to relax. Perhaps she could talk her way out.

She had opened her mouth to speak when there was a thud at the door and the SS man was jarred aside. A burly soldier pushed in, surprised to see another man in the way, but in too much of a rush to care. He muttered something and hurried to a cubicle, fumbling with his pants as he did so. The cubicle door banged shut and he crash landed on the seat, unleashing hell on the clean bowl a second later.

The SS man's lip curled with distaste and he opened the door, giving Carla a last look before disappearing. Carla took a deep breath and thanked her lucky stars. Despite the grunting from the cubicle and the stench wafting out, she would happily clean that man's toilet all day.

Carla finished up as fast as she could before heading back to the maid's cleaning cupboard, emptying her bucket of dirty water down the drain and washing her hands thoroughly.

The near-miss with the SS man had wound her tight again, as it did every time such a thing happened. It seemed to be every day these things happened.

She didn't know if it was happening more or if she was just more aware of it, but the whole place seemed to be just a cesspit of evilness, predators and leches at every turn. Wiping her hands on a towel, Carla forced herself to suck down a breath and get herself together.

There was no point in worrying about what didn't happen. There was enough to worry about already. The Nazis had something afoot, something big. The Polish pilot was there, and Major Wolf had arrived overnight. She had heard the whispers about the stolen plane

– the Nazis boasted about it openly, the younger ones at least. So cocksure they couldn't keep their mouths shut.

Carla had diligently fed that back to London, and she had no doubt the English would hatch some kind of plot. What could they do though, this far into Germany itself?

Carla hung the towel back on its hook and gave a sigh. There was no time for wondering what might be; she still had work to do.

6

Napier stared at himself in the mirror as he shaved.

The usually clear blue eyes were ruptured by red cracks and his skin was drawn. He wasn't surprised – the last few months had been damned hard. It had taken a toll on him that he wasn't sure he'd ever recover from.

Had to make it through the war first, and now there was this insane mission he'd been thrown into. He understood why he was involved, he just didn't understand how Captain Jensen thought they had a hope in hell of pulling it off. Sure, he spoke German and was competent enough in a Mossie, but getting their hands on the damn thing was the challenge.

Jumping deep into a country chocka-block with slathering Nazis who wanted to rule the world, urged on by a dwarf with a ridiculous moustache and only one nut? It was madness, pure madness.

Mind you, from what he'd seen and heard of him so far, his companion seemed to relish jobs like this.

The SAS were mavericks in every sense of the word, and ruthlessly efficient warriors who struck deep behind enemy lines like it was a cakewalk. The new unit was no place for a dandy. On top of that the man was a Kiwi, and they were all mad anyway. A bit like the

Celts, Napier mused as he washed the traces of soap from his face. They were all mad too, even the ones his Pa employed on the family estate.

Napier cupped cold water into his hands and washed his face, pausing to let the coolness soak into his eyes. He dried his face on a gritty towel and checked the mirror again. Slightly better. No chance of getting a girl if he didn't sort himself out. Mind you, he thought, not much point getting a girl if he wasn't going to be coming back.

He'd had a quick fling a month back, when he was in London for a few days. A cute little WAAF – Women's Auxiliary Air Force – with bouncing curls and a bouncing bosom to boot. He chuckled at the memory. She'd been a real little firecracker.

Maybe after all this was done and dusted he'd get down to Kent and catch up with Dickie Bird and the lads from 41 Squadron. He'd been with them for some time in mid '40, when it was all go on the coast, and they'd always been up for a lark. It was just what he needed right now.

He wiped the sink down before wrapping the towel around his waist and opening the door.

————

Hastings hadn't spent a lot of time in Cairo, and he figured he wasn't going to see much of it this time either.

Not that it bothered him; sightseeing wasn't his purpose in being there. He'd seen the pyramids from a distance, had no interest in going back to see them. He'd spent enough time in the desert to have any great interest in camels or Bedouin or bloody sand. Sand that got everywhere, wrecking engines and clogging up weapons. Shit stuff, it was. Only good if you were lazing on a beach, watching waves roll in and a girl in a swimsuit.

He sighed, his eyes heavily-lidded. He was still fully clothed aside from his boots, which sat on the floor beside him. He had barely moved in the hour or so they'd been in the room.

The bed was too soft but better than a bedroll on the rocky

ground. Following the old military adage of grabbing sleep when you could, he was starting to drift off when Napier finally emerged from the bathroom, a towel wrapped around his lean waist and his skin glowing pink. He swept his wet hair back and ran a comb through it, standing at the foot of twin beds so he could use the mirror on the dressing table.

'Well I don't know about you, old boy, but I'm famished.' The pilot began carefully combing his moustache.

Hastings cracked an eye to squint at him. His colleague – partner? associate? – seemed somewhat better for a long soak in the tub. Hastings had to admit, the news must have been a body blow.

Fly boy or not, he sympathised with Napier. Not that he'd tell him as much. It didn't seem right either, an NCO sharing a billet with an officer, even if he was only RAF. The digs weren't half bad though, so there was that.

'What's on for dinner, d'you think?' Napier said. He finished with the comb and turned, idling scratching himself as he waited for a response.

'Dunno.' Hastings closed his eyes again. 'Something with mutton or goat, I reckon.'

'Hmmm.' Napier scratched himself some more. 'Don't say much, do you?'

'Huh.' Hastings grunted, his eyes still closed. 'Not to a bloke with one hand on his bollocks.'

Napier chuckled and stopped scratching. 'Sorry, old man. Childhood habit. I haven't got crabs, if that's what you were thinking.' He grabbed a shirt from the clothes he'd laid out on the bed, and began dressing himself. 'So what's your story, then? One of these fabled SAS chaps, I see.'

'Yup.'

'Uh-huh.' Napier buttoned his shirt and searched for clean underwear. He stepped into them and pulled them up under his towel, not wanting to offend his new companion any further by appearing naked in front of him. He noticed that Hastings had yet to call him "sir", but he suspected that wouldn't be coming in a hurry.

The soldier was obviously a rugged sort. 'From the looks of that tan you've been in the desert, I take it?'

'That's it.'

Napier dropped his towel and pulled up his trousers. 'Well it's going to be a jolly boring trip if that's all you've got to say.'

Hastings sat up with a slight grin. 'What d'you wanna know, then? I'm twenty-three years old, I'm a farmer from Oamaru – that's in North Otago, in case you didn't know – I signed up as soon as I could and I've been fighting ever since. My hobbies are blowing shit up, killing Jerries and shooting guns. I like cold beer and hot women, I'm a handy rugby player and I can drive and fix most things with an engine. That do ya?'

Napier laughed, his blue eyes sparkling. 'Very good,' he said. 'You're a year older than me. And I do, actually.'

'Do what?'

'Well not really, not Oamaru itself. But I know where North Otago is.'

Hastings looked doubtful.

'I do,' Napier insisted. 'Geography; we learned about New Zealand and Australia. I've a good mind for details, you see. Don't remember Oamaru, though. Sounds a funny little place.'

'It is. Only really went into town for shopping and church though.' Hastings leaned back against the wall and began to deftly roll a cigarette. 'What about you? School in Switzerland, wasn't it?'

'That's right. The last three years, anyhow. For some reason Pa thought I needed toughening up.' He ran the comb through his hair again, checking the look in the mirror. 'Still don't know why he thought that.'

Hastings raised an eyebrow but kept his thoughts to himself. '*Pa* some landed gentry, is he?'

Napier noted the undertone in Hastings' voice. Whether it was sarcasm or jealousy, he wasn't sure, but it was there.

'I guess you could say that. Not a working farmer, mind. Family land.'

'Where?'

'Well, we live in Surrey, near Guildford if you know it.'

Hastings didn't, so stayed silent. Napier put the comb down and fished in a pocket for his cigarettes.

'I finished school and was supposed to go to university. Pa wanted me to study finance.' He pulled a face. 'Doesn't set me alight, I'm afraid. I spent a year chasing girls and doing sod all else, then the war happened.' He moved onto his suitcase, unable to find his cigarettes. 'So I signed up, doing the patriotic thing, and here I am.'

'Here.' Hastings held out a hand-rolled smoke. 'Fill yer boots.'

'Thanks.' Napier took it and accepted a light as well. He studied the cigarette with amusement. 'Bloody clever, I wouldn't know how to do that.'

Hastings gave a smirk. 'Probably never needed to, did you?'

Napier shrugged. 'True.' He smiled then let out a short laugh. 'You know something else? There's a town in New Zealand called Hastings, and right next door is a town called Napier. Did you know that?'

'Yup.'

'A bit odd that we're stuck together then, don't you think?' Napier took a draw on his rollie and nodded appreciatively. 'Not bad at all.'

Hastings grunted. 'I think what it means is that we're the two dumb bastards handpicked for a suicide mission, that's what it means.' He got to his feet. 'Come on, let's go find some grub.'

'You're not going to have a bath first, old man?' Napier flushed when Hastings frowned at him. 'I mean, you know...haven't you just been living in the desert?'

'I have, but I'm hungry,' Hastings said firmly. 'First things first, *old man.*'

He opened the door and was met by a burly MP. The copper glowered at him.

'Where d'you think you're going then, sunshine?'

'Grub.'

'Yer wha'?' The MP glowered harder, and Hastings wondered if he was one who they had tangled with the previous night.

'Food, Corporal,' Napier said over Hastings' shoulder, smiling breezily. 'We're off to get something to eat. Show us the way to the dining room, would you? There's a good man.'

The MP took on the squint of a bulldog chewing a wasp.

'There is no dining room, and you two are not allowed to leave this room.' He ran his eye up and down Napier's smart dress. 'Governor's orders. *Sir.*'

Napier's smile never faltered. 'Not a problem at all, Corporal. Thanks for letting us know. Any chance of having something sent up?'

'Not from me there ain't, no.' The MP shifted his scowl back to Hastings, who was close enough to smell his stale coffee breath. 'My job is to keep you two gents isolated an' secure, nuffing more. A'ight?'

Hastings felt his hackles spring to attention, but Napier moved in smoothly.

'No bother at all, Corporal, you're doing a marvellous job,' he said, edging the door closed. 'Sorry to have troubled you.'

He closed the door and ushered Hastings away from it, shushing him with a finger to his lips.

'That...' Hastings started to say, and Napier grinned.

'Don't worry about that prat,' he said, jerking a thumb at the window. 'There's more than one way to skin a cat, old man.' He paused, and sniffed. 'But first, you need a bath.'

7

Tuesday afternoon

T he man that Ahmed had gone to see had paid him well for the information. Not only was it news to him, but he knew Ahmed to be reliable and credible.

The man had lived in Cairo for a long time, but his origins were lost in the mists of time. Some thought him Spanish, some Moroccan. It mattered not to him; the here and now was what mattered, and he knew he was sitting on a hot potato. The details Ahmed had gathered were sketchy on their own, but built into the bigger picture they filled some significant gaps. This was classic SOE stuff, and the man knew that Captain Jensen was donkey-deep in the outfit.

A quick phone call had been made from the room above his market, and the man who answered had listened intently. It was potentially dangerous to make a phone call, always the chance that the British may have tapped either end, but the man had operating in Cairo so long that he was confident of his cover. The British had no idea who he was. They bought his goods, they chatted, they drank coffee at the same cafes. For heaven's sake, he even screwed the same whores as them.

The man at the other end, the one with the guttural accent, paused after receiving the information. 'Wait there,' he said. 'I will call you with instructions.'

Before the man had a chance to discuss a price the line went dead. He sat and waited, the sounds of the street drifting up through the open window. He looked across the rooftops and waited. All good things came to those who waited, and he was a man of patience. He wondered why the German was calling him back; it wasn't usual. He would normally call with information, agree a price and a dead-drop, and that would be that. He would collect his fee from the drop the same day and carry on working his market.

Not so today. Today was different. He could feel it in his bones, an electric charge that made his fingers tingle. Without knowing the whole picture, he knew he had struck gold. The two strange men and the appointment time made sense to his German contact, who had been unable to keep an edge of excitement from his voice.

The phone jangled and he grabbed it quickly, putting the receiver to his ear but saying nothing.

'I will see you tonight,' the German said abruptly. 'Six o'clock. Same as last time, *ja*?'

The man nodded to himself, his mind racing. This was bigger than he'd thought. The only other time he'd ever met the German face to face, since being recruited, had been to receive a payment in jewels. That had been a special deal, a one-off. Today must really be special.

'Yes,' he said. 'Six o'clock.'

No need to discuss a fee any further. The line went dead.

———

A year of living in Cairo as a white man had taught Klaus Bergmann the life-saving skill of melting into the background.

Unable to conceal his European features in a sea of brown faces, he had instead embraced it. Most people knew him as Claude Berg, the somewhat eccentric middle-aged travel writer and explorer. It easily explained his regular forays around the country, popping up in the most unusual of places, always ready with a smile and a friendly gift, and in the midst of a feature article he planned to sell to Reuters or one of the other big news outfits.

An acrimonious divorce had sent the Swiss freelancer to seek a new life elsewhere and, as a confirmed bachelor, he was always eager for a chat. The occasional raised eyebrow was always placated by a profuse apology for intruding, it's just the way these eccentric types are, you know...

It was the perfect cover for a dedicated fascist and member of the *Abwehr*. Sergeant Bergmann was a skilled intelligence operative and had built a solid network in Cairo, including a number of members of the criminal underworld – they were ideal because they knew everyone and had few scruples when it came to cold hard cash. People like the contact who had just called him.

For a long time now, things had gone well. Intelligence weas gathered in bits and pieces, all fed back to his masters in Berlin. Big pictures were built from such scraps and Bergmann knew that his work contributed to the overall war effort. Cairo was such a melting pot of competing interests that often the same people were playing for several teams and feeding false intelligence to the lowest payer. Playing these games had become an art form for Bergmann and he prided himself on having the upper hand on the Allies.

This business with the SOE troubled him, however. They were still a new outfit but he recognised their expertise, despite having out-manoeuvred them on several occasions. He was aware of the operation to steal the Mosquito fighter and had no issue with such an audacious plan but, if Ahmed was to be believed, it was apparent that the British were planning something even more daring as a counter-attack.

He had no reason to doubt the shifty hotel manager; his information had always been solid gold before.

Sitting in the basement room under a single light bulb, Bergmann drummed his fingers on the desktop and churned over what he knew. Just two men, but specialists. Perhaps they were the leaders and there were more men with them, but he somehow doubted it. It didn't feel right. Ahmed had described these two men in great detail, and Bergman recognised the type. An airman and a soldier, sure, but they were more than that.

Why? It always came down to the why. The obvious answer was that they were going to try and steal back the Mosquito. Bergmann grunted to himself. It would be a hell of a ballsy move to try that. The SOE were known for their cavalier daring – they weren't called The Circus for nothing – but still, it would be madness to try such a thing. The English with their stiff upper lips and pompous attitudes would be loathe to sacrifice even just two men on such a foolhardy mission.

It couldn't be that. Bergmann leaned back in the rickety old chair, hearing it creak under his weight. One day soon it would break, but he had no time to fix it just now. There was too much going on, and that crafty old bastard Captain Jensen was behind it all.

He knew Jensen's file well, and knew he was a formidable opponent. Experienced, hard-nosed and brave. If anybody was to try such an operation it would be Jensen.

Bergmann rocked forward on the chair and stood suddenly. He knew what he had to do.

He made his way up the single flight of narrow steps to the single door. Extinguishing the light, Bergmann stood in the pitch blackness and listened for a full minute. Satisfied, he opened the door towards him and checked at the peep hole in the wall. Peering through the tiny aperture, he could see that the storeroom was empty.

The section of wall swung open on concealed hinges and Bergmann pulled the internal door closed behind him. He eased the "wall" back into place, being careful not to disturb the boxes of cleaning supplies and old newspapers and odds and ends that filled the shelves lining the wall.

After double-checking that the hidden door had clicked back into place, Bergmann let himself out into the bookshop. The dusty shelves were lined from floor to ceiling with books of all sorts, every genre known to man and in many different languages. All part of the cover, it added to the illusion of the eccentric writer and travel enthusiast.

The hidden cellar room made it even safer to conduct his business from here.

Bergmann grabbed his coat and hat from the rack behind the counter and headed for the door. He knew the key to whatever the Allies were planning was Captain Jensen himself.

Sometimes, the quickest way to kill a snake was simply to cut off its head.

Bergmann opened the door and stepped out into the noise and smells of the street. He had a man to see.

8

The room they'd been given was on the second floor of the hotel.

Doors opened out to a small balcony, just large enough to squeeze a couple of chairs onto if they sat shoulder to shoulder.

While Hastings finished dressing, Napier stepped out onto the balcony and wondered if this was such a good plan. He was an officer after all. Certain standards were expected of officers, and rightly so.

Hastings could get away with it, he had no doubt about that. That was the thing with these SAS johnnies – piratical and proud of it. But RAF officers were different. He was already walking a thin line after the dust-up the night before, and it didn't look good on an otherwise perfect record. He was beginning to reconsider his idea when he spotted movement in his peripheral vision.

It was a girl on the next balcony, several feet away. He glanced over. She was sitting on a chair, reading and casually smoking a cigarette. She was a hell of a girl. Flame-red hair and full lips and the blouse of her uniform was filled out very nicely. Very nicely indeed.

He couldn't see any insignia so could only guess her unit. A signaller, perhaps, or an admin girl. It mattered not. She was the best-looking girl he'd seen in months. He was so caught up in his lustful thoughts that he didn't realise she'd turned his way.

'Hello,' she said coolly, taking a lazy drag on her cigarette.

Napier caught himself awkwardly. 'Err, hello.'

'Tell me,' she said. She cocked her head and exhaled smoke over her shoulder, ever so coolly. 'Do you always stare at a girl?'

Napier felt his mouth go dry and he stuttered involuntarily, 'Um... err, well...ahh...'

The girl laughed, a confident and carefree laugh that sent a thrill through his core. By God, she was a beguiling girl alright. He was about to speak when he heard a chuckle behind him.

'She's got your card marked, mate.' It was Hastings, fresh from the bath and smelling much better than he had. Weeks in the desert on hard routine was clearly not good for one's hygiene.

Napier turned and forced a grin, doing his best to cover up his embarrassment. 'She's quite a trick, alright,' he said. 'No time for chit-chat though, let's get a move on, shall we?'

Hastings gave a smirk that told Napier he'd seen right through the bluff, and went to the railing. He looked down at the next balcony below them.

'Easy,' he said. He gave Napier a cocky grin. 'And if you fall, at least you've got wings.'

Napier heard the girl laugh again and steadfastly avoided her gaze. Hastings threw his legs over the railing, lowered himself until he was hanging by his hands from the bottom rung, and swung himself onto the landing below.

Napier carefully climbed over after him, risking a glance down as he did so. People bustled along the street below and the odd car horn honked.

'Is this how you keep yourself amused?' the girl asked, leaning over her own railing to watch.

Napier edged his hands down, praying his sweaty fingers didn't slip. Soaring high in a plane was one thing, but he'd never been good with heights.

'All the time,' he managed, reluctantly letting his feet hang. He dangled there in mid-air like a pendulum that had stopped, and gave his feet a kick. He could feel his grip slipping as his body swung forward, and he let go, hoping like hell he had enough momentum to make it.

Hands grabbed him round the waist and he landed on the balcony, letting out his breath in a whoosh. By God that had been scary. He caught Hastings' grin and straightened up, shaking himself up.

'Thanks, old man,' he huffed. 'But I had it.'

'Of course you did.' Hastings was over the next railing like a climbing monkey, sliding his hands down then dropping to the street below. He looked back up at Napier. 'Come on chap, easy as pie.'

Napier took a breath and climbed over, steadying himself before inching his hands down the railings. At least he didn't have as far to fall now, he figured. He dropped his feet and let his weight hang, licked his lips and dropped. Hastings caught him by the arm to keep him upright.

'Easy as pie,' Napier echoed, straightening his jacket. He looked back up, seeing the girl still watching.

She applauded and he felt himself grin, getting some of his composure back.

'What's your name?' he called out, and she shook her head, her hair bouncing playfully.

'You first.'

'Freddie,' he called back. 'The name's Freddie.'

She laughed that gay laugh, sending another thrill through him.

'Lovely to meet you, Freddie,' she called down. 'I'm jolly pleased you didn't break your neck.'

His cheeks went scarlet but he was on a roll now. 'What's your name?' he persisted.

'Abigail,' she said, giving him a cheeky grin. 'Ti-rah, Freddie.'

And with that she was gone from sight. Napier turned to Hastings, who'd been watching and waiting silently.

'She's a hang of a girl, Jack,' Napier grinned, unable to contain himself.

Hastings gave him a nudge. 'Come on Romeo, I'm hungry.'

There was a café next door to the hotel, with a number of Allied personnel inside. They made their way in and Hastings collared the first waiter he saw.

'We're Lieutenant Littlewood's group,' he said. The waiter looked quizzical. 'He should have a reservation here for us,' Hastings went on.

The waiter checked the reservations book at the door and shook his head. 'No reservation, sir.'

'Littlewood? You're sure? A table for four.'

'Sorry, sir. No reservation.'

'He must've forgotten it, blast him,' Hastings said. He chewed his lip a moment, looking thoughtful. 'He's coming down anyway, should be here any minute. We'll just wait for him, okay?'

'No problem, sir. This way.'

The waiter showed them to a table for four. 'You like a drink?'

Hastings looked to Napier, who shrugged. 'May as well, eh sir? Mr Littlewood'll sort it out when he gets down.'

'Sure,' Napier heard himself saying. 'Two beers thank you.'

The waiter scurried off and Napier chuckled.

'You're a bloody bad influence, Jack. First we escape from our hotel, now we're running up a tab? I don't know what's got into me.'

'Could be dead tomorrow,' Hastings shrugged nonchalantly. 'Today's for living, mate.'

Napier pondered that as he scanned the room for anyone he knew. There were a couple of RAF lads at the bar, but it mostly Army. He turned his attention back to his companion.

'So why exactly did that ruckus kick off last night?' he said. 'I mean, it seemed a bit bloody over the top, don't you think?'

'Huh.' Hastings grunted and started rolling a cigarette. 'That was nothing; you should see a ding-dong between Army and Navy, mate. Ever played services rugby?'

Napier shook his head. 'The odd game at base, but not inter-services, no.'

Hastings shook his head and grinned. He licked the paper to seal the cigarette and tucked it behind his ear so he could start rolling another one.

'The hardest rugby I've ever played,' he said, 'no quarter given and none asked for.' He grinned again, finishing the second cigarette. 'It's brutal – blokes going off with blood noses, covered in sprig marks, broken bones. Bloody brilliant stuff.'

'I see,' Napier mused. It certainly gave him a measure of the man. 'So the ruckus last night then? You Army chaps really seem to have it in for us, don't you?'

Hastings chuckled and sparked a match. He lit a cigarette and took a puff, then handed the second one to Napier, who looked surprised and took it. Hastings held the match for him to light up.

'You ever heard the saying about the stars?'

Napier shook his head.

'The Navy navigates by the stars, the Army sleeps under them, and the Air Force use them to rate their hotels.'

Napier couldn't help laughing. 'Well, I don't know if it's really true but I get your point.' He paused while the waiter delivered two ice cold beers. Napier took one and raised it. 'Well here's to better relations then, eh?'

'Yup.' Hastings clinked his glass and took a long draught, smacking his lips with approval. 'I'm still not gunna call you Sir, though. Just so we're clear.'

'Fine by me, old man,' Napier grinned. 'Freddie's the name, anyway.'

Hastings waved the waiter over. 'Better order some grub before we get sprung, eh?'

'Why not?' Napier raised his glass and took a sip. 'Could be dead tomorrow.'

Hastings cocked a grin and raised his own glass. 'Now you're getting the hang of it, *old man*.'

9
———————

T he alleyway behind the market was narrow and smelled like rotten cabbage and dog crap.

Jensen made his way towards the main road, placing his cane and feet carefully to avoid the rubbish. His head was thumping and he desperately needed a few minutes of fresh air to clear his mind. It was always like this at the final stages of an operational phase. He was five minutes away from the hotel now, nearly time to go back.

Littlewood was rushing about making some last-minute arrangements – weapons, kit, all the bits and bobs that two men would need for a few days of field work. Jensen had allowed himself half an hour to stretch the legs and clear the head. That funny little man, Ahmed, had offered to organise a car for him but Jensen was insistent on walking. He only liked to be driven by his own driver, who had the afternoon off.

He had asked Ahmed to find him a brandy for when he returned – *no problem, Colonel-sir* – and Jensen wondered not for the first time whether his drinking was getting away on him. But a man had to have a release somehow.

When you had men about to launch into action, it was a hefty responsibility. Not that he had any particular affection for the men he sent out there, but he was acutely aware of the part he was playing in their lives.

He was so absorbed in his own thoughts that he nearly missed the man.

Standing in a doorway just ahead, looking towards the main road. Something about his body language was furtive, cagey. Jensen instinctively slowed, his hackles rising. He eased to the side, pressing his shoulder to the wall. He was still maybe twenty feet away from the man, not quite able to make out who it was.

Jensen stayed there, watching as the man melted back into the doorway without looking his way. Who was he and what was he doing? Could just be a street urchin, or a crook looking for an easy target. Well Jensen wasn't that. He slipped a hand under his jacket to the little Beretta .25 tucked inside his waistband. It was a pea-shooter but it would do the job up close. He watched as the man moved about in the doorway, not coming out far enough to properly see what he was doing. Jensen couldn't tell if the man had seen him, and after a minute or so, decided it didn't matter anyway. He gave the pistol a reassuring pat.

Backtracking down the alley would take him longer to get back to the hotel; pressing on forward was the quicker route and besides, his paranoid mind was undoubtedly playing tricks on him.

He pressed on, pushing off the wall and heading towards the top of the alley, another thirty feet or so past the doorway where the man lurked. Jensen felt his senses pinging, the little alarm bell that had kept him alive so long starting to ding clearly in his head.

He kept the cane in his left hand, accentuating his gammy gait for the sake of any onlookers, and carefully edged his right hand under the jacket again. He palmed the Beretta as he neared the doorway, snicking the safety off and keeping wide of the doorway. Only a few feet away now, he could see the man side on, leaning in the doorway with his back to Jensen. Oblivious to his approach. Long coat and a slouchy hat, brown hands that told Jensen he was a local.

Coming up even to the doorway now, Jensen shot a sideways

glance. The man was looking down, ignoring him. The smell of urine and body odour reached Jensen's nostrils and he wrinkled his nose. Disgusting creature.

The alarm in Jensen's head quietened and he was past the man, focussing now on the top of the alley. These hobos were everywhere, and sometimes it was hard to tell them from the real locals. Jensen started to slip the Beretta back into his waistband.

The attack came faster than he could have anticipated, one quick step then the strike. The knife in the hobo's hand was long and wicked and it flashed through the air, slashing at Jensen's neck. If he hadn't heard the footstep and started to turn, the blade would have taken him across the side of the neck. It connected instead with his upper arm, slicing in hard and causing Jensen to stumble to the left.

Not registering the pain yet, he managed to get the Beretta out as he turned, but the man was behind him and he couldn't turn in time to get off a shot. The man booted him hard in the lower back, sending him crashing into the wall, the pistol falling to the ground with a clatter.

Jensen rolled against the wall, turning to face his attacker. He could see him clearly now, a wild-eyed older man, maybe older than Jensen himself, grey showing in his shaggy beard. Jensen's eyes flicked from his attacker's face to the knife he was thrusting forward, aimed straight at Jensen's chest.

He moved again, crabbing sideways along the wall, his gammy leg barely able to hold him. He felt the leg give out and he was going down, the knife missing his chest and instead ramming hard into his right shoulder. Jensen let out a gasp and dropped on his left knee, helpless now.

The man let out a wild, unintelligible shriek and jerked the knife out, cocking his arm for another strike. Jensen looked up at him, knowing there was no way he could escape. The next strike would finish him.

His left hand still gripped the heavy cane and his fingers moved without thought, lifting it parallel to the ground as if to ward off the attacker. He pressed the concealed button under the grip with his forefinger and there was a distinct click from the foot of the cane.

A three-inch blade, wickedly sharp, leaped from the end of the cane, locking into place. The attacker was too focussed on killing Jensen to notice, and he lunged forward again with the knife.

With the strength of a desperate man, Jensen jabbed the cane forward, using the extra length it gave him to get to his attacker before he was stabbed himself.

The rapier rammed into the attacker's gut just below the rib cage and impaled him. His eyes bulged and he stopped where he was, surprised by the sudden attack. He looked down to see blood on his clothing. He dropped the knife and put both hands to the implement in his gut, yanking it out to reveal the short, bloodied blade.

The man looked at Jensen who stayed where he was, breathing heavily and bleeding from the dual wounds to his right arm and shoulder. His cream suit jacket was drenched in blood down that side. The man muttered something and looked back to his own wound, not quite believing how things had turned so quickly. This wasn't how it was supposed to go.

The man clutched his wound and stepped back, his mouth moving soundlessly, took another step and fell backwards. He landed on his backside and sat there, staring at Jensen and speaking soundlessly.

Jensen forced himself to crawl to him, his right arm hanging uselessly at his side and every movement sending horrendous pain bolting through him. He bit his lip and blocked it out, concentrating on his attacker instead. He got face to face with him, both men wheezing and sweating.

This was no street robbery; he had been ambushed, and he needed to know why.

'Who are you?' Jensen grated. 'Who sent you?'

The attacker's mouth moved but no words came out. His lips were becoming bloodied and Jensen could hear a bubbly wheeze in his lungs. A punctured lung meant death unless he got to a hospital fast, and that wasn't going to happen.

'Give me a name,' Jensen managed. 'Who sent you, man?'

The attacker's eyes were wide with panic but he was losing focus, and his gaze shifted off to the side, past Jensen and somewhere off into the ether.

'Damn it,' Jensen growled. He grabbed the man's shirtfront with his left hand and shook him. 'Tell me who sent you, you filthy mongrel.'

The man's head lolled to the side and he went limp. Jensen let him fall back and sat back on his heels, sucking in air. By Christ he hurt, but he knew he couldn't wait around here. The locals wouldn't take kindly to a Brit killing one of them, and there was always the chance of a back-up team coming to finish the job.

He got the cane in his hand, retracted the blade and thanked his lucky stars he'd had it with him. It was just an interesting gadget from one of the boffins that he'd never thought he'd actually use. He got it upright and heaved himself to his feet. The Beretta was next and he got himself to the side of the alley, leaning heavily against the wall while he tried to catch his breath.

He needed to get back to the hotel, or at least to the closest patrol where he would be safe, and they needed to get the body picked up so they could try and identify the attacker. With any luck, that would tell them why the attack had happened and who was behind it.

A man appeared at the top of the alley and stopped, staring towards Jensen. He was a white man in a dark coat, a fedora low over his eyes. The pain and exertion were pulling Jensen's senses down into a tunnel, but he could feel the man's gaze on him. Boring in, seeking information. The man's hand slid across his body and under his jacket.

Jensen grunted with the effort but he raised the Beretta and pointed it at the man. The man's hand froze where it was, but didn't retreat. Jensen kept the Beretta on line, focussing hard to block out the pain and concentrate on the man. He knew without a doubt that if he lowered the gun, the man would kill him. He didn't know who he was, but names and ranks didn't matter. The man was a killer and Jensen was the prey.

The man slowly withdrew the hand from under his jacket, displaying both palms to Jensen to show he wasn't a threat. Jensen kept the Beretta on him, pushing himself more upright against the wall. He knew he couldn't hold this much longer, but he was determined to go down fighting.

The man slowly raised one hand and made a finger pistol, pointing it at Jensen. He "fired" it, smiled and was gone a second later.

Jensen lowered his trembling arm and leaned heavily against the wall. His shirt was soaked with sweat and blood and his head was floating. He could only assume the operation was compromised.

He needed to get somewhere safe, and fast.

10

Hastings and Napier emerged from the café with full bellies and a sense of mischief developing. Lieutenant Littlewood would be receiving a bill soon enough, but hopefully they would be long gone by then.

Napier couldn't quite believe he'd actually done it, but it reminded him of the hijinks he and the lads he used to get up to on base between flights. He'd already filled Hastings in on the incident involving the farmer's daughter and the tractor, and he had the sense this evening was going to go the same way. They just needed to find some girls, but that could be the challenge.

'The girl on the balcony.' He grabbed Hastings' shoulder. 'That's the ticket! Did you see her? She was quite a packet, don't you think?'

Hastings nodded approvingly. 'Quite a packet,' he said.

'I should go and see her,' Napier said. 'Knock on her door, what d'you say?'

'I think it's a terrible idea,' Hastings said, digging out a smoke.

'Why?' Napier looked hurt. 'Where's your sense of adventure, Jack?'

'Two good reasons,' Hastings said through a mouthful of smoke. 'One, you're half cut. Two, I've been drinking too.'

'Hang on, we drank the same amount,' Napier said.

'Yer, but I can handle it. You're a nancy-boy when it comes to drinking.'

'Is that bloody so?' Napier's cheeks flushed and he stepped back, his eyes flashing. 'I can hold my own, I'll have you know.'

'That so?' Hastings picked a flake of tobacco from his lip and flicked it away.

'Yes it bloody is so,' Napier snapped. 'And I've a good mind to...to...'

He fumbled for words, and Hastings laughed.

'Calm down, mate,' he said, 'I'm only winding you up. You RAF boys are a bit sensitive, aren't you?'

'Oh my God...' Napier pushed past him, rushing past the café towards a growing crowd of people near the next corner.

Hastings went after him, tossing his smoke aside. Through the crowd he could see someone on the ground, someone in a cream suit. Napier reached the crowd and started pushing his way through, but it wasn't until Hastings dropped a shoulder and barged in that they managed to force a way through to the fallen man.

Sure enough, it was Jensen, slumped against the wall and looking ready to pass out. His clothes were heavily bloodstained and he was clutching his cane and a small pistol, not that he looked in any condition to use either.

A local was in the act of slipping Jensen's watch from his wrist when the two men arrived, and Hastings went for him, snatching the man's hand away and giving him a hard shove backwards. The man went down but was up again quickly, whipping a knife from beneath his robes.

Hastings' hand had already flashed to his own hip and he jerked the Enfield No. 2 from its holster. The revolver was up and pointing at the thief's face before he realised what was happening.

'Get back,' Hastings bellowed, his tone and body language leaving no doubt that he was prepared to fight. 'Everybody, get back.'

The crowd backed away, some running for cover, the heartier of them preferring to stay put.

'He doesn't look good,' Napier said from behind him. 'He needs a medic.'

'Here.' Hastings thrust the revolver at him. 'Keep them back and I'll take him.'

Napier kept an eye on the crowd, the muzzle of the .38 following his gaze, while Hastings got down and lifted Captain Jensen onto his shoulder. The man groaned but was too weak to resist as Hastings rose to his feet with the wounded man over his shoulder.

'Let's go.'

They could hear running feet and the blast of a whistle and a few seconds later a squad of MPs arrived, a thick-necked sergeant in the lead.

'What's goin' on 'ere?' the sergeant demanded in an accent straight out of Cornwall.

'He's one of ours and he's wounded,' Napier said. 'We need a medic, sharpish.'

A command car raced around the corner, blasting the horn to clear a path, and Hastings hustled to it. The Redcaps helped him to carefully place Jensen in the back seat, before the sergeant barked a set of instructions to the driver that Hastings barely understood.

The car took off at speed for the nearest doctor, and the MP sergeant turned to Napier and Hastings.

'Right then,' the sergeant said, planting his hands on his hips and glowering menacingly in the way that only the Redcaps seemed to. 'What the 'ell's goin' on and who're you two then?'

He looked from one to the other, then did a double-take at Napier.

'An' why exactly 'ave you got two pistols, sir?'

Napier looked down at the Enfield in his hand, then at the identical weapon still holstered on his hip. He passed Hastings' pistol back to him, feeling foolish that he'd clean forgotten he was armed himself.

'We only needed one,' Hastings butted in, 'and the boss here helped me out.' He could see the doubt in the MP's face but it didn't matter. 'Look, we really need to go. Haven't got time to explain, sorry.'

'Look 'ere, sunshine,' the MP said, 'nobody's goin' anywhere until I get some flamin' answers, is that understood?'

'Look, chum.' Napier's voice had suddenly got posher and more authoritative. 'I know it's ghastly, and I simply hate to pull rank, but we're with the Circus and we can't talk right now.' He glanced around pointedly, the crowd still close enough to be an issue. 'Too many ears, what? It's all Top Secret and all that, you know how it is old man.' He nodded firmly to Hastings, who had been listening in silent admiration. 'Come along, Sergeant, there's a good man. We need to get a wriggle on and get back to HQ lickety-split. You've faffed about enough as it is.'

With that he marched off with Hastings following dutifully behind, leaving the MP sergeant staring bemusedly after them. He'd heard of those fellas they called the Circus, but it still didn't explain what had just happened.

Mind you, maybe it was best not to know. He rolled his shoulders, hearing his joints pop and crack. His men were busy moving the crowd on, and he noticed a white man in amongst the locals. Well dressed, dark coat and a hat. As his gaze settled on the man, the sergeant got the distinct impression the man was watching the MPs. On second thoughts, no. He was watching the RAF officer and the Army sergeant walking away towards the hotel. The MP sergeant pondered that for a moment, shooting a glance towards the two men.

When he looked back, the watcher had gone. He scanned the crowd again, but the man was like a wisp of smoke. The sergeant mentally shrugged and brushed it off.

Probably another of the spooks from the Circus.

Best not to worry.

———

Bergmann watched the two men striding away towards their HQ. He knew where they were going; no need to follow them.

He noticed the military policeman clock him and instinctively melted back into the crowd. There was no point in hanging around.

The assassination attempt on Jensen had failed, and his hand was now tipped. Bergmann didn't like that, not one bit. He needed to regroup and move to Plan B – once he figured out what exactly that was.

As he sifted away into the background, Bergmann's frustration at the failed attempt was overridden by confidence in one thing. He had plenty more assets in play and this game was not over.

Not by a long shot.

11

The interrogation room door opened and two men emerged. One was a doctor, tall and thin in his white coat, greying hair falling over his forehead. He left without a word, heading down the dungeon-like corridor towards a heavy steel door at the end where a soldier stood guard. The second man watched him go, waiting for the door to clang shut behind the doctor before clasping his hands behind his back and rocking thoughtfully on his heels. His black SS uniform was wrinkled from hours spent in the cramped confines of the room behind him.

As the clang of the door echoed down the corridor, the SS man turned back into the interrogation room. A single bare bulb dangled from the ceiling, fighting against the fug of cigarette smoke that hung like a cloud in the room.

The only furniture in the room were three rickety wooden chairs and a matching table. On the table was a bulky recording device. The recorder was a back up to the stenographer, who had already left before the doctor arrived.

Captain Fischer did not know why he had to be so careful with men such as Squadron Leader Karol Jankowski, nor did he care. To him Jankowski was just another interrogation subject. True, he was willingly giving up information, but Fischer knew he would have got it anyway. Traitors had no honour and deserved no special treatment. There should have been no need for a doctor, simply because the man complained of chest pains. It irritated him that the powers-that-be wanted him treated with kid gloves.

A sudden thrill ran through him as he imagined what he could do to a man like Jankowski. Or Major Wolf. The legendary Major Wolf, who had arrived today and would be meeting Jankowski tomorrow. Things would really pick up once he got involved, and it would be a great honour to watch a master in action.

His gaze fell on the traitor slouching in one of the chairs. He was a stocky man with thinning dark hair and a drawn, pale face. He looked exhausted. Feeling Fischer watching him, he looked up slowly with sunken eyes.

'Are we done?' he rasped.

Fischer smiled thinly. 'Of course, my friend,' he said. 'You have done very well today. You must feel like you have earned a good meal and some sleep.'

Jankowski lifted himself to his feet, moving like an old man despite his relative youth. He straightened up and looked at Fischer tiredly.

'I still don't feel well,' he said.

Fischer held his tongue, instead saying, 'The doctor is satisfied that you are okay, Karol. All you need is some rest.' His lizard-like eyes spoke volumes. 'I suggest you go now and take it.'

Jankowski nodded wearily and shuffled towards the door. He manoeuvred round Fischer to get through the doorway. Once he was in the corridor, Jankowski paused. Turning his head, he spoke over his shoulder.

'I am supposed to be a guest here, you know,' he said. 'I have already given you a lot of information, even back when you had me as a prisoner. Strangely enough, I still feel like one.'

Fischer arched an eyebrow but said nothing.

'Do you treat all your guests like this, *Captain*?' The venom in his tone was unmistakable.

Fischer had had enough of the whining Pole. It had been a long day already and the man needed an attitude readjustment.

'You have a lot more talking to do yet, Squadron Leader Jankowski,' he said. 'Guests must still earn their keep.'

Jankowski opened his mouth to object, but Fischer's next words stopped him cold.

'A cow that produces no milk is of no use to the farmer,' Fischer said softly. 'You would do well to remember that, my friend.'

Jankowski turned away without looking at him, straightened his shoulders and headed down the corridor towards the steel door.

Fischer watched him go, his mind ticking over.

———

Sometimes Carla managed to avoid Hilde the ogre, but tonight was not one of those nights.

Seated at the long table between two of the other girls – Mary, a quiet girl with the hint of a moustache, and Angela, a bubbly chatterbox with long braids – Carla focussed on forcing down the thin cabbage soup and staying out of the conversation around the group.

As usual, Hilde was leading it. Close to thirty and a good five stone overweight, she had the moustache of a teenage boy and piggy eyes that were almost hidden by rolls of fat. Loud and overbearing, she went one better on every comment anyone made, and she always had the final say. All the more reason to stay out of it, in Carla's view.

'That Major Wolf is a scary man,' Angela was saying. 'I do not think he ever smiles.'

'Oh, he smiles at me,' Hilde declared. 'He is not so bad for those of us who know him.' She flicked her hair and spooned some soup into her mouth. A tiny dribble made its way down her furry chin but nobody told her and she didn't seem to notice.

'I think he is quite a dish,' one of the other girls giggled. Irma, a local girl who roomed with Hilde. A silly girl, in Carla's view, and not someone she would confide in.

'He is certainly very handsome,' Hilde agreed, giving her roommate a squint. 'But I do not think he will be interested in just a maid, Irma.' She gave a superior sneer. 'I had a nice chat with him today, in fact. He is a very nice man.'

Carla swallowed and bit her lip. Major Wolf made her skin crawl, and Hilde was all talk. Still, talk was good.

'I heard the Englanders are coming,' Angela continued, and Hilde gave a frown.

'What a load of nonsense,' the supervisor declared. 'We are all over them and the war will be over in a few months, everyone knows that.' Still, Carla noted, there was a trace of uncertainty in her voice.

'No, silly,' Angela gushed, 'I just heard it before I finished work. I was talking to Pieter, you know the skinny one who does the radios? He was telling me.'

Carla paused with her spoon in mid-air, aware that the atmosphere had suddenly changed. She put the spoon to her lips and took a mouthful. This was certainly interesting and, even better, Hilde seemed to know nothing about it. She willed the girl beside her to continue, but Hilde cut her off.

'Well your friend Pieter shouldn't be talking to domestics like that,' she spat, her cheeks flushing. 'And you will hold your tongue too, Angela. It is not our place to talk out of school about things we hear.'

'I didn't hear it,' Angela protested indignantly. She was a little older and more confident than Carla, who would never have dared speak to Hilde like that. 'He told me.'

Carla snuck a glance at Hilde across the table, seeing the older woman's jaw set. Her shoulders were tight and the look on her reddened face told Carla that Angela was reading this all wrong.

She put a warning hand on Angela's arm, but Angela was in full flight now.

'In two nights the English are coming,' she said defiantly. 'Parachutists will be landing here...'

Hilde flew across the table with her soup spoon raised.

Crockery was thrown and soup spilled as the table rocked, and the spoon arced through the air. There was a loud crack as it struck Angela across the face and knocked her sideways into Carla. Both of them toppled off the bench seat, landing in a tangle of arms and legs on the floor of the kitchen.

Carla was trapped beneath the older girl, with her legs still hooked over the bench seat. A flailing elbow caught her on the temple and black spots burst across her vision. In the far distance she could hear shrieks and yelling, and suddenly a mountain fell on her, smashing the air from her lungs. The mountain was shuddering on top of her and she feared she may be squashed before she could take another breath.

Desperate for air, Carla tried to heave Angela off her, but it was impossible to even move. It took her a moment to realise that Hilde was on top of them both, and the shuddering mountain was actually Hilde raining down blows on Angela, who was the unwitting meat in the sandwich.

Carla could hear Angela screaming and someone else shouting and the dull thud of impacts somewhere close to her head and someone was shrieking and she couldn't breathe. Angela's hair was in Carla's face and the head beneath it was rocking and jerking and moaning. Carla couldn't see through the tangle of hair but she could feel hot, sour breath in her face and she instinctively knew it was Hilde.

Without warning the weight was lifted off her and she saw the other girls there, pulling Hilde away and lifting Angela to the side. Carla lay where she was, gasping to get air into her crushed lungs. She could taste copper and felt wetness on her face, but she didn't care – that wouldn't kill her.

Struggling onto her side, she propped herself up on one elbow and sucked in breaths, each intake easing the steel band around her chest ever so slightly.

Looking to her side, she saw Angela slumped against the wall. Two of the girls were tending to her, but Carla could see she was in a bad way. Blood was flowing freely down her face and neck from an open wound on her cheekbone, and already her white uniform blouse was soaked. The eye above the gash was red and swollen and rapidly closing up. The girl herself was moaning and weakly trying to move, but she looked nearly dead.

Carla took a deep breath that made her torso shudder, and looked past the injured girl to where Hilde stood at the end of the table. Two more of the girls stood near her, tentatively watching, clearly too afraid to actually hold her back.

Hilde's face was flushed and sweaty and her knees were grazed, and she still clutched the soup spoon in one beefy fist. The look on her face sent an arctic chill through Carla's core – she was staring down at her victim with a hateful glare, her eyes gleaming like an animal about to pounce on its prey. It occurred to Carla that not only had the older woman reacted with extreme violence, but she had enjoyed it.

Hilde turned her gaze to Carla and fixed her in a beady stare, almost challenging her to say or do something, anything. Anything to allow her to react again.

Carla forced herself to roll over to her knees and avoided Hilde's gaze as she struggled to her feet, Mary helping her up. The table was covered in broken dishes and spilled soup and Carla guessed that dinner was over.

12

‘Captain Jensen has a couple of decent wounds, but he's been sewn up,' Littlewood said, pacing the hotel room. He clutched a tennis ball in one hand and Hastings noticed he was squeezing it constantly. 'He's resting now and wants to be back here, which the doctors have said no to. Knowing him, he'll be back here by morning.'

He managed a tight-lipped smile, but the tennis ball was still taking a thrashing.

'It's all a bit odd, don't you think?' Napier said. 'I know Cairo's a dangerous place, but the timing seems a tad off, doesn't it?'

'Indeed.' Littlewood nodded. *Squeeze, squeeze.* He turned and started another length of the room.

Napier was propped on his bed, while Hastings stood near the window. Littlewood had caught them just before they hit the sack, both tired from the night before and having full bellies. Hastings had changed his uniform, his clothes having been bloodstained from carrying the Captain over his shoulder.

'Do many men get mugged around here?' Napier said.

'There's often a spot of bother, as you both well know. But attacks like this are not so common.'

'Is it connected to the operation?' Napier said. He swung his legs over the side of the bed and sat up. 'You know, was he targeted d'you think?'

'I wouldn't think so,' Littlewood said. *Squeeze, squeeze.* 'No, we're pretty bloody careful and this one's so far on the down low only a handful of people know about it. We've changed things up a bit as well.' He finished a length and spun on his heel to come back. 'We wouldn't normally have our agents in the hotel here, for starters.'

At the window, Hastings raised an eyebrow but said nothing. He could see a flaw in the plan straight away.

'So we're to continue as normal?' Napier said.

'Absolutely,' Littlewood said. He stopped his pacing and took a breath, tossing the tennis ball now in his hand. 'Yes, carry on as you were. Get your heads down, tomorrow's a busy day.' He looked to Napier. 'Jump training for you, chum. And I have your request for weapons and bits and bobs,' he told Hastings, who gave a short nod. 'I'll get all that sorted out and will see you in the morning.' He cracked the door and gave them a wave as he exited. 'Cheerio.'

'Cheerio,' Napier echoed, turning to Hastings. 'Well, a good bit of excitement, eh? Not as convinced as old mate there seems to be, but I suppose they know what they're doing, what d'you think?'

Hastings's face was dark.

'That wasn't pure chance the Captain got attacked,' he said. 'Not a hope in hell.' He pushed off the wall. 'We better watch our backs.' He grabbed hold of the heavy dressing table and dragged it across the floor until it blocked the door.

'What're you doing, old man?' Napier said, watching him with amusement. 'You don't seriously think we might get attacked, do you?'

Hastings straightened up and gave him a hard look.

'I'll sleep better knowing I've covered my arse,' he said. 'Law of the jungle – kill or be killed.' He started yanking the covers off his bed. 'Do what you like, but I'm sleeping on the floor.'

Napier chuckled to himself. 'Not me, I'm afraid. I'm a sucker for a good bed.' He watched as the Kiwi made himself comfortable on the floor. 'I'll see you in the morning, bright and early.'

Hastings lay down, fully clothed, the Enfield beside him within easy reach. He tucked a pillow under his head and stretched out. It had been a while since he'd slept in a proper bed, but he figured one more night wouldn't hurt him. He closed his eyes and was asleep within seconds.

Napier kicked off his shoes and padded across to switch off the light. The room fell dark and he went to the window. The shutters were open and he stared out at the city.

Cairo, the ancient city of mystery. Pharaohs and pyramids, traders and travellers. A place of legend, a place that made your blood tingle with excitement. A place of war and deception.

He wondered what the next day would bring. He wondered how the hell they were going to get their hands on Jankowski, if they could even get into Alpenbad. He barely knew the man on a personal level, just another chap he was thrown together with because of the war. A skilled pilot, though. And a tough bugger in the hot-headed way that Poles were.

The bloody Germans. Merciless bastards. He'd seen vicious acts before, stricken aircraft being driven to the ground rather than letting them go.

One of the squadron, young Leo, had bought it during the Battle of Britain. Many had bought it, but Leo had always stuck in his mind. He'd been badly hit over the Channel, one engine on fire and out of the game. He'd turned and made for home, every man in the air desperately hoping he could make it. Even though the kite was buggered he could bail out and be picked up soon enough.

But a 109 had jumped on his tail and harried him, getting ever closer despite Leo's best efforts to shake him. Black smoke pouring from the engine, he was losing speed and manoeuvrability fast. Probably should have just bailed out, but he had no chance.

The 109 had raked his Spitfire from tail to nose, sending Leo down to the drink in flames.

Napier had chased hard after him, driven by a blinding thirst for revenge, but he'd got away. He felt his teeth grinding as he thought about it now. This was what they were dealing with.

His new companion, Hastings, obviously didn't think much of the RAF. He'd clearly done his bit down below, but he had no idea what Napier and the others had been through.

Yes, there were hijinks and adventure on the squadron – of course there were. But it had also been bloody nerve-wracking. Constant ops, little sleep, relentless pressure. The ever-present risk of death or crippling injuries, or capture.

Fear.

One of the boys had been horribly burned in a crash landing, wounds so terrible they didn't think he'd survive. He had, but perhaps he'd have been better off not making it. Another had broken his back putting his kite down in a field and would never walk again. Then there were the ones who didn't make it back at all.

Napier loved it on the squadron, even when he woke with a gnawing dread in his gut. Now he was off on some madcap bloody mission with a man he didn't know, a man who didn't respect him. A mission he clearly wasn't prepared for, and one that they were highly unlikely to survive. His short time on the run had taught him one thing – he definitely didn't want to be stuck behind the wire. He wondered if Hastings knew, and whether he would care anyway. Probably a no on both counts, he decided. Jensen would undoubtedly know; the man seemed to know everything. It hadn't been a great time – in fact, it had been hellish – and it was yet another bloody good reason not to go on this ridiculously dangerous mission.

Napier sighed. Hell, he'd got this far. Maybe they'd be okay.

He lay on the bed and laced his hands across his stomach, closing his eyes. Tomorrow was another day.

13

Angela shared a room with a couple of the girls in the same dorm that Carla was in, but Carla hadn't seen her since the disastrous end to dinner.

After helping tidy up the mess Hilde had made and clean the kitchen, Carla had gone to Angela's room, hoping to satisfy her curiosity. The loose talk that had thrown Hilde into such a rage was obviously of importance, and she knew she had to determine what exactly was going on.

But Angela wasn't there and her bed was still made, and Mary – timid at the best of times – had been reluctant to talk, preferring to busy herself with getting ready for bed. Carla had prodded her gently but quickly gave up for fear of raising alarm bells. Backing out of their shared room, she made her way down the hallway towards her own room.

Passing by the bathroom, she broke her stride to pause, the smallest sound coming from behind the door. Carla listened for a few seconds before she heard a second sound. It was the whimper of a wounded animal, and she knew she had found who she was looking for.

Pushing open the door, she found Angela at the basin with a

facecloth in her hand. The water in the basin was stained a dark pink and the cloth itself was bloodied. The girl with the long braids turned slowly to see who had come in, and Carla took an involuntary step back when she saw the girl's injuries.

The left eye was completely swollen shut and was already a dark purple-black. The wound below it was sewn shut but the stitches looked rough and unfinished. The whole left side of her face was swelled in a misshapen mess, dragging that side of her mouth into a morbid grimace.

Angela looked away quickly, putting the facecloth back to her eye.

Compassion overrode Carla's revulsion at the injuries, and she swiftly moved to the girl's side.

'Here.' She pried the cloth from reluctant fingers and dabbed it carefully at the dried blood around the eye.

Angela winced at the touch and Carla put a hand to her shoulder, shushing her softly as she would a scared child. It took several minutes of careful attention before the worst of the dried blood was cleaned away, but eventually Carla pulled the plug. Rinsing out the facecloth, she gave Angela an encouraging smile.

'There,' she said. 'You look a million times better already.'

Angela gave her a winsome smile in return. 'They were so rough,' she said, her speech distorted by the swelling. 'One of the doctors did it, but...I don't think he cared.'

Her good eye welled up with tears and Carla pulled her close, letting the girl cry on her shoulder. She stroked the girl's back and shushed her softly, providing what comfort she could. Once she'd regathered herself, Angela wiped her nose on her sleeve and sniffed hard.

'I look like a freak,' she said. 'And I don't even know...why? How could she do that?' She was on the verge of breaking down again. 'How could a woman be so horrible?'

Carla shook her head in sympathy. 'I don't know,' she said honestly. 'Perhaps she is not quite right in the head; I don't know.'

Angela managed a smile. 'You are right, I think,' she slurred. 'She is not right in the head. I would never hurt someone like that.'

'And it was nothing,' Carla said, 'just nothing. I mean, what? One of the boys tells you something and you tell us at dinner. So what?' Her stomach fluttering, she gave an indifferent shrug. 'It probably wasn't true anyway.'

Angela looked up quickly. 'Oh, it was definitely true. Pieter never lies; he is a good boy.'

'I can't believe the English are coming,' Carla prodded. She felt sick to do this but she knew she must – it was the only way to know. And if it were true...well, it meant something. 'What are they going to do, invade us?'

'He didn't say they would invade us.' Angela paused to dab at her eye again with the facecloth. She winced at the touch. 'He said they were coming in two nights, Thursday.'

Carla managed a disbelieving look. Her throat felt like sandpaper and she really needed to wee. But the door was open now and she had to go through.

'How can he know this?' she said, 'and if it were true, surely we would all be on high alert?'

'It is true,' Angela said defensively. 'Nine o'clock tomorrow night he said.'

Carla nodded, her mind racing. The specific detail certainly sounded true, and she had no reason to believe either Angela or Pieter would lie. But what did it mean? Pieter was a radio operator, a skinny boy with an oversized Adam's apple and crooked teeth – everyone knew him. He must have heard this information through his work, probably a radio message. But where from?

'What else did he say?' she asked without thinking, and immediately realised her mistake.

Angela looked at her closely now, her one good eye narrowing. 'Why? Why do you want to know, anyway?'

'Nothing,' Carla said, flustered. 'It just...you know, it's just nothing. Whatever he said to you is no reason for Hilde to do this.' She gestured towards the girl's facial injuries. 'I mean, come on. That was just vicious.'

Angela nodded sadly, close to welling up again. She lowered her head and touched the facecloth to her eye. 'I don't understand it...'

Carla pulled her in for a hug, patting the girl's back sympathetically. 'I know, I know,' she whispered soothingly.

Her heart was pounding in her chest. That was too close – she had almost blown it with her over-eagerness. Hopefully she had covered it well enough to satisfy any suspicions Angela may have had.

But now that she had the information, she needed to do something with it.

She eased Angela up and gave her a smile. 'You will be okay now,' she told her. 'You should get to bed and rest. Tomorrow is another day, yes?'

Angela nodded and managed a small, lopsided smile. 'Thank you, Carla,' she whispered. 'You are a good friend.' She paused, reconsidering. 'You are a good person,' she said firmly. 'Thank you.'

'No problem.' Carla gave her a quick hug before heading for the door. 'I will see you in the morning, okay?'

As she closed the bathroom door and moved towards her own room, planning how she could get to the hidden radio and send a message back to her spymasters, Angela's words echoed in her head. *You are a good person.*

Right now she felt like anything but a good person.

———

There was a knock and the door opened before Littlewood had even responded.

A look of irritation crossed his face. A fresh-faced young signaller rushed in, waving a piece of paper in his hand, his cheeks red from running.

'Sir, sir, you need to see this.' He reached the desk and thrust the paper at the officer.

The office, much smaller than Captain Jensen's, was lit only by a single desk lamp that threw long shadows.

Littlewood frowned, unused to such interruptions. It was the first chance he'd had for some quiet time all day, and he had a freshly brewed mug of tea and a piece of shortbread – God only knew where Ahmed got hold of these things, but he managed somehow – waiting to be savoured.

He looked at the young signaller, making sure he got the message, and took the note from him. It was handwritten and as he read it, the blood drained from his face.

'Oh good Christ,' he muttered, looking up sharply. 'When did this come in?'

'Just now sir, two minutes ago. I ran straight up here, sir.'

Littlewood ran his eye over it again, making sure he'd read it right. There was no mistaking it.

ENEMY KNOW ATTACK THURS 2100.

'Oh, good Christ,' he said again, shoving his chair back hard and making for the door. 'Where're Napier and Hastings?'

'I don't know, sir. Probably in their room.' The sig was hard on his heels and they collided when Littlewood stopped suddenly in the door.

The Lieutenant's face was ghostly white. Running through his head was a flashback to the afternoon, of the phone call he'd taken. The realisation sucker punched him and Littlewood felt the wind leave his lungs.

He whirled and practically ran back to his desk. Sure enough, scrawled there on the blotter was a note. He'd scribbled it down himself when he took the call from the airbase, confirming the time after the crew had checked the up-to-date weather report. *2100hrs Thurs.*

There in beautiful Indian ink, written by his own hand with his own fountain pen. Unmissable to anyone standing over the desk.

Thursday was the day and 2100 hours was the ETD for the Operation Fusilier flight. Meaningless to anyone unless they knew something else. There was obviously a spy in their midst, but the question was who?

Everyone in the SOE was closely vetted, but he guessed there was always the chance a rogue could slip through. Even though this job was held tight to a close circle, to comb through every possible leak would take time they didn't have. Of course, he reflected bitterly, it didn't help that he'd left a note lying about.

By Christ, Jensen would have his guts for garters if he ever found out.

His mind made up, he looked back to the young signaller.

'What's your name, Corporal?'

'Smith, sir. Eben Smith.'

'Find those men, Smith,' Littlewood barked. 'Find them immediately and get them downstairs. Bring their kit with them. I'll be waiting.'

The young signaller dashed out and clattered down the stairs, leaving Littlewood to stare at the transcription again. The agent they had in place was damn good, and so far had proved one hundred percent reliable. There was no reason to doubt them now.

But if they were right, Operation Fusilier had a major problem on their hands.

Littlewood ripped the section off the blotter and struck a match, watching the paper curl and burn before dropping it in the ashtray.

14

The hurried footsteps in the hallway woke Hastings well before the frantic banging on the door.

He rolled to his knees, snatching up the Enfield and moving away from the door. The room was dark and he felt like he'd been asleep for only a few minutes.

'Open the door,' a man was saying. 'Lieutenant Littlewood needs to see you urgently.'

Napier was up now, also grabbing his pistol and coming to Hastings' side.

'Who is it?' Hastings called out.

'Corporal Smith, sir.'

Hastings shoved the dresser aside and opened the door, but stayed offline so he could cover whoever was out there. He recognised the young signaller and relaxed.

'What's going on?'

'You better speak to Lieutenant Littlewood, sarge. He needs to see you both urgently.'

'Wait a moment.'

Napier had slept in his underwear, so quickly dressed and put his shoes on while Hastings and Eben Smith waited impatiently.

Smith led them downstairs and out to the road, where a black Humber Super Snipe waited with the engine running. Smith opened the rear door and ushered them both in. The car started off immediately, and they could see Littlewood in the front passenger's seat. The subaltern looked pale and the tennis ball in his hand was being rapidly strangled to death.

Hastings peered at the driver, realising it was a woman. Not just any woman, either. It was the girl they had seen on the balcony earlier, the one that Napier had been so enamoured with. *Abigail, was it?*

She caught his eye in the rear-view mirror and he thought he saw her stifle a smile.

'Things have had to move up, chaps,' Littlewood said as the girl guided the big car through the darkened Cairo streets. 'We've got up to date intelligence that means we have to move you tonight. We can't wait.'

'What's the int?' Hastings said.

'It appears we've been compromised somehow,' Littlewood said, carefully avoiding any mention of his own carelessness. 'No idea how and it doesn't really matter right now, but you'll be safer out here, and you'll still have tomorrow for your training. Just means you'll be going a day early. And there are a few other things you need to know.'

He turned in his seat properly so he could see them both.

'Our agent on the inside, White Rabbit. You will need to get them out and bring them back with you.'

Hastings said nothing, and even Napier managed to stay silent. Things were happening fast and they both sensed the barely-controlled panic in the air.

'The agent will make themselves known to you once you're on the ground. This mission will almost certainly blow the agent's cover and they will need to get out before they are captured.'

'So is the plan still to be stealing back the Mosquito and flying out, then?' Napier asked. 'Failing that, we destroy it?'

'That's it,' Littlewood agreed.

'And if we can't?' Hastings interrupted abruptly. 'What then?'

Littlewood frowned. 'What d'you mean?'

'What if the Mosquito's not there? What if we can't destroy it?' His dark eyes probed Littlewood's face. 'You expect us to what, walk out? Give ourselves up as POWs?'

'Well...'

'I mean, you're now talking about four people. I suppose we could shove them in the bomb hold. And what are we going to be up against? They won't let us just fly off into the sunset. What kind of planes do the Jerries have there, exactly?'

'There's a small airfield nearby, only a few miles from Alpenbad. That's where the Mosquito is.' Littlewood said. 'It was built specifically for troops coming and going from there. There are always aircraft on the ground there, and our most recent int is that they have at least a flight of He111's on the deck.' He looked pointedly at Napier.

'Really?' Napier shot Hastings a look in turn. 'Well, that makes sense, then.' He shook his head. 'You cunning buggers.'

Hastings frowned. 'What d'you mean?'

Napier sat back in the seat. 'Two days ago, I was taken out to RAF Almaza by some of the intelligence chaps, and they had a Heinkel He111 there, apparently captured from the Jerries. Anyway, I've never flown one before obviously, but I was given the opportunity to give it a whirl.' He hiked his shoulders. 'Flies pretty well actually, for a bomber. Not that I'm an expert.'

'Well I hope you get to be an expert pretty bloody quick,' Hastings said.

'I'm sure someone of your calibre will be fine,' Littlewood said, with more confidence than either of the passengers felt. 'They don't give out DFCs to any Tom, Dick or Harry.'

'And what about this parachute jump, then?' Napier persisted. 'I get the feeling the training's going to be a bit rushed.'

Hastings snorted. 'Rushed?' he said. 'That's being kind.'

'It will be rather brief,' Littlewood allowed. 'But there's not much you need to know, frankly. You'll be jumping from 500 feet, so you'll be down before you know it.'

'Five hundred feet?' Napier looked aghast. 'I shan't even have time to breathe!'

Hastings gave a grunt. 'Don't worry mate, just follow me. She'll be right.'

'She'll be right?' Napier stared out the window morosely. 'Well, it's been a good life up until now...'

Soon enough they arrived at RAF Almaza in north-east Cairo, the same airfield Napier had been at to test-fly the Heinkel just days ago. The girl behind the wheel showed credentials to the guards and was waved through, steering the Humber across the airfield to a darkened hangar. An Avro Lancaster was on the tarmac nearby.

The Humber pulled up beside the hangar and the girl killed the engine.

'Here we are gentlemen,' Littlewood said. 'Your home until you fly out. I suggest you make the most of getting your heads down while you can. There won't be much rest after this.'

15

Wednesday morning

The tiny shed had half-collapsed with decay over time, and the remains were almost entirely overgrown by weeds and roots from the surrounding undergrowth.

Years before it had been used to store feed for the animals, but the farmer and the animals were all long gone. Carla had found it while out walking – anything to be free of the walls of the Imperial Hotel – and it had proved to be quite the find. Not only did nobody ever go there but it was roomy enough inside for her to hunch over the radio she stored there.

The radio itself was a big machine, and getting a good reception sometimes meant stringing the aerial from a nearby tree. It had been given to her a year ago by her father's friend, Josef. Perhaps *given* was too loose an interpretation – inherited was more appropriate. Inherited when the Gestapo kicked in his door at dawn and dragged him through the streets to the Imperial.

Carla had seen him there, bloodied and terrified as the plain-clothed brutes dragged him to an interrogation room in the cellar. Like many before and since, he had never seen daylight again.

Carla had spent three days petrified that she would be revealed as his collaborator, but he had held strong. His heart had given out, so they said. Carla had no way to know if it was true or whether they just tortured him to death, but the point was moot. Josef had died and she spent the next week looking over her shoulder, jumping at every shadow, waiting for the hammer to fall.

It never did.

Eventually she had plucked up the courage to recover the radio hidden in his garden and move it to the dilapidated shed just outside town, near the lake. The first message she had sent to the unseen British at the other end had been to inform them of Josef's capture and murder. They had already known, and in an instant her fears had been allayed – he had been exposed because of an off-the-cuff comment he had made to the wrong person.

The Nazis hadn't known he was a spy, so they had no cause to think he had an accomplice. He was just another left-leaning academic who had spoken out against the Fuhrer. As much as the news was welcome, it had also enraged Carla even further. Having grown up with educated people, she was well aware of the hardships her beloved Deutschland had suffered after the Great War. She was also well aware of the threat that Hitler and his demented cronies posed to her people.

Her parents were dead because of them, her beloved brother had been killed while serving a Fuhrer he didn't believe in, and she had seen many friends die in the bombings, sent to the front or pressed into slave labour to support the war effort.

At nineteen years old, Carla played her own part for the country she loved. As a hotel maid at the Imperial she worked long, hard hours and was well thought of. She managed to avoid most of the wandering hands of the guests and never complained. She always volunteered for extra duties and did it with a smile.

Little did her employers know that what she saw as playing her part was very different to their own interpretation.

She had no doubt that Germany could well win this war, but she saw nothing but more pain if they did.

While other girls her age were googly-eyed over the diminutive Fuhrer, Carla felt nothing but disdain and disappointment. Her dream of becoming a teacher and educating the next generation slipped further away with each battlefield success.

She had no desire to live in England either, and if they did somehow overcome the power of the German military machine, she had no doubt they would once again crush the German people under a well-polished heel. If that happened, she could only hope for the best.

It had been a year since Josef, a former colleague of her father, had reached out to her.

He knew her well, had known since she was a child, and knew the pain she was feeling. Not only had Franz been killed in action, but her mother's always-fragile mental state had taken a turn for the worse.

Finding his wife hanging from the rafters had been the last straw for Franz Senior, and his already-broken heart had given out on him. Forty-three years old and dead from a heart attack, joining his beloved wife and only son in the afterlife, leaving poor Carla on her own.

All of this had taken place over two short months a year ago. As far as Carla could see, the three people she loved most in the world had died at the Fuhrer's hand. It had left her empty, distraught and vulnerable. Josef had been a welcome shoulder to lean on.

He had taken her in and cared for during her grief, when everyone else turned away. Many nights they sat up talking, and eventually – when he believed she had reached a point of trust – he had divulged a secret to her. Not only was he a proud German, but he was also a spy. An agent for the British, spying on his fellow countrymen in order to help the English win the war. It had seemed strange to Carla at first, but the more they talked the more it made sense. And the more she wanted it.

He had managed to get her to a small town near the Swiss border where they met an Englishman. For two days he had taught Carla skills she would need to survive in the role she had volunteered for.

Signalling, codes, and basic – *very* basic – spycraft. Returning home to Alpenbad, Carla had quickly proved herself. The snippets of conversation she overheard, the faces she saw, the scraps of paper she took from rubbish bins – bits and pieces here and there that helped to build a complicated jigsaw.

Now she was on her own.

This far into the heart of Germany, the Nazis were overconfident. They saw no need to use direction-finding equipment in a town that was as fascist as it was beautiful. Still, common sense dictated that messages were kept short and sharp, and Carla always took precautions to ensure she was in the clear before ducking into the shed to keep her scheduled radio appointment.

Major Wolf was staying at the hotel, and that was important to the British. She didn't know exactly why it was, but she didn't need to. They always wanted to know who was staying there. Carla wondered if one day they would ask her to kill one of them, and she wondered if she could.

Her breath clouded in the damp, earthy air as she huddled over the radio, the red-lensed penlight held in her teeth allowing her to see what she was doing. It also made her drool and her mouth dried out in the cold. It was hardly ladylike, she reflected as she waited with a pencil poised over her pad.

The response came within a minute and she quickly scribbled it down, deciphering it as fast as she could. She was wary of the Nazis unexpectedly deploying DF kit, providing more impetus to get the job done quickly.

NEED TO KNOW JANK EXACT LOC. URGENT. 2000HRS.

Carla sat back on her haunches for a few seconds, her mind buzzing. No mention of Wolf, the feared Nazi interrogator. Instead they were still interested in the Pole, Jankowski. They needed to know his exact location and she needed to supply it at eight o'clock that night; why?

There was only one reason Carla could think of.

Perhaps this was it – they were going to task her to kill him. But what then? She would never get out alive, so he must be a very important target.

She fired a fast acknowledgement and turned the radio off. She would be due to get replacement batteries soon, the cold being no good for them. Josef had had spares so she'd never been resupplied. Just another hurdle to overcome in a life that wasn't turning out how she'd ever imagined it.

Little Carla Bettelheim, the girl with the pigtails and a passion for drawing flowers and skimming stones. A spy against her own people. She wondered what her parents would have thought of it.

Pushing the thought aside, she closed up the radio case and slid it back into the potato sack. She shoved it into a depression in the ground, the small hole lined with scraps of wood and an old woollen coat, then closed a flap of moss-covered matting over the top. Unless someone lifted the flap, the radio was hidden from sight.

The spruce was easy enough to climb and Carla scrambled up like an overdressed monkey, recovering the long wire aerial she had hooked up only minutes ago. From her vantage point she could see the rooftops of town, smoke curling from chimneys in a bid to fight the ever-present cold. She wondered what the chimneys were like at the concentration camps she had heard of. To think that her own people believed it appropriate to burn Jews to death was incomprehensible; another justification for what she was doing.

Letting the wire drop down through the branches, Carla was about to follow suit when movement caught her eye. Coming around the edge of the lake was a single, black-clad figure. Ramrod straight back, head upright and scanning. A peaked cap, gun on the hip.

Carla froze, pressing herself against the trunk of the spruce. A lump of snow dislodged above her and dropped on her neck, but she daren't move.

Even at this distance she recognised the form of Major Wolf.

The icy softness gradually slid below her collar but she held where she was, eyes fixed on the man as he steadily moved around the edge of the lake, getting ever closer to her position. When he reached the closest point he would be just two hundred yards away.

What had seemed like a cheekily genius position now seemed ridiculously dangerous, and Carla cursed her stupidity for being so brazen.

What kind of fool sent secret spy messages from, literally, under the Nazis' noses? The kind of stupid fool who was asking to be tortured, that was who. She had heard whispers at the hotel of what the SS did to people in interrogations – beatings, electrocution, burning with cigarettes, injecting truth drugs. Nothing seemed beyond them; she had even heard of women being raped by the more sadistic of them, and she had no doubt it was true.

Hanging there in the tree, her back freezing as the snowy sludge wormed its way down her spine and her breath clouding in front of her, Carla began to consider her escape options.

If she moved now, he had to see her. If he came closer, could she get away? Run? She doubted she could outrun a soldier, especially in her ugly-but-functional work uniform and clunky shoes. Could she fight him off, maybe kill him hand to hand? Carla almost laughed. To do so was nothing but a silly girl's dream.

Wolf reached the exact point where he was closest to her, just an expanse of white between them broken only by a few tracks to the foothills, dirty spider veins across the porcelain face of beauty. He stopped there and looked around.

Carla stopped breathing and held perfectly still, feeling the sudden urge to pee.

He reached into his pocket and brought out a packet of cigarettes. Getting one going, he puffed happily, blowing clouds of grey into the frigid air. In a few moments Carla caught the whiff of exhaled smoke and breathed it in; it reminded her of her father and his evening routine of two cigarettes with a harsh black coffee while he marked papers.

Wolf stayed there until he had finished his cigarette, three long minutes in which Carla's palms and armpits sweated and her fingers and the tip of her nose froze. Eventually he casually tossed the butt aside and continued on his walk, hands clasped behind his back as he continued on towards town.

Perhaps he was just out taking some exercise. Perhaps he was scouting something out, perhaps it was Carla and her hiding place. She didn't know and it didn't matter either way; she needed to get back to work fast before her absence was noted and questions were asked.

She shimmied down the tree and dropped to the snow below, rolling up the aerial as fast as her frozen fingers would allow before stashing it back in the radio case.

Skirting her way through the scrubby trees at the edge of the forest, she reached the lake path and hurried back towards the Imperial. A pair of soldiers lounged against a wall at the entrance to the alleyway she used as a shortcut to the rear of the hotel. Smoking and chatting, they saw her coming and one made a comment that brought a snigger from the other. Carla didn't catch it, but she didn't need to. They were just young boys, maybe even younger than her – silly boys who thought their ill-fitting uniforms made them men.

She ignored them and strode between them into the alley, nearly at the hotel now.

'Why the rush?' one of them said to her back.

Carla blanked him and kept moving, the exercise feeling good after the chill of the tree climb.

'Hey! I'm talking to you, woman!'

Hurried footsteps came up fast behind her and she half-turned before one of the boys grabbed her roughly by the arm. He spun her to face him and she saw the acne on his sallow cheeks up close, his breath reeking of cigarettes and bad coffee.

'You do not ignore a member of the Fuhrer's forces when he speaks to you,' he spat, 'do you not know who I am?'

Carla tried to yank her arm free but his fingers dug in hard, causing a sharp flash of pain up to her shoulder. Realising she had no chance of outgunning him, she went for disdain instead. With a dismissive glance at the shoulder straps bereft of any rank insignia, indicting he was just a *soldat*, she gave a sneer that was harsher than she had intended.

'Not much, from what I can see,' she said, and his cheeks flushed red. His friend chuckled as he approached, and the boy holding her threw him a scowl.

'You smart-mouthed bitch,' he snarled, turning back to Carla. 'Who do you think you are?'

He lifted his hand to slap her and Carla instinctively pulled back, but he only gripped harder. She braced herself for the strike, but the moment was broken by a sharp shout from the other end of the alley.

'You! Stop that now!'

The soldier boy looked past Carla and she saw his face drop. He immediately dropped his hand and stepped back, but did not release her arm.

Jackboots clicked towards them, not hurrying but moving with authority. Carla sensed another person behind her but she kept her gaze on the boy holding her arm. The second young soldier had fallen back, sullen-faced and waiting.

She heard a slow breath almost in her ear, then a calm voice.

'What do you think you are doing, soldier?'

'This woman, she was...' The boy fumbled for words that didn't want to come, and she felt his grip loosen on her arm. 'She was...I mean...'

'And since when do enlisted men not salute officers?' The voice was cold and very calm – eerily so.

The boy finally let go of Carla's arm and both soldiers snapped to attention, throwing up sharp salutes.

A hand touched her shoulder and Carla jumped. The man behind her a soft chuckle, and she turned to see Major Wolf barely a foot behind her, his pale blue eyes watching her with some amusement. His black uniform was spotless, the creases sharp enough to cut paper. The blonde hair beneath his peaked cap was impeccable and his skin was drawn taut across high cheekbones.

'I am sorry, *fraulein*,' he said, his hard face registering no regret whatsoever. 'I did not mean to startle you.'

'Th-thank you, sir,' Carla stammered, not needing to put it on. 'I am okay.'

'These men didn't hurt you?' He hadn't stepped back when she turned, and they were so close his chest was almost touching hers. She could smell the cigarette she had seen him smoking, mixed with cologne – something expensive, she guessed.

'Not so much, sir.' Carla tried to force her heart to slow down, but it was racing. It was turning into a hell of a day. 'Thank you, sir.'

'That is good.' Major Wolf's voice was almost a purr. He regarded her up close for a long moment, then flicked his gaze past her to the two boys. 'But that is not what I saw.'

He eased around her and she turned to follow him until they were shoulder to shoulder, facing the two young soldiers. They had dropped their salutes but remained at attention.

She could feel their tension and felt the tiniest bit of sympathy for them, but just the tiniest.

Despite her instincts, she also felt a bizarre sense of gratitude towards the Nazi standing beside her. She had no doubt that things would have gone bad if he hadn't come along when he did.

'Have you seen action yet, son?' He addressed he closest boy, the one who had grabbed Carla's arm.

'No sir, not yet. But I very much would like...'

'I have no interest in what you would like, son.'

The soldier fell silent again, and Carla felt a kick of pleasure at his embarrassment. How quickly the tables had turned on the two bullies. Major Wolf switched his attention to the second boy.

'And you?'

'No sir.' At least this one showed more smarts than his friend, and kept his answer short.

Major Wolf gave a slow, considered nod.

'It will come soon enough. You will both fight on the front, and test yourselves in battle against men determined to kill you. You will add to the glory of the Fuhrer and the Fatherland.'

Carla could see the boys stand a little straighter, their chests pushed out a little more. Just as she had thought the tables had turned quickly, in the blink of an eye they had gone from expecting a dressing down to receiving a pep-talk.

'When a man has faced the hardships you will face,' Major Wolf continued, 'he knows his own limitations and capabilities. He has earned the right to walk with pride.'

The boy closest to Carla allowed the slightest of smirks to cross his lips, and she felt a growing unease in her gut. Slipping a quick glance over her shoulder, she realised that she was completely alone with these men.

'A man like myself has faced many hardships and fought bravely for our Fatherland,' Wolf told them. 'A man like me knows what he is entitled to and will happily take it.'

With that he reached across his body and grasped Carla's breast firmly through her coat. She jumped with fright and pulled back, but he placed the other hand on her hip and held her in place.

'You see, men,' he told the two boys, who were now openly smirking. 'I have earned the right to take what I want.' His hand squeezed hard and Carla gasped in pain, but she dared not resist. The two young boys were one thing, but this man was something else altogether. She knew that resistance would only bring more pain.

'You, however, have not.'

'Yes, sir.' The closest boy nodded and caught Carla's gaze.

She felt her stomach roll at the lecherous look in his eye.

Major Wolf released her and Carla stumbled to the side, clutching herself tenderly as she welled up. She glared at him reproachfully and he gave a short laugh.

'Run away, *fraulein*,' he told her. 'Go and get to work, you silly little girl.'

Carla turned tail and ran down the alley, hot tears breaking the dam to roll down her cheeks. Her rescuer had turned out to be no better than the two young boys. The laughter behind her spurred her on, and a thought pushed to the front of her mind – *if the Englanders ask me to kill him, I'll say yes. I will say yes!*

She wiped her eyes on her sleeve as she ran and drew in deep breaths, trying to get herself together before she got to work. Reaching the back door, she left herself in and hurried to the cloakroom. She was almost there when Hilde appeared from a side door, her bulk filling the hallway and making it impossible to pass.

She regarded Carla with a glare.

'Where have you been, Carla?' she demanded. 'Do you think the rooms will service themselves?'

'No, no,' Carla said, her heart still racing. 'Of course not, Hilde.'

'Then get on with it,' Hilde snapped. 'Everyone must do their bit for the effort, even an idiot like you.'

As Carla squeezed past her, Hilde cuffed her across the head.

'Hurry up, you ugly bitch.'

Carla grit her teeth and took it; just another insult on an already bad day. She knew it was important to keep up the pretence of being a willing worker, and fighting with Hilde would do her no good.

But, as she hung up her coat and grabbed her apron, she knew that Hilde's time would come too. She would make sure of that.

16

N apier hit the sand with a thud, knees together, and rolled to the side. The roll absorbed much of the impact but still his body jarred, for what seemed like the hundredth time that night.

Standing on a platform some twelve feet above the mat, two men watched him.

'Much better,' the Flight Sergeant instructor called out. 'Go again.'

Napier got to his feet, dusted himself off and ran a hand through his hair, smoothing it into place.

'Is that really necessary, old man?' he asked. 'I mean, I feel I'm going to injure myself before I even get there.'

Hastings scowled and pursed his lips. Beside him, the Flight Sergeant's face darkened.

'Get your bloody arse up 'ere and do it again,' he barked, dry spit flying from his lips. 'And you'll keep doing it until I say you're good enough.' He glowered down at the bemused officer. 'You're not laird of the manor 'ere, sunshine, so get a bloody move on.'

Napier shook his head and moved to the ladder to climb up again.

The Flight Sergeant moved aside to make room, and Napier edged to the lip of the platform.

'Isn't it almost time to go?' he said. 'I mean, we've been at it for...'

He pulled back his cuff to check his watch, lurching suddenly from a firm push in the back. He uttered a short cry and went over the side, managing to get his knees together just in time to hit and roll. He scrambled to his feet, furious to hear the other two men laughing.

'What the hell d'you think you're doing?' he sputtered.

'That were a sudden gust of wind,' the Flight Sergeant said with a smirk. 'You weren't paying attention, Mr Napier.'

'You're a nasty bastard,' Napier retorted.

The Flight Sergeant shrugged carelessly. 'Maybe so,' he said evenly. 'But I'm the nasty bastard tryin' to keep you alive.'

Napier caught Hastings' eye, getting a cool stare in return. He was completely unruffled – probably looking forward to the jump. Napier took a breath.

'Fair enough,' he said, trudging towards the ladder to climb back up. 'Let's go again.'

Hastings nodded to himself. He felt a twinge of sympathy for the bloke; the parachute training he'd had as a pilot was about as long as it took to down a pint and finish a smoke. There was a world of difference between that and being prepped for an operational jump.

'Come on,' he said, stepping aside to let Napier onto the platform. 'One more then we best crack on.'

17

Littlewood hurried into the hangar, puffing under the weight of the gear dragging both shoulders down. Behind him on the tarmac an aircrew were bustling about, preparing the Lancaster selected for the mission. Corporal Jones tagged along behind him with an ammo can in each hand.

The seven-man crew would drop the two men over the target zone then head straight for England. The Avro Lancaster had a range of about 2500 miles, just enough for the long journey as long as everything went to plan. If it didn't, well, they'd probably have to ditch it and hope for the best.

He spotted Hastings and Napier against a wall, talking quietly and poring over a map spread out on a table. The cots they'd used the night before were folded away beneath the table, with their meagre possessions on top.

They looked up as Littlewood and Jones got to them, and gave them a hand to place their loads on the table.

'Did you manage to get everything?' Hastings asked, running an eye over the items. Littlewood straightened his shirt. 'I think so.'

Hastings frowned, wondering what the admin boffin had left out from the list he'd given him, and got straight into sorting out what they had.

Two each of the Sten MkIIs and the excellent Browning Hi-Power automatics. Half a dozen magazines for each of the rugged, ugly submachine guns and two each for the pistols. The weapons were all 9mm, meaning they only had to carry one calibre of ammunition. It also matched the Schmiesser submachine guns and Walther and Luger pistols they knew the Germans would be carrying. If necessary, they could scrounge enemy ammunition.

Eight No.36M Mills bomb grenades – four each, but Hastings had already decided that the airman wouldn't be much use with one, let alone four, so he'd keep most of them himself. A couple of bayonets in case they were needed, and Hastings carried his own wickedly sharp Fairbairn-Sykes fighting knife.

Rummaging through the items, he found what he was looking for and gave a grin.

'You like that?' Littlewood asked somewhat nervously, and Hastings gave a nod of approval. 'Good work.'

It was one of the new Welrod pistols, a fully-suppressed .32 bolt-action. He'd never got his hands on one until now, but had heard good things. It was an almost-perfect assassination weapon, so he was pleased to have it.

'What about the other bits?' he said, sorting the weapons into two piles.

'Here.' Littlewood gingerly lifted a wooden box and a smaller cardboard box onto the table. He stepped back as if it might bite him. Hastings ignored him and opened both boxes. It wasn't enough to take out a building, but should be enough for their purposes. Plastique, detonator caps and chargers, and a collection of pencil timers with fuses of various lengths. 'That'll do.' He nodded and moved the boxes to the pile he'd allocated himself.

'I say, old boy.' Napier peered at the pile Hastings had slid in front of him. 'My pile's a tad lighter than yours, don't you think?'

Hastings grunted and pushed a wooden box of loose 9mm ammo towards him. 'Here, make yourself useful and load some magazines.'

'How many?'

'All of them.'

Corporal Jones watched the two men, lingering on the dark Kiwi as he worked.

Littlewood raised an eyebrow, harrumphed to himself, and cleared his throat. He looked at Hastings expectantly, but the Kiwi was busy thumbing rounds into a Sten magazine. Littlewood cleared his throat again. Standing shoulder to shoulder with Littlewood, Corporal Jones's red lips twitched with amusement. She paused thoughtfully, leaned slightly towards the lieutenant, then straightened up again. The hint of amusement disappeared from her face.

Hastings continued loading the magazine, but gave the lieutenant a sideways glance.

'You alright?' he said.

'Are you alright, *sir*,' Littlewood said pointedly.

Hastings finished the magazine and slapped the spine against the palm of his hands to seat the rounds properly. He picked up another empty and grabbed a handful of loose rounds.

'Sergeant?'

'Yes?'

Littlewood stiffened and Napier caught on.

'It's okay,' Napier interjected, but Littlewood scowled at him.

'Actually, it's not okay,' Littlewood said. 'We have a rank structure for a reason, Sergeant Hastings. I would appreciate if you showed it the respect it deserves, and address myself and Flight Lieutenant Napier as *sir*, is that understood?'

Napier saw a twitch in Hastings' temple, and took a mental step back. He could see what Littlewood was getting at, but he had completely misread the situation and was on his own.

Hastings continued thumbing in rounds while he spoke.

'When were you in combat, sir?'

'I don't think that's really relevant, Hastings,' Littlewood huffed.

'Well I think it is, you see. I've spent the whole war so far in combat. Even the RAF blokes have seen a bit of action – this joker even got a DFC, so he's done *something* worthwhile, right?'

Napier resisted the urge to smile at the back-handed compliment.

'You heard of our boss, Colonel David? Well he's officially Lieutenant-Colonel Stirling, see, but the men call him Colonel David. It's a mark of respect, because he's been out there with us, getting his hands dirty. Fighting the Germans.' Hastings finished loading his second magazine, slapped it into his palm and picked up another.

'So you don't respect me because I haven't been in combat, is that what you're saying, Sergeant?' Littlewood had straightened up, shoulders back and chest out.

'I'm just saying respect is earned, *sir*,' Hastings said. 'If it makes you feel better that I call you sir all the time, then that's what I'll do when we're in company.'

'I see.' Littlewood seemed to ponder that, but Hastings wasn't finished yet.

'But if you're sending me and the Flight-Lieutenant here out together, then we're cobbers. We're not doing the whole rank business when we're out there, just trying to avoid getting our balls shot off.' He glanced at Napier, who was just finishing loading his first magazine. 'Isn't that right, Freddie?'

Napier couldn't resist a grin now, with Hastings unexpectedly using his first name.

'That's right,' he said. He slapped the spine of the magazine against the palm of his hand as he'd seen his companion do, put it down and grabbed a second one. 'No time for formalities when we're dodging old Jerry, eh?'

'They don't call us Special Forces for no reason, do they? It means we're a bit special. Different to the others.'

'So you're above the normal rules and regulations?' Littlewood said, perhaps a slight sneer coming into his tone. 'They don't apply to you, is that it?'

'We're a bit different,' Hastings said again. 'One thing Colonel David is hot on is his tenets. Rules we follow. One of them is, "The SAS brooks no sense of class". Means we're all equal.' He gave Napier a dead-pan look. 'Even the RAF.' Hastings turned back to Littlewood. 'Is there anything else, sir, or should we get on with organising ourselves here?'

Littlewood cleared his throat self-consciously, hesitated, then nodded. 'Yes, very good, Sergeant. Carry on.' He glanced to Jones, who had stepped back and was waiting. 'Come along, Corporal.'

He turned and stalked off with the redhead NCO in his wake, and Napier gave a little chuckle.

'Well that was interesting,' he said.

Hastings put down his third loaded magazine. 'I don't have bloody time for his feelings,' he said. 'A man's gotta know his limitations, and he's got plenty.' He glanced at the single full magazine in front of Napier. 'Come on, get a move on Freddie. Jerry's waiting.'

18

They were soon out on a makeshift shooting range near the edge of the airfield, with discarded boxes slapped together with bits of wood as makeshift targets.

Hastings walked Napier through the basic operations of the Browning first, then the Sten.

'Lucky it's a very basic weapon,' he said. 'It's built for untrained Resistance fighters to use, so even a pilot should be able to hit something.'

'Well I'll do my best, old man.' Napier cocked it, tucked the skeletal butt into his shoulder, and squinted down the stubby barrel at a target ten yards away. 'Shall I go?'

'Hit it.'

Napier squeezed the trigger and the Sten jumped in his hands, spitting out an angry barrage. The target twitched as a couple of rounds punched through it, but the dirt bank behind it took most of the impact.

Napier lowered the weapon. 'Stroppy little thing, isn't it?'

Hastings raised an eyebrow. 'Is that it?

Napier looked doubtfully at the target, only relaxing when he saw the two holes in it. 'Got it,' he said with a grin. 'Bloody good.'

'You only scared him,' Hastings growled. 'While you're patting yourself on the back old Fritz has come and smashed your head in. You're no use to me if you're bloody dead, mate.' He jabbed a finger at the target, locking an angry gaze on his companion. 'You wasted nearly half a magazine and you only wounded him. He's still coming at you, his mates are still coming and I'm highly pissed off because now I have to shoot all these bastards. And when I'm done there I might just bloody shoot you myself.'

Napier blinked. 'Perhaps you could show me how you'd do it then?'

Hastings glowered. 'Step back, nancy-boy.'

He cocked his Sten and ran a quick eye over the six targets. 'Let's go,' he muttered.

The Sten came into the shoulder and he put a short burst into the closest target, shifted and blasted the next one with another three rounds and swung to the right to nail the third target. Crabbing sideways he dropped the fourth and fifth with one long burst, the submachine gun snarling and spitting out a steady stream of ejected casings as he moved fast and smoothly.

The sixth target was to the far left and Hastings moved that way, pumping another burst into a target that hadn't fallen yet. The cardboard shredded under the impact and the wooden stake holding it upright snapped in half.

The sixth target took the last half a dozen rounds from the Sten and fell to the side. The whole process had taken maybe five seconds and Napier almost applauded, but Hastings wasn't done yet. He let the Sten fall on its sling and he whipped the Browning from the holster on his hip. He fired a shot into the sixth target's head then moved back to the others and repeated the process, before turning to face Napier. Smoke curled lazily from the barrel of the pistol in his hand and he fixed Napier with a hard stare.

'That's what you need to do,' he said. 'Kill the bastards, not play with them. Because sure as eggs, they'll kill you without a second thought. Then they'll kill me, and that'll really piss me off. Got it?'

Napier nodded, reality starting to set in.

'Good. Then let's go again.'

Hastings reloaded and holstered his weapon then fixed the targets upright again, ramming the one with a broken stake into the ground.

'That's one's on his knees but he's still shooting,' he said. 'Do it.'

Napier brought the Sten up and began again, nailing the first two targets with a burst each. He moved sideways like he'd seen Hastings do it, getting the third target with a long burst. He swung to the fourth target and made to fire but the trigger was slack. He paused and looked at the weapon, unsure what to do.

'Your mag's empty,' Hastings said. 'What're you gunna do now?'

Napier started to eject the magazine so he could change it, but was stopped by a shout.

'Shoot them! They're coming to kill you!'

He dropped the Sten in confusion and scrabbled for the Browning on his belt. He got it out, remembered to thumb the safety off, and blasted away at the last two targets. Both took hits and he heard Hastings shout at him to stop.

Napier lowered the pistol, breathing hard. He felt himself grinning as he saw he'd managed to hit all five targets, even the one on his knees.

Hastings moved up beside him, surveying the damage.

'Better,' he said, and Napier felt his grin get bigger. 'But you're still shit.'

Napier looked hurt.

'Don't worry, we've got a few hours. Time enough to make you good.' Hastings gave a crooked grin. 'Or at least less shit, anyway.'

19

Wednesday afternoon

Afte r a brief stop for lunch it was back into the hangar for more jump training.

Napier had managed to achieve a basic level of skill in close quarters shooting and Hastings was satisfied that at least he wouldn't shoot either of them in the foot. For all of his toffy mannerisms and speech, he was smart and determined to learn fast, and Hastings found him easy to instruct.

The jump platform was raised higher and Napier soon found himself dangling in a parachute harness, refreshing on how to untangle twisted lines, steer the chute by lowering the left or right toggle and how to flare just before impact.

'It'll probably all turn to rat shit,' the Flight Sergeant told him cheerfully, 'but at least I can say I told you how to do it.'

'Well that's the main thing, isn't it?' Napier said, grunting as he untwisted his lines. 'Don't worry about me, will you?'

The Flight Sergeant grinned. 'Never fear, guv'nor. We're all in this together.' He turned to Hastings, who had been watching quietly. 'Your turn, I reckon. Show us how it's done.'

Hastings dutifully rigged up and went through the same routine as Napier, dropping from various heights and executing a perfect landing each time. The Flight Sergeant nodded approvingly.

'That's how you do it,' he told Napier.

'Show off,' Napier muttered.

Seeing how skilled his companion was at parachuting, he wondered gloomily how exactly he was going to survive this damn mission. The sooner he was back behind the controls of a Spitfire the better. The Kiwi could go back to running round the desert blowing up fuel dumps, and whatever else his outfit of pirates did.

By late afternoon they had run through everything they needed to and found a shaded spot beside the hangar. Napier broke out a pack of Players and they lit up, lounging on a bench seat scarred with cigarette burns and tea stains.

Napier drew thoughtfully on his cigarette, feeling his shoulders relax as he dragged the smoke down into his lungs. He exhaled and watched Hastings from the corner of his eye. The SAS man was toying with his dagger, alternately flicking it in the air to catch it by the blade and tapping it on his knee.

'You nervous, old man?' Napier said, tapping his ash.

'No.' Hastings gave him a quizzical look. With his beard, unkempt hair and a dart clinging to his lips, he looked like some kind of wild man from the mountains. 'Why d'you ask?'

'Oh, I don't know.' Napier gestured towards the Fairbairn-Sykes as it spun through the air to be snatched by a weathered, gnarly hand. A man so young shouldn't have hands like that, he thought. 'All this here, this knife throwing business.'

'No.' Hastings gave a short laugh, his dark eyes glittering with amusement. 'I just want to get going. The sooner we're there the sooner we're into them.'

'Don't you get nervous, though?' Napier shifted so he was partially facing the other man. 'Come on, everyone gets the old butterflies before a big show.'

Hastings shrugged carelessly and patted the flat of the blade against his knee.

'Of course,' he said. 'But it's what you do with it that matters, isn't it? Some blokes chain smoke, some blokes need a piss every two minutes.' He gave Napier a meaningful glance. 'Some blokes can't stop talking.'

Napier gave a rueful chuckle. 'Point taken, sorry.' He took a puff and licked his lips. 'It's just I'm not used to all this, you know? I go to war in the air, not on the ground. I don't have to look old Jerry in the eye when I kill him, I just blast the bugger from a distance and hope nobody's on my tail.'

'Well, this'll be different then, no doubt about it.' Hastings exhaled smoke as he spoke. 'Chances are we'll be in amongst it and it'll be up close and very bloody personal. You've gotta hit the bastards before they hit you, mate. No time to fanny about getting a nice angle, just line 'em and drop 'em, quick as you can.' He flicked his butt away and stood. 'It won't be all "chocks away and home for tea and medals", that's for sure.' He gave a smirk as he turned away. 'This is real war, mate.'

Napier was on his feet in a flash, discarding his own cigarette. 'That's what you really think of me, is it? Some glory-hound with no idea what it's really like, this "real war"?'

Hastings paused and turned back to him, a sardonic look on his face.

'It's a fair summary,' he said. 'A nice bed, hot meals every night and someone to iron your uniform for you – not a bad way to spend a war, I'd say.'

Napier bristled, his jaw clenching. 'Don't pretend you know what I've been through,' he snapped. 'I flew more sorties than I can bloody remember, every bloody day up there fighting those bastards, watching my back every bloody second, waiting for the hammer to fall. I saw my friends go down in flames.' Dry spit flecked his lips now and his cheeks were flushed. They were stood almost nose to nose. 'D'you know how many of my intake made it to their first year? *None*. I'm the last man standing, Jack. The last man. So don't talk to me as if I don't know.'

Hastings' lip curled. 'You're still a toff,' he said, as he began to turn away.

Napier grabbed him by the shoulder and jerked him back around. Hastings saw red and threw a fast right hook at his face, but Napier was faster and the punch sailed past his ear instead. The pilot landed a solid right jab to Hastings' jaw and rocked him on his heels, following up with a snappy left-right to the gut. Hastings rolled with it and returned another right hook, stealing the wind from Napier's sails and sending him staggering back.

He tackled the airman and they crashed to the ground, fists flying as they rolled on the dusty ground, neither man prepared to give an inch. Hastings was heavier and stronger but Napier was surprisingly fast and hard to contain, using his greater height and reach to any advantage he could get.

No sooner had Hastings got him pinned on his back than Napier had bucked his hips to throw him off-balance and wriggled sideways, hooking a leg over Hastings' and shoving an elbow into his face. Hastings took the elbow with a grunt and responded with a vicious headbutt that split Napier's eyebrow.

'Oi, knock it off you two!'

Running feet sounded as the Lancaster crew rushed over, and Hastings managed to get another jab into Napier's gut before hands roughly grabbed him. As he was being pulled up, Napier hit him with a last wild fist, landing square on the soldier's nose.

The flight crew grabbed both of them to their feet and separated them as a Squadron Leader came storming over. He was a short, tubby man with a florid complexion and an impressive moustache.

'What in the devil is wrong with you two?' he bellowed, looking first at Hastings then at Napier. 'I will not have men scrapping on this base like a pair of junkyard dogs, is that clear? This is a military base, not the backstreets of Stepney!' He glared at them both. 'I've a good mind to hand you both over to the MPs. In fact, tell me why I shouldn't do just that.'

'Apologies, sir,' Napier said, dabbing blood from his eyebrow with a handkerchief. 'Just a silly argument that got a bit out of hand. Won't happen again.'

The Squadron Leader glowered at him. 'And you an officer, too. Disgraceful.' He turned towards Hastings then did a double take back at Napier. 'Oh, it's you.' He paused for a moment as if he'd lost his train of thought. 'I see...'

Hastings wiped blood from his nose and cleared his throat.

'Yer,' he said, 'sorry about that, sir. Just a bit of biffo, no harm done.'

'Well I don't know about that,' the Squadron Leader huffed. 'Both of you get yourselves seen to, you look like you've been scrummaging against the blasted All Blacks.'

Hastings gave a short nod. 'Righto, will do.'

'Will do, *sir*,' the Squadron Leader snapped. 'Now get to it, Sergeant.'

'Yes sir,' Hastings growled.

He headed off and the Squadron Leader sent a couple of the aircrew along behind, with instructions to make sure he got there without getting into any further mischief. The two young crew whispered among themselves as they made their way towards the headquarters building.

'That's Freddie Napier,' one of them was saying, 'he's a bloody legend, he is.'

'You're not wrong, pal,' the Scots lad agreed. 'He's a flamin' ace, alright.'

Hastings pricked up his ears and turned, the two crew almost bumping into him.

'He's an ace, is he?' he said. 'How's that?'

'Got six confirmed kills to his name, he has,' the first lad said. 'Plus whatever else they couldn't confirm, like.'

'So you kill six Germans and they call you an ace, is that it?'

'Five confirmed kills,' the second lad said. 'You gotta take down five enemy planes, sarge.' He held his hand up with the fingers splayed, just in case Hastings didn't get it. '*Five.*'

Hastings raised an eyebrow, his top lip curling. 'Is that it? I've killed more than five Germans and nobody calls me a bloody ace.'

'It's harder to shoot down a plane than a man on the ground, innit,' the first lad said obstinately.

'That so?' Hastings decided it was an argument he could make all day without getting anywhere, so he gave a shrug instead. 'So you reckon he's pretty sharp, eh?'

'Pretty sharp alright,' the first lad agreed. He chuckled. 'Consider yourself lucky, me old mucker – he was air force boxing champ an' all.'

'That right?' Hastings was surprised that he wasn't more surprised; the bloke definitely had a good punch on him, he could attest to that.

'That's right,' the Scots lad chimed in. 'Last fight he knocked out the Navy champ, flat on his back in the first round.' He gave a broad grin, proud as Punch. 'Consider yerself lucky alright, pal. He's an ace and a bloody boxing champ.'

'He is, is he?' Hastings rubbed his jaw thoughtfully as he stared back to where Napier was chatting with the Squadron Leader. 'Well, well, well...'

20

O ne did not survive long in the intelligence game without razor-sharp instincts, and Captain Jensen's instincts were better than most.

The attempted assassination in the alleyway had not just set him on edge, it had sent him into overdrive. Operation Fusilier was so damned important he'd barely paused for breath anyway, but now everything was heightened in the extreme. Not only did it seem that the enemy were onto them – the white man in the hat was clearly German – but they had a hole they needed to plug; if only they knew where it was.

Wheeling through the Cairo backstreets on the way back from the hospital to the office, he kept his head on a swivel. Every movement brought a fresh stab of pain, but damn it to hell, he couldn't just sit around. The hefty Webley .455 in his hand was ready to go at the first sign of trouble, and there was a Tommy gun on the seat beside him. Corporal Jones – Abigail, at least occasionally – was behind the wheel. He knew she also had a pistol on her belt and knew how to use it.

Without shifting her attention from the road, the redhead girl spoke over her shoulder.

'We delivered the kit to the men, sir,' she said.

'Very good.' Jensen didn't move his eyes from his surroundings.

The girl slowed to manoeuvre around a horse and cart loaded down with God-only-knew-what. Could have been a Spandau hidden there under a blanket, and he willed her to hurry up. She did just that, accelerating and moving smoothly through the gears. Jensen let out his breath; his blasted nerves were jangled and no doubt about it.

'They seem well-prepared,' the girl continued.

Jensen threw her an irritated look in the rear-view mirror. It wasn't like her to make idle chitchat.

'Something on your mind, lass?' he rasped.

She looked away quickly, took a breath, and caught his eye again.

'I don't know...'

'Spit it out, Corporal,' he snapped. 'I'm getting older by the second.'

'I'm not sure if I should say something, sir. It's not really my place.'

Jensen scowled then grimaced as a stabbing pain buried itself in his shoulder. He grit his teeth against the pain. 'Just say it, Abigail.'

Encouraged by the informal invitation, the girl opened up, and Jensen's day took a turn he'd never seen coming.

'Mr Littlewood has a lady-friend, sir.'

Jensen grunted. 'I didn't realise he had a lady friend.'

The only interesting thing about that was that a man wasn't a homosexual, which he had long suspected. It was hard to tell with some of these admin-types.

'I don't who she is,' Jones continued, 'but she uses cheap perfume.'

Breathing through the pain and wondering just how sensible his self-discharge had been, Jensen pricked up his ears.

'What're you getting at?' he inquired, wondering if he'd missed something. Abigail was not only a good driver; she had proved herself to be a trusted confidant. Jensen was well aware of the value of a woman's intuition, and he knew that her seemingly innocuous comment was anything but. It had obviously taken some guts for her to even mention it.

'Mr Littlewood's lady friend, sir,' Jones said coolly, steering the Humber through the busy Cairo streets. 'She wears cheap perfume and he's never mentioned her, at least not to me.' She gave him an inquiring look as if inviting him to provide something to the contrary. He didn't, and his mind began to tick over.

The girl had met his gaze in the rear-view mirror, giving nothing away but speaking volumes.

'I don't know that it's an exclusive relationship, sir,' she said. 'On her part, anyway.'

Jensen sat up a little straighter, a sharp jolt of pain causing him to let out a gasp. 'Are we talking a business relationship, Abigail?'

She gave a slight shrug. 'I would suspect so, sir.'

'How long have you known?'

'I smelled it today for definite. I've caught a whiff before but wasn't quite sure. It's the same scent, though.' She screwed her pretty nose up. 'Nothing I or my friends would wear, sir.'

Jensen sat back and turned it over in his head until they reached the office, the silence between them perfectly comfortable. He knew that Abigail had passed on the message she had; now it was over to him what he did with it.

Sitting at his desk now with a strong coffee at hand, Jensen cursed aloud. Ladies of the night were particularly busy in this town, everyone knew that. Not only was it damned poor form for an officer, any officer, to indulge themselves in the vice scene, but it was foolish beyond the pale for an intelligence man to do such a thing.

If Abigail was right – and she usually was – then Littlewood had inexcusably compromised himself. Jensen had no idea yet whether it had led to a compromise of the operation, but he was certainly going to find out. What he did after that, well, who knew? But the mission had to proceed, of that he was certain.

He took a draught of the coffee, savouring the instant hit so strong that his nerves jangled. By God, you could run a truck on the stuff.

How Ahmed got his hands on the stuff was just another mystery in a city of secrets.

Jensen put the cup down and regarded it thoughtfully for a long moment.

Ahmed. The helpful little man, Ahmed. The finder of good coffee and quality biscuits. The local who knew everyone and was ever so obliging.

Jensen felt his pulse kick as he ran his tongue over his gums, the thick and heavy coffee taste everywhere.

Iced tea. Iced tea on ice. The iced tea Ahmed had brought him yesterday had been on almost-melted ice cubes. Even in this weather, ice shouldn't melt so fast.

His mind raced back to that moment. Opening the door to find Ahmed there, about to bring in the tray of drinks. No need for guards on the door, so no one could say how long the little man had even been standing there.

Could he have been listening at the door? If so, he could well have heard everything. He'd seen Napier and Hastings – hell, the man had been right there in the office with them.

Jensen felt a growing sense of dread in his gut, a heaviness that he knew he wouldn't shake.

He reached for the phone on his desk and lifted the receiver to his ear. He dialled one number and waited only a second before it was answered.

'Corporal? I have a job for you.'

21

Wednesday evening

The second glass of brandy brought a warm glow, and Littlewood felt himself melting back into the wing chair in his rooms. It was too small to be considered a suite, but as an officer at least he got his own digs.

He liked his own space, and it certainly made it easier when he was entertaining. His favourite entertainment in recent times came from a girl who he'd met through Ahmed, the chap from the hotel. Like many of the local call girls she used an English name, although for some reason unknown to him she'd chosen Maude.

He'd never found Maude to be a very titillating name, but the girl was something else. Hell's bells, she was something else alright. She'd introduced him to practices he'd never come across before, things he was sure would send him straight to hell – but, by God, it was intoxicating.

Relaxing now after a short but vigorous session, he watched her lazily as she rolled across the rumpled bed and got to her feet. She was short and slim and her jet-black hair fell almost to her waist. She ghosted across the floor to where he sat naked, leaned down with her hands on his thighs, and looked him in the eye. Her loose hair drifted across his bare skin, sending tiny tickles of electricity through his nerves. Soft light flickered across the walls, leaving deep shadows outside the golden cones.

Her nose brushing his, Maude gave that sultry smile that never failed to get him.

'Are you happy, lover?' she whispered. Her breath was warm on his skin. Her English was excellent, the result of having trained as a teacher in England before the war. She had seen some of the countryside, even visiting his home town of Bognor Regis in Sussex.

'I'm always happy when you're here, my darling,' Littlewood replied. He brushed the back of his hand across her shoulder and up to her neck. She eased the tumbler from his other hand and tilted it to her lips, taking a tiny sip.

'You make me happy too, my lovely man.'

She gave him the tumbler and ran a fingernail along his left thigh, up his stomach to his chest. Littlewood twitched under her touch.

'You seem stressed,' she said softly. She raised her eyes from his toned torso back to his eyes. Her own eyes were dark and warm and empathetic, and Littlewood felt himself melting into them. 'What is wrong, my darling man?'

Littlewood shrugged. 'Nothing's wrong,' he said. He took another sip of his brandy, the heat easing down his throat and relaxing him even more. 'I just have a lot on my plate right now, that's all.'

He saw the spark of excitement in her eyes and felt himself lift, buoyed by how he knew she looked up to him. Her, a poor local girl, and he an officer. Not just any officer, but an officer responsible for planning secret operations. She knew he was important and showed him the respect she knew he deserved.

'It must be so exciting, doing what you do,' Maude told him, her finger brushing through his chest hair.

Littlewood shrugged again, but his grin belied the nonchalant gesture. 'Oh, we all do our bit for the effort, don't we?' he said. 'I'm just a small cog in a big machine, my dear.'

Maude's fingernail traced a line down his chest to his stomach and rested lightly there. Littlewood felt his abdomen contract. Her hair brushed across his face as she leaned in to softly kiss his lips. He responded, leaning in for more, but she pulled back with a wicked smile.

'Tell me,' she breathed. 'Tell me what you did today. You must be doing something very exciting, I know it.'

Littlewood felt a twinge in the back of his mind, but he pushed it aside as he so often did. He knew he could trust her, and besides, he never told her anything terribly much. Well, maybe a little more than he knew he should, but she was sound as a pound. Besides, it felt good to have someone to confide in. A man needed that in times like this.

'Just a little job,' Littlewood said. Condensation from the tumbler of brandy was dribbling down his inner thigh. 'Just a couple of men, that's all.'

Maude's eyes glistened with excitement. 'Is it dangerous?' she said. She eased down to straddle his knees. 'Did you send these men behind enemy lines?'

Littlewood chuckled, his eyes fixed on her naked body. 'You know I can't confirm that I'm sending these two men behind enemy lines,' he said. Had he been watching her face rather than her body he may have seen the look of intense concentration cross the prostitute's face as she committed everything to memory. 'And yes, it's dangerous. Bloody dangerous, in fact.'

Maude wriggled slightly further forward onto his thighs. 'You don't have to go with them, do you?' Her hands moved to his hips as she settled her weight onto his legs. 'Please say no, darling man.'

Littlewood sat up straighter, passing the tumbler over to the coffee table beside the wing chair. 'No, no,' he said. 'Not me. Just two men.' He gave a short laugh. 'And can you believe, one of them can't even parachute? How absurd is that? Well, he'll find out all about it any moment now.'

Maude smiled and bent her head down to kiss him again. 'You are so incredible,' she told him. 'So strong and so important...'

22

The girl that Littlewood knew as Maude walked briskly from the officers' quarters through the backstreets to the working-class area where the locals lived.

She was completely comfortable in her surroundings but felt on edge regardless, the excitement buzzing through her. She knew her brother Ahmed would want the information she had from the blabbermouth British lieutenant – the silly little man who she knew was in love with her – and she had to get it to him quickly. He hadn't exactly spilled his guts with the whole operational plan, but he'd said enough that she could fill in some of the blanks; Ahmed would fill in even more.

She knew the British had been betrayed by a traitor who had stolen some kind of special airplane, and it was obvious that Lieutenant Littlewood was sending men after him. Not just that, but it was tonight.

Reaching Ahmed's dingy flat in the back room of a carpet store, Fatima let herself in with her key. Ahmed was waiting in the darkness, wide awake as he seemingly always was, and she paused just long enough to lock the door behind him.

'What is it?' His tone was urgent as he guided her to the wobbly table he had been sitting at. The rest of the flat was in darkness, just the slight glow of a paraffin lamp turned down low giving enough light for her to see.

Fatima quickly reeled off the information she had gleaned from Littlewood, her brother listening attentively. He took no notes but she knew it was all committed to memory as if he was photographing her brain.

When she was done, he asked a couple of questions to clarify he had it all, before giving her a short nod and indicating she should go. As she moved towards the door, he grabbed her arm and Fatima jumped. Turning, she saw he was holding his hand out. With a sigh, Fatima removed the money she had taken from Littlewood from the hidden pocket in her sleeve and handed it over. Always the businessman, Ahmed.

He counted it and gave her back a single pound, before opening the door and ushering her out.

'Go,' he urged her, 'I have work to do.'

Five minutes later, as she neared home, Fatima started to get a prickly feeling up her spine. She threw a quick glance over her shoulder, but the street behind her was practically deserted. She hurried on, her head buzzing with the activities of the evening. Not only had she gathered some intel for Ahmed from the hapless Albert, but she knew it was valuable. The look in her brother's eye told her all she needed to know.

Smiling to herself, she concentrated on getting home without being rolled up by the patrolling soldiers. It didn't pay to be caught out at this time of night, and she had no other clients to see so would get to bed earlier than usual. Bliss.

She turned the last corner towards home and walked straight into someone coming the other way.

Even as she started to mutter an apology, strong hands grabbed her by the arms and pushed her hard against the wall. Gasping in surprise, Fatima was powerless to resist as she was brusquely turned around and her face was pressed against the rough wall. All she knew was that the strong hands belonged to a man who smelled of cigarettes and onions.

He secured her wrists behind her back in handcuffs and spun her back around to face him.

Expecting to see a soldier, she was surprised to find two men in dark suits and trilbies facing her. Both faces were blank and hard, cold eyes boring into her and sending a chill through her core.

'So, Miss Fatima,' the man gripping her arms said. 'You have some explaining to do.'

'I...I...' she stammered, hoping she could play the bewildered girl and talk her way out of what promised to be a very sticky situation.

'Don't try and bullshit me, girl,' the man growled, digging his fingers into her arm. 'It's the end of the road for you. You know the penalty for spying?'

Fatima tried to swallow but her throat was tight and drier than a wizened date. She managed a slight shake of her head.

The second man stepped forward now, bringing his hand up quickly. She felt the cold steel of a pistol muzzle pressed against her forehead, directly between her eyes and ever so slightly higher than the cartilage of her nose.

'Death,' the second man rasped.

The first man leaned forward to stare intensely into her eyes.

'Talk or die,' he said simply. 'What's it going to be, Miss Fatima?'

23

Wednesday night

At eight o'clock sharp, Carla connected with the controller at the other end. The reception was not great but she hoped not to be live for long.

She quickly tapped out the first message, giving the exact room where Jankowski was staying. That done, she flicked off the red-lensed torch and sat back on her haunches to wait for the response. The shed was freezing cold and the woods outside were still, the rustle of a breeze through the trees the only sound in the darkness. Carla shivered in her coat and willed the operator to hurry up. She lifted the collar of her coat and exhaled down her front, the warm breath bringing the slightest relief.

She flicked the torch back on a few seconds before the response came, and was ready with a poised pencil. Scribbling the code down as it came in, she started decoding it before the message was even done. The message was longer than normal and ended with a request for acknowledgement. Presumably the other operator was worried she would miss some of it.

Carla fired away a fast and simple *ACK*, before turning her attention back to the message and decoding the rest of it. The reception had distorted a few letters but she was able to fill in the blanks. When she did, she did a double-take at what she'd written down and felt her chest constrict.

DROP TONITE. RV 0600. PREP TO EXFIL. YOUR MISSION OVER. ACK MSG.

Carla's heart was racing as she absorbed this message, having to read it several times before it sunk in. The British were coming and they were taking her back with them. She was leaving not only the Imperial Hotel and Alpenbad, but Germany itself.

The prospect of getting away from the Nazis took her breath away, but her stomach churned at the thought of abandoning her beloved homeland. Was that what she wanted? Surely this was her home, for better or worse? She didn't know how she really felt about the plan; things were happening so fast.

The radio interrupted her thoughts with a short burst. *ACK*. The other operator was getting impatient. Carla tapped out a quick *ACK STANDBY* and drew a deep breath, trying to get her thoughts together.

She needed to compose herself before she responded, and the operator and their controller would just need to wait. After all, it was her neck on the line here, not theirs. Sitting back there – wherever *there* was – safe and warm with the inevitable cup of tea at hand while she was freezing her backside off here in the woods with Nazis all around.

Taking a few moments to focus gave her the clarity she needed, and she realised that an attack of any sort this deep into German territory would have to bring reprisals. The Nazis would have to know there was a spy amongst them and they would be ruthless in their search for that unfortunate soul.

Carla knew that she could not hold out against their interrogation, and even though she knew very little, it wouldn't matter. With Josef gone she didn't know of any other spies in the area

– or any other spies at all, come to that. But she would be forced to tell them about her training, who she'd met back then, how she did what she did; everything would come spilling out. She would try to hold out, of course, but this was the Gestapo – they were brutally cruel.

No. Her mind was made up. The only option would be to get out and get out fast. If the escape or rescue or whatever it was failed, well, she would be on her own and she'd have to come up with a Plan B. This was it. Her mission as a spy against her own nation was about to end, the next morning. A new future lay somewhere else and maybe one day she could return home. Maybe.

Taking another deep breath, Carla tapped out a brief message. *ROGER RCVD.* Received and understood. It sounded so formal, so military-like. Little Carla Bettelheim, the silly little girl who lost her family and tried to be the hero. Nobody would have ever picked her to be anything remotely military-like.

The next message came quickly, giving her a set of coordinates that she immediately recognised as the shed she was currently in. Making sure she didn't think they were coming to her dormitory or something silly like that and screw it all up. She was to meet the agents there at six a.m. the next day, or failing that, the same time the next day. There was no chat or niceties about it, just a set of simple orders in black and white.

Carla responded and shut the wireless down. Tucking it away in its hiding place, she wondered if she would ever need to use it again. There would be no need for replacement batteries now. Tearing her pencilled notes into tiny pieces, she shoved them into her mouth and followed it with a hand-numbing scoop of snow. Her teeth jumped at the frigid assault and she screwed up her face as the snow softened and washed the coded messages in an icy cascade down to her stomach.

After reeling in the aerial and checking everything was cleared away, Carla eased the cover back and slipped from the shed. She took several steps away until she was in the shadow of the trees, then paused. Holding her mouth half open to widen her ear canals, she cocked her head to the side and listened intently. Only the sounds of the forest reached her but she stayed stock still for another five minutes just to be sure. It would be gut-wrenching to make a mistake now, so close to the end.

Satisfied that she was clear, she headed down towards the lake track. She couldn't afford to be out too long.

24

Waiting until the footsteps were nearly upon her, Hilde stepped out of the shadows of the alleyway and grabbed at the girl.

Carla let out a scream of fright and jumped back, flailing out at her attacker, but Hilde moved with surprising speed and pinned her against the opposite wall.

'What are you doing?' she demanded. 'Why are you out so late?'

Carla seemed to relax slightly on hearing Hilde's voice, but the head maid wasn't giving her an inch. She shook the girl by her arms, hard enough to bang her against the bricks.

'What are you doing out?'

Carla's voice quavered when she answered. 'I was just out walking, Hilde,' she whined. 'I wasn't doing anything.'

'Don't lie to me, you little bitch,' Hilde snarled, doing her best impression of the SS men she so admired. 'I know you're up to something. Always sneaking out, you're up to something and you better tell me what it is.'

Carla cowered away from her, defenceless. 'I'm not, Hilde,' she pleaded. 'Honestly, I was just taking a walk for exercise. I didn't realise it was so late. I'm so sorry for being out late, I really am.' Her voice took on a really pathetic whine now. 'Please, Hilde. I'm not causing any trouble, you know me.'

Feeling a surge of power over the pathetic girl before her, Hilde squared her shoulders. This girl and others like her might be the pretty ones, but they had nothing between their ears. They didn't understand the way things worked, the way the Fuhrer was carrying them all forward. They were silly girls who were only good for sins of the flesh; nothing more. Admittedly, Hilde may be ever so envious of the way the men leered at them, but it meant nothing. The men in power needed powerful women behind them, not silly girls like this.

She cuffed Carla across the side of the head and shoved her towards the mouth of the alley.

'Get inside,' she snarled. 'If I catch you out again after dark, I'll report you.'

Watching Carla scurry away, Hilde planted her hands on her wide hips and felt herself smile. She would report the girl anyway – one could never be too careful. Plus, it would curry her more favour with the Commandant.

She would do that first thing in the morning.

25

T he second sharp rap sounded at the door before Littlewood reached it, his towel clutched around his waist.

Mid-wash, he was in no mood for visitors at this time of night. If it was that urgent he'd have got a phone call, so whoever was at the door was about to receive one hell of a dressing down.

He took an involuntary step back when he opened the door to find Captain Jensen and his driver, Corporal Jones, standing there. The Captain filled the doorway and was leaning heavily on his cane. He held himself stiffly due to his recent wounds, and Littlewood was reminded yet again what a stubborn old bugger the man was.

The red-haired girl stood behind his shoulder. While her face was blank, Captain Jensen's was anything but. It reminded Littlewood of thunder clouds rolling across the moor shortly before unleashing hell on those below. He had the distinct feeling that he was the one below.

'Ahh, sir...hello...'

'Step aside,' Jensen growled, lumbering forward and into the room.

Littlewood did so but raised a hand to stop the driver. 'Just a second there, Corporal,' he said, 'I don't think there's any need for you to come into an officer's quarters.'

He turned to Jensen for support and got a scowl in return.

'She's with me,' Jensen snapped. 'And everything that is said in this room, she is witness to.'

Corporal Jones shut the door and stood in front of it. Littlewood noticed that she was carrying a holstered pistol on her hip, and the holster was unsnapped. He gave Jensen a confused look.

'Sir, if I may just put on some clothes...'

'In a minute,' Jensen said. He steadied himself on the cane and looked his subordinate square in the eye. 'You've been a bloody fool, Bert.' His jaw was clamped so tight he could barely get the words out. 'Your man Ahmed led us to a German here in Cairo, a spy living right under our very noses. He was just intercepted sending message via a hidden wireless set. Unfortunately, he got at least part of the message away before they got their hands on him.'

Jensen's eyes were black as coal and Littlewood felt his guts drop. He opened his mouth to speak but nothing came out.

'God only knows what gen he's been sending the enemy, eh? How many men have gone to their deaths because of that slippery little bugger?'

Littlewood managed to lick his lips, acutely aware that he was standing there in only a bath towel. That unbecoming fact alone was enough to tell him he was in serious trouble.

'In about two minutes some of our colleagues from Intelligence with be coming through that door,' Jensen told him, lowering his voice. 'You will be taken for interrogation on suspicion of treason and spying for the enemy.'

Littlewood finally found his voice. 'I object most strongly, sir,' he squealed. 'That's a ludicrous accusation!'

Jensen's eyes narrowed. 'Is it, Mr Littlewood? I wouldn't be so sure. Who found us Ahmed as our man Friday?' He jabbed a gnarled finger at Littlewood's pale chest. 'You did.'

Littlewood's jaw trembled but he thought better of speaking again.

'Who's been screwing Ahmed's prostitute sister and pillow talking secrets to her?' Another jab with the gnarled finger. 'You have.'

Jensen took a lumbering step forward now, getting right up into Littlewood's personal space and forcing him back towards the wall. 'She's been taken into custody by the secret squirrels,' he growled. 'Funnily enough, she's got a lot to say for herself.'

Littlewood's knees wobbled and his bladder threatened to let go. He fought to stay upright, and reached out a hand to the wall for support.

'You're done, Mr Littlewood,' Jensen said. He straightened up, his hard stare never leaving Littlewood's face. 'Whether it was intentional or just plain stupidity, it matters not. I would like to think you were just stupid but I really don't care. Either way, you've aided the enemy and sent good men to their deaths.'

A warm trickle made its way down Littlewood's inner thigh and he felt his cheeks glow hot. He tore his eyes away from the senior officer to glance over to the girl at the door. She lifted her gaze from the puddle slowly forming around his feet to meet his eyes. The look of disdain simply added fuel to the fire of his humiliation. He looked back to Jensen, a cold sweat breaking out across his forehead.

'Sir, you really must believe me...'

Jensen's lip curled. 'I believe the facts, Mr Littlewood,' he growled. 'And if I had the choice, I'd shoot you right now myself.'

Footsteps sounded at the door, followed by a sharp knock. Corporal Jones opened the door to let in two men in dark suits, accompanied by a pair of uniformed sergeants. The two sergeants took up posts on either side of the door. The second man gave a short nod to Corporal Jones and stood aside, hands clasped behind his back.

The lead man crossed the floor to where Jensen and Littlewood stood. He nodded to Jensen.

'Sir.'

Jensen stepped back, relinquishing control to the newcomer. The other man turned to Littlewood, who by now was openly sweating. The stench of fresh urine was noticeable.

'Lieutenant Albert Littlewood?' the man said, and Littlewood gave a quick nod. 'Come with me, Albert.' The man took him by the arm, pausing to glance down at the puddle at Littlewood's feet. 'I see.'

He looked back up to Littlewood. He was average size and maybe forty years old and completely unmemorable. But, even in his current state, Littlewood was smart enough to know that he was not a man to be messed with. 'We'll get you dressed before we go anywhere.'

Littlewood nodded again, watching as Captain Jensen made his way to the door. Pausing there with the red-haired girl beside him, he turned and looked back.

'To say I'm disappointed after all our work together is a huge understatement, Mr Littlewood. This is goodbye,' Jensen rumbled. 'But if they hang you, I'll see you one more time.'

Maybe it was the flickering half-light, but Littlewood could have sworn he saw sadness in the older man's weathered face. Jensen paused as if he was going to say something but thought better of it and turned away.

He moved into the hall, the girl following and closing the door behind them.

Littlewood turned his attention to the unmemorable man in front of him. His pulse was slamming in his head and he felt like he was about to pass out.

The unmemorable man gave a cruel smile.

'Now you're all mine, Albert,' he said. 'All mine.'

———

Emerging onto the street, Jensen let out his breath and stared at the night sky for a long moment.

Feeling eyes on him, he snapped back into the moment and glanced at the young Signals corporal who was guarding their car.

'Thank you, Smith,' he said, climbing into the back as the boy held the door for him.

'Good night, sir.'

The Humber moved off, leaving behind the two cars for the other men. Abigail Jones broke the silence.

'Do you think he bought it, sir?'

Jensen raised his eyebrows. 'Have you been reading those cheap detective novels, Jones?' he inquired. 'That's very American of you.'

Jones caught his eye in the rear-view mirror and chuckled. 'Sorry, sir. And yes, I have. But do you, sir?'

Jensen nodded to himself. It was a fair question. Ahmed had indeed taken the Intelligence chaps to a German spy – some kind of Swiss bookseller, apparently – and they had found a secret room with a wireless set. But they hadn't captured him at all; the slippery bugger had got away.

God only knew where he was now and how much damage he had caused. Hopefully either Ahmed, his prostitute sister Fatima, or even Albert Littlewood himself could shed some light on that. Without something more, they were flying blind.

'I hope so, Abigail,' Jensen said softly. He watched buildings flit by in the darkness. 'I damn well hope so.'

26

The click of Major Wolf's jackboots was the only sound in
the room as he strode across the wooden floor and
snatched the slip of paper from Colonel Weiz's hand.

There were no niceties about it, no deference to a man of superior
rank. Wolf was SS and what the SS wanted, the SS got.

Weiz stayed where he was beside his desk, clasping his hands
behind his back. He was aware that it made his portly belly protrude
even more, but it concealed the trembling hands. He had no desire to
give the dreaded interrogator any more cause to doubt him, not after
receiving the message just minutes ago.

He stayed silent while the hard-faced man in the black uniform
read the message, the ice-blue eyes flicking across the page from top
to bottom then back again. Digesting the contents of the message,
Wolf stalked slowly to the hearth where a fire sparked and flickered.
He stood and stared at the blank wall above it, his arms folded across
his chest and his lips pursed thoughtfully.

Colonel Weiz waited, flicking a nervous glance to the other two
men in the room.

Squadron Leader Jankowski sat in one of the plush velvet
armchairs near the fire, a snifter of fine port in one hand and a

cigarette smouldering in the other. They had been into their second round when the runner had come calling, and Weiz's glass now sat on the corner of his desk, unloved.

The fourth man in the room stood by the door, wordlessly waiting for his next order. The runner, a fat private who had first brought the message to the Commandant and had then been dispatched to fetch Major Wolf.

The silence in the room seemed to last a lifetime, and a trickle of sweat was beginning to worm its way down the Commandant's back. He glanced again at the runner, who was making a detailed study of the floor. A private didn't get to be fat or this far from the front by being either nosey or noticed.

Jankowski caught Colonel Weiz's eye and gave an elaborate shrug. Weiz inwardly wished the Pole would play it down – Wolf would have noticed the gesture and filed it away, no doubt to be used against him at a future date. Men of the Waffen-SS were not known for their sense of humour, and Wolf was the worst.

Feared by his own side as much as the enemy, he was not known to have any friends, not even a confidante. No wife or girlfriend – legend had it he had once choked a man to death for suggesting he was a homosexual – but happy to avail himself of the spoils of war, including women.

Weiz looked away from the Pole, who was now coolly taking a draught of his port and savouring it. He made a show of swallowing with a lip-smacking sigh of contentment, and looked from Weiz to Wolf.

'So what is the problem?' he asked, speaking expansively with his hands. 'I have the feeling we have bad news.'

Wolf's back stiffened, and Weiz felt his heart sink further. All he wanted was to see out the war in this cushy number, hosting the crème-de-le-crème of the Third Reich for their R&R. The elite of the Fuhrer's chosen ones. He had no wish to return to the front, no thirst for battle. It had long been beaten out of him, knocked down and then kicked to death by the lavish meals, flowing wine and soft furnishings of his current role as Commandant of the Alpenbad garrison.

All that was looking rather tenuous just now. He felt his shoulders tense up as Major Wolf turned slowly from the fireplace and faced him.

'It is right that you brought this to my attention,' Wolf said softly. He flicked a glance to the fat private by the door. 'You are dismissed.'

The runner nodded respectfully before disappearing like a shot, leaving the three officers in the large drawing room.

Wolf put his hands behind his back, mirroring Weiz's stance although, noticeably, he lacked the matching belly. He stared at Weiz for a long moment before speaking.

'That is an interesting turn of events,' he said coolly.

'Indeed, Herr Wolf,' the Commandant agreed, his jowls wobbling as he nodded.

'But not an unexpected one.' Wolf continued as of the other man hadn't even spoken. He gave a slight shrug. 'It is simply something I must deal with.'

'Absolutely. Agreed, indeed. We must deal...'

'I.' Wolf's voice cracked like a whip and Weiz pulled back as if he had been slapped. '*I* will deal with it, Herr Commandant.' His eyes narrowed. In the shadows of the heavily-furnished room it gave him an almost hawk-like appearance.

Hawk or wolf, it didn't matter, the Commandant thought to himself. They were both predators.

'This is my domain,' Wolf continued. His tone was flat and unemotional. 'I will, of course, receive the full co-operation of the garrison.' It wasn't posed as a question, and the Commandant made the appropriate noises and nods.

'Of course, of course. Every courtesy...'

A chuckle came from the man on the armchair, and Jankowski looked from one to the other again. 'What?' he asked. 'Perhaps someone would like to share with me?'

Weiz frowned subtly, hoping the man would pick up on the cue and shut the hell up before he got them both in the shit. Wolf smiled benignly at the Pole.

'It appears we have a spy in our midst,' he said calmly. 'And the Englanders are sending two men to come and kill you. In fact, they will be here tomorrow.'

Jankowski did a double-take, visibly blanching at the news. 'Are you sure?' he said.

Wolf's smile, for what it was, dropped. His eyes bore into Jankowski's skull like searchlights in a stormy night sky. The Polish pilot took the hint and stopped talking. He took a drag on his cigarette instead and avoided the man's gaze.

The silence hung heavily in the room until Wolf finally broke it.

'We have nothing further on this,' he said, 'but we must take it as completely credible. Our source has always been one hundred percent reliable before, so there is no reason to doubt them now. That means that we have work to do, and I will begin immediately.'

Jankowski took another drag on his cigarette and muttered something under his breath.

'Excuse me?' Wolf spoke softly but there was no mistaking the menace in his words.

Jankowski looked up, blew smoke and tossed the butt into the fireplace. He turned back to face Wolf, clearly shaken but with something to say.

'I thought I was safe here,' Jankowski said angrily. 'I did everything asked of me – I brought you a new prototype plane, I have talked to your people constantly since I got here and told them everything I know from...well, from when I first entered into service until now. *Everything*.' He got to his feet now, splashing port onto his hand and cuff as he did so. He stepped away from the armchair, which handily also gave him space from the SS officer who was watching and listening silently.

'This is how the game is played,' Wolf replied evenly. 'We spy on them, they spy on us. Each of us hopes we have the better spies.' He shrugged nonchalantly. 'Naturally ours are better.' He paused half a beat for effect. 'But at the end of the day, they are all traitors.'

Weiz saw Jankowski's head come up sharply, reacting instinctively to the obvious jibe.

'This is not a game for me,' Jankowski said, spinning on his heel and facing Wolf now. 'This is my life. I do all this for you, and what do I get from it? I get hunted down like an animal.'

Wolf raised his pale eyebrows, his face a mask of disdainful surprise. 'What do you get from it?' he said softly. 'What do you get from it?' He tapped a finger on his chin thoughtfully and pursed his lips. 'Do you mean aside from being well recompensed in gold and valuables? Aside from us dealing with personal issues for you, assassinating various enemies you have made over the years. If memory serves me correctly, one of them was even a girl cousin who rebuffed your advances when you were just fifteen years old. One was a schoolteacher who gave you a bad grade when you were sixteen years old.' Wolf slowly began to advance across the floor towards him as he spoke. 'One was a political opponent of your father who accused him of corruption.' He advanced closer and Jankowski stayed rooted to the spot, watching the predator closing in.

Colonel Weiz swallowed hard and tried to speak, but could not manage it.

Wolf stopped barely a foot from Jankowski now. His voice remained soft and calm and dripping with menace. 'One was your own father.'

Jankowski's Adam's apple visibly danced a jig. Wolf cocked his head slightly to the side.

'Have I missed anything?' he asked gently.

Jankowski tried to hold his gaze but failed, turning away to examine the wall instead.

'I thought not. It was entirely predictable that someone would turn against us. It has happened before and I have no doubt it will happen again.' Wolf allowed himself a smile, but it was the hungry smile of a beast of prey, devoid of any humour. 'And, as it always is, such an act will be dealt with with extreme prejudice.' He leaned in close to Jankowski's turned-away cheek, the man still steadfastly refusing to look at him. 'Just as the Englanders are wanting to do with you, Herr Jankowski.'

Colonel Weiz thought he could see a tremor run down the Pole's body as the major stared at him.

'Herr Wolf?' His voice came out scratchy and uncertain and he quickly coughed to try and cover it before trying again. 'Herr Wolf.'

Wolf stepped back from Jankowski and turned his way. A more relaxed demeanour came back across him. *'Jawohl*, Herr Commandant?'

Weiz swallowed nervously, unsure if the man was now belittling him with his formalness. Deciding he probably was but there was nothing he could do about it, he bumbled on.

'I will leave it in your...very capable hands to deal with this... matter,' he stumbled. 'You are quite right; this is your domain.' He nodded, his jowls flopping with the effort. 'And very fortunate we are to have such a man available, I must tell you.'

Wolf ghosted a smile but said nothing.

'I know our valued guest is safe in your hands, and you will get to the bottom of this. For now, though...' Weiz managed a conspiratorial smirk, 'I think Herr Jankowski would do well to get to his quarters for the night. Such news is quite upsetting and I know that no harm was intended by his...sharing his thoughts with us.' He stared at Jankoswki, eventually catching his eye. 'Isn't that right, Karol?'

Jankowski gave a cautious bob of the head, licked his lips and, as if finally catching on, he nodded again with more enthusiasm. 'Absolutely correct, Herr Commandant,' he rasped. 'Absolutely correct.' He flicked a quick glance in Wolf's direction. 'No offence intended at all, Major.'

Wolf gave a gracious nod and smile, and moved towards the door. 'I will see you in the morning, Herr Commandant.' He turned the handle and paused to look back at the Pole before he opened the door. 'Sleep well, Herr Jankowski. You are perfectly safe here.' Again the ghostly smile. 'The Englanders can try, but there is not a chance of them reaching us here in the heart of the Fatherland. You have nothing to fear.'

With that he wafted through the door, there was a soft click of the latch and he was gone.

Weiz took a deep breath to try and calm his nerves before turning to his companion. Just minutes ago they had been enjoying a stiff drink and a smoke. How the mood had changed.

Jankowski stared back at him, his body stiff as a board and the stress pounding off him in invisible waves.

Weiz smiled weakly, feeling the sweat running down his back to his waistband. His armpits felt damp. 'Everything is fine, Karol,' he said with more confidence than he felt.

Jankowski's glass exploded against the wall, port splashing wide and fragments of glass scattering in all directions. He spun on his heel and stalked from the room.

27

The propellors were whirring and the engines were warmed up and ready to go.

The crew waited on board, impatient to go. Out there in the darkness of the airfield, beyond the lights of the Humber, sentries stood guard.

Napier and Hastings had loaded their kit on board, and came back onto the tarmac when they saw the Humber pull up. Jensen lumbered out of the back seat, the redhead corporal taking his elbow to help him out. A grimace of pain crossed the man's face as he straightened up, leaning heavily on his cane.

'Gentlemen,' he called, as the two men approached at a trot.

They were clad in battledress with helmets and parachutes, each man seemingly armed to the teeth. Dark camouflage paint was smeared on their exposed faces to reduce the glare of the oils in the skin. The whole effect combined to give them a cut-throat appearance.

'Good luck, gentlemen,' Jensen told them. He shook hands firmly with each of them before resting back on the pommel of his cane. Corporal Jones' hand was light on his arm until he had himself right, then it was gone. He gave a nod of thanks without looking at her.

'Thank you, sir.' Napier's boyish face was glowing in the glow of the headlights, mottled pink and ghostly white beneath the camo cream. It made his blue eyes all the more noticeable. 'Very good of you to see us off, sir.'

'You know what to do, boys,' Jensen said, leaning in towards them and making eye contact with each in turn. 'Go well, go hard, and we'll see you back here when you return.'

'Absolutely, sir.' Napier beamed, but it seemed half-forced. Jensen guessed the young airman was probably shitting himself about now.

'Righto, boss.' Hastings finally spoke, his laconic drawl bringing a wry smile to Jensen's lips. 'See you in a bit, eh?'

'You will, Mr Hastings,' Jensen told him. 'Now best you get aboard.' Looking past the two young men he could see a crew member waving at them to hurry up. 'I think they're ready for you.'

'Absolutely, sir. Cheerio.' Napier leaned to see past the Captain. 'When I'm back, Corporal, perhaps we could have a nice dinner somewhere, what d'you say? A nice meal and a bottle of wine?'

Jensen cocked an eyebrow as he glanced sideways at his driver. He noticed her cheeks had flushed and she was almost squirming.

'Good luck, sir,' she replied uncomfortably. 'See you both when you get back.'

Napier's smile faltered but he quickly caught himself and turned to his companion, clapping him on the shoulder with an exaggerated laugh. 'Enough chitchat, Jack – come on. Let's get a wriggle on.'

He turned and hurried towards the Lancaster. Hastings gave Jensen and Jones a last look before turning and following the airman. From the corner of his eye, Jensen noticed Jones watching Hastings go. His lips twitched under his whiskers, but he said nothing.

They stayed where they were, watching the big bomber taxi down the runway before turning and preparing for take-off. The engines roared, dust and sand billowed, and the Lancaster barrelled down the runway like a charging beast.

Watching it lift into the dark night sky, Jensen spotted the escort flight waiting high above. They would make sure the Lancaster got safely part-way before breaking away to help stage a diversion elsewhere. It was all smoke and mirrors, this game, he reflected to himself.

As the Lancaster disappeared into the darkness, Jensen turned to his driver. She was fixed on the tail of the long-gone bomber, only breaking away when she realised he was watching her. Her cheeks flushed again.

'I hate this part, sir,' she blurted, going scarlet as soon as the words left her mouth. 'It sickens me to see them go like this.'

Jensen gave a comforting smile and laid a fatherly hand on her shoulder. 'They'll be back, Abigail. They'll be back.'

'How can you know that, sir?' There was a catch in her voice. 'They're jumping into Germany. They might as well be jumping into Hell.'

Jensen nodded slowly. 'I know, lass. I know.' He squeezed her shoulder. 'Now let's get back. I don't know about you, but I could do with a good stiff whiskey.'

Jones managed a smile. 'Make mine a double, sir,' she said.

28

The thumping of his heart was almost loud enough to drown out the drone of the Lancaster's engines.

Napier concentrated on running through the aircraft's specs, using the technical data as a distraction from the absolute sheer bloody terror he was feeling. His guts were churning and he needed to pee again. Good God, how many times had he been up over enemy territory? But this was different. This time he was in the hands of a crew of seven men he didn't know, in a plane he'd not handled himself, with no control over his destiny whatsoever.

At least when he had control of the kite he knew what he was doing, and it was down to his own skill and luck whether he made it home or not. Right now he had none of that, and was just praying they'd make it. No doubt the crew were very good, but still...

It was 1500 miles to Alpspitze, which at a cruising speed of 200mph would take them seven and a half hours or thereabouts, all going well. The Lancaster could hit 282mph of course, and probably would get close on the way back to London, but on the way to the drop zone it was important not to waste fuel unnecessarily, in case it should be needed. The Lanc couldn't outrun a German fighter, and the escort flight of Spitfires would peel off before too long due to their shorter range – must faster and more agile, of course, but not built for long range strikes. After that they would be on their own, relying on the cunning and skill of the pilots. A diversionary raid was being made fifty miles away, in the hope of drawing in any enemy in the area.

Pressing his back against the airframe as he huddled on the canvas seat, Napier clenched his fists and ran through the technical data again. A ceiling of 21,000 feet, but they were well below that, close to 13,000. They would be jumping from about 500. Damned close to the ground, too close if anything went wrong. At least it would be quick. So dark out there he wouldn't even see it coming.

He threw a glance at Hastings, slouched beside him. The man could have been asleep, with his chin on his chest and his eyes closed. They were both bundled up with white paratrooper smocks over several layers, but it was still cold. Napier could barely feel his feet. How Hastings could sleep was beyond him. He was tired and the nervous anticipation was making him tremble, but there was far too much adrenaline coursing through his system for sleep to come anywhere near.

Corporal Jones' reaction to his dinner invitation had been disappointing, and he mentally kicked himself for throwing it out there. She was a hang of a girl, though, and he knew they'd have some good laughs if she would give him a chance. He should've kept his big mouth shut until they got back; hard to say no to a man who'd pulled off something like this.

He peered closer at Hastings. The man was definitely out like a light. Bloody soldiers; if they weren't fighting or boozing, they were sleeping. Napier forced himself to take a deep breath and let it out slowly. His mind wandered to what he knew of being captured.

The short time he'd spent recently with the Intelligence bods had been interesting, to say the least. Maybe that was what had opened his mind to things like this mission; all the secret squirrel stuff, the cloak and dagger mystique of it all. Spies and counter-spies. Maybe it was all part of Captain Jensen's plan, to draw him into the intelligence web like a spider with a fly.

He'd learned a bit about POWs and the camps, and it reinforced to him what he'd always thought. If he ever got captured, as soon as he'd been taken he'd be looking for a way out. There was no way Freddie Napier would play nice for old Fritz, that was for sure. Some of the prisoners gave up and just muddled their way through each day, but most still had their fighting spirit.

Mostly RAF of course, some Fleet Air Arm. Only the occasional soldier or sailor. Airmen had little chance once they were shot down, and had to accept that they weren't going to fight their way out. Few, like him, were lucky to make it on the hoof. Soldiers, on the other hand, had to lay down their arms to be taken prisoner. The shame of that must have been crushing. They were a different beast, alright.

Considering the slumbering Kiwi beside him, Napier confirmed the idea in his mind for the hundredth time in the last day. And these SAS chaps were different again.

He took another breath and leaned back against his parachute, trying to get comfortable. One of the crew came through, hurrying somewhere to do something important. He grinned when he saw Napier's ashen face in the dull light of the hold, and gave him a thumbs-up. Napier responded without enthusiasm.

The crew member paused, dug in his pocket and produced a slightly bent block of Cadbury's. He offered it to Napier, who shook his head.

The crew member shrugged. 'Suit yourself,' he said loudly.

Napier smiled apologetically. 'Sorry chum, it's just I may well throw up if I eat anything.'

'I'll have it.' Hastings had lifted his head an inch and cracked open an eye. He held out his hand and took the chocolate from the grinning airman. 'Thanks, mate.'

The airman chuckled and moved on, leaving Napier to watch bemusedly as Hastings made short work of the chocolate. Napier wondered if anything ever bothered the man, or did he just have ice in his veins?

It must have been a hell of a life out there in the desert, attacking airfields and racing away into the darkness, hiding during the day and hoping no Jerry fighters spotted them. Death waiting at every turn. It was different to being in the air, that was for sure. That had been nerve-wracking as hell – plenty of pilots were nervous wrecks, no doubt about that – but he had always felt in control to some degree.

Not now.

He shook the thought from his head and forced himself to take a slow breath in. He let it out again, and noticed that Hastings had stopped eating and gone back to sleep.

By Christ, hurry up. Napier squeezed his hands together and willed the flight to be over.

29

He didn't know who exactly had slipped up, but it really didn't matter. The network was in chaos and his cover was blown.

Bergmann had seen the Englishmen at his shop, with that slimy little Ahmed in tow. The traitorous dog had sold him out for one reason or another. Bergmann had watched from the shadows as they tore the shop apart, emerging triumphantly with his radio set. He was always confident of bluffing his way through a challenge, but the hidden radio sealed the deal and he knew there was no coming back from it.

It was over.

He had disappeared quickly into the night, using back alleys and side streets to avoid patrols and make his way to a one-room apartment he kept above an empty shop. There was a second radio stashed there and he had got away a quick message. That done, he took the small suitcase from the cupboard – enough clothes and food to last him a few days – and the package taped up beneath the kitchen sink. A Flemish passport and a wad of cash, a good start to escaping and evading the forces he knew would be after him.

Locking the door behind him, Bergmann paused in the darkness of the street to take stock. The plans he had put in place were about to pay dividends, but one thing was nagging at him. Unfinished business.

Jensen had survived the assault in the alleyway, and had even prevented Bergmann from finishing it himself. Technically, that was two attempts. Bergmann hefted the small Walther in his pocket, his mind made up.

He wouldn't survive a third.

———

The sponge bath he'd given himself had done little to ease his pain, either physically or mentally. It had been a hell of a couple of days, and the week wasn't over yet.

Jensen emerged from the bathroom in his gown, his hair rumpled and damp. He didn't care; right now, all he wanted to do was slip into bed for a long, dreamless sleep. He would tidy up the glasses in the morning – Corporal Jones had stayed for a drink before bidding him goodnight and heading back to barracks. Not entirely for a young female NCO to be in his quarters, of course, but for God's sake. He was old enough to be her father.

He shuffled painfully across the room to extinguish the lights before turning to the window. It led to a fire escape, rickety though it was, and he was paranoid about ensuring it was locked. Ideal place for a burglar to climb in, if they didn't break their neck on the fire escape first.

Funnily enough, it was insecure. Jensen frowned, sure he'd set the catch earlier. He sighed and did it anyway. The painkillers mixed with booze probably weren't helping his memory.

It seemed to take an age to cross the room to his bedroom door, and when he got there he paused.

With one hand on the doorframe, Jensen stood stock still. The bedroom itself was in total darkness. And in the darkness was a man. He could sense him there. Framed in the doorway, even with no light behind him, Jensen knew he was a sitting duck.

'Yes, Captain Jensen,' a soft voice came from the darkened bedroom. 'You would do well to stay right there.'

Jensen stiffened. The bedside light came on, and he saw the man quite clearly now, standing beside the bed. Dark suit, fedora. A gun in his hand.

It was the man he'd seen in the alleyway, the man who had been there to kill him.

'You,' Jensen rasped.

The man didn't smile. 'Yes. You were lucky then; but not now.' He gestured with the barrel of the pistol. 'Get that hand out of your pocket. If you have a gun, I will kill you now.'

'You'll kill me anyway.'

The man shrugged. 'Yes. But first I would like to talk. Step back.'

Jensen backed up slowly, keeping his hands in plain view. At least if the man wanted to talk there was some chance that Jensen could overpower him. Slim, but slim was better than none. He backed into the living room of the apartment, his mind moving fast. Controlled, not panicking, but working options and angles with such speed that they were barely conscious thoughts.

'Don't do anything silly, Captain Jensen.' Bergmann paused, keeping several feet away from the older man. 'I am a desperate man. The last thing I am going to do before I disappear is to deal with you.'

Jensen made a scoffing noise. 'You must be desperate to climb in my window to try and kill me. Our people know who you are; they're everywhere. You won't last five minutes out there now, especially if you kill me.'

Bergmann angled away from him, reaching down to turn on a side light near Jensen's armchair.

'They don't know who I am,' he said confidently. 'I know you have my contact and he is singing like a canary, as they say, but unfortunately for you he knows nothing. Not enough to help you now, anyway.' He straightened up, the barrel of the Walther never wavering. 'Once I am finished here I will be gone and they will never find me. It is like trying to grab hold of a wisp of smoke, Captain Jensen. And it is why the *Abwehr* is so much better than your S-O-E.' He laboured over each letter, the disdain in his voice unmistakable.

'Your lock took me all of thirty seconds to defeat and I walked right in the front door.' Bergmann smirked now. 'I am not some petty burglar who climbs in people's windows.'

'But I am.' A girl's voice came from the shadows behind Bergmann. 'Drop the gun.'

Bergmann didn't move. 'Or what?'

'Or I'll cut you in half where you stand.' Abigail Jones stepped out from behind the heavy drapes with Jensen's Thompson in her fists. At this close range and with a 50-round drum attached, it was no exaggeration.

'If you shoot me, I will shoot him,' Bergmann countered. 'I may not wish to, but my natural reaction will be to squeeze the trigger. I cannot miss. Is that what you want?'

'Of course not.'

'Then put down the gun,' Bergmann told her. 'Unless you want to be responsible for killing your superior officer.'

'I didn't say I wouldn't,' she responded coolly. 'I just said I didn't want to. You might hit him. I will most definitely kill you.'

'You won't dare,' Bergmann said confidently. The Walther still hadn't moved offline from Jensen's chest.

'This is your last chance,' Jones said. There was no uncertainty in her voice.

Bergmann extended his arm, the barrel of the Walther barely a couple of yards from Jensen now – too far for the older man to reach, but close enough for a certain kill shot.

'And this is yours, *fraulein*.' Bergmann tried to see her from the corner of his eye, but she had shifted sideways out of his peripheral vision. 'Unless you want the blood of a dead officer on your hands, put down your weapon and step away.'

'Sir?'

'Yes, Corporal?'

'I'm terribly sorry, sir. But I think it's best that I do as he says.'

'Corporal Jones...'

'I don't want to get blood on your chair, sir.'

There was a rustle of movement and Bergmann glanced that way for the slightest of milliseconds.

In that millisecond, two things happened.

Jensen lurched towards the armchair on his right, and the Thompson submachine gun roared. The armchair went over with a crash under Jensen's weight as a .32 bullet whistled past him. A long burst of .45 rounds smashed Bergmann's legs out from underneath him and he screamed as he went down. The Walther fell from his grasp and was the least of his concerns as he writhed on the floor and grabbed at his shattered legs. Blood was everywhere and a cloud of gun smoke hung in the dimly-lit room.

'Keep the bastard alive, Jones,' Jensen wheezed, scrabbling across the floor towards the screaming German spy. 'We need him alive.'

Footsteps thundered in the hallway outside and fists hammered at the door.

'Come in! Come in!' Jensen bellowed. 'Get a medic!'

He reached Bergmann as a pair of soldiers charged into the room, and he clapped a hand onto an open bullet wound in the spy's thigh. Bergmann shrieked in agony as Jensen applied pressure to stop the bleeding.

Jones carefully put the Thompson down and slowly came to help. Catching her eye, Jensen gave her a short nod.

'You did good, lass,' he rasped. You did good.'

———

Waking with a start, Hastings was momentarily disoriented in the dark hold of the plane. He wasn't sure what had woken him, but the hairs on the back of his neck were prickling and he had a sense of danger.

He looked at Napier beside him, who was either praying or sleeping – probably the former, he figured – and not bothered by whatever had disturbed Hastings.

A crew member was coming past and Hastings grabbed his arm.

'How far out are we?'

The airman bent down to reply, and at that moment the Lancaster was rocked by a long burst of cannon fire.

The airman standing before him was thrown backwards by a hit, and cannon rounds smashed through the fuselage, causing the bomber to judder and sway.

Hastings felt the Lancaster drop and could hear both the rear gunner and the mid-upper gunner open up with their heavy Brownings. He held on tight as the plane banked hard right and threw him off-balance, and Napier shouted something he couldn't understand.

More rounds smashed through the fuselage and pieces of the airframe pinged about, each piece of flying steel enough to take one of them out before they knew it. A fighter screamed past deafeningly close and the mid-upper gunner let rip just above their heads. The flash of elation that Hastings felt disappeared just as fast when another fighter opened up on them and raked the Lancaster from side to side.

To a ground soldier it felt like the plane was going to split in half, and Hastings knew then that they were in the shit big time. He grabbed Napier's rig and pulled him close.

'Get moving!' he bellowed. 'We're going down.'

Napier didn't argue; that much was obvious. It didn't matter right now where they were, they just needed to get out. They got to their feet and staggered together towards the side crew door. The gunner above them was still pumping out bursts of fire and the rear gunner hadn't stopped, the noise combining with the roaring engines and wind blasting through the bullet holes to create a deafening atmosphere.

The Lancaster shuddered again and the hold was filled with screaming rounds, shrapnel and sparking ricochets, causing both men to throw their hands up and stagger back, in the hope of not getting hit. Miraculously neither was, but the rear guns went silent. Flames flickered from that direction and Hastings pushed Napier back the way they had come.

The bomber started to level out then pulled up, only to be hit hard near the front. It immediately banked left and Hastings was thrown to the floor, Napier tripping over him in the darkness. They fumbled their way to their feet and grabbed the fuselage for support.

'Side door,' Napier shouted, and Hastings pushed him in that direction.

Hastings stumbled again, falling over their packs which were lashed together with a parachute of their own, to be dropped separately. Strapped between them was the cumbersome wireless set, padded out to protect it. He dragged the heavy bundle behind him and followed Napier's bulky figure to the side crew door. The wind rushed in as the door was thrown open, and Napier was sucked forward by the slipstream. Hastings seized hold of him just in time, jerking him back with his left hand while holding onto the packs with his right. He snatched the rip cord for Napier's 'chute and clipped it onto the wire above the door, then did the same with the rip cord for the packs. Lastly, he hooked himself up.

The Lancaster came out of the banking manoeuvre and levelled to a degree, and he wondered if somehow the attackers had pulled back. Another shuddering burst of fire answered that question and he could smell electrical smoke now, even see it in the darkened interior, rolling towards them like a fog from the front of the aircraft.

It was time to take their chances and go.

He clapped Napier hard on the shoulder. 'Go!'

Napier disappeared out the door and Hastings heaved the packs out a couple of seconds after him. He took a final look around the darkened interior of the Lancaster, an acrid burning smell now ripping into his nostrils, then hurled himself out into the darkness of the night sky.

30

'Go!'

The bellow in his ear made Napier jump with fright, and a firm hand on his back shove him out into empty black space. His heart hit the back of his throat as he plunged through the air, deafening noise enveloping him – the rush of the wind, the howl of tortured metal, roaring engines and the thunder of machine guns. All around him tracer rounds were ripping through the sky.

The next second he felt a hard jolt upwards and his stomach flip-flopped again, wondering if he'd been shot.

Craning his head up, he could just make out his lines beneath the billowing parachute. The silk canopy looked to be the right shape and he couldn't see any tangles in the lines.

So far, so good.

The Lancaster was already gone from above him and banking away, an angry hornet on its tail with its guns flashing, a second fighter standing off and waiting for a turn.

He saw flames from one of the bomber's engines, the sky so black he couldn't even tell which wing. Muzzle flashes from the top of the Lancaster told him that the gunner there was still in the game.

'Get the bastards!'

It was Napier's own voice screaming in the night sky, but it sounded disembodied even to him.

He turned his attention to where he was going, knowing they had jumped much higher than planned. No idea how high or where, though – so dark and mountainous it could have been anywhere, could have been a mile away or just a few yards.

Napier craned his head up again, scanning to see if Hastings had made it. Another 'chute was over to his right but he couldn't see if it was a person or a bundle at the end of it.

Knowing he could only worry about himself right now, he peered down past his boots, realising quickly that the inky blackness was gone and all he could see was a dark white dotted with black patches.

Trees covering a mountainside, valleys and ridges around them, no lights in sight. He was heading for a long slope and it wasn't clear.

Oh sweet Lord, here it is.

He could see terra firma rushing up at him and he grabbed at the toggles, flaring at the last second and feeling a gentle tug back up before his feet hit, knees together, and he was down. Tumbling in a heap in the snow, Napier knew he hadn't broken anything, at least nothing he could feel yet.

He scrambled to his feet awkwardly, fell over, and tried again.

Looking around in the luminescent glow of the snow, he realised he was close to a thatch of spruce, the boughs heavily laden with snow. He was lucky he hadn't landed in one of the trees. Looking harder, he could see a parachute caught up in one of them, a dark shape swinging beneath it.

He was about to move towards it when he heard a rustle above him. He turned just in time to see Hastings flare and float expertly to ground, running a few paces before falling in the snow.

'Nice night for it,' Napier said breezily, trying to appear unruffled.

The Kiwi got to his feet, gave a grunt and started pulling in his parachute and ropes.

'Go grab the kit, would ya?'

Napier shrugged out of his harness and did as he was told,

climbing the tree that the packs were dangling from, the movements clumsy and awkward kitted up as he was. He managed to slash the ropes with the bayonet he carried – not as stylish or cool as Hastings' commando dagger, but it did the job – and send the packs to the ground with a dull thump, then it took an eternity to disentangle the silk itself and drag it down.

By the time he finally got his feet on the ground again, Hastings was ready and waiting. He had his Sten in one hand and his pack on his back, and was checking a compass. The wireless set was at his feet, housed in a plywood box that had sustained some damage on landing.

'Don't mind me,' Napier muttered, 'I've got this.'

Hastings gave him a blank look. 'Good.' He jerked a thumb over his shoulder. 'We're going that way, and you need to hurry up. The Jerries'll know where we are and it won't be long before there's ground troops on our arse.'

Napier wiped sweat from his face, the skin instantly feeling colder, and shoved the bundled parachute at him.

'Here, sort that out then will you, old man?'

Hastings added it to the bundle at his feet and buried the lot in a narrow crevice, kicking snow over it while his companion got himself sorted. Pack on, weapon cocked and ready and slung across his chest, sidearm checked and good to go. Napier hoisted the wireless set on top of Hastings' pack, securing it in place with a pair of straps. He grunted with the exertion.

'Forty-five pounds,' Hastings told him. 'Just be pleased you're not carrying the bastard.'

'Oh, I am, old man.' Napier gave a chuckle. 'Let me know if you need a spell, though. I'll do my bit.'

Hastings gave a nod, unsure if he was being sincere or not. 'Follow close behind,' he said in a low voice, conscious of sound carrying in the still conditions. 'Give me a tap if you need to stop, or we won't be stopping. We've got ground to make up. It's oh-two-hundred now and we've got about five or six hours of darkness to make ourselves scarce. I'm not sure where we are, but I'm guessing we're well short of our target. That means a tough job just got tougher, and we've got shit to do. We're gunna have to bust our balls to get on target tonight, so no shagging about. Any questions?'

There didn't seem any room for doubt, so Napier kept his mouth shut. He had the feeling they were in for a hell of a night, and there was nothing to do but just get on with it.

31

Thursday morning

T he trek up the mountainside started off tough and, as Hastings had predicted so succinctly, it just got tougher.

Hastings set a steady pace, eager to gain distance from their drop site but knowing that they probably had a good walk ahead of them, followed by the infiltration and mission itself. They made their way through the forest to the closest peak, using the trees to cover their trail from an aerial observation in daylight.

The darkness soon became comfortable as their eyes adjusted and they made good time, blowing hard by the time they emerged from cover and found themselves just below a ridgeline.

Pausing at the top, Napier planted his feet and sucked in air. His lungs and legs weren't used to such exertion, and he wondered how far they had to go. It had been some time since he'd been in the mountains and he'd forgotten what hard work it was.

He took a water bottle from his belt kit and drank greedily, not realising how parched he'd become during the flight and the subsequent walk. The butterflies in his stomach were still going hell for leather but at least his hands were steady and he'd lost the desperate urge to pee.

He watched as Hastings checked the map by shielded red light, checking his compass and the sky above as he tried to get their bearings.

'Are you navigating by the stars there, Captain Ahab?' Napier said, putting his bottle away and coming over.

'Can't see much with the cloud cover,' Hastings said, 'but I'm pretty confident I know where we are.' He turned the map so Napier could see it, and stuck the torch in his teeth so he could point. 'We're here...our target's here.'

'Oh.' Napier blinked. 'There looks to be a fair bit of ground between here and there, don't you think?'

'Yep. About a hundred miles as the crow flies.' Hastings indicated a valley on the other side of the mountain, leading down to what might have been a village or hamlet. 'We'll drop down that way, see if we can liberate some transport from somewhere, and head this way.'

Napier squinted at the map. 'By road?'

'Yep.'

He raised an eyebrow quizzically. 'Bit risky, isn't it?'

Hastings gave him a look. 'Mate, we're in Germany. The Germans don't like us much, and we're here to ruin their day. No one said it'd be easy.' He folded the map and tucked it back into his smock, giving a devilish grin. 'Besides, they won't expect a couple of the good guys to be strolling about here, will they?'

'No, not at all,' Napier said, trying to sound confident. 'They'd have to be mad to be here, wouldn't they?'

'That's right mate.' Hastings killed the light and tucked it away too. 'Stark raving bonkers. Give us a hand.'

They lowered his pack and he opened up the radio. Napier kept watch while Hastings powered it up and got out his ciphers. He tapped out a quick message to HQ, informing them of the attack and their safe landing a hundred miles off target, and their intention to continue on.

'Stand by,' he muttered, resting back on his haunches.

He knew there were radio operators and cipher clerks manning the network constantly, so it shouldn't take long to get a response. He assumed they would already know of the plane being attacked and probably shot down, unless the plane's radio had been taken out.

There had been no point telling HQ their exact location, as they could work that out for themselves. There was also no point wasting time telling them that they intended to lay low during the day – that would be a given, considering where they were. The sooner they got moving the better; he didn't know if the Germans would be using direction-finding kit this far behind their own lines, but it wouldn't pay to find out the hard way.

The response came back within a minute and Hastings concentrated hard, scribbling the code down on a slip of paper with the torch held between his teeth. The message was in Morse, but encrypted with a code known only to the two agents on the ground and the radio operators at base.

He decoded it as fast as he could. It was short and to the point. He read it aloud to Napier.

'Roger. Proceed with mission. Contact 1900.'

He tapped out a fast response acknowledging receipt, then packed up the radio. He tore the paper he'd used for the coding into little pieces and shoved it into his mouth, washing it down with a swallow of water. Getting to his feet, he heaved the load onto his back.

'Well that's that then,' Napier said. 'They didn't offer to swing by and pick us up, then?'

'Not a chance, mate. We've still got a bloke to rescue and a traitor to kill. Happy days.' He clapped Napier on the arm and began to move off. 'Come on, let's get on with it.'

Napier let out a sigh of resignation and fell in behind him.

'Stark raving bonkers indeed,' he muttered.

They followed the ridgeline a short distance before dropping down onto a snow-covered track cutting down at an angle towards the valley Hastings had identified. More snow was lightly falling, the flakes gently floating down, hopefully enough to cover their tracks.

There was no air activity, no fighters scrambling to strafe the mad invaders. That was a good sign, surely. Napier hoped the Lancaster crew had managed to fight off their attackers, but he knew in his heart it was highly unlikely at best.

Right now they were all probably either dead or captured. Maybe one or two were on the run, but he doubted they'd get far if they were. The escape and evasion training he'd had was pretty rudimentary and, when he'd been shot down, he'd been running on instinct more than training.

The sense of failure for being shot down and fear at being captured or killed had been huge, threatening to overwhelm him. At one point all he'd wanted was to be at home with his mum, curled up on the sofa by the fire, warm and comfortable and secure. Instead, he was running for his life, pursued by blood-thirsty Nazis in a foreign land with threats and danger all around.

On reflection, it was not too dissimilar to the position he found himself in now.

The track they were on dropped down sharply and the going became slower, both men tripping and falling a number of times, unseen obstructions catching their boots beneath the covering of snow. The mountainside dropped away on a broad white expanse to their right as they followed the track.

'It didn't have this on the brochure,' Napier said at one point, dusting himself off after yet another tumble.

Hastings gave a grin, his teeth glinting in the sparse moonlight. 'Not all jolly old hockey sticks, what?' he said, his tone mocking. 'Gets a bit tricky when you're down in the mud.'

Napier pursed his lips, the jibe too pointed to miss. He bit his tongue, deciding to keep his thoughts to himself. For now, at least.

'What're you waiting around for?' he retorted instead. 'Let's get moving.'

Hastings pulled a face of mock surprise.

'Oh, ready are ya?' He turned to go. 'Try and keep up...'

Napier felt a flash of anger and shoved the other man from

behind. Hastings staggered forward a couple of steps before whirling with his fists up.

'Really?' he growled. 'You didn't get enough last time?'

'If that's what it takes for you to keep your stupid bloody mouth shut,' Napier snapped, 'then have at it, old son.'

He was set and ready to go, and he wasn't going to back down. He'd had enough of the Kiwi's cheap shots about the RAF, about being a toff, and everything else that came out of his mouth. He knew it wasn't the ideal time to make a stand right here and now, but it was happening anyway.

Hastings shucked off his pack, putting it to the side carefully to protect the wireless. Napier followed suit.

'Don't say I didn't warn you,' Hastings said, weaving as he closed in.

'I should let you know, I happen to be the middle weight inter-services champ,' Napier said, watching him carefully.

He didn't know if Hastings had any formal boxing training, but he was certainly a tough bugger. He'd have to watch every – *crack*. Hastings caught him flush on the jaw, the snap punch so fast that Napier only saw the blur at the last second, pulling back just enough that he wasn't knocked over. Still it sent him back a step and he blinked hard, blocking the follow-up jab with his forearms.

He threw a fast one in response, more to give his opponent something to think about than anything else, and managed to brush Hastings' temple.

They closed up now, both men throwing body blows in a melee of grunts and swinging arms, neither willing to budge an inch. Punch after punch was blocked or absorbed, every strike followed up with another until they were grappling more than sparring as fatigue set in fast.

Napier's forearms were aching from blocking hard hits and he'd cracked his knuckles on Hastings' Sten, causing a rocket of pain to shoot up his wrist. He let go of Hastings' smock and shoved him hard in the chest, getting some space.

'Enough,' he panted, keeping his guard up. 'This is ridiculous.'

'You wanted it, *old chap*,' Hastings said, breathing hard. 'You saying you concede?'

Napier snorted. 'It's all about winning with you, isn't it? Got to win, got to have the last say.'

Hastings gave a grunt. 'You started it, mate. Now you don't want to finish it?'

Napier pondered that for a moment, knowing that if he conceded he would never hear the end of it. Hastings took his silence as a sign of surrender, and dropped his hands.

'All talk, no bloody trousers,' he said, turning his head to spit. 'Typical air force.'

He turned just in time to catch a right cross on his jaw as Napier lashed out. His head snapped to the side and he staggered back, his legs going wobbly beneath him. The bugger could punch, alright. He tried to catch his balance but instead stumbled off the track towards the open side, the world spinning around him.

There was a loud crack followed by a rushing swoosh, and the ground beneath his boots gave way.

Hastings dropped like a stone, plummeting down in a rush of falling snow.

'Oh, bloody hell!'

Napier leaped to the side of the hole that had appeared just off the side of the track, seeing his companion's dark head disappearing away in a cloud of white powder. The snow had been covering a crevice and Hastings' weight had been enough to cause a cave-in.

Dropping to his knees to peer down into the hole, all Napier could see was darkness. God only knew how far down it went, and he doubted that Hastings could have survived the fall. It probably dropped straight down the mountainside and his companion would now be lying smashed on rocks, somewhere down there in the depths of a frozen hell.

He dug out his torch and removed the red lens filter, shining it down into the abyss. All he could see was reflected white and the occasional black patch of rock.

'Hastings? Hastings, are you there? Hastings!'

He cocked his head and listened, the silence broken only by the crunch of ice beneath his knees and the gentle sift of loose powder in the well-like hole below him.

'Hastings! Are you alright?' He listened again. Still nothing. Oh Christ, this was not good. 'Hastings, are you there? Speak up, man!'

The narrow black hole gaped back at him like a mouth in a silent scream. Napier eased back on his haunches, flicking off his torch. He rubbed a hand over his face and took a deep breath to calm his nerves.

It was not good at all. He was deep behind enemy lines, unsure exactly where, on a mission he probably wouldn't make it back from and now his companion was dead. And from his own hand, to boot. If he hadn't lost his rag and thrown that last punch...good Lord, he could never own upto that.

If he made it out of this, he'd have to tell Captain Jensen that Hastings either fell down a cliff or his parachute didn't open properly and he died on landing. Maybe he died in combat...that was it, a skirmish with the Jerries and he copped it, fighting bravely to the end. Napier could put him forward for a medal – that'd really piss him off.

Napier was so lost in thought that he never heard the footsteps approaching up the track until they were only a few yards away. His head snapped up and he grabbed at the Sten, falling on his backside as he tried to bring the weapon to bear.

Hastings looked down at him with a smirk. 'You alright there, nancy-boy?

'I...I thought...Jesus.' Napier scrambled to his feet, not quite believing he'd ever be so happy to see the other man again. 'I thought you were dead.'

'Yeah, well.' Hastings gave a nonchalant shrug and jerked his thumb back down the track. 'It was just a little ravine, I slid down on my arse and popped out down there a ways.' He brushed snow off the sleeve of his smock and adjusted the Sten on its sling. 'No drama.'

'Oh...right.' Napier got himself together, doing his best to hide his relief. 'Jolly good, then. Glad you're okay and all that.'

Hastings shouldered his pack, settled the load, and eyed him.

'That was a cheap shot, though. Caught me when I wasn't looking.' He jutted his chin forward and Napier wondered if they were heading for Round Two. The Kiwi cracked a grin instead. 'So if you're finished blubbing and feeling sorry for yourself, let's crack on, eh?'

With that he turned and led the way down the track.

32

S nowflakes were wafting gently to the ground, settling on his bare head as Karol Jankowski stared out over the town.

His pulse was slowly coming down and the knot in his gut was easing. Screw that German bastard, Wolf. It had been unnecessary and left a foul taste in his mouth, ruining a perfectly pleasant evening.

The rooftop was easily accessed and it was peaceful up there, a good place for a contemplative smoke after another day of debriefing. God, it seemed to go on for ever. Questions, endless questions. Wolf had been there for a short time but the other officer, Fischer, had been the main interrogator today. Relentless, thorough, and with the personality of a dried turd, the SS officer had a cruel look about him.

The run-in with Wolf had unnerved him somewhat, if he was honest with himself. An assassination plot? Doubtful. He had the feeling the Nazi was messing with him, getting inside his head. Any advantage was a good advantage. How easily the man had humiliated him, though. And in front of Weiz, too. The Commandant was no friend of his, but at least he could talk to him.

Jankowski took a deep drag on his cigarette, holding the smoke in his lungs for several seconds before exhaling through his nose. He had no love for the Nazi men he was dealing with, but they were a necessary evil. They were his ticket to freedom; for now, at least.

He took a last drag on the cigarette and flicked the butt aside, watching it arc over the side of the side of the hotel roof. Beneath his feet was his room, comfortable enough without being plush. More comfortable than a wooden bunk in a room shared with ten others. He shrugged his shoulders in the heavy coat, shifting the collar higher on his neck. It was cold here, but his belly was full and he had a warm bed to go to. If Colonel Weiz was playing the game right, there'd even be a girl for him. Hopefully a working girl and not one of the staff from the hotel next door – he wasn't squeamish about getting rough, it was just easier if he didn't have to.

The town was in darkness, not a light to be seen. Even this far behind their own lines, the Germans were careful.

Jankowski took a deep breath of the cold air, feeling himself eventually smile. The only thing he needed to worry about here was maybe a bombing a raid or, more likely, not getting the clap from one of the working girls.

Small things. Wolf and his mind games aside, life here in Alpenbad was pretty decent. Tomorrow would be more debriefing, but Weiz had promised him a spa and a massage at the end of the day. It was just what he needed right now; the tension in his neck and shoulders was as bad as it had ever been. He closed his eyes and turned his face to the sky, feeling the soft flakes brush his face as they drifted down. He breathed in the cold air and felt a shiver run down his spine. The chill felt cleansing, and helped him to push aside the negative thoughts.

Tomorrow was another day. Another day of opportunities to prosper.

Jankowski turned and headed for the rooftop access door. He had things to do and it was far too cold to be out tonight.

———

The hamlet they reached beneath the mountain was barely big enough to even warrant the name, and it was obvious that anything they did there would be quickly noticed.

They carried on past instead, sticking to a track that gave them good space from the houses. Not even a dog barked and soon they were gone, two shadows in the dark. They marched in silence, shifting back to the main road once they were clear of the hamlet, with Hastings setting a cracking pace now that they were on the flat.

The next village was larger, at least according to the map, and he hoped to find some kind of transport there. They were well behind schedule and had only about an hour until daybreak.

When that came they would be horribly exposed, so they had better either be on target or hunkered down somewhere safe well before that happened.

It was dangerous to be on the main road but he doubted the Germans would normally have roadblocks set up, not this far behind their own lines; there would be no point, and the Germans were nothing if not efficient. Mind you, if they thought the Allies were there, the two men were just as likely to stumble into an ambush. It was frustrating not knowing what the enemy knew.

They would make their best time by taking the most direct route and keeping their eyes and ears open for any sign of trouble. It was bloody risky, but it was a chance they had to take.

They were delayed by at least a day, if not longer. For all they knew that would be too late, so they needed to get on target as fast as possible.

The cold was a good motivation to keep moving too, and he deliberately kept the few stops very short. If he'd had his way they'd have kept moving and not stopped at all, but he knew that Napier – or Balfour-Napier or whatever the hell his name was – was neither as fit as him nor used to marching.

Time would tell how useful the pilot actually proved to be, but Hastings wasn't holding his breath. He had the distinct impression that the officer would faint dead away at the first shot fired. It was one thing to be zipping around the skies playing war, but quite another to be down there amongst it.

What he wouldn't have given to have a section of SAS lads with him rather than some toff pilot, even if he could throw a decent punch. A Bren gun, a stash of grenades and they'd be into it. The Jerries wouldn't know what had hit them.

The next village came up before they knew it, and Hastings moved to the shoulder of the road beneath the lee of a bank. Standing with his mouth half open and his head cocked, he closed his eyes and listened. Many was the time he'd located a lost lamb in the hills by using this trick, and he'd discovered in war that it worked just as well on men.

Right now, all he could hear was Napier breathing heavily and rustling his clothing. Hastings frowned and concentrated. There was a scrape then a glug of water, and Napier slurped at his bottle. Hastings frowned harder and cracked one eye open.

'Would you shut up?' he hissed. 'I can't hear a damn thing.'

Napier wiped his mouth on his sleeve. 'Sorry.' He held still for a few moments, watching as Hastings went back into his listening pose.

A belch erupted from Napier's gut quite unexpectedly, and he clapped his hand to his mouth. Hastings opened his eyes and glared at him.

'Shut – up,' he grated.

'Sorry, old man. No idea where that came from.'

'And keep your voice down; d'you want to wake every Fritz in the bloody village?'

'Sorry.'

'And stop saying sorry. You sound like an idiot.'

'Sor...' Napier stopped and thought for a second. 'My apologies. I'll try to be less idiot-like.'

Hastings pulled a face as if to say he doubted that could happen. 'Come on, watch our backs and stick close.'

They moved forward, the night still pitch dark as they headed towards the edge of the village. The only sounds they could hear was the crunch of their boots on the icy ground. Napier desperately wanted to sniff but settled for wiping his nose on his sleeve instead. The snot would probably freeze so hard he'd scratch himself on it later. The thought made him giggle but he quickly stifled it before Hastings turned on him, knowing it was just nerves.

The high street of the village was snow covered and in darkness, the businesses closed and the houses all shut up, blackout curtains in place to stymie any Allied bombers venturing this far. Hastings figured they were less likely to be seen by any insomniac locals if they avoided the residential areas, so he led the way straight up the main drag. They stuck to the shadows and moved quickly, but he knew it was still helluva risky. If they got spotted they'd have to leg it and hope for the best. And if they got rumbled, it was all on.

They were nearly through the village when he heard a low growl from his left. He paused and peered into the darkness, quickly spotting the source of the noise. A German shepherd dog, standing in a yard, nose above a low fence. Ears and hackles up, eyes locked on Hastings. Its shoulders were tensed, ready to spring into action.

Another low growl sounded from its throat. It would only be seconds before the beast erupted into a bark, bringing all manner of attention they didn't want.

Hastings glanced at the building they were outside. A small, shabby brick building with a sign hanging over the door. *Polizei*. He groaned inwardly; just what they needed. The village policeman probably lived on-site. Beyond the dog was a kennel in a tiny yard. Judging by the size of the building, the occupant would be sleeping only a few yards away.

Hastings made a soft clucking with his tongue and avoided eye contact with the dog. It was already on alert, and he didn't want to antagonise it by appearing as a threat. It was the big dog here and they were intruding on its territory. He clucked again, hoping Napier didn't do anything stupid.

They could always shoot the animal if they had to, but it was obvious and would immediately ring alarm bells on discovery. The Jerries would know someone had been there. More than that, it went against his grain to kill an innocent animal for no reason. The dog was doing what it was supposed to do. They just needed to keep it calm and make space.

Hastings stepped back, keeping the dog in his peripheral vision but not eyeballing it. It could be over that fence in a flash and then there'd be trouble. He sensed Napier following his lead, moving back into the street. The crunch of their boots on the frozen ground seemed deafeningly loud in the silence of the sleeping village.

The dog's growl rumbled again, long and low as it watched the two strangers back away. Hastings was unsure if the growl was the dog exerting its authority over them, getting the last word in as they backed down, or if it was the precursor to a full bark.

He edged his right hand to the Welrod pistol he had tucked in the front of his belt. The SOE-designed weapon was almost fully silent, but the lightweight .32 rounds would lack the necessary punch to put a charging dog down with one shot. He would need to be fast and accurate to get the job done.

Reaching the roadway, Hastings kept his head down and slunk past the dog, making sure his body language was completely submissive. In a few seconds he was past it and melting into the shadows, the light footfalls behind him letting him know that Napier was right there.

Once they were out of sight of the dog, Napier came alongside him.

'Well that was bloody close,' he whispered. 'I thought the blighter was coming over that fence for a piece of old Black Jack Hastings.'

Hastings cocked an eyebrow. 'Black Jack?' he said.

Napier shrugged, keeping pace beside him. 'It suits you. You remind me of a pirate. I could see you in days gone by on the high seas with a bunch of rogues, pillaging and looting and what have you.'

Hastings gave the slightest chuckle. 'I thought someone must've told you. That's my nickname.'

It was Napier's turn to raise an inquisitive eyebrow. 'Really?'

'You burn pretty dark in the desert,' he said. 'Some of the boys thought I was a Maori.'

Napier chuckled. 'Ergo, Black Jack,' he said. 'Fair enough.'

'What about you?' Hastings adjusted the Welrod in his belt, wishing he had a holster for it. With that and the Browning on his hip, the dagger and the submachine gun, he guessed it was no surprise Napier saw him as a pirate. 'Got a nickname?'

'No, not at all,' Napier snorted. 'I have enough trouble with my normal name, let alone a bloody nickname.'

'You don't like having a double-barrelled name?'

'It's a pain in the bloody arse,' Napier said bluntly. 'Who needs two names anyway? I'd be happy if I was just plain old Jim Smith. Balfour-Napier? What kind of handle is that? Quite the mouthful. Bloody ridiculous, if you ask me.'

Hastings nodded to himself in the darkness. His companion's depth of feeling on his name surprised him, but he kept his thoughts to himself. In his experience toffs always seemed to have ridiculous names, so he guessed Freddie Napier was about as plain as he could get.

They walked on in silence for half an hour, following the main road towards the next town. They kept the pace up, Hastings determined to maintain at least five miles an hour.

Dawn was creeping quickly closer.

33

As the grey light of dawn oozed skyward, Hastings took them off the road and into the foothills of the mountains again. This time, given they were so close to the road and the snow had stopped falling, he took more care to avoid leaving any sign behind them.

Moving carefully, they trekked uphill a mile or so, deliberately taking a route away from the most likely, making their way through heavier undergrowth and being careful not to dislodge the snow-laden lower tree branches.

Pulling up short in a scraggy ravine, Hastings ran his eye over the ground. 'This'll do,' he whispered.

'Time to build a bivvy?' Napier shucked off his pack and rolled his shoulders, hearing a satisfying series of pops as his joints loosened up.

Hastings nodded. 'Better get cracking too, the sun's not far away. And keep your voice down.'

Together they worked fast to build themselves a hide that would both conceal them from any observers and also protect them from the elements. The temperature was bitingly cold, all the more noticeable now they had stopped walking and dropped their packs. It wouldn't take long to get hypothermic in these conditions if they weren't careful.

A good-sized spruce had fallen from above the ravine, and its rotting trunk lay at an angle from the lip of the ravine, creating a natural hide in the hollow beneath. The branches fanned out to give it width.

Hastings broke off a pair of small branches from beneath it and backtracked to sweep away the little sign they had left behind them. They scooped out snow to make the hide deeper and create walls around them, then tossed in any loose fronds and leaf matter that they could find to create a layer of insulation from the ground.

Burrowing in first, Napier took out their blankets and laid one down on the makeshift flooring. The other could go over the top once they were settled in. He arranged their packs and cleared some more branches from the underside of the tree trunk to give them room to move without losing an eye in the process.

Hastings came in last, sweeping behind him to be sure they were as undetectable as possible. He hunkered in beside Napier, who was busily getting a meal sorted. He had only brought minimal rations, but a tin of bully beef scooped onto hard biscuits would keep the wolves at bay.

'Rather snug isn't it, old man?' Napier observed, trying and failing not to elbow his companion as they got themselves organised.

'Watch it,' Hastings grumbled. He unslung his Sten and laid it at the ready. 'Here's our front arc of fire.'

'Uh-huh.' Napier gave a cursory nod and set about opening his tin.

'Are you looking?' Hastings pointed out beneath the tree trunk, where a small gap allowed them a decent view of the slope below them. 'Any Germans will either come up here or down from above us. If it's from above us, we won't see them until it's late.'

'Oh.' Napier stopped and blinked. 'Well what happens then?'

'We're buggered then, aren't we? They'll probably drop a grenade in and blow us to smithereens. Least, that's what I'd do, anyway.'

'I see.' Napier nodded thoughtfully. 'Jolly good, then.'

Hastings shook his head to himself and decided he'd better just deal with anything that came up on his own.

'What d'you reckon about a little fire?' Napier inquired, prying the lid off his bully beef.

'No.'

'Not even a little one?'

'No.'

'Haven't seen anyone since we landed, old man. I doubt they'll be poking around looking for us, don't you think?'

Hastings gave him a look. 'Two reasons why not, fly boy. One, you'll smoke us out in here. Two, the smell'll carry for bloody miles. We've got no idea if there's no Germans for miles, or if there's a garrison of the buggers a hundred yards down the road. So, no fires – eat it cold.'

'Very well,' Napier muttered, propping himself on an elbow and awkwardly using a biscuit as a spoon. 'No need to be so grumpy, old chap.'

Hastings grit his teeth and wriggled forward a bit further. 'I'll take first watch. I'll wake you when it's your turn. Once it gets close to dark we'll send a signal back to Jensen.'

'Jolly good.' Napier munched on his first mouthful. It was no *foie gras*, that was for sure.

'Oh.' Hastings looked over his shoulder at him. 'If you need a piss, do it in the snow down the far end. And if you need a shit, don't.'

Napier nodded again and swallowed. 'Got that. Wees yes, poos no. No problem.'

Hastings turned back to cover the arc, the Sten in his hands. He was cold and knew he would get colder, but right now it didn't matter.

Someone needed to keep watch and he was it.

'What's your issue with medals?' Napier asked after a few minutes.

'What?' Hastings grunted.

'Medals. You know, the shiny things they pin on you.' Napier shovelled more bully beef and biscuit into his mouth. 'You don't like them?'

Hastings gave a snort. 'Don't need 'em,' he said curtly.

'Nice to be recognised for what you've done though, don't you think?' Napier prodded. 'Everyone likes a pat on the back, don't they?'

Hastings grunted again and shot him a look.

'I don't need bloody medals to tell me I done a good job. One man can't do everything on his own; it's a team effort. If they want to give me a bloody gong, they should give all the boys one as well.' He paused, checking the arcs before adding, 'I'm nothing bloody special. I'm just a farm boy like anyone else, trying to get through this thing without getting my bollocks shot off by some dirty Hun.'

'Fair enough.'

Napier nodded silently to himself. It made more sense now. He wondered if that was an Antipodean thing; they were certainly a different breed, these wild men from New Zealand and Australia.

He recalled his initial thoughts on the man back in the Cairo hotel. Definitely not too different to the Celts. It was as if they were basically from the same stock as the English but wilder, more rugged and perhaps a little more towards their caveman origins.

There'd been a few in the RAF and he had to admire their tenacity and skill, not to mention their balls-out bravery. Al Deere had been one he had much admiration for, among others.

His thoughts drifted back to the issue of medals. He knew Pa had been incredibly proud when he won his DFC, and Napier had revelled in the adulation it brought within his family. Even if his actions were never recognised again, he had a medal that would always have pride of place within the Balfour-Napier family.

After the war he would be rolled out for formal functions, resplendent in his number ones with a cross on his chest that was polished to within an inch of its life. It was something that could never be taken away from him.

Of course, his older brother may well overtake him. Squadron Leader Christopher (never Chris) Balfour-Napier (both names, thank you very much) of Bomber Command, several years older and regular force before the war. He'd already been in a command position when '39 happened, and although he'd flown a few missions he was largely behind the scenes.

Pulling the strings and making strategic decisions to protect the country, their father said. Didn't need to be out there putting his neck on the line; he'd done that and his superior intellect meant his skills lay elsewhere.

All nonsense, as far as Napier was concerned. It was all very well being tucked away in an ops room somewhere making plans for others to execute, and quite another to be up in the clouds dodging tracer and hoping the old kite held together until you could nurse it home. Still, here he was on this insane mission, a mission he would probably never be able to talk about and for which he doubted there would ever be any medals given.

Hastings should be happy with that; the man didn't seem to like talking at the best of times.

Napier tucked away his tin and tidied up, before settling down under the blanket.

He had the feeling it was going to be a long day.

34

M ajor Heinrich Wolf had learned to take small pleasures when he could. A man of war led a busy life, never knowing when the next moment of rest may come. The next meal, the next breath of fresh air.

The Imperial's dining room was pure luxury compared to what he'd experienced – high ceilings, tall windows with ornately carved sashes, luxurious drapery. A fireplace on the far wall, chandeliers above the linen-laid tables.

He was a man well used to enclosed spaces, tight, airless rooms that reeked of fear and desperation. Places he enjoyed, taking a grim satisfaction from the work he did in these places. The move from the regular force to the Waffen-SS had been a good move for him. Adept as he had been as a battlefield soldier, he was in his element in the elite unit.

It brought with opportunities well-suited to a man of his skill and inclination.

Draining the china cup of the last vestiges of thick, black coffee, Wolf lifted a white linen napkin to wipe his mouth. As he did so, he spied the portly figure of Colonel Weiz waddling across the Imperial Hotel's dining room towards him.

He sighed inwardly. The man was disappointing in many ways, not least in the slovenly way he carried himself. The florid complexion and fat gut told Wolf that the man was ready to drop dead at any moment. He was no man of war, that was for sure. Perhaps, once Wolf's mission here in Alpenbad was done, he may suggest to his superiors that the man could be re-assigned to somewhere a little more demanding. It paid to keep men on their toes, especially in times of war.

Wolf folded the napkin carefully and placed it back on the tabletop. He was eating alone, which suited him just fine. He had no need for company or pleasantries. He forced a smile onto his face as Weiz reached him. The colonel leaned against the back of the chair opposite Wolf, breathing heavily. Wolf made no effort to hide a look of distaste.

'*Guten morgen*, Herr Wolf,' the Colonel wheezed.

'*Guten morgen*, Herr Commandant.' Wolf folded his hands on the table before him. 'Another beautiful day here in the paradise that is Alpenbad, isn't it? A raid was repelled last night, and an enemy bomber was shot down in the mountains. I take it you heard?'

'Yes, of course.' Weiz wiped a handkerchief across his damp face. 'Another success to our excellent Luftwaffe.'

'Indeed, Herr Colonel. There is no doubt in my mind that this supposed incursion by the English was stopped dead in its tracks by that one action.'

Ignoring the waitress who came to refill the SS man's cup, Weiz looked doubtful. 'Really, Major? What makes you say that?'

'At least one parachute was seen descending from the aircraft,' Wolf explained slowly, as if he was speaking to a child. 'I suggest this would have been either the crew, or these supposed paratroopers. Either way, there is no way they could survive up there in the Bavarian mountains.' He gave a short laugh, watching the waitress' backside as she moved away. 'Whatever the English think they could achieve here in Alpenbad, I suggest their dreams are dashed. No Englishman is hardy enough to survive out there.'

Weiz still looked doubtful, but he nodded and made all the right sounds anyway. It paid not to disagree with the SS.

'Anyway, my apologies. What can I do for you this morning, Herr Colonel?'

'I have some information I think you may find interesting.' Weiz pulled out the chair and flopped into it gratefully.

Wolf subconsciously edged back from the table.

'One of the domestic staff came to see me this morning.' Weiz paused to wipe his forehead with a handkerchief. 'I rushed down here immediately to tell you.'

Wolf waited silently. In the absence of a platitude of some sort, Weiz forged ahead.

'She caught one of the staff sneaking in the back door last night. After curfew.'

Wolf's face remained impassive as he listened.

'When my...the woman...she asked her what she was doing out late, she said she was going for a walk.' Weiz leaned an elbow heavily on the table, angling in conspiratorially. Wolf shifted back almost imperceptibly. 'She believes the girl was up to no good, and told me immediately.'

Wolf arched a blonde eyebrow. 'Immediately, Herr Colonel? She told you last night then? And you are only telling me this now?'

Weiz's jowls wobbled as he shook his head. 'No, no, of course...I mean...well, perhaps "immediately" is not quite accurate...she told me first thing this morning, just now in fact. Of course, I came and told you straight away.'

'I see.' Wolf pursed his lips and turned the information over in his mind.

The existence of a spy in their midst was deeply troubling, and this tid-bit of information could well be the crucial link in the chain. Or it could just as well, and more likely, be nothing more than gossip and innuendo. So what if a girl was caught out after curfew? She was probably returning from an illicit liaison with one of the troops, as was commonplace.

'Who is this girl?'

'The maid? A girl called Carla.'

'And your informant?'

'She is a supervisor.' Weiz lifted his chin proudly. 'I promoted her myself. Very trustworthy, very trustworthy indeed.'

'This is not the supervisor who put one of the domestics in the infirmary last night, is it? Hilde Schenken?'

Weiz paled and sat back in his chair. 'Why...yes, I mean...yes, it is her.' He frowned quizzically at Wolf. 'She put one of the domestics in the infirmary, you say? How is this possible?'

'The better question is how is it possible that you did not know this, Herr Colonel,' Wolf said coolly. 'I knew of it last night. She beat a girl nearly to death in the kitchen. Quite a nasty wound, so I am told,' he paused, then added, 'by *your* staff.'

Weiz's jaw trembled but no words came out.

'Perhaps you may want to reconsider the level of trust you place in your source, Herr Colonel. Regardless of that, and naturally I am no prude when it comes to the application of violence, but there is an issue beyond this that goes to the root of last night's incident.'

Weiz was breathing heavily now, and his forehead was gleaming. He looked like he wanted to be anywhere else but right here, right now. Wolf couldn't deny the thrill of excitement that gave him.

'One of the signallers housed here has been talking out of school about his work. It was he who spoke to the girl who was assaulted last night by your friend, *Fraulein* Schenken. This girl, Angela, she in turn blabbed about it over dinner, leading to the incident.'

Colonel Weiz looked positively sick now, and Wolf had the abstract thought that perhaps the man would have a heart attack right here at the table. He dismissed the thought immediately; if he did, then so be it. He should have kept his house in better order.

Looking past Colonel Weiz to the open entrance doors of the dining room, Wolf saw two of his men striding past with a young signaller between them.

'In fact,' he said, rising to his feet. 'It appears I must go. I have somebody I wish to speak to. We will talk again later about this information you have.' He clicked his heels together as Weiz stood, and gave the fat man the Nazi salute. 'Heil Hitler, Herr Commandant.'

He ignored Weiz's feeble attempt at a salute and headed for the door.

Striding through the door into the foyer, he passed by a pretty, dark-haired maid who was wiping a mirror on the wall.

Carla watched him in the reflection as he went out the front doors, the same way Pieter had just been taken. She felt like throwing up, but forced herself to concentrate on cleaning the mirror. It was a fine-looking piece with intricate gilt edging. Hearing footsteps behind her, she spotted movement in the reflection.

Emerging from the service hallway were two more black-clad SS men. Each was holding the arm of a young girl who was being hustled along.

Carla's heart dropped when she saw the girl's beaten face with the swollen-closed eye.

35

I t was mid-afternoon before they came for Carla.

She was rinsing cups in the sink when two men entered the kitchen. One she immediately recognised as Major Wolf. The other was a sharp-faced Captain she had seen before but who's name she did not know.

'*Fraulein* Bettelheim,' Major Wolf said, closing the door behind them.

'*Jawohl*, Herr Major.' Carla put down the cup she had been rinsing, and wiped her hands on a cloth. She kept the cloth in her hands as she faced them. Both men stopped just inside the door, and Carla wasn't sure, but she thought she saw a flicker of recognition cross the major's face when he looked at her. Just the sight of him twisted her gut into knots.

'I am Major Wolf of the Waffen-SS,' Wolf said stiffly, throwing out a sharp Nazi salute. 'Heil Hitler.'

Carla returned the salute with much more enthusiasm than she felt.

'This is Captain Fischer.'

The man beside him, bearing the rank insignia of a Hauptmann, gave her a brief nod but said nothing. He was maybe ten years younger than Wolf, maybe five years older than Carla herself.

'How may I help you, sir?' Carla kept her voice as calm as she could, but her mind was racing a million miles an hour.

Pieter and Angela had been taken for interrogation; now they were here for her. An interrogation was obviously to follow, and she knew that would only end one way. It was one thing if she was some dumb fool who knew nothing, but she wasn't. They would know that she knew something and they would get it out of her – one way or another.

Angela must have told them she had asked questions; what a stupid fool she'd been. She couldn't blame Angela for it. It had been her own eagerness that got carried away, and now she would have to face the consequences of her stupidity. She had been naïve to ever think she could play this game of spies and walk away a winner. She was just a silly girl playing a game she didn't know the rules to.

A tiny bird was trapped in her chest, its wings beating frantically to be let out. She stared at the hard-faced men before her.

'You are anxious, *fraulein*?' Wolf's tone was soft, but his eyes never missed a trick.

'Yes sir,' she said honestly.

'Why are you anxious, Carla?' His manner was that of a kindly uncle, and it was at that moment that a switch tripped in Carla's brain.

He wasn't here on solid evidence – he was trying to trip her up. If they knew what she'd done, they would have dragged her out of there in chains. It was only a guess but it somehow seemed right to her. That single thought gave her the tiniest bit of confidence and she felt her pulse drop ever so slightly.

His eyes were still on her. They were the pale blue of hard-frozen ice.

'I do not know, sir,' she said, looking into his face then quickly away. 'I am not used to speaking to men...powerful men like you, Major Wolf.'

'I see.' He hesitated for a fraction of a second, as if her answer had thrown him.

Her mother had told her a long time ago that men were simple creatures; all it took to get your way to bat your eyelids and stroke their ego. Her mother had laughed when she said it, that carefree laugh that she had, and Carla had thought at the time it was a silly thing to say. It couldn't possibly be true. As she matured into womanhood, she realised that never had a truer word been said.

Josef had told her many things as part of the informal training he gave her, and one of them had reinforced her mother's message of long ago. They had been walking in the forest when he told her this, the birdsong cheerful around them as they discussed the dark arts of espionage.

'Men don't believe a woman can defeat them. That goes double for a young girl. This is why women are the best spies.' He had smiled, his eyes crinkling but sad. 'Men's egos are their worst weakness. You must play on that every chance you get.'

'But how can I do that, Josef?' Carla had feigned innocence. 'I do not know how to do this.'

He had laughed and clapped his hands, his eyes crinkling now with delight. 'I think you will know, Carla, I think you will know.'

The twin memories flashed through Carla's mind in a split-second, and she felt herself lift inside.

I can do this. I must do this.

'You spoke to a girl called Angela last night,' Wolf said. 'Yes?'

'Yes sir.' Carla nodded without hesitation. 'That is true.'

He waited, but she didn't fill the silence, forcing him to continue.

'She said some things here, at dinner.' He looked about him as if noticing the kitchen for the first time. 'Here in this very room.'

'Yes sir, that is also true.' Carla pulled a face. 'It was horrible.' She gave a shudder at the memory, which required no acting.

He nodded slowly, his eyes never leaving her face. 'We will talk about that later. You spoke to her later, up in the bathroom at your house. That is correct?'

'Yes Herr Major, at our dormitory.' She nodded her agreement enthusiastically. 'I helped her to clean her face up after the...' she gestured vaguely at the table..., 'the...what happened.'

'Yes, I see she was injured. Quite badly, it seems.'

'Very badly, sir, yes.'

Carla was speaking without hesitation to show her willingness to co-operate, all the while holding her hands clasped together with the dishcloth in front of her. Not only did it make her seem non-threatening but it served to push her breasts together, and she had already caught Major Wolf's gaze flick down to the hint of cleavage she knew would be peeking out from the top of her blouse.

It revolted her to do it, but as her mother had said, men were simple creatures.

'You asked her questions about what she said,' Wolf said.

'I asked her how she was, sir. Yes, I did ask that. She was very upset.'

'You asked her about what she said at the dinner table.' A flat edge creeped into his voice, and she pegged it straight away; she knew he was getting to the point.

'No sir.' She shook her head firmly, and looked him in the eye. 'I asked her nothing about that, sir. It was just silly nonsense, just gossip. She said the Englanders were coming, but they are not.' She spread her hands expressively and looked around the room. 'I do not see any Englanders here, sir. She was talking nonsense.'

Wolf's gaze did not falter.

'She tells me you asked her specifically about it. You wanted to know when they were coming and how she knew this.'

'No sir.' From the depths of her belly, a firm undertone burst out. 'I did not. That is not true, sir. I did not believe what she said, and I have no reason to talk to her about it.'

Silence fell and the pressure of it bore down on Carla's shoulders. She desperately wanted to fill it with more explanation, but she knew it would be a mistake. It was best to appear co-operative and just a little less smart than the interrogator. The best lies are those based on truth, with just enough untruth thrown in to muddy the waters; another lesson from dear Josef.

Carla clenched her hands together around the dishcloth and mentally dug her toes in, holding on for dear life.

Eventually it was Wolf who had to break the silence.

'I see,' he said softly. 'Tell me then, *fraulein* – why would your friend say this about you? It is a serious accusation to make.'

'It is, sir,' Carla agreed. 'It is not a nice thing for her to say that, but it is not true, I assure you.'

'I am not a man who takes these matters lightly,' Wolf said calmly. 'The SS is not an organisation that people should tell lies to.' He caught her eye and held it. 'Is it, *fraulein* Carla?'

'No sir, absolutely not.' She shook her head vigorously. 'I know that.'

'Tell me what happened then.'

'I helped her clean her face, I made sure she was alright, and I told her to go to bed.' She shrugged. 'Then I went to bed myself.' She looked up at him dolefully. 'That is all, sir. That is what happened.'

'I see.' Wolf pursed his lips and tapped a finger against his chin thoughtfully. 'Tell me then, why would she say this? Why would she tell me, an SS officer, that you were unusually interested in what she had said?' He leaned in close enough for her to smell his coffee breath. 'Her words, Carla. "Unusually interested".' He leaned back again. 'Why would she say that?'

Carla considered her response for a moment, hoping that it gave her the appearance of racking her brains. She knew what she was going to say, and she knew the possible consequence of it. But there was no other way. *The best lies are based on truth, with just enough untruth thrown in to muddy the waters.*

'I can only think of two things, sir,' she said carefully. 'She had a big hit on the head last night. Maybe it affected her brain...you know, her memory.' She tapped her temple for emphasis. 'I don't know.' She shrugged and dropped her hand back down. 'Or she has simply lied to you.'

'Lied to me?' Major Wolf gave her a surprised look. 'That is a bold accusation to make, is it not?'

'It must be true, sir. I did not make her say those things at dinner, none of us did. She said it all herself. Now it seems she is in trouble for it.' Carla looked him straight in the eye again. In her peripheral vision she could see Hauptmann Fischer standing back, watching and listening silently. Taking no part in the conversation; this was Major Wolf's show. Carla ignored him.

'Perhaps she wants to talk her way out of it, perhaps she thinks saying someone else did something wrong will be better for her.' She did not blink. 'But I did not do that, sir. She is either wrong or she is lying.' She gave a final nod. 'I think it was the bang on the head, sir.'

'Interesting.' Wolf took a long, slow breath. 'Very interesting.' He turned to look at Fischer. 'What do you think, Herr Fischer? It seems someone is telling us lies.'

Carla felt her left leg suddenly begin to tremble, as if she was having a spasm. It felt as if it was about to give out on her. She pressed her knuckles against the front of her thigh as hard as she could without drawing attention to herself. Praying it would stop just as suddenly, she barely dared to breathe.

The Englanders had failed to appear at the 0600 rendezvous that morning, and she had been on edge all day since. Wondering what had happened. Waiting. The gossip around the hotel had been that a raid had happened some distance away, and a bomber had been shot down. Of itself, that wasn't unusual. But this bomber had been alone, miles away from the raid. Perhaps it was lost, but regardless, it had been shot down over the mountains. As usual, Carla had listened to the gossip, sifting out the known facts from the opinions and guesswork. She had been careful not to ask any questions this time, and only commented to praise the brave Luftwaffe for protecting them from a bombing raid.

She knew little of such things, but a gnawing feeling in her gut told her that was the plane the paratroopers were coming from. And now they were gone. She could only pray that she was wrong. At six o'clock tomorrow morning she would know for sure.

Pushing the thoughts aside, she turned her attention back to the SS men.

Fischer licked his lips and sniffed. He gave an indifferent look to his superior.

'I would suggest someone is telling us something that is perhaps lies, sir,' he agreed. 'Or perhaps, as the young lady says, this girl is mistaken.'

The trembling eased and Carla gave her leg a surreptitious shake, willing the tingly feeling away.

Fischer looked from Wolf to Carla. 'Unless the young lady is indeed a spy?' He stared hard at her. 'Are you a spy, *fraulein*?'

Carla's leg nearly collapsed under her and she pressed down hard to try and keep it in place. She'd never experienced this before, but she'd never been interrogated before either.

A girlish titter escaped her lips before she could stop it, and both looked at her curiously.

'Did I say something funny?' Fischer inquired coldly.

'No, sir.' Carla's cheeks burned hot and she put a hand to her mouth, the weak leg quickly replaced by another almost-calamity. 'Not at all. It's just...I am not a spy, sir. I am just a hotel maid.' She shook her head with obvious embarrassment. 'I know nothing of these things, sir. I am just a girl.'

Wolf chuckled and turned back to her. 'Thank you for your time, *fraulein*. We will let you get on with whatever it is you were doing.' He cast an eye around the kitchen then back to her. 'Washing the dishes, was it?'

'Yes, sir. Thank you, sir.' Carla bowed her head subserviently.

'Oh.' Wolf paused as he began to turn away. 'One more thing, *fraulein*.'

Carla stayed where she was, the dishcloth in her hands. She was gasping for a glass of water.

'I understand you were caught coming in late last night. After curfew.'

Fischer gave a quizzical frown, obviously unaware of this piece of information. Carla's mind raced but the response was ready without even needing to think about it.

'It was just before curfew, yes sir. Only a couple of minutes before.

Hilde, my supervisor, she was somewhere outside and she saw me.' She looked suitably apologetic. 'I would have been inside on time if she hadn't stopped me, sir.' Wolf was giving nothing away, but she had the feeling she was responding okay on this one. Almost as an afterthought, she added, 'I don't know where she'd been, sir, but I was at the door before she got there. It is not best advice to argue with her though, sir, as you have heard for yourself.'

She gestured again towards the table, as if they could see the result of Hilde's assault on Angela for themselves.

'I do my best to stay out of her way, sir. With respect, I mean... well, you know...'

Wolf's eyes flickered, and he spoke to Fischer while still watching Carla.

'Hauptmann Fischer? Do you have any more questions for this young lady?'

'No, sir. Thank you.'

'Well.' Wolf gave a smile that would have been charming if she couldn't see the evil behind it. 'Thank you for your time, *fraulein*. We will be going now.' He reached out and touched the back of his hand to her hair, running it slowly down to the end, where it rested just above her breast. Carla trembled but fought with every fibre of her body not to pull away. 'I will see you another time, *fraulein* Carla.'

'Thank you, sir.'

He turned sharply and headed for the door, waiting for Fischer to open it for him. There was a click as the door closed behind them, and Carla slapped a hand onto the edge of the table to catch herself before she collapsed.

Breathing hard, she leaned there for several seconds, her stomach churning and her mind screaming at breakneck speed.

Feeling a surge inside, she lunged for the sink and vomited uncontrollably.

36

Walking down the service hallway, Major Wolf pondered his conversation with the girl.

He remembered her clearly from the alleyway – she was the sort of pretty girl you didn't forget in a hurry. He remembered the firm touch of her body. Perhaps later...he shook the thought from his head. He had more important things to worry about just now.

Fischer paused at the exit door.

'What d'you think, sir?' he asked.

Wolf pursed his lips. 'I am not entirely convinced either way at this point, Klaus. The indomitable Colonel Weiz seems confident in the trustworthiness of his informant, however I do not have the same confidence.'

Fischer sneered. 'Weiz is a bumbling fool,' he said. 'I wouldn't trust him to tie his own shoelaces.'

Wolf smiled. 'That is a fair assessment, I would suggest. The other girl, Angela – she seemed genuine. She certainly believed what she was saying. However, this one,' he tossed his head back towards the kitchen, 'she makes a good point. If that fat fool of a woman hadn't tried to cave her head in with a damned spoon, things would be a lot clearer.'

'Agreed, Herr Major.' Fischer nodded. 'This girl Carla seems quite genuine to me. And really,' he gave an arrogant smirk, 'what are we talking about here? A bunch of cleaning women?' He made a scoffing noise. 'I doubt any of them could spell their own names, sir.'

Wolf smiled at the younger man's arrogance. He was not as inclined to dismiss someone based simply on their standing in life, but the man made a fair point.

'Come on,' he said. 'I need a coffee before I speak to this idiot Weiz again.'

37

Thursday evening

By the time night fell, both men were more than ready to get up and moving. The lack of sun and the cold permeated up through the frozen ground had contributed to an uncomfortable day, even laying side by side to share body warmth.

Sleep had been sporadic while not on watch, but both had managed to grab a few hours off and on. Talk had been at an absolute minimum, which had clearly suited Hastings. His ability to lie absolutely still for long periods of time was apparently matched only by his ability to stay silent for the same time. Napier had eventually given up trying to make whispered small talk and resigned himself to the fact that he was partnered with a voluntary mute.

As soon as darkness descended they were on the move, scooting out of their hide and moving downhill towards the road again. Aside from the odd military vehicle on the road, they had not seen or heard any sign of enemy activity. They still took their time though, stopping to watch and listen in case they walked into an ambush. They'd done well so far, and neither man was keen to get caught short now.

With the way clear, they hit the road and moved with a trot.

Napier was taking a turn carrying the wireless set, and he certainly felt the weight on his shoulders and neck. He focussed on keeping his footing and maintaining a steady pace, using the urgency of their movement to distract himself from the discomfort he was feeling.

He had spent a good part of the day trembling from the cold – he told himself it was just the cold, not fear – and his energy was flagging.

Hastings was a few yards ahead of him, his head on a swivel as he scanned every which way. He moved with the controlled athleticism of a hunter, his Sten going everywhere his eyes went. It was comforting for Napier, who knew he was most definitely playing second fiddle when it came to combat.

After lying down for so long they felt reenergised to make up ground, and both were soon warmed up and oblivious to the cold. They had roughly an hour before their next radio transmission, and they put it to good effect. They had travelled close to five miles before Hastings led the way off the road. They hadn't seen a soul in that hour, and the night was fully dark and quiet. Even the insects had hunkered down for the night.

Reaching a spot off the road where they were shielded from view by a small hill, Hastings helped Napier unload the wireless. Napier dropped to his knees and sucked in air, the relief of having his pack off making him feel lighter than air – if his shoulders and back hadn't been throbbing.

He watched as Hastings quickly got the wireless going, stringing out an antenna over the top of the hill. Atmospherics was always the issue and sometimes it was hit and miss as to whether things would work properly or not.

Hastings frowned as he concentrated on fixing the right frequency. He checked his watch – 1900 hours on the dot.

Settling on the frequency, he tapped in a short message to identify himself and confirm they were clear to communicate. He included their co-ordinates this time, so the operator would know exactly where they were.

The response came straight back and he scribbled it down. It only took a minute to decipher it and his eyes widened with surprise. It was a set of co-ordinates and a time followed by the word "Wimbledon". Wimbledon was the code word to indicate an agent meet, and he had a pretty fair idea where the co-ordinates would lead them.

'Not asking for much,' he muttered.

He paused for a few moments while he composed his reply. He had a few short words that would have worked well in the circumstances, but it would have been pointless. The order had been given and they had no choice but to follow it. He tapped out a fast reply.

ACK.OUT.

Just in case they came back with a follow-up message, he left the wireless on while he ripped up his note and went through the process of swallowing the pieces. Nothing came through so he switched off and packed up.

Napier slid down the hill from where he'd been keeping watch and snacking.

'What'd they say?' he whispered.

Getting out the map and his compass, Hastings quickly identified their goal.

'Here,' he said softly. 'They want us to be pretty much on target by oh-six-hundred to meet the agent.'

Napier balked. 'Are you bloody serious, old man? Are you sure you did your code thingie right?'

'Dead certain.' Hastings folded the map and tucked it away again, then checked his watch. 'That means we've got eleven hours to get there. Nearly a hundred miles.'

'That's bloody ridiculous,' Napier said, shaking his head in frustration. 'Call them back and tell them. There's no way we can walk that far tonight; it'd take days.'

'We need transport,' Hastings agreed. 'The next village is about two miles; we'll be there in half an hour. We need to try and get our hands on something there.'

'And if we don't?' Napier said.

'We go to Plan B.' Hastings stood and started strapping the wireless set to his own pack.

Napier stood also, his back stiff. 'What exactly is Plan B?' he said.

'Don't know yet, mate.' Hastings gave a wolfish grin. 'Let you know when I figure it out. Come on, let's go.'

38

Accompanied by a hubbub of hushed voices, the footsteps on the creaky wooden stairs were heavy and slow, and Carla immediately knew.

She opened her door and watched as Angela was helped up the stairs by Irma and Mary, each girl holding an elbow. Her footsteps were a painful shuffle and she held herself as if she expected to fall apart at any second. Reaching the top landing, they paused so she could catch her breath.

Trudy and Martha came from the bathroom, where they had been getting ready for bed. The single bare bulb from the bathroom cast a yellow glow into the otherwise darkened hallway. At the far end of the hall, Hilde's door opened and she filled the doorway. The nightgown hung off her like a half-collapsed tent and her wispy hair was loose and untamed. She looked first to Carla, saying nothing, then to the three girls at the top of the stairs.

Lit up by the bathroom light, Carla became the focus of their attention.

Fixing her with a stare from her one good eye, Angela licked her lips gently. Slowly and painfully, she forced herself up as straight as she could get, staring at Carla all the while. Every movement caused a new twitch of agony to cross her pale face, but she seemed determined to succeed.

Easing herself free from the helping hands, Angela shuffled forward, her heavy shoes dragging loudly on the cold floor. Carla stood transfixed, unable to speak or move. It was a terrible thing to see such a vibrant, friendly girl reduced to this. A shadow of her former self. A wreck. Besides her eye and the roughly-sewn gash beneath it, she had obviously suffered fresh injuries. Ribs, by the look of how she carried herself, possibly broken. As she gradually entered the cone of light, Carla saw her hands. The left hand was held stiffly before her, held up like the neck of a swan as if to protect it. The fingers were puffy and she could see that at least one knuckle was deformed.

Bile rose in the back of her throat. Carla forced herself to breathe, unable to break away from Angela's stare.

The girl shuffled closer. As she did so, she gently turned over the hand she held so delicately. When it hit the light, Carla almost gagged. The flesh had been seared by something hot, scorched black around the edges of a wet, pink and white circle in the centre of her palm.

The vicious bitterness of the bile hit the back of Carla's throat, and she clamped a hand to her mouth to keep it in. She swallowed hard, the motion making her want to vomit again.

'You,' Angela said, her voice cracked and unsteady. 'You did this.'

Carla shook her head – whether she was denying the girl's accusation or trying to shake the vision from her head, she didn't know. 'No,' she whispered. 'It's not true.'

'You did this.' Angela's voice was stronger, more insistent.

Behind the physical injuries, Carla detected a strength. An anger in there. An anger directed solely at her.

'You lied to them.' Angela's voice was the only sound in the cold hallway. 'You told them I lied.'

Carla could feel everyone's eyes on her. Watching – accusing. She was frozen to the spot.

'I told them the truth,' Angela continued, her fury gathering momentum. 'I told them the truth! And then you...you lied to save your own skin.'

'I didn't,' Carla whispered. 'Your head...'

Angela gave her a scathing look. 'Don't – don't pretend you care, Carla. You don't care...you're nothing to me. You mean nothing.' She leaned in, her breath sour on Carla's face. 'I thought we were friends.'

'We are...'

Angela spat then, flecks of dry white spittle hitting Carla's face. Carla flinched but took it. It seemed like the least she could do. Angela peered at her with the good eye, examining her as a scientist would a specimen in a laboratory.

'You're not even sorry,' she said softly, 'are you?' The eye, green and shadowed and curious, glistened as a single tear appeared in the corner. The tear toppled over the edge to dribble down the side of Angela's nose. 'You did this to me...you made them do it. And you don't even care.'

Her bottom lip wobbled, then her jaw trembled. More tears sprang forth, running freely down her face.

'I...I...' The words stuck in Carla's throat, and she felt herself welling up too. All she wanted to do was to take the girl in her arms and soothe her pain, to make it alright. To fix it. She knew she should but she couldn't.

'Why?' Angela's battered face crumpled properly now and she sobbed, bringing her other hand to her face as huge, painful sobs wracked her broken body. 'Why, Carla?'

Irma and Mary came to her now, taking her by the arms again and beginning to lead her towards her room. Carla watched them go, a turmoil of emotion pounding her head and heart alike.

She shifted her gaze to the cousins in the bathroom doorway. Trudy and Martha stared back at her, their faces identical masks of disappointment and disdain. Trudy slowly shook her head before turning away. Martha stared a moment longer then stepped back. She closed the door and the hallway fell back into darkness again. Angela's door closed and a line of light appeared beneath it. The girls would be tending to her wounds, calming and comforting her before putting her to bed.

Carla knew that sleep would not come easily, for any of them. Tomorrow was another day, but what kind of a day would it be? What kind of a future awaited Angela now? More interrogation and torture?

And what of herself? What could she expect?

The whisper of movement yanked her from her thoughts, and she jumped when she realised Hilde was right there. The supervisor's podgy face was pale in the darkness.

'I know what you said,' Hilde said. 'I'm not crazy.' The weight of her stare was intense and a fierce hatred burned from within it. She raised her right hand to chest level, and Carla caught a glint of steel. The woman was gripping a small pair of nail scissors in her fist. Her grin was tight and nasty. 'You talk about me like that again...and I'll kill you.'

Carla managed to nod, transfixed by the sharp point of the scissors. It would only take a second for the mad woman to plunge them into her neck, and she didn't trust her not to do it.

Hilde pushed her face right up to Carla's, her soft, heavy body pressing against her.

'I'll kill you,' she hissed.

Carla nodded again, and as soon as the weight was gone, she stepped back into her room and shut the door. Her heart wanted to explode from her chest and her legs had gone weak again. She leaned against the wall, breathing hard and clutching her arms around her.

It was an age before she crawled into her bed and dragged the covers over her. Muted voices sounded outside in the hallway as the other girls conferred. With any luck one of them actually would kill her tonight, just to put her out of the misery that had engulfed her.

No. She fought the thought down. *No, she would not give up.* She could not give up. To do so would dishonour everything her family had stood for. Everything she and Josef had worked so hard for. She hadn't risked everything like this just to give up now.

Lying there in the darkness, her breath fogging in the cold, Carla prayed and waited for dawn to hurry up and come.

39

The short time frame injected a tangible sense of urgency into their trek, and they moved at a fast clip.

Napier was forced to practically jog to keep up, despite Hastings carrying the heavy radio set. He held the Sten in both hands and settled into a steady rhythm, keeping one eye on their surroundings but unable to resist a nagging thought that had been bouncing around his head all day.

Jankowski, the Pole. Serving bravely in the RAF, like Napier a veteran of the Battle of Britain. Shot down and captured, thrown in a prison camp. Legend had it – or at least, how Jankowski told it – he'd escaped from a camp in Salzburg and made his way on foot across country back to the lines, after escaping from a military hospital. He'd been welcomed back with open arms of course, debriefed and all that bollocks, revered as a hero by his fellow airmen.

He'd been through Hell and made it back. But how much of it was true? To suddenly turn out to be an enemy spy was a quantum leap. Had he been a spy all along? Had he even been captured at all? There were too many questions and not enough answers.

Napier had some idea of what his colleague had apparently gone through, after being shot down over France. He'd managed to avoid capture by the skin of his teeth, but it had been a hell of a time, dossing down in barns and sheds by day and walking alone at night, scrounging food from rubbish bins and gardens he found along the way.

He was in occupied territory in an RAF uniform with just his wits, a basic escape kit and a plan of bluffing his way through using his language skills. Getting stopped by a patrol would have been fatal, so he'd winged it and relied on his animal instincts. Three days later he'd reached the coast and accidentally made contact with a British commando unit doing a recce ahead of a raid. They'd got him home and he'd been immediately taken by the Intelligence bods who siphoned every bit of gen from him they could, even things he didn't think he knew.

That was barely two months ago.

It had felt very different to his current situation; he'd been trying to get away then and risked being thrown in a camp if he was captured. Now, it felt like he was heading into the eye of the storm, and a painful death was the only outcome should they be captured. That idea sent chills down his spine and he tried to force it from his mind.

So lost in his own thoughts was he that he didn't notice Hastings stop walking and he carried on past him. He jumped when Hastings grabbed his arm and pulled him to the side, into the shelter of an overhanging tree.

'Easy, old man,' Napier said, 'you gave me a bloody fright.'

'Ssshh.' Hastings held a finger to his lips and cocked his head to listen, pointing down the darkened road ahead of them.

Napier listened keenly but heard nothing. He looked inquisitively at his companion.

'What is it?' he whispered.

The hairs on the back of his neck were prickling now; Hastings must have detected the approach of Germans, some stealthy mountain troops sneaking up to slit their throats.

Their mission would be over before it even really began.

In the faint moonlight he saw Hastings grinning. Not a pack of approaching killers, then.

'You know how to ride a horse?' Hastings whispered.

'I play polo,' Napier said.

Hastings rolled his eyes.

'Of course you do.' He jabbed a finger towards the darkness again. 'There's horses up ahead. We're going to borrow a couple. Ever ridden bareback?'

'Once or twice,' Napier said. 'I wouldn't say I'm an expert.'

'Well, now's the time to learn. Come on.'

Hastings led the way and seconds later they were letting themselves into a paddock where several horses were resting in an open barn. Leaving Napier at the gate to keep watch, Hastings approached the animals calmly, letting them know he was there and posed no threat. One harrumphed and shook its head, watching him as he entered the barn and came closer. Hasting spotted a barrel of feed against the wall, and scooped some into a container, offering to the horses as he approached them. A young colt leaped to its feet and darted away, whinnying at the stranger.

Speaking quietly to the animals, Hastings ignored the skittery youngster and focussed instead on a couple of older mares. They stayed quiet and let him get close, first one then the other nuzzling into the food container to snaffle an unexpected feed. They weren't old enough to be retired, and he didn't recognise the breed, but they were sturdy working horses. He guessed they were on a farm, so the animals would be strong and healthy and used to heavy work.

As the animals emptied the feed container, Hastings stroked their necks and spoke softly to them, building their trust. He filled a couple of pockets with more grain before using his red-lensed torch to find the saddlery down the back of the barn.

He wanted to conceal the reason for the missing horses, so he ignored the saddles and bridles, and instead grabbed a rope hanging from a nail. He sliced it into two lengths using the Fairbairn-Sykes, and quickly fashioned two makeshift bridles.

Even in the dark it was easy, borne from having done it through necessity back on the farm. His family never had extra money for fancy gear when he was growing up, and makeshift anything was the norm. He slipped the bridle onto the first animal, firmly taking control so she knew who was in charge. That done he whistled for Napier and fitted out the second animal.

'Here.'

Hastings handed the first set of reins to his companion and nimbly leaped on the back of the second horse. She shook her head and gave a little dance, unsure about this stranger on her back. He patted her neck soothingly and waited while Napier tried unsuccessfully to leap up as he had done.

The horse skittered and harrumphed at him and his second attempt ended with him falling on his backside as the horse moved away. Hastings shook his head and came alongside. They needed to get moving and the way Napier was going, they'd wake the farmer and end up with buckshot flying.

The mare settled once its buddy was alongside, and Hastings guided it gently towards a pen with a sagging gate. Using the gate, Napier managed to climb aboard and they spent another couple of minutes calming the horse before moving out. Hastings led the way, softly calling the other horses to follow behind.

'What're you doing?' Napier hissed. 'We don't need all of these, do we?'

'I want them loose,' Hastings whispered. 'Then the farmer won't know straight away how many we've taken.'

'Oh, right.' Napier nodded, feeling stupid for not thinking of it. 'Good idea.'

Hastings grunted. 'I thought so,' he said.

Reaching the road, he left the gate open behind them and led the way down the shoulder of the road, sticking to the softer ground to avoid the click-clack of shod hooves on the roadway. The other horses had got up and watched them, but none made an immediate move to leave their shelter. He shrugged to himself and left them to it – they didn't have time to waste and he didn't want to risk creating noise that would bring attention.

They moved past the farm and the barn was soon lost in the darkness behind them. Hastings nudged his ride into an easy trot to warm it up, and he waved Napier up beside him.

Side by side they left the farm far behind them and rode deeper into enemy territory.

40

The night went without incident, the two riders carefully making their way past the tiny settlements and working farms that dotted the countryside. They stopped regularly to rest the horses and water them from troughs or streams that they came across, and took the opportunities to refresh themselves as well.

They kept the horses moving steadily, alternating between a trot and a canter, Hastings estimating that this would average about eleven miles an hour over time. Given that they had started off close to a hundred miles from Alpspitze, he reckoned it would take them about nine hours to get there at that rate, although they had started behind the eight ball with having to trek down the mountain then hike until they came across the horses. They could possibly sneak in by the 0600 hours deadline, but they'd be cutting it fine.

They had lost valuable time, and if they could get their hands on a vehicle they'd be far better off.

Not only would it be faster but it would be a hell of a lot more comfortable. Both men were happier when the horses got a canter on, rather than bouncing around at the trot. It was some time since either of them had ridden at all, let alone bare-back, and the lack of padding from a saddle or even a blanket was doing them no favours.

The temperature was somewhere below freezing and the light breeze added to their misery, the cold biting through their smocks, woollen jerseys and the layers beneath. Both men wore woollen hats and heavy gloves, and had scarves pulled up over the lower halves of their faces. Despite this, as the night wore on and the temperature dropped further, they were both cold to the core and losing feeling in their extremities.

Eventually Napier called a halt.

'Need to stop,' he mumbled.

He let his mount wander off to the side of the road and he slid off it clumsily, staggering on numbed feet. Hastings followed suit with reluctance, eager to get on target as soon as possible. They had miles to make up yet, but he was frozen too and knew that exposure could be the death of both of them before they even got near Alpenbad. He'd seen it in the mountains before, hunting in winter past the snow line. Men went down fast and it was hard to haul them back.

Looking at his companion, he could see Napier was in a bad way. His own feet felt like blocks of ice in his boots, and his hands were clumsy lumps of meat being operated by someone else. He tethered both horses to a tree branch and guided Napier into the undergrowth. Using his torch, he quickly scouted out a clear spot beneath a small drop which acted as a natural windbreak. They would still be visible from the road but, having not encountered any other traffic all night, he was confident enough they'd be safe for a while. Besides, a dead pilot wouldn't be flying him home.

He parked Napier and got his blanket out, wrapping the other man in it and thrusting a hard biscuit at him.

'Eat that while I get a fire going.'

Napier did as he was told, watching as Hastings rapidly threw together a small fire using a fire-starting kit from his pack and any dry tinder and kindling he could find. In a few minutes there was a decent fire going and Napier huddled close to it, the warmth of the flames an unbelievable relief. Hastings filled a mess tin with snow and got it boiling, directing Napier to throw coffee and sugar into his mug.

'More sugar,' he urged.

Napier worked with fingers that were slowly thawing and wrapped his hands around the hot mug, letting the steam waft up onto his face.

'Here.'

Hastings produced a tin of condensed milk and cracked it open, spooning some first into Napier's coffee then his own. He stirred it in and took a sip, relishing the hot sweet-bitterness. He hadn't realised how cold he'd got until they stopped, and he saw now that they couldn't have gone on any longer. He scoffed down a biscuit himself and used his spoon to eat some of the condensed milk.

'You came prepared,' Napier noted, finishing his coffee and digging out another biscuit.

'Always. They say it's a one-day job, so come prepared for three.' He mixed another coffee in Napier's mug. 'You warmed up, mate?'

'Much better.' Napier took the mug back with a smile. 'Thanks.'

'I've met some bastards in my time, y'know Freddie,' Hastings said, mixing a second drink for himself. He preferred tea but coffee would give them more of a boost. 'It's not until you go hunting with a bloke that you really get to know him, is it?'

Napier thought of his own hunting experiences for a moment. Rousing quail and pheasants with Pa's friends was probably a bit tame compared to what he imagined Hastings got up to.

'True,' he said.

'I went hunting once with my best mate. Good bugger, salt of the earth. Went after some stags not far from home, spent a couple of nights up there. Took my usual gear, had a pretty good plan what we were going to do.' Hastings took a long slurp on his drink. 'Got up there, got nothing the first day but some pretty good sign we were in the right area. Bunkered down in a hut for the night, and y'know what?'

Napier shook his head.

'The useless bugger forgot to bring his food with him.' Hastings shook his head in amazement at the memory. 'So no problem, I shared what I had. We ate dinner, went to bed. I'm sleeping away and all's well, right? Well, come morning time, bugger me if most of the food's gone. Old Stan'd been up before me, see. I ask him where the left over food is and he says he's got no idea. No idea, I says? Well it wasn't me, I was asleep.'

Napier smiled, nursing the last of his drink. His insides were defrosted now and he felt a million times better.

'So I hunt around and can't find it, so I says to him where is it? Y'know what he tells me?' Hastings didn't wait for a response. 'He tells me the possums must've got in overnight and nicked it.' He shook his head again. 'No bloody way it was possums, mate. He ate it, and that's all there is to it. And y'know what? He went from being a good bugger to a bastard, like that.' He snapped his fingers. 'Lying prick. Needless to say it was a short hunting trip. We came out of the bush separately and I never spoke to him for six months after that.' He shook his head again then threw back his drink. 'Lying bastard.'

Napier drained his own mug and accepted the tin of condensed milk. He took the first spoonful and savoured it. It was sweet enough to set his teeth on edge but it was everything his body was craving just now. If that didn't get him going, nothing would.

'Did you see him again?'

Hastings face darkened and Napier was sure he saw a touch of sadness there.

'Saw him on Crete,' he said. 'Different outfit to me, but we ran into each other. Got killed the next day near Maleme.' He went quiet, staring into the flames as they flickered across his dark face. 'Poor bastard,' he muttered.

Napier nodded silently, spooning the thick sweet milk into his mouth. He didn't want to intrude on the man's memories.

'Anyway.' Hastings looked up and gave a self-conscious smile. 'We better get moving, eh?'

They both stood and started getting their kit together again.

'You know what?' Napier said, crouching over his pack. 'I think you just said more words to me than the whole time I've known you.'

'Don't get used to it.' Hastings put away his mess tin and mug. 'I was only trying to keep you awake so you didn't die on me. I didn't want to have to carry you out.'

'Charmed, I'm sure. Anyway, thanks.' Napier looked him in the eye. 'I mean that.'

Hastings gave a short nod and shouldered his pack. He pulled on the gloves he'd had tucked into his smock. 'Good to go?'

'Hang on a sec.' Napier rummaged in his pack and produced a bundle of something. 'I'll just throw these on.'

Hastings peered closer. 'That your long johns?'

'Yep. Probably time to get them on, I think.' Napier started to shed his top layers.

'You didn't think to wear them at the start?' Hastings glowered at him in the dying firelight. 'What with the mountains and snow and whatnot?'

Napier pulled the top on then quickly started dressing again. 'Didn't think we'd need them, so I just brought them in case.' He caught Hastings' glare. 'I thought we'd be in and out,' he said defensively.

Hastings shook his head and kicked snow over the fire, throwing them back into darkness.

'Like I said, I've met some bastards in my time,' he said. 'And you're a classic dumb bastard.'

Napier finished dressing and laced up his boots again. The long johns definitely added a layer of warmth and he mentally cursed himself for not wearing them from the start. He stood and straightened himself out, grabbing his pack and giving Hastings a self-conscious grin.

'There we go, right as rain. Shall we off, then?'

'Huh,' Hastings grunted. 'Look at this first, in case you get lost.'

They huddled over the map and Hastings used a twig to direct his attention.

'We're about here I reckon. It's now nearly oh-four-hundred and we're still about twenty five miles out. We need to get to the meeting point before oh-six-hundred and scout it out, in case our contact's been compromised and we get rumbled. Means we need to get a wriggle on. No more stops unless you're dying, alright?'

Napier gave a nod. 'And if we do get rumbled?'

'We're that close now that it'd be pretty obvious what we're here for. We can't bluff it out now. If we get rumbled we've gotta just push through it, disengage as quick as we can and try to make sure the bastards don't get a signal away. Then we just go hell for leather and hit the target, come hell or high water. Even if one of us gets it, the other one's gotta just go for it. Fair enough?'

'Yep.' Napier gave a nod and set his jaw firmly. It was getting very real and the butterflies were having a party in his guts. 'Fair enough.'

'Let's go.'

41

Friday morning

At 0547 hours, Napier stood at the edge of a spruce forest and gazed down the mountainside.

Ahead of him was a wide expanse of clear ground where the mountainside dropped away down to Alpenbad and the target of their mission.

Napier stared down, barely making out any lights where he knew the town was. Even this far behind their own lines, in their own country, the Germans were careful. They were smart, a formidable foe alright, no doubt about that. He felt an eerie calm come over him, standing here in the silent stillness of the mountain, within spitting distance of their goal.

The adrenaline was still pumping but he had regained a grip on himself now. This was how he felt when he was flying into combat.

No turning back now; it was game on. Do or die.

Darkness was their friend for now and they needed to get their agent meet done and be in play well before dawn. Any later and they would be screwed worse than an East End madam.

Hastings had secured the horses in the forest, feeding them and letting them drink from a tiny brook he had found that moved fast enough not to freeze over. The horses were exhausted after the ride and it was doubtful how much further they could have ridden.

If the agent meet turned out to be an ambush, they needed to be free to run and fight and not give the enemy any advantage at all, if and when they were either captured or killed.

Hastings joined Napier now at the edge of the forest, lifting a pair of binoculars to his eyes to scan below them. He could make out the dark shape of buildings in the town, a lake to the west of it, but not much else.

No sign of the agent they were to meet.

'Let's get moving,' he whispered. 'You take the left and rear; I'll cover the front and right. Let's go.'

He moved off and Napier fell in behind him, the Sten in his hands and his head on a swivel.

The trees provided cover and it was pitch dark, but Hastings moved with the nimble-footed confidence of a mountain goat, never hesitating and never making a sound. He was like a wraith in the darkness and Napier had to focus to keep on his tail, knowing he'd quickly be lost if he didn't.

They moved deep into the forest, careful not to disturb anything or make a sound as they headed downhill. It was possible that the Germans would have sentries posted around the town, given the high value of their guests who came and went, although hopefully the agent on the ground would know enough to avoid them. It was some minutes before Hastings stopped.

The forest would take them down a valley to a point only a mile or so from the town, with the lake between them. There they would meet their contact and covertly infiltrate to wherever Jankowski was. That would be the sharp end of the operation, and their escape was in the lap of the gods after that.

Napier was under no illusions that any of it would be easy, but the degree of calmness he had felt a few minutes earlier was hanging in there, at least for now.

The going downhill was easy enough, although each of them

slipped and took a tumble, tripped by some unseen obstacle beneath the snow.

Napier had always loved the mountains, skiing without a care in the world, breathing in the clear, fresh alpine air. It was invigorating and refreshing and a bowl of thick, steaming soup was always welcome at the end of it, usually followed by a stiff drink with his feet up in front of a roaring fire.

His time in Switzerland had been both horrendous and wonderful, the heartache for being wrenched away from his family balanced by the new experiences and the sense of independence. So many firsts had taken place in his years at boarding school, not least of all his first love.

She had been older, the sister of a school chum. Sixteen and worldly with it. He was certain that he wasn't her first, but it didn't matter. For two glorious months they had been together every minute they could manage, talking and laughing and sharing themselves in every way possible. She had taught him things that only a girl with experience could know, and he had been a willing student – if only his masters had known how willing he was, they'd have been horrified.

He smiled inwardly at the memory, cradling the Sten in his hands and sweeping his left arc. If only she could see him now. Would she be impressed at young Freddie, he wondered?

Little did it matter, he figured. She was long gone and he was here on this crazy mission. The chances were high that he wouldn't live to see another dawn break, let alone love another girl. He pushed the morose thought aside and focussed on the task at hand.

There'd be plenty of time for chasing skirts later – he needed to get home in one piece first.

42

Easing the door closed behind her with barely a click, Carla pressed herself against the wall and waited, eyes and ears straining in the darkness. Only the sound of her heart crashing against her ribs could be heard.

After a moment's hesitation – she was so close now, she could almost taste the freedom – she pushed off and hurried along the road, hugging the shadows. The pre-dawn chill was cold on her exposed skin and she was hungry, but the thought of eating made her stomach churn.

She prayed that she would be back before the girls woke and her disappearance wouldn't be found out. It had been a sleepless night, constant visions of Angela's injuries flashing to the forefront of her mind. Listening for any sound, the tiniest creak of a floorboard that might indicate Hilde was coming with her scissors.

She knew that she couldn't get through another day here, not now. The girls had all turned against her, that much was obvious. And she couldn't blame them, not really. Trudy and Martha had ignored her when they came into the room last night. She had wanted to speak to them but knew it would just cause more recriminations, so she'd feigned sleep instead. They had only stayed long enough to gather bedding before going down the hall to Angela's room, where they stayed the night.

It was a show that solidarity that Carla knew Angela needed, and she knew it would be appreciated. It was the right thing to do, and ironically, it made her job easier. She had managed to slip out of her room without disturbing anyone, and was now on what she hoped would be the last leg of her mission.

How many times had she made this journey to the falling-down hut with the hidden radio? Too many to count, and she'd never been sprung. God forbid it would happen now, the last time. The Gestapo weren't known for their understanding, even with their own countrymen.

She hurried on through the deserted streets, not even a soldier in sight at this hour. The odd light could be seen creeping around the blackout curtains as workers started to rise for the early shift, but she was confident enough that she wouldn't be seen.

In just a few minutes she would be safely at the rendezvous point to meet the agents sent in, and things would unfold from there. What that would entail, she didn't know.

But she knew it would be the end of the line.

So caught up in her thoughts was she that she did not see the young soldier. Watching from a shop doorway on the street she turned onto, he paused with an unlit cigarette between his lips and a match poised to strike. He was a sallow-faced youth in an ill-fitting uniform with his rifle slung over his shoulder. He recognised the girl from the alleyway, the one who had embarrassed him in front of his friend before the splendid Major Wolf had happened along.

The smart-mouthed bitch.

As Carla disappeared around the next corner, she was oblivious to the soldier falling in behind her.

43

Half a mile from the RV, they came to a sudden stop.

Hastings lowered himself slowly to a crouch, pulling Napier down with him. He held a finger to his lips, cupped his ear and pointed off to their ten o'clock.

Napier strained his eyes and ears, half opening his mouth to improve his hearing. He was amazed at how well he could see in the dark forest, and he knew that sound would carry far in the mountains.

It was several seconds before he heard the faint crunch of a boot on snow. He zeroed in on where he thought the noise had come from, holding completely still. It was another minute before he spotted the tiniest of movements, a single branch moving when everything else it around it was still. It was in the same direction but closer, although he still couldn't see anyone.

His heart was pounding in his chest and his mouth was dry.

It couldn't be Germans, surely? Not so soon? But it had to be – there was no one else here. The agent was supposed to meet them at the RV, not in the forest. They had made a wide sweep of the RV before committing to the last move, and were still a few hundred yards away from the meeting point.

Napier felt his cheeks get hot. To get so close and be foiled already would just be too much to handle. It would be off to the SS for a dose of scopolamine and a brutal interrogation.

Squinting now, he spotted movement ahead. A person was heading directly towards an area just inside the treeline, which would put them right at the RV.

It had to be the agent, and they looked to be in a hell of a rush. Understandably, he guessed.

In a few seconds the figure was out of sight, and he began to rise.

Hastings touched his arm and leaned in to his ear.

'Wait.'

Napier lowered himself carefully again, the urgency in his companion's voice unmistakable. Whatever Black Jack had seen or heard, he would trust him to be right. Hastings raised a hand and pointed back to where the first figure had come from.

Peering hard, it took Napier a moment to see the second figure. Rising cautiously from a crouch, the second figure scurried forward several yards before dropping down again. He could make out the rifle and the coal-scuttle helmet, and his heart jumped into his throat.

They'd been burned, just when they were so close. He could taste the bile in his mouth – the bitterness of defeat. He felt his fists clenching and glanced to Hastings.

'What do we do, Jack?' he whispered.

Hastings was still as a statue, his eyes everywhere.

'There's only one,' he breathed. 'There he goes again.'

Sure enough, the soldier moved ahead again, closing in on the RV point.

'We need to get the agent,' Hastings whispered. 'Regardless of what this bloke's up to – we can deal with him, no worries.'

Napier nodded numbly, feeling horribly out of his depth. 'White Rabbit,' he muttered.

Hastings gave him a quizzical look, almost smiling.

'The agent,' Napier whispered defensively, realising he was blabbering. 'White Rabbit.'

'I know,' Hastings murmured, heavy on the sarcasm.

They both saw the soldier disappear from sight exactly where the first figure had just gone.

'Whatever's going on here,' Hastings whispered, 'that joker's on his own, and we can't sit around like a bunch of ninnies. We need to do this meet regardless, right?'

Napier nodded.

'Stick behind me.'

They moved cautiously forward, making their way along the edge of the forest towards the RV point. Hastings dropped to a knee and pulled Napier close so he could whisper in his ear.

'Hold here.'

Napier gave the slightest of nods and kept his eyes to the front. He knew that Hastings must have moved off but he never heard a sound. One second he was there, the next he was gone.

The metal of the Sten was cold in Napier's hands. He rested his thumb on the safety, ready to flick it off and unleash hell.

44

Soldat Hildebrandt watched the girl duck into some kind of cover, a lean-to perhaps, under the overhanging trees.

Whatever she was up to, he knew it was something she shouldn't be. Nobody was out and about at this time of the morning, and certainly not running off into the forest. He tightened his grip on his rifle. He would capture her and drag her off to see Major Wolf, maybe after having a little fun with her first. After the way she had dismissed him last time, she needed to be taught a lesson.

Maybe she was a spy of some sort. If she was, well, that was an open invitation to an Iron Cross, wasn't it? Capturing an enemy spy would be the pinnacle of any soldier's career, and a sure-fire path to promotion as well.

Hildebrandt pushed up to his feet and began to move forward, his eyes locked on what he could see now was some kind of an overgrown shed.

45

Through the shadows and branches Napier finally saw a proper movement, the soldier moving from his left across the last piece of open ground towards the RV.

Maybe only thirty yards away now, moving slowly and carefully. Napier's shoulders tensed and he held his breath. The stubby barrel of the Sten was pointing directly at the figure and he was ready to go. Even as he was trying to figure out where Hastings was, there was a flicker of movement from the figure's left.

A shadow leapt on the figure and dragged it to the ground in one fast, silent move. Napier leaped to his feet and raced forward, reaching the tussling pair in a couple of seconds and training his weapon on them.

There was no need.

The soldier was bleeding profusely from an open wound in his side, and Hastings was removing his dagger from the man's other side when Napier arrived on the scene. Both stab wounds had penetrated deep up under the ribs and Napier could see the soldier would be dead in seconds. His eyes were open and glassy and his mouth was gaping silently.

Napier felt his gut flip-flop and he looked away.

Hastings got silently to his feet and paused to wipe his blade on the dead soldier's jacket. He breathed heavily as he stared down at the dead body, then spat to the side and put his dagger away. Swinging his Sten forward into his hands, he looked at Napier with his eyebrows raised.

Napier gave a short nod, and Hastings jerked his thumb behind him.

———

Carla froze when she heard the soft footfall outside the shed. It occurred to her that she should really have waited outside rather than in here, with no escape route. It had been a terrible decision, but hopefully one she would live to regret.

'I love Brighton in the summer,' came a man's voice from just outside the door. He spoke flawless German, and her insides went cold.

It was a trap.

Somehow, she had been followed and ambushed. Caught at a secret RV point, with a radio at hand no less, she was done for.

Bursting from the shed, Carla ran for her life.

———

Napier jumped when the figure exploded from the shed and ran. The person managed to get several yards before Hastings was on them, tackling them to the ground and rolling in the snow.

Napier raced after them and almost tripped over a loose leg as he raised his Sten.

Hastings had wrapped his legs around the figure and had the person's head arched painfully back, his Fairbairn-Sykes dagger at the exposed throat. The person stopped struggling immediately at the touch of the blade on their skin.

Napier could make out the person trying to speak, immediately detecting a German accent. And a female one, at that.

'Stop stop stop,' he said quickly, before Hastings had a chance to slice the girl's throat.

Hastings paused, the blade still at the girl's throat.

'You're joking,' he muttered, but didn't let go.

Napier leaned down so he could keep his voice down.

'I love Brighton in the summer,' he hissed in German.

Replying in English, the girl's voice was strained.

'I prefer Dover,' she managed. Her German accent was strong but the English was faultless. 'The beaches are quieter.'

Napier felt a surge of relief accompanying his confusion.

'I'm always there by ten,' he said. 'What about you?'

'Ten is too early,' she said. 'I swim at one o'clock.'

Napier straightened up, keeping the Sten on her. Hastings shifted the blade from her throat and rolled to his knees, still holding her down. He pulled the hood from her head, revealing long dark hair and a pale, terrified face.

'What the hell are you playing at?' he hissed. 'You've compromised us straight away.'

'You're already compromised,' she snapped back, her eyes flashing angrily at him. 'They know you're coming.'

Hastings and Napier shot each other a look.

'How do you know that?' Hastings said.

The girl scowled. 'I'm your contact, aren't I? I'm a spy – I'm supposed to know things like this.'

Napier almost laughed at her indignation. She was 100% right, of course. There was more to know, but he believed she was who she said she was.

'Get up,' he said.

They both got to their feet and the girl glared at Hastings as he sheathed his dagger.

'Did you have to be so rough?' She touched at her throat gingerly, checking her fingers for blood.

He gave her a grim smile.

'Count yourself lucky,' he said. 'I killed the other bloke.' He jerked his head past her towards the dead soldier lying in the snow.

The girl's eyes went wide and she crossed to where the man lay. Peering down at his face, she covered her mouth to stifle a gasp.

'I know him,' she said. 'He is not a nice boy.'

'Well, he followed you here and now we need to get rid of the bastard,' Hastings growled.

———

Carla rubbed her neck and eyed the two men.

The one who had nearly broken her neck was very strong and tough-looking. The other one was softer, perhaps more of a gentleman, if there were such things in the British Army. He cut a dashing figure and no doubt had many girlfriends. He still had a submachine gun pointed at her belly, though.

She got her racing pulse under control, the terror of being grabbed and nearly killed gradually subsiding. She was glad they were here, even if they still had her at gunpoint. The dead soldier was not good news, though – although, she had to admit, she wouldn't mourn his passing.

'I cannot stay long,' she said. 'I must get back, or I will be found out and there will be trouble.'

'Get over here,' the tough one said, directing her further under the cover of the trees.

46

The three of them huddled under the snow-laden boughs of a spruce, their steamy breath mixing in one cloud as they stood close together.

'How do they know we're coming early?' Hastings said.

'I don't know where from, but they got a message somehow. There is a spy in your organisation, a traitor I think.'

Napier pulled a face. 'I doubt that very much,' he said.

Hastings hiked his shoulders. 'Could be,' he said. 'They know somehow, don't they?'

'Yes, but...'

'No buts about it,' Hastings cut him off. 'Some bastard's cutting our lunch.' He turned back to the girl. 'What exactly was the message? Do they know why we're here?'

'They know you are coming to rescue or assassinate – this is the right word, yes? Assassinate?'

Hastings gave a short nod. 'That's it.'

'They know you are coming to rescue or assassinate someone, a man staying here. The Polish man.'

'Staying here?' Hastings queried her. 'Not held prisoner?'

'No, not a prisoner. He is one of them. They eat and drink together, like they are old friends.'

'Jankowski.' Napier almost spat the word.

'Yes, that is him. Jankowski.' Carla pulled a face. 'He is not a nice man, very...creepy. He thinks it is a big joke, I think.'

Hastings gave a snort of disgust.

'Well our mission just got easier,' he said. 'We're definitely not rescuing the bastard – we're killing him.' He turned back to Carla. 'The other man, Major Wolf – is he here?'

She nodded vigorously. 'Yes, I know him. He is here. He is not friends with the Commandant, though. He is not a nice man.'

'Who's not nice, Wolf or the Commandant?'

'This Major Wolf. He is a very mean man, very horrible. He is like him.' She pointed towards the dead soldier. 'There are many men like that here, horrible men. They are not good German men. The Commandant is not like that, he is just...weak. He is a weak man.'

'Where's Wolf staying?' Hastings said.

'He is in the house next to the Commandant's house. It has the green door.'

'Does he have security? Bodyguards?'

'He's not the main target, Jack,' Napier said.

'I know, but if we can get him too then all the better. One more dead Nazi.'

'He has no bodyguards,' Carla said. 'He does not need them. Only a driver.'

Hastings nodded, filing away the information. If they had the chance he'd have a crack at the SS officer too, but Napier was right – they had one primary target and he couldn't afford to lose focus.

'Do they know what time we were coming, any details like that?' Napier asked.

The girl nodded. 'They know what time, they know you were coming by plane. But there was a big air raid, I don't think they think you made it. There was a plane shot down.'

Napier's jaw set hard. 'Shot down in the raid, or on its own?'

'On its own, not far from here.'

'The poor blighters.' His voice was thick with emotion. 'The poor bloody blighters.'

Carla put a hand on his arm. Her eyes were wide as she recognised his anguish. 'I am sorry. Were they your friends?'

He sniffed hard, fighting to keep his emotions in check. This was no time for blubbing like a silly school girl.

'When was this?' he asked instead.

'Yesterday,' she said. 'They were very happy about it.' She squeezed his arm. 'I am sorry. Not all Germans are like this.'

He gave a nod, touched by her empathy. Both men realised it must have been shortly after they'd been dropped. Hastings gave a dark scowl, and caught Napier's eye.

'Don't worry mate,' he growled. 'We'll make the bastards pay.'

'So they're not on the lookout for us, then?' Napier said.

The girl shook her head. 'I don't know. They think your plane got shot down. I heard one of them in the bathroom – they always talk in the bathroom – I heard one of them say the information they got must have been wrong. A day early, he said.' She shrugged. 'They still have guards posted everywhere though. I don't know.'

'They've got to play it safe,' Hastings said. 'Just in case we did make it. There's no way to know if we were dropped or not, unless they saw us, so they had to shoot the plane down and still look for us. That's what I'd do.'

'How do you know all this?' Napier asked.

'I work there,' Carla said, as if it was obvious. 'I serve these men their drinks and I change their beds. They think I am a good loyal *fraulein*.' Her face pinched. 'I am a good loyal *fraulein*, but I am not a Nazi pig like them. Instead I do my work and keep my eyes and ears open.'

Hastings felt a surge of admiration for her. The girl had guts, no doubt about that.

'You have a radio?' he asked.

She nodded.

'We need to destroy it before they find it. We also need to get rid of old mate over there.'

'It's in there,' she pointed back towards the dilapidated shed.

'We'll get a message back to say we're here, but there's a mole. They need to fix that at the other end. We'll carry on and do our bit. I need you to go from here to a new RV. We need to get to the airfield and get our plane back, so we need transport. Can you drive?'

She nodded vigorously.

'Good, can you get your hands on a car?'

Her brow furrowed before she shook her head. 'I don't think so. No one has a car except the soldiers. I could try and steal one perhaps?'

'Do you know how to steal a car?'

'No.'

Hastings almost grinned. 'Then now's not a good time to learn. Leave that to us. We'll come and get you from a rendezvous point.'

'No.' Her tone was sharp, taking them both by surprise. 'I cannot go back.'

'But you...' Hastings began, and she cut him off.

'They think I'm a traitor. One of the girls...she was tortured yesterday by the SS. Major Wolf. I had asked her questions, and she told them. I had to tell them...' Her eyes welled up and she bit her lip. 'I told them she lied. So they...they tortured her.'

Hastings looked to Napier, his jaw set hard. An unspoken message passed between them. 'Did they kill her?' Hastings spoke surprisingly softly now.

'No.' She shook her head and wiped her nose on a delicate lace handkerchief. 'But she is not...she is not good.'

'Then she'll live.' Hastings put a hand on her arm and bent down to look her in the eye. 'She will be okay, this girl. You did the right thing. We needed you to do that to protect yourself, and it was the right thing to do.' He squeezed her arm. 'Don't worry, we'll make them pay for that.' He gave her his best attempt at a reassuring smile. 'You trust me on that?'

Taking in his weapons, his camo cream-smeared face, and the aggressive way he carried himself, Carla nodded.

: said quietly. This was a man she would never want to
ith.

we need you to carry on, love,' Napier said, and she turned her
attention to him now. 'If anything's out of place, they'll know
something's up. We can't afford to blow it now.' His reassuring smile
was the real deal, enough to lift her spirits and bring a small smile to
her face. 'Can you do that for us?'

Carla nodded again, happy to be looking into his kind blue eyes.
'Yes, of course. I'm sorry. I will do that.'

They quickly worked out that they would need to go past her
dormitory to get to the airfield, so chose an alleyway around the
corner to meet.

'But you look like Englishmen,' Carla said doubtfully, gesturing at
their uniforms. 'They will shoot you on sight.'

'They'll be too busy worrying about themselves,' Hastings said
with a piratical grin.

'But surely...'

'As soon as you hear shooting, get yourself there, right?' Hastings
spoke firmly. 'Don't wait for anyone. Understand?'

'I can do that.' She nodded vigorously. 'I must get back though,
before I am noticed.'

'Of course, of course.' Napier gave her a winning smile. 'You've
done a cracking job, you know. Very brave.'

Carla blushed and looked away shyly. She was used to unwanted
attention from the Nazi pigs, of course, but not attention from such a
handsome, genuine man. This attention was very welcome indeed.
She looked back to Napier and held his gaze for an eternity, neither
of them speaking yet both of them knowing.

'Is there any change to where we will find Jankowski?' Hastings
asked, shattering the moment. 'We were told he's in the main house
where the Commandant is.'

'Yes, that is it. He has a room there, he is next door to the
Commandant.'

'Right.' Hastings quickly ran through the security of the house
with her, wanting to take his time but knowing he couldn't

218 | ANGUS MCLEAN

compromise her any further. Once he'd got what he needed, he looked to Napier. 'Any other questions?'

'Nothing.'

'Right.' He looked back to the girl. 'Are you good?'

'Yes, of course. I am fine.'

'There'll be trouble once they realise one of their men is missing, and definitely once we do what we came to do.'

'I know.'

'You've got to make sure you meet us, right? We can't afford to wait if you're late. Is that understood?'

Carla nodded again, trembling despite the warm coat.

'How will I know when to leave?'

Hastings' dark eyes glittered. 'We'll be making a lot of noise, you won't be able to miss it. As soon as you hear any sign of trouble, you get to the alleyway and wait for us there.'

'I understand.'

'I hope like hell this joker was just acting on his own,' Hastings said to Napier, a frown creasing his brow.

'I am sure he is,' Carla interrupted. 'He is not nice. He tried to... you know...do things to me.' She swallowed. 'Just yesterday...maybe the day before. No, yesterday.' She gave a nervous smile. 'I am sorry, there is so much happening to remember things.'

She filled them in on the incident in the alleyway, talking rapidly and with obvious embarrassment. She avoided their gazes when she told them how Major Wolf had grabbed her. The two men frowned at each other.

'Just another reason to put a bullet in that bastard,' Napier muttered.

'If we have to go without you, they'll come looking for a spy, it could mean you all get interrogated. What will you do?'

'I will not tell them a thing. I would rather die first.' There was a steely determination in her tone that both men picked up on. 'I think it will be okay,' she said, 'but thank you. It is nice to be thought of like this.'

'You better go.' Hastings gave a nod and a crooked smile. 'Thank you, and good luck. See you at the RV.'

'Yes, good luck.' Napier smiled warmly and gave her a wink.

She smiled back, lingering on his face before turning away. They watched her hurry back towards town, disappearing into the gloom of the almost-dawn.

'Quite a girl,' Napier said.

'Hmmm.' Hastings nodded, staring thoughtfully after her. 'Interesting.'

Napier cocked an eyebrow. 'You don't believe her?'

'I do.' Hastings rubbed his jaw. 'First we're told we're coming in to kill or capture Jankowski, who's a traitor. We get compromised before we even get off the ground, so the plan changes and we come in a day early. Now it looks like they were expecting us anyway.' He frowned at his companion. 'The goal posts keep shifting, and we don't know if we're Arthur or bloody Martha.'

Napier nodded reluctantly. 'Certainly seems that way, old boy. What d'you think, then?'

'We bury that joker and destroy her radio. Then we get amongst it and do what we came to do,' Hastings said, hefting the Sten in his hands. 'Time's ticking. Let's crack on, mate.'

47

On the flat between the base of the foothills and the town, they veered left and followed a well-worn track for a short distance.

Hikers and skiers obviously used the path to get up into the mountains, and although Hastings was loath to use a recognised track, it was going to be faster than cutting across country and leaving obvious signs in the snow. As it was the ground crunched underfoot as loudly as snapping twigs, and they had to slow their pace to reduce the noise, taking careful, exaggerated steps like a drunk walking down stairs.

It was still dark, the kind of bottomless dark you only got in the wilderness, and they needed to make the most of the cover it provided. The snow had stopped falling and a cutting wind had picked up, coming head-on as they circumvented the periphery of the town. It slapped the exposed skin of their faces and hands, enveloping them in its soul-freezing chill and quickly numbing the exposed extremities.

They had left the horses behind, loosely tethered in the forest. If they needed them, they had a method of escape. If not, the animals would be able to get loose easily enough. The dead soldier was buried under snow along with the smashed radio. It wasn't a permanent solution but it would do for now.

Hastings led the way for half a mile before stopping and turning his back to the wind. The pack operated as a windbreak for him, and he lowered himself to a crouch. Napier closed in and they got their heads together. Hastings opened the front of his smock, using it as a shield to hide the light from the red-lensed torch as he checked the folded map.

'The Commandant's house is here.' He identified the location in the middle of town with a frozen finger. 'We could go directly there, be about twenty minutes I reckon.'

'There'll be patrols,' Napier whispered, and Hastings nodded. They knew the town itself was laid out in an open design around the town square, which the Commandant's house was off.

'Better to go this way.'

He traced a route around the outside of the town, leading to a narrow lane that ran close to the Commandant's house. It would take them around the lake and then cut back in, and they would be hitting the target right on the crack of dawn.

It was cutting it damned fine but it was all they could do. The other option was to just balls it out and walk straight through town, which would undoubtedly end in a gun battle within minutes.

'We hit that hard and fast,' Hastings whispered, 'walk straight in like we own the joint. Take out anyone who gets in the way, and get our hands on Jankowski.' His eyes were dark as he studied Napier's face. 'We definitely know he's a traitor now, right?'

'We do.' Napier gave a brief nod.

'So we get in there and take him out. No messing about.'

'Got it.' Napier nodded again, avoiding his gaze.

Hastings grabbed his arm. 'You might have to do it yourself,' he hissed. 'Are you up for it?'

Napier hesitated a second then nodded a third time. 'Yes,' he said. He swallowed, then repeated himself more firmly. 'Yes, yes.'

'Good. We'll only have one chance. As soon as that's done we'll hit the SS place next door, but only if we have time. Otherwise we just leg it to the airfield as quick as we can, and leave the place in chaos behind us.' He gave that wolfish grin again. 'Nick a plane, get in the air and bugger off. Pretty simple, eh?'

Napier cocked an eyebrow. 'If you say so, old man. I don't know that I'd call it simple.'

'Simple and effective,' Hastings said firmly. 'The more basic the plan, the less likely it is to get ballsed up.'

'Righto,' Napier nodded. 'Let's do it.'

Folding up the map, Hastings felt a hand on his arm. He looked up sharply. Even in the darkness he could see that Napier had a soft look on his face.

'Jack, I just wanted to say...good luck. I never thought I'd be doing something like this, but you can rely on me.' He held Hastings' gaze. 'I'll do everything I can to get us out of here, and I'll be right beside you every step of the way, old man.'

Hastings tucked the map away. 'Good on ya, mate.'

He stood, shifting the weight on his back. Napier stood too, waiting. The wireless set was like a dead weight on his shoulders but he felt somehow lighter. He felt good for having said that; Hastings needed to know that he wasn't in this alone, even if he thought pilots were all a bunch of pampered sissies. He would probably have something equally meaningful to say, a few well-chosen words of encouragement and solidarity.

Hastings straightened his smock and gripped the Sten in both hands.

'Keep low and move fast,' he said. 'Let's go, nancy-boy.'

48

They were a quarter of the way around the lake, roughly halfway to the apex, when they heard it.

A dog barked, not too far behind them. A man's voice, low and muffled, German. An eager whine from the animal, something else from the man, then one word that Napier heard quite clearly.

'*Suchen!*'

'Oh bugger,' he muttered. 'He gave the command to "seek".'

They could hear the dog now, powering towards them. Somehow it had detected them and the handler had let it loose to find them.

'Get in the water,' Hastings hissed, darting to the edge of the lake.

They had just come past a clump of trees that partially overhung the bank, and ahead of them was an open stretch towards the top of the lake. He stomped through reeds into the shallows, Napier close behind, a torch beam flashing on the track behind them. Hopefully the soldiers with the dog were too far behind to see them, but the dog definitely knew where they were. It was a black and tan arrow through the darkness, zeroing in fast.

The water was freezing cold but they carried on regardless, hoping the dog would be confused and scoot on past.

'Get under,' Hastings hissed, struggling out of his pack as he dropped down. He let the pack fall away and was trying to draw the Welrod from his belt when the dog arrived. It was a good-sized German shepherd, strong across the shoulders. Its ears were up and it was honed in on the figure of Napier, who was still lumbering amongst the reeds, trying to shuck off his pack and the cumbersome radio set in its plywood box.

The dog gave a growl and launched itself through the air.

Napier was slammed from behind and went under, his arms trapped in the straps of his pack and his legs tangled in the reeds. The extra weight of the dog forced him face first beneath the surface.

Seeing the dog latch on his companion's pack, Hastings started to move to help him, but stopped when he heard the approach of running feet. Only one set of boots; that was good. The soldier must have been patrolling alone, confident of dealing with any problems with just him and the dog.

Pulling back away from the thrashing commotion, Hastings finally got the Welrod free from his belt and eased himself down in the reeds, backing gently into the cover of the trees and keeping his eyes on where he knew the soldier would appear.

The dog was tearing at Napier's pack and there was a hell of a commotion as the pilot tried to avoid either getting bitten or drowning.

The soldier came into sight, a torch in one hand and a rifle in the other.

'*Raus! Raus!*'

Raising the long barrel of the Welrod, Hastings sighted in. He had to ignore the dog for now and deal with the man. He was about fifteen yards from the soldier, who was now at the edge of the lake, shining his torch on the dog and whatever it was attacking.

'*Englander?*'

He sounded surprised, and in that second Hastings shot him. The Welrod was almost completely silent and all he heard was the faintest *phut* followed by a slap as the .32 bullet punched the soldier's chest.

The soldier staggered backwards a step and looked down at

himself. Hastings worked the toggle to chamber another round and squeezed the trigger a second time, putting the round higher. It clipped the side of the soldier's neck and caused him to cry out, dropping his torch and rifle as he grabbed at his neck and dropped to his knees.

Pushing up from the water and reeds, Hastings got a third round up the spout and closed in. He fired the third round from only a few yards away, punching it straight into the man's right eye as the soldier turned to look at him.

The body flopped back on the ground, silent.

The German shepherd yelped when the bullet slammed into its shoulder, the only part of the animal that Hastings could see clearly. The dog released its prey and turned to look behind it, shocked and in pain from the sudden attack.

Smashing the pistol across the dog's snout, Hastings knocked it sideways into the water. He got around Napier, tripping over his thrashing legs, and closed in on the dog which was scrabbling for a foothold in the water. The dog found its feet and launched itself up in a frenzy, pain and rage driving it to attack the man who was hurting it.

Its powerful jaws locked onto Hastings' left forearm as he blocked its attack from reaching his throat and it forced him over backwards, down into the dark, freezing cold water.

The cold wasn't enough to numb the burning pain in his forearm, and he couldn't cock the Welrod with one hand, let alone underwater while being mauled by a dog.

Scrambling to get a hold, Hastings felt the dogs' claws ripping at his legs and torso. He rammed the barrel of the pistol into its side, jabbing it as hard as his sodden clothing would allow him to move. It seemed to make no difference. The dog shook its head, thrashing at his arm and growling harshly.

He managed to get a foot down and threw his weight sideways, rolling the dog off him to his left. It stayed locked on his arm but it now also had no footing. He knew the quickest way to kill it would be to spread its front legs and stab it in the chest, but he had no way of doing that just now. He pushed harder, using his leg strength and body weight to force the dog into the water then under it.

Getting a knee onto the animal beneath the surface, Hastings pinned it down and forced down on his left arm, which was screaming in pain. He held the dog down, ignoring the claws that continued to rip at him as the animal fought for its life. It released his arm, obviously realising there was a bigger issue at play, but it was too late. Hastings held it down, pinned to the bottom of the lake, feeling the resistance gradually easing as the dog became weaker.

After what seemed like minutes, the animal lay still.

Breathing hard and with his left arm in agony, Hastings rolled off the animal and let it float to the surface. He awkwardly worked the toggle on the Welrod and chambered another round. Pressing the muzzle against the underside of the dog's jaw, he squeezed the trigger and put a bullet in its brain.

Leaning on his hands and knees in the shallows, Napier watched as he heaved up water. Sucking down air, he wiped his mouth and spat.

'Bit...harsh...old man?' he wheezed.

Hastings slid the pistol back into his belt and looked down at the lifeless animal.

'Needed to make sure,' he said quietly. 'I didn't want it to suffer.' He took a breath, his chest feeling tight. 'Only doing its job.'

He moved the dead dog over beneath the trees, wedging it in beneath a branch so it wouldn't float away. He touched the animal softly on the head, saddened that he had been forced to kill it. He had no beef with animals, and felt sick. It felt completely different to killing a man. He moved onto the bank and dragged the dead soldier over to join his dog. By the time he'd finished, Napier was on his feet and arching his back with a grimace.

'Jesus Christ,' the pilot panted. 'I twisted my back under that blasted thing and swallowed half the bloody lake. I'm buggered, as you'd say.'

'You think I swear too much?' Hastings gave him a quizzical look.

'No, not at all...'

'Well you're not as buggered as you could've been.' Hastings said. 'Or as buggered as the radio.'

His own pack was somewhere in the water, and Napier's was completely waterlogged, as was the wireless set.

'Well, I say, that buggered it, alright,' Napier said, a sudden laugh escaping his lips.

'You're not wrong. And we've lost more time.' Hastings cast a look around. 'We need to get moving, and we need to get round this lake.'

He cocked his head, listening.

'What is it?' Napier tried to wring out his smock, but it was absolutely drenched. The chill of the water was settling into his bones.

'An engine.' Hastings stared into the darkness, his keen eyes picking up a glow of light near the apex of the lake. 'There's a sentry post up ahead, and we're heading straight towards it.'

'Oh bugger.'

There was no way they could get past the sentry post by road. They couldn't go back the way they had come.

'Only one option,' Hastings said quietly. 'How's your swimming?'

49

I t was about three hundred yards from where they started to get across the lake and be clear of the sentry post.

From there it would be a hop, skip and a jump into the town to get on target. Time was very short and already they could see the sky lightening on the horizon. The lake wasn't cold enough to have frozen over, but it certainly felt somewhere south of zero. They would have to move fast as soon as they got out of the water, both to use the little remaining darkness as cover and to avoid dying of hypothermia.

Leading the way with powerful one-armed strokes, Hastings knew the situation was getting desperate. Jensen hadn't been kidding when he'd said they probably wouldn't make it. Damned if he was going to die here in a lake, though. The least he could do was make it to shore and go down fighting.

His left arm ached like a bastard, and he used it only to push his bundled kit ahead of him. Wrapped up in his smock was his Sten, Browning, ammo, boots and most of his clothing. It was wrapped up and tied off to a branch, the air in the bundle helping it to float. He wore only his trousers and shirt, with the Welrod in his belt and the Fairbairn-Sykes dagger on his hip.

The cold was all-consuming but he tried to push it to the back of his mind. They were a third of the way across, closer now to the sentry post than their intended landing site. He kicked hard, unable to touch the bottom now, nudging his bundle ahead.

Glancing back, he saw Napier just behind him. The airman was swimming confidently, pushing a similar bundle ahead of him. They had ditched the wireless in deeper water and weighted down their packs along with it. There was nothing there they needed, although it would have been handy to have the explosives. Never mind, they'd have to make do. He knew how to make bombs without needing gelignite or plastique.

As long as they could shoot and run, they were still in the game.

Breathing hard, Hastings could feel his nose oozing with the cold. His fingers and toes were numb and it felt like he'd swallowed a block of ice. He kicked harder, the weight of the sodden trousers making it difficult. Half way now, he reckoned.

Another glance behind, seeing Napier's pale face a bit further back now. He was moving awkwardly, his head just above the surface.

'Okay?' Hastings hissed, his voice sounding ragged to him.

A shake of the head and a pained expression. Napier stopped swimming and just floated, hanging onto his bundle. His face was screwed up and he let out a muted moan.

Hastings turned and stroked back towards him, reaching him in a few seconds. He bobbed beside him, kicking to stay upright.

'What's wrong?'

'Cramp...my back...Jesus...'

Napier was taking shallow breaths, obviously in pain.

'Can you swim?'

Looking towards the shore, Hastings gauged they were probably about in line with the sentry post just now. The last thing they wanted to do was go ashore there.

'In a...minute...shit...' Napier rolled his torso gently, trying to relieve the cramp. 'Twisted my back...that bloody wireless...too heavy.'

Hastings trod water beside him, conscious that every second they stayed put the higher their chance of being spotted. And every second in the water, the colder they got. He could feel his arms and legs freezing up now that he wasn't swimming, and his face was numb. They needed to get moving or they would die right there.

He pulled Napier in close, so they were face to face in the freezing water.

'Listen, you toffee-nosed git,' he hissed through chattering teeth, 'Jensen told me about you.'

Napier squinted at him in the darkness, his whole face trembling. 'What's that, old man?' he muttered.

'He told me about you...shot down. Three days E and E...behind the lines.' Hastings paused to take a breath – his chest was constricting in the cold. 'You made it; got home...takes balls...' He gave his companion a shake, the water sloshing between their faces from the movement. 'So I know you can do it...stop being a fuckin' girl's blouse...get on with it.'

'Okay...okay.' Napier rolled onto his side and took a deep breath, letting it out slowly. 'Should be okay.' He managed a tentative grin. 'Bit chilly for a dip, old chap.'

Hastings grunted and gave him a push in the right direction.

'You go first, I'll watch our backs.'

They started off again, doing their best to get the noise to a minimum. It was a tough ask with sodden clothing and limbs made clumsy by the numbing cold. For a long time the shore seemed to be moving away, and Hastings even wondered for a moment if perhaps the lake was tidal, but suddenly they were almost there. He moved with a renewed vigour now, spurred on by the thought of getting out of this icy death trap.

He overtook Napier, who had slowed right down and was moving sluggishly. He got his feet under him and waded up onto the shore, dropping to his knees in the icy mud past the reeds. He fumbled the Welrod out and scanned their surroundings, checking for any sign that they'd been spotted.

It was silent aside from the throb of an engine somewhere off to their left, where he had pegged the sentry post as being. No barking dogs, no shouts of alarm.

Nothing.

He turned to see what Napier was up to, and saw his companion crawling through the shallows, moving with the enthusiasm of a dying hippo. Hastings scrambled back to him and hooked his hand under Napier's arm, helping him up out of the water. Napier was shivering so hard that Hastings could feel it. His bundle was floating at the edge of the water and Hastings quickly recovered it before they lost that too.

'Come on.'

He hauled the airman to his feet and hustled him up to the roadside. With nothing in sight, they staggered across and clambered up the low bank on the other side, Hastings practically dragging Napier with him. There was a narrow ribbon of clear snow between the road and the woods and they crossed that too, getting alongside the edge of the woods.

'This way.'

Hastings half-carried Napier with him as he stumbled his way back towards the sentry post. He had a very simple plan in mind. Dawn was only minutes away and they would lose all element of surprise then. Napier was clearly going down fast and if they carried on, he'd be dead before the sun was up. Hastings knew he needed to either get the man operating again or get him into medical care, but medical care meant surrendering and inevitably execution. That left only one option.

Dropping down, he pulled Napier down to a crouch. The man's face was pale against the back drop of the trees and he was shivering violently.

'There's Germans just ahead,' Hastings whispered. 'Stay here.'

He put his sodden boots on and left Napier with his bundled clothing and weapons still attached to the branch. He wasn't planning on a gunfight and had the Welrod and his knife just in case. He moved off in a crouching stumble, the closest he could get to a run just now, before dropping to his hands and knees.

The rumbling of the engine got louder as he crawled across the icy-hard ground. It wasn't moving, just idling in the road, occasionally revving ever so slightly. He eased himself up the side of the low crest at the roadside.

Even in his frozen state, Hastings recognised what he was seeing. A truck with sentries posted, keeping watch on a sector. Looking for them. But not looking too hard. The truck should have been off and the sentries should have been on foot, keeping watch properly. But soldiers weren't like that, especially young ones. Young cold soldiers were even worse. That was why, as he crested the rise in the ground and looked down onto the sentry post, he felt himself smile just a little.

The truck lights were off but he could hear the heater going on full blast. Two cigarettes glowed in the cab and he heard the chatter of the two sentries. They were keeping warm, giving the engine the occasional boost to keep it running hot, and doing a crap job at keeping watch. They could probably see okay straight ahead, but nothing behind or to the side.

They were asking for trouble, and if he was their sergeant he'd have kicked their arses. As it was, he needed what they had, so he would kill them instead.

He eased back from the crest, crawling back to where Napier waited. The airman was shivering hard and Hastings knew it was only a matter of time before he was past the point of no return.

'Two guys in a truck,' Hastings whispered, putting his mouth close to Napier's ear. 'I'll go deal with them. You stay here.'

Napier nodded, at least managing to comprehend that.

Hastings gave him a pat on the shoulder and stood slowly, his limbs protesting as he straightened up and started swinging his arms about. It was slow and painful at first but he got his shoulders and arms moving, then his back, legs and feet. He still felt frozen to the core but at least he could move properly – if he couldn't move, he couldn't fight.

He slid the Fairbairn-Sykes knife from its sheath, flexing his fingers on the cold steel, and moved away from Napier. He cut parallel to the truck for a short way, keeping the woods to his right and the road to his left. His feet felt like lumps of frozen meat and each step was an effort at first, but he knew he needed to keep moving and get it done. Napier couldn't afford for him to wait.

Once he was thirty yards or so behind the truck, Hastings crawled to the top of the rise and scanned. No sign of anyone else, and no indication he'd been seen. He slid over on his belly, sliding down to the shoulder of the road before crawling out to the middle of the road. The darkness behind him meant he wasn't backlit, so even if the guards bothered to check their mirrors he would be just another shadow.

Moving steadily, he zeroed in on the tailgate of the truck and got there as quick as he could. He paused at the back of the truck, breathing hard from the exertion. He took a few seconds to roll his shoulders and neck, limbering up before he slipped around the left side of the truck. The driver had the steering wheel restricting his movements, so the passenger was the danger man.

That made him the first target.

Hastings eased his way along the side of the truck, the crunch of each step as loud as shattering glass to him. He reached the passenger door and paused, taking a couple of fast breaths to get the blood pumping as he hefted the knife in his hand.

He reached up and took hold of the door handle, braced a boot on the step, and wrenched the door open.

The passenger was mid-stream in conversation when the door beside him flew open and a dishevelled, wild-eyed soldier launched himself up into the steamy cab. The passenger actually let out a cry of fright before Hastings rammed the Fairbairn-Sykes up under his chin and through the roof of his mouth.

The driver recoiled back in horror, fumbling for his weapon.

Hastings got on top of the passenger, ripping the knife from the man's throat and free of the hands grasping desperately at it. The passenger was gurgling and gasping and out of the game, so Hastings turned his attention to the driver, who had got both hands on a rifle that had been leaning against the bench seat between them.

The weapon was too long to easily bring to bear, and the driver realised too late that he'd committed to an action he couldn't complete. He tried to back away as Hastings lunged across the cab at him but found himself trapped against the door with his legs tangled in the gear stick and the rifle sling.

Hastings thrust the knife into the man's chest, yanked it out and scrambled closer to get a better angle. The driver managed to throw a fist at him but Hastings barely registered it, focussing instead on what he needed to do. The second stab pierced the side of the driver's neck and he grabbed at it, trying to stop the attack that both men knew was the end.

Hastings leaned into it, twisting the knife with both hands, the driver's face screwed up tight against the excruciating pain and terror that was ravaging his body. He shuddered and gasped and Hastings held on for what seemed a lifetime until the driver began to sag. His hands dropped away and his body went slack, and Hastings pulled back, kneeling between the two bodies.

His hands were covered in blood and he was breathing hard. He wiped the knife carefully on the trousers of the driver and re-sheathed it. He clambered back over the passenger, who was staring at him with glassy, sightless eyes. Hastings could smell the coppery stench of the blood soaking the man's front.

He climbed back down into the cold, dragging the dead passenger with him, then removed the driver and hauled him around to the side of the road beside the passenger.

Closing the cab to keep the warmth in, Hastings fumbled with numb fingers to strip the men of their greatcoats. He struggled into one and hugged it to him, the wool rough on his skin as he buttoned it up. He climbed back into the cab and grabbed the men's weapons – a Schmiesser MP40 and a Karabiner 98k rifle. Fortunately neither man had got his hands on the MP40 before he'd taken them out. He slung the rifle over his shoulder and hung the submachine gun across his body, hugged the second greatcoat to him and hustled back to where he'd left Napier.

'Here, get up.'

He helped Napier to his feet and got him into the greatcoat, the man shaking so much it took an age to get his arms into the sleeves.

That done, Hastings pulled him into a bear hug and rubbed his hands vigorously up and down Napier's back and arms, trying to stimulate some warmth. Napier grunted and Hastings felt his own hands warming up, and after a while Napier pulled away.

'I'm okay,' he muttered. 'I'm okay.'

'Good, come on then.'

They hurried back to the truck as fast as Napier could move, and Hastings helped him climb up into the cab. The rush of warm air that escaped the door was like a beacon in a deadly sea storm to Napier and he shuffled across the seat until he found the vent. Huddling over it, he held his hands to the air and sucked the warmth into his lungs.

As inviting as the warm cab was, Hastings' work wasn't finished yet. He handed the rifle up to Napier and closed the door, turning his attention to the two soldiers he'd killed. He felt no regret about killing them – they were the enemy and the job needed to be done. If they'd had the chance, he and Napier would be dead right now.

He fumbled them out of their uniforms, stripping the boots, trousers, jackets and shirts off first one then the other. Like he and Napier, both men were average sized. By the time he'd finished their undershirts were soaked from the snow, so he left them in their undergarments and opened the door again.

Napier looked up, a little more alert now thankfully.

'Here, get changed.'

Hastings thrust the German uniforms onto the seat and climbed in, shutting the cold outside again. He noticed that the cab was cooler from the opening and shutting of the door, but it couldn't be helped.

Napier gave the uniforms a doubtful look.

'You want us to disguise ourselves as Jerries?' he said, his teeth still chattering. 'D'you think that's wise?'

Hastings shucked off the greatcoat and started to strip out of his sodden uniform.

'You think being here at all is wise?' he said. 'At least their kit's dry. If you want to die of hypothermia, stay as you are. I'd rather go down fighting.' He took a second look at his companion's face. 'We better clean this cam cream off, too.'

He pulled on the shirt and field tunic, feeling instantly better despite the blood that made the clothing sticky and wet. With obvious reluctance, Napier began to follow suit. By the time Hastings was fully dressed, Napier was still struggling into his trousers.

'I'll sort those bodies out,' Hastings said. 'Back in a minute.'

He left the warm cab again, feeling much better prepared now for the gasp-inducing cold. The bodies looked almost white in the dark, as if they'd been there forever. He grabbed one by the wrists and dragged it up the bank into the snow.

After several yards he dropped the body and returned for the second one. It wasn't a fool proof hiding place by any means, but it would do for now. The second one was heavier and he was puffing and sweating by the time he laid it beside the first.

He straightened up and sucked in breaths, feeling the sweat trickling down his back. If nothing else at least he was keeping warm. The sweat felt good, even though he knew it would soon turn cold.

He took a moment to get his thoughts together.

Napier was beginning to seriously worry him. He could understand that almost drowning then just managing to dodge hypothermia could happen to anyone, so he didn't hold that against him. Well not much, anyway. The guy just seemed reluctant to get his hands dirty, and he lacked killer instinct. That, now more than ever, was what they needed. The determination to drive forward and keep going.

He had it himself; he'd always had it, probably from his tough upbringing.

But the toff pilot? Hell no. Hastings decided there and then that if Napier was going to hold him back, he'd have to leave him somewhere safe and do the job himself.

He started trudging back to the truck, the stolen jackboots snug on his feet. Headlights blazed from the left, the direction of town, and he instinctively stopped still. Standing where he was, he would still be invisible to the oncoming vehicle, but any sudden movement like ducking down would be out of place with the environment. Trees and shadows didn't move suddenly like that.

He lowered himself down to a crouch, swinging the MP40 forward on its sling. He checked the readiness of the weapon – safety on, magazine seated properly. He presumed that the soldier he'd taken it from would have had a round chambered, but assumption was the mother of all cock-ups, so he worked the bolt anyway. He couldn't see a round eject in the darkness but at least he was ready now.

The vehicle came down the road towards the truck, slowing as it approached. Hastings kept it in the periphery of his sight, not wanting to destroy his night vision, and moved forward in a crouch. The car was a Horch 108, a jeep-like vehicle he knew the Germans used as a staff car.

It pulled up behind the truck and both front doors opened. The engine remained running, the headlights illuminating the two soldiers as they moved towards the driver's side of the truck. Hastings shot a quick look, recognising that one was an officer of some sort in a peaked cap, the other a burly soldier with an MP40 in his hands.

Napier was seriously in the shit now, he realised, and it was only seconds away from hitting the fan.

Hastings moved to his right, heading for the front of the truck. He needed to get there fast or Napier was dead.

51

The driver's door opened and a round-looking young officer stared up at him. Off to the side was the other man with a submachine gun at the ready.

'Everything alright, Private?' The officer had a nasal tone and looked to be maybe twenty if he was lucky.

Napier nodded dutifully and responded in German. '*Ja*, sir. No problem, thank you.'

The officer nodded then peered past him. 'Where is the other man?' He squinted up at Napier, still holding the door open with one hand. 'He better not be asleep.'

'No no, sir.' Napier gestured vaguely off into the darkness, fighting to stop his teeth from chattering. 'Call of nature, sir.'

The officer nodded again, glanced away as if he might see the other soldier watering a tree, then turned back to Napier.

'Stay alert, Private. This is a crucial time for us and there's every chance the British pigs will try and attack us.'

'Yes sir.' Napier patted the 98k across his lap. 'Don't worry sir, they won't get past me.'

The officer gave a smile, then the burly soldier with him spoke in low tones. Napier couldn't catch what was said, but he detected the urgent edge in the soldier's voice. He saw the officer stiffen as he listened, and he knew the game was up. What exactly had tipped them off didn't matter right now – maybe the soldier knew the two guards posted here, maybe he'd seen something. It didn't matter.

Napier was about to be sprung and all three men knew it.

He had no chance of getting the rifle around in time, not with a submachine gun so close. He'd be dead in a second. His best option was to get out the other side and run like hell. With any luck Hastings was lurking around somewhere and the mad Kiwi would get amongst it.

Napier licked his lips, took a breath, and prepared to move.

———

The crunch of a boot on ice was the first indication of trouble for the young Leutnant Krammer. He started to turn but it was too late.

The MP40 barrel cracked him across the back of the head with full force, sending him staggering as his attacker swept past him. The officer grabbed hold of the side of the truck for support, his legs like jelly beneath him. He watched with a detached fascination as a German soldier attacked his driver, the burly Unteroffizier Rache.

The soldier rammed the MP40 into Rache's face as the driver was backing up, almost knocking him off his feet and dislodging his helmet. Rache recovered enough to bring his weapon up but it was too late. The other soldier knocked the weapon aside and kicked the corporal in the guts, sending him staggering again. Rache went to a knee and the other man was on him, smashing the MP40 onto his skull again and again until Rache sagged to the ground.

Leutnant Krammer got himself upright, his vision blurring as he tried to think. He had to defend himself. He felt for the holster on his hip, finding the comfort of the Mauser's grip. He tugged it free, trying hard to focus on the man who was beating Rache to death.

Raising the Mauser, Leutnant Krammer prepared to fire.

———

Gripping the 98K in both hands like a staff, Napier balanced on the step with both feet and slammed the butt of the rifle into the side of the officer's head.

It dropped the man like a sack of spuds and Napier overbalanced, falling to the ground with a grunt. He scrambled clumsily up from the slushy roadway, picking up the rifle he'd dropped, ready to attack again.

There was no need. The officer was lying motionless on the ground, a pistol hanging limply from his outstretched hand. Hastings turned, breathing hard. The other soldier lay dead at his feet. Even in the low light Napier could see the wild look in his eyes.

'He dead?' the Kiwi said, striding towards the fallen officer.

Napier swallowed hard. 'I think so.'

Hastings nudged the officer with his boot and the man's head lolled unnaturally.

'Yep,' he said with some satisfaction. 'Broke his neck. That did it alright.'

Napier nodded numbly, and tried to swallow again. His guts were churning and he turned away just in time to avoid his companion when he projectile vomited. He heaved and went again, splattering the roadway with the contents of his stomach. Hastings left him to it and set to stripping the two new bodies of their uniforms.

By the time Napier had recovered himself and finished spitting, he had a new set of uniform to wear.

'It's a lot cleaner than what we've got on,' Hastings explained, 'plus you get to be an officer. You should feel right at home.'

Napier showed no hesitation this time, just got busy getting changed. Hastings was right, the uniform was unbloodied and felt a lot cleaner, albeit a bit tight across the shoulders. The corporal had been a bigger man than Hastings so he had to tuck his shirt in and cinch the belt tighter, but it was a nice change from the blood and sweat of his first attempt at disguise. Hastings also found a wound dressing and a bandage in the soldiers' kit and got Napier to patch up his arm. The dog bite would need to be cleaned properly and re-dressed, but all that could happen later – if there was a later.

In short order they were freshly changed and had dumped the two other bodies in a different place under some trees, kicking snow over them for a short-term hide. They bundled their own wet uniforms and the bloodied uniforms from the sentries together and buried them in a snow drift.

They kept their own weapons, concealing the Browning pistols beneath their greatcoats. Hastings slipped the Welrod into his own belt and attached the Fairbairn-Sykes dagger to the belt as well, making sure both weapons were well hidden.

That done, they turned their attention to the vehicles.

'Someone'll be expecting these chaps back at some stage,' Napier said, tugging the Leutnant's cap onto his head. 'They wouldn't have an officer coming to do a stint on watch; he must be doing the rounds.'

'So either the next OP will be expecting him,' Hastings said, 'or he'll be due back at base some time soon. Could only be a few minutes until someone notices them missing.'

'This could be the last one,' Napier agreed. 'Or it could be the first.' He cast an eye towards the mountains. 'And the sun's almost up.'

'We need to get our arses in gear.'

Hastings grabbed up the MP40 dropped by the dead corporal, and tossed it to Napier. He followed it with the webbing, which carried six magazine pouches, a bayonet and a canteen. Usually there was also an entrenching tool and a bread bag, but not being out in the field meant the soldier had left that off his kit. He secured a similar rig from the sentries around his own waist and took a few seconds to check all the magazines were loaded.

Satisfied that he was good to go, he checked that Napier was set up properly – being RAF, he couldn't be trusted to look like an infantryman properly. He had to admit though, his companion was a quick study and was looking good. He even had the Leutnant's Mauser holstered on his hip.

'Right, watch my back,' Hastings said.

He drove the truck down the road a little further until he found a narrow track off into the woods. He bumped along until the truck was well under cover of the trees, and turned it around in case they needed it later for a getaway.

Leaving the keys in the sun visor, he hurried back to where Napier was waiting by the Horch, his submachine gun ready. Maybe it was Hastings' imagination, but the airman gave the impression of having got himself together. He could only hope – they would certainly need to be on their game when they hit the village.

'Nothing doing?' Hastings paused to wipe sweat from his brow and take a drink from the water bottle on his stolen belt kit.

'Not a thing.' Napier nodded towards the car. 'D'you want to drive or shall I?'

'You're the officer, so better be me.' Hastings opened the driver's door and gave him a grim look. 'Just be sure to *sprechen sie Deutsche* if we get stopped, eh?'

Napier didn't bother telling him that was actually a question, just climbed in the front passenger seat and closed the door.

With the MP40 on his lap, he took a deep breath and let it out slowly. He was warming up properly now that he was dry and had fresh clothes on, and the heater was on full blast, for what it was worth. Despite all that had happened so far on this insane mission, he had the feeling that the real business was about to begin. They were heading straight into the belly of the beast, and there would be no turning back.

St Joseph of Cupertino was the patron saint of pilots, and although Napier wasn't the most dedicated churchgoer, he'd always thought it handy to have a little spiritual guidance. He muttered a quick prayer now as Hastings cranked the car around and straightened up with the nose towards town.

'Good to go?' the Kiwi asked. 'Your back okay?'

Napier nodded, hoping the other man hadn't heard his quick prayer. He probably didn't even believe in God. He hadn't even thought of his back, what with all the killing that had just happened. Somehow it seemed irrelevant now.

'Yes,' he said, with more conviction than he felt, 'let's do it.' He gave a self-conscious grin, trying for nonchalant but failing. 'Chocks away, old boy.'

Hastings smiled darkly. 'Right,' he said mockingly. 'This is it. Remember this; keep calm, do the job at hand, and if it all goes tits-up, mallet the bastards before they mallet us, right?'

Napier's Adams apple bobbed but he managed to nod. 'Of course.'

Hastings punched him lightly on the shoulder. 'For an RAF woofter, you're not a bad bloke, Freddie.'

Napier swallowed again and took a breath to calm his nerves. 'I'll take that.' He shifted the MP40 in his lap, the weight of it comforting in the dark. 'Let's go.'

52

Rounding a bend in the road as they closed in on Alpenbad, they were hit with blinding headlights.

Both men threw their hands up to shield their eyes and Hastings hit the brakes, slowing the car before they crashed into the truck he could just make out behind the lights.

Framed by the lights were at least a couple of soldiers with Schmiessers, the weapons pointing directly at them as they slowed to a stop.

'Oh, bloody hell,' Napier groaned. 'This is not good at all.'

'Stay calm,' Hastings muttered from the corner of his mouth. 'We're gonna blag our way through it, right?'

Napier gave a sound that may have been a choking squeal.

'That posh education of yours,' Hastings muttered, watching a soldier approaching the driver's window. 'Now's the time to bloody well use it.'

The soldier reached the door as Hastings cranked the window down. He peered into the car, getting a glare from Hastings in return. The soldier opened his mouth to speak, and that was when Napier burst into action. He leaned across Hastings and addressed the soldier in faultless German, with all the haughty arrogance he could muster.

'Turn those damn lights off you imbecile, you're blinding me!'

The soldier hesitated, caught off guard by the angry officer. This wasn't quite how things were supposed to work.

'Well hurry up,' Napier snarled, 'or I'll shoot the damn things out myself. Are you all stupid?'

The soldier gestured to his comrades, and a few seconds later the lights were dimmed. He went to speak, but was again cut short by the irate officer.

'I haven't come all this way for you idiots to nearly make us crash,' Napier ranted, getting red in the face. Veins popped in his temples and neck. 'What sort of fool blinds a driver like that?' He jerked a thumb towards Hastings, who remained blank-faced throughout the exchange. 'I already have the misfortune of being assigned the laziest village idiot I have ever met as my driver, now you nearly run me off the road. Honestly, you make him look smart.'

Hastings didn't have much clue what was being said, but he was impressed. Hopefully the Jerries bought it. He slowly eased his hand down to the MP40 beside his seat just in case. If things went pear-shaped he would have to act fast.

The soldier blinked and cleared his throat.

'Well what're you waiting for, man?' Napier snapped. 'Move aside and let us by!'

'I am very s-s-sorry, sir,' the soldier managed. 'We have been t-t-told to stop any v-v-vehicles, sir.'

Another soldier was coming forward now, a scowl on his face and his submachine gun at the ready. Hastings sensed trouble and slipped his hand onto the MP40, curling his fingers around the pistol grip.

'What is the problem here?' the new arrival rasped, peering suspiciously at the two men in the car. He was about thirty and grizzled with it. He wore a Sergeant's insignia, and Hastings had the impression he was a seasoned battler, probably a career soldier. He wasn't good news for the two intruders.

Napier gave the man a furious glare.

'Are you in charge of these bumbling idiots?'

'Yes sir.' The sergeant was completely unruffled.

'Then get them out of my way,' Napier thundered. 'I don't have time to waste being questioned by stuttering buffoons like this.' He jabbed an accusing finger at the first soldier. 'I'm on an urgent mission for the Field Marshal himself.'

The sergeant's eyebrows rose. Hastings didn't understand much of what was being said, and just hoped his partner knew where the hell he was going with this line.

'Which Field Marshal would that be, sir?' the sergeant rasped, a touch of doubt creeping into his voice now.

'Field Marshal Rommel,' Napier said, giving a sigh of exasperation at the man's obvious ignorance. 'Feel free to ask him yourself, if you like. He'll be here in the morning, and he's expecting everything set up how he wants it.'

'I don't know anything about him coming, sir.'

'Of course you don't know, *sergeant*,' Napier snapped. 'Do you think one of our greatest commanders tells *everybody* his movements? Now get this blockade out of my way before I take this any higher.'

The sergeant hesitated, glancing doubtfully at Hastings. Hastings gave him a sympathetic eye roll, NCO to NCO, as if to say "What can you do?"

The sergeant relented, and took a step back. It was clear he was getting nowhere with this pompous idiot. Their orders were very clear and, being the career man that he was, his instinct was to demand papers and go through the whole rigmarole. But he could see a massive headache right there.

He didn't know these two, but that meant nothing – people came and went from here all the time. They sounded and looked genuine, the Leutnant in particular. A typical officious prick, like most officers. He pitied the poor bastard who'd been stuck with him, even if he was the village idiot.

Besides, he had doubts about the intel they'd been given. Surely nobody would be stupid enough to try and attack them here in the heart of Germany? To do so would be suicide, and he knew the Englanders wouldn't be so stupid.

He turned to his section and gave a wave.

'Let them through,' he said. He turned back to the car and gave the Leutnant a salute. 'Thank you, sir. Please go through.'

Napier returned the salute. 'Thank you, sergeant.' He sat back in his seat and drummed his fingers on his knee.

Hastings waited as the truck moved to the side of the road, keeping his gaze straight ahead. He ignored the German sergeant, praying that Napier had been obnoxious enough that the man wouldn't try to make small talk. As soon as the truck was clear, Napier turned and glared at him.

'Well hurry up, man,' he snapped. 'What're you waiting for? Idiot.'

The only word Hastings understood was *dummkopf*, and knew it was directed at him. He clenched his jaw, gave the sergeant a sideways look, and started forward. The soldiers watched them as he eased the car past the truck, and he was just waiting for a stream of bullets to smash into them.

They cleared the side of the truck and he steered into the middle of the road, accelerating and changing down gears. He kept it steady as they gained space, and in the rear-view mirror he saw the truck moving back into position on the road.

'Bloody hell,' Napier muttered, 'I can't believe it.'

'You did good,' Hastings said, relief hitting him like a wave. They weren't out of the woods yet but at least that was one hurdle down.

Napier chuckled and shook his head in amazement. 'I can't believe it.' His chuckle grew into a laugh, and Hastings felt himself smiling too.

'Calm down,' Hastings said, 'the fat lady hasn't sung yet.'

Napier stopped laughing, caught his breath and gave him a sideways look.

'You're just full of good cheer, aren't you?' he said. 'You had to rain on my parade.'

Hastings grunted, his eyes fixed on the dark road ahead.

'Laugh it up later,' he said quietly. 'We've got work to do yet.'

53

The sound of a car sliding to a halt outside the dormitory building was the first sign of trouble.

Carla had opened the shutters already, even though it was practically still dark outside. There was no way she would get back to sleep now, so she figured she may as well get things in order. She would never be coming back to this room again. Either she would be swooped away by the two Englishmen or, if they failed in their mission, she would be on the run.

Peering down to the road now, she realised there was a distinct third option.

Hilde was there, speaking to Major Wolf and Captain Fischer. She turned and gestured excitedly towards the house, the excitement doubling when she saw Carla looking down at them from the window. Wolf and Fischer both looked up too, and Carla instinctively pulled back.

She knew it was too late though; Hilde had called them here, and there was no way out. Perhaps she could try and escape across the neighbouring rooftops. It was the only possible way other than the front door, which she now heard opening. A pair of motorcycles rumbled to a halt outside as well, and she heard the first footsteps on the stairs.

'Shit,' Carla cursed to herself. 'Shit, shit, shit.'

Even though she knew they were coming, she still let out a squeal when her door banged open.

Major Wolf was impeccable in his black uniform, the swastika proudly worn on his arm, the peak of his cap polished. Fischer peered over his shoulder, and she could see the helmets of other men there too, Hilde's head bobbing up as she tried to get a view past the men.

'So, *fraulein* Carla Bettelheim.' Wolf stepped into the room, a pistol at his hip levelled at her. 'I did not think we would be speaking again so soon. If I am honest, I am disappointed.' He allowed himself a thin smile. 'In myself, not you. That charade you put on yesterday was quite the performance.'

Carla felt the dressing table bump against her back as she edged away from him. She was in the corner now; nowhere to go.

'It will not happen again, I assure you,' Wolf said. 'When something happens once, *fraulein*, it is happenstance. Twice is coincidence. Three times...' The pale blue ice of his eyes bore into hers. 'Three times is enemy action.'

'But sir, I...'

'No, no, no.' He wagged his finger like she was a naughty child. 'The time for this is over. You lied to me yesterday – to *me*.' He put his free hand to his chest, as if he was personally affronted by her. 'Now this morning you have been seen sneaking in and out of your house. It is time for us to talk properly, *fraulein*.' The thin smile came back again. 'And this time, I assure you, you will tell me the truth.'

Trapped in the corner with a squad of SS men facing her, Carla felt her gut drop through the floor. This was it; the end. There would be no fairytale ending for her. No nice Englishman with the beautiful eyes and the kind face. No escape from the hell that was Alpenbad.

The only thing she could do now was pray.

54

Early dawn light was creeping over the town.

The Horch eased to a stop several doors down from the Commandant's house.

There was a sentry posted at the front door who cast a lazy eye in their direction then looked away, recognising the car and detecting no threat. The car with two German soldiers in it was a familiar sight and his shift was nearly finished.

Napier had his hand on the door handle when Hastings spoke.

'Wait,' he said. 'Change of plan.'

'What?'

Napier was aghast. He'd psyched himself up to get to this point; he was ready to roll, and roll now. He followed Hastings' gaze towards the next house past the sentry, where a soldier was leaning beside the front door. They could see the tip of a cigarette glowing orange as he inhaled.

'The Nazis are right next door,' Hastings said. 'They've got a guy at the door too. If we take out the sentry and bowl into the Commandant's house, we're going to have a swarm of bad bastards on our arses before we even get inside. We need to deal with them at the same time.'

'Jesus man, you could've decided that earlier.' Napier licked his lips, feeling his forehead getting damp under the cap.

'Sometimes you just gotta fly by the seat of your pants, mate,' Hastings said. 'I'll deal with the SS jokers; you take the main house and I'll come in behind you. I'll take out the sentry for you first. Okay?'

'Ahh....'

'Good.' Hastings cracked his door. 'Follow my lead, you'll be fine.'

He got out, grabbing the Sten and slinging it over his back out of sight. He kept the MP40 in full view, and concealed the Welrod down by his side. Napier alighted on the other side and they fell into step side by side as they approached the Commandant's house.

Recognising an officer, the sentry snapped to attention. His rifle was at his side, no immediate use to him.

'*Guten morgen*,' Napier said, reaching the base of the steps.

Three stairs and a landing before the front door, which was closed. The sentry was standing to one side of the door.

'*Guten morgen...*'

Phut. The sentry's greeting was cut short by a .32 round punching into his chest. He gave a gasp and staggered back against the door.

'Go,' Hastings hissed, as Napier grabbed the dying sentry and helped him to the ground, out of sight of the sentry at the next house.

He moved quickly past, locking onto the man he'd seen smoking. The man was watching him but didn't seem alarmed – at least not yet. The soldier pushed off the wall as Hastings came closer, straightening up and flicking his cigarette aside. He took a step forward, something arousing his suspicions, but it was too late.

The Welrod came up, Hastings whipped the toggle back and the long barrel gave a tiny *phut*. The bullet took the soldier in the gut and he cried out as he folded forward, clutching at the wound. Working the toggle again, Hastings sensed eyes on him and snapped his head up. A second man was framed in a window on the second floor, looking down at him. Hastings saw his lips moving and heard a muffled shout of "*Achtung!*".

Things were about to go noisy.

He fired another round into the side of the wounded soldier's head then rammed the Welrod into his belt, snatching the M40 forward on its sling. He sent a short burst through the window where the soldier had been looking down, then dropped the gun on its sling and yanked a German potato-masher grenade from his belt kit. Gripping the wooden handle, he tugged the pull string downwards to prime it.

He hurled the grenade overhead through the smashed window and charged up the front steps. The grenade exploded at the same time as he booted the door in. Someone upstairs screamed.

The stairs directly in front of him switched back out of sight from the landing ahead. A soldier was running down the bottom flight of stairs towards him, a pistol in his hand. Hastings dropped him with a burst and turned to his right, where an internal door was starting to open.

Through the gap he could see the grey of a German uniform and the barrel of a weapon. He didn't hesitate. A 10-round burst smashed through the door and knocked the soldier off his feet, swinging the door open at the same time. It was a bedroom and there was another soldier there, struggling into his pants. Hastings blasted him off his feet onto the bed, sensed movement behind him and spun on his heels, dropping low.

Bullets thudded into the wall above him as a man in a black SS uniform opened up with a machine pistol from the stairs. Hastings returned fire, scrambling sideways for a better angle. More fire came from the guy, who ducked back out of view on the landing, and Hastings raked the balustrade and ceiling with fire, emptying the magazine.

There was another door to his left off the entranceway and he booted it hard beside the handle. The doorframe splintered but didn't give, and he booted it again. A pistol shot sounded from inside the room, and the door crashed open. Another bullet came his way as he swivelled to the side, dropping he MP40 on its sling and snatching another grenade. He tugged the charging cord and lobbed it through the doorway, ducking back again and grabbing hold of the Sten.

There was a cry of alarm then the grenade exploded and smoke and dust billowed out the door. Hastings was through the doorway a split second later, spotting a wounded soldier leaning on the wall with a pistol in his hands. He was half-clad in his black uniform.

Hastings put a burst into him and scanned the room – nobody else. A glance out the doorway brought a long burst of fire from the stairs that blasted splinters from the doorway near his head. One ripped across his right cheek, opening it up with a sharp sting.

He swore and pulled back. There were shouts from upstairs as the Nazis got themselves organised, and more fire rained down on the doorway. He heard a thump and saw a potato-masher bounce off the floor of the entranceway, hitting the door he was standing beside.

'Jesus!'

Hastings booted it back and slammed the door, covering his head as the grenade exploded in the entranceway. Feet sounded on the stairs and he threw the door open, keeping low as he leaned out and opened fire.

The Sten chattered and jumped in his hands as he raked a long burst into a Nazi who was almost at the door, knocking the man backwards then swivelling to engage two more who were halfway down the bottom flight of stairs.

One opened fire but the rounds went high, and Hastings cut him in half with a sustained burst. He folded and fell forwards down the stairs as his mate shouted a warning and swung a rifle towards Hastings. The weapon was too long and cumbersome for close quarters fighting, and Hastings emptied his magazine into the man, sending him tumbling down too.

Ducking back into the room, Hastings scrambled for a magazine. Both submachine guns were empty and he needed to reload fast.

There was an ominous thump followed quickly by a second, and he glanced down. Two grenades had hit the floor just outside the doorway, barely two feet from him.

55

N apier moved quickly up the steps as the sentry slid down the wall, slumping to the ground. A dark stain was spreading across his chest.

He heard a shout then a burst of fire, spinning to see Hastings grabbing a grenade from under his great coat. His guts dropped to his boots and he knew it was all on now. Grabbing the MP40, he stepped past the fallen sentry and opened the door into a high-ceilinged entranceway.

Art decorated the dark panelled walls and a wide mirror gave him a view of the man coming through the front door. He was a wide-eyed German officer who looked terrified but surprisingly determined, and Napier gave himself a short nod.

Time to do it.

There were shouts from upstairs and the sound of running feet both above him and on the stairs directly ahead.

There was an explosion and automatic fire from next door and he swallowed hard. This was very real now and he knew there was no backing down.

A pair of soldiers half-clad in field grey charged down the stairs, one with a Luger in his hand and the other with a rifle.

'What's going on?' yelled the one with the pistol, hooking his suspenders over his shoulder as he came down the last flight.

'I don't know, a fight I think,' Napier shouted back. 'Where is the Pole?'

The man looked at him, realising he was a stranger, but the uniform and fluent German momentarily threw him off.

'Jankowski?' Napier prompted.

'Who are you?'

The man's eyes narrowed and he threw a quick glance at his comrade, who was moving past Napier towards the door.

'Where is he?' Napier said, injecting an authoritative edge into his voice.

The man started to look behind him then focussed back on Napier. 'I don't know...'

He was cut off by a short burst of fire as Napier pumped rounds into his gut. The man grunted and fell backwards, firing an involuntary round into the mirror and causing it to explode into a thousand pieces. The other soldier whirled, trying to bring his rifle around, but Napier nailed him with a loose burst, more rounds peppering the open front door than his target.

Barely daring to breathe, Napier bolted up the stairs, knowing the element of surprise was now gone. A fat older man in uniform trousers and an undershirt, his greying hair mussed up from bed, appeared at the top of the stairs.

'Herr Commandant?'

'Yes? Who are you? What is going on?'

'We are under attack, sir.' Napier bounded up the stairs to him. 'I've been sent to secure you and Herr Jankowski.' He cast a quick look around, seeing three rooms off the top floor landing. A hallway extended off to his right and there were another couple of doors off that. Four of the five doors were closed.

'Where is Herr Jankowski, sir? I must make you safe. We have no time.'

The Commandant gestured down the hallway behind him.

'His bedroom is down there, but I don't see...'

The barrel of the MP40 poked into his soft belly, just below his navel.

'Call him to come out, Herr Commandant,' Napier said softly, his voice colder and calmer than he'd ever heard it.

'What? What is the meaning of this?' The Commandant looked down indignantly at the barrel of the weapon, then into Napier's eyes. Realisation hit him like a sucker punch. 'You...you are...'

'Yes,' Napier whispered urgently. 'Now call him out or I'll kill you right now.'

The Commandant craned his head to call over his shoulder.

'Jankowski! Jankowski, come out. We have to go!'

More gunfire sounded from next door, then a pair of almost-simultaneous grenade explosions. The Commandant visibly flinched and Napier pushed the barrel harder into his guts.

'*Schnell!*' the Commandant almost shrieked. 'Karol!'

A door crashed open downstairs and someone came running up the stairs. Napier stepped to the side, turning quickly. A black-clad SS member was racing up with an Erma machine pistol in his hands. The Commandant saw his opportunity and grabbed for Napier's MP40.

Napier instinctively squeezed the trigger and the Commandant screamed and jerked as he was opened up by a dozen rounds. The SS man looked up, realising what had happened, and started to bring his Erma up. He was on the half-way landing, barely ten feet from Napier.

The Erma fired, chattering loudly as rounds flew past Napier. The pilot shoved the dying Commandant away and turned, bringing the MP40 to bear.

The SS man got his Erma on line and fired again.

56

Hastings hit the floor hard, landing on his shoulder and sliding half under the bed.

The two grenades exploded behind him, slashing shrapnel through everything in sight and sending a double concussion blast rolling into the room.

Completely deafened, he rolled to his knees, coughing at the smoke and dust from the blasts. He couldn't hear any shots but he saw pieces of the door and frame getting blown off as rounds came. He couldn't feel any injuries from the grenades, at least not yet.

A soldier burst through the doorway, keeping low and leading with a spray of fire from an MP40.

Hastings snatched the Browning from his hip in one smooth movement, thumbing the safety off as the pistol came up. He fired four fast shots one-handed, nailing the man with the last bullet. The guy dropped to the ground and Hastings shifted his aim to the doorway, waiting for the back-up to arrive.

A second man was almost into the room before Hastings shot him, two rounds in the side that knocked him sideways against the wall. He turned towards his attacker, staggering sideways across the front window, and Hastings shot him again. The soldier crashed back into the window, shattering it and slumping there, stuck in the frame.

Hastings dropped the Browning at his feet and quickly slammed a magazine onto the Sten. He cocked it then reloaded the MP40 as well, ready to go. He holstered the Browning again and crept forward, the complete deafness in his ears slowly being replaced by a loud, foggy ringing.

He didn't know how many more men were in the house, but he had to get next door to help Napier. Risking a peek around the doorframe brought a barrage of fire from the stairs and he pulled back, bullets and splinters flying everywhere. He wiped at his right cheek where he could blood running down into his collar. The wound stung but there was nothing he could do about it just now.

There was a shout then suddenly the wall above took heavy fire, burst after burst punching through and showering him with dust and more splinters.

Crawling forward, Hastings grabbed the first soldier by the arm. The guy was in a pool of blood but still alive, and he looked at Hastings with terrified eyes. Hastings ignored him and hauled him to his feet, ignoring the bullets still smashing through the wall and the weak attempt at resistance.

Hustling the guy to the doorway, Hastings grabbed him by the belt and the back of his collar and propelled him out into the entranceway.

Automatic fire erupted and the wounded soldier took numerous hits from his comrades as he fell to the floor. Hastings swept into the doorway with the MP40 up, opening fire on the stairway. Two SS men there with Erma machine pistols were still firing on their fallen friend, and Hastings raked them with a long burst, blasting both of them.

Behind them was an officer with an MP40 who immediately returned fire, but Hastings was faster. The officer was smashed backwards into the wall and he sent his own rounds up the stairs into his own men. One tumbled down the stairs to land at his feet and someone else screamed.

Not waiting to see what happened, Hastings raced onto the bottom flight of stairs and cut loose with the MP40, emptying the magazine in four short bursts into the shadows up the top. Someone grunted and fell and shouts sounded.

Dropping the MP40 on its sling and grabbing the Sten forward, Hastings charged onto the half-way landing.

57

The Erma opened up and blasted holes in the wall beside Napier's shoulder, causing him to flinch and step away while firing his own weapon.

The SS man ducked and started up the stairs, firing again. Napier side stepped, firing, tripped over the Commandant's foot and stumbled, firing another long burst, falling to one knee. The SS man pumped rounds past him and Napier traded bursts with him as the man came ever closer.

The Erma fired one last burst that shred the air past Napier's head, then fell silent. Napier squeezed the trigger and the MP40 put a single round through the SS man's sleeve, ripping a pair of holes but missing his arm altogether.

The two men stared at each other for a second, neither able to believe they'd missed with an entire magazine at almost point-blank range. Then the SS man leaped up the last few steps, snarling out some kind of battle cry as he charged.

Napier came up from his knee at full speed, bringing a thundering uppercut with him. It caught the SS soldier under the chin and snapped his head back, his eyes rolling back in his skull as he stopped dead and wobbled on his feet. He toppled sideways into the top balustrade, over balanced and went over the side, his jackboots swinging towards the ceiling as he upended and plummeted.

There was a loud thump as he hit the bottom stairs, bounced and lay still.

With trembling hands, Napier changed magazines on the MP40. He chambered a round and checked the Commandant on the floor. His front was a mass of red and he was staring at the ceiling with sightless eyes.

'*Achtung, Herr Jankowski!*' Napier shouted. '*Schnell!*'

He paused, listening as well as he could with ringing ears. There was no answering call and no hint of movement. Napier took a breath and let it out slowly. The bastard was here somewhere – he was going to have to go and get him.

58

Aside from a dead soldier the top landing looked to be clear, but Hastings was taking no chances. There had to be at least one more guy up there, and whoever it was knew he was there.

He plucked a grenade from his belt kit, realising it was his last one. He placed it at his feet and quickly reloaded the MP40 – down to only one spare magazine for that, too. He checked the angles above him, seeing one closed door off to the right and a hallway to the left. With no lights on and smoke and dust hanging in the air, it was like trying to see through fog. He'd have to take his chances and make an educated guess.

Weapons ready, he primed the grenade. He took two long paces upstairs and tossed the grenade around the corner into the hallway. Swivelling, he booted open the closed door behind him and sprayed a burst into the bedroom beyond it. An SS man in full black uniform was kneeling in there with a Luger aimed at the door. He got off a single round that tweaked Hastings' flapping greatcoat, before a bullet took off his jaw and dropped him.

The grenade exploded and a grey cloud billowed down the hallway. Hastings gave the wounded SS man a short burst in the chest and turned his attention to the hallway, where he could hear someone moaning.

Moving in a crouch, he pumped two bursts into the smoke cloud and advanced. A door was swinging open to his left and he peeked around it, seeing a dazed black-shirt leaning against the wall and shaking his head. He saw Hastings but gave no sign of comprehension. Hastings dropped him with a burst and cleared the rest of the room – no other threats.

The door across the hall was hanging off its hinges and he could see the room was empty. Straight ahead was the last door, and it was closed. Hastings stayed in the doorway where he was and fired a burst into the door, blowing out the locking mechanism. It swung open and he could see a sink against the far wall, shattered by his bullets and leaking water onto the floor.

There was a smear of blood on the floor.

'*Kaput!*' Hastings shouted, one of the few German words he knew.

There was no response.

He could see that the bathroom opened off to the right. He crabbed forward carefully, the floorboards creaking beneath his weight. Reaching the doorway, he could hear laboured breathing beyond it. He eased the barrel of the MP40 around the frame and was rewarded with the pop of a small-calibre pistol.

Hastings angled the MP40 as far as he could without exposing himself and awkwardly squeezed the trigger. The submachine gun jumped in his hands and he heard bullets pinging off metal. There was a grunt and a sliding sound, and he pushed himself forward, getting through the doorway on his side and giving another burst into the dead space to his right.

A soldier dressed only in his underwear was slumped in the bath against the wall, shaving soap still on his face. He had taken hits in the chest and was staring blankly at Hastings. His chest rattled wetly as he struggled to breathe.

Hastings pushed up to his feet and gave him a single shot in the head. He turned and hurried down the hallway. He needed to get next door and help Napier.

———

The Commandant had indicated down the hallway when Napier had asked for Jankowski, so he moved in that direction.

The hallway was dark and both doors there were closed. One was straight ahead, the other to the left. Napier let the MP40 hang from its strap and drew the Browning instead, figuring it would be easier to use in such close quarters.

He tried the handle of the door to his left, stepping back as it swung open. It was a bathroom – sink, bath, a wet towel on the floor. No one there. Focussing on the door dead ahead, Napier trod as softly as he could.

'Herr Jankowski?' he called out. 'I have been sent to pick you up, we must move quickly.'

There was the sound of movement in the room ahead of him, and he thought he heard the click of a pistol being cocked.

'Herr Jankowski?'

'Who are you?' came the reply, a little shaky but trying to hide it by being loud. 'Who has sent you and where are we going?'

A siren began wailing from somewhere within the town, no doubt alerting more troops. This was not going as well as they had hoped. He could still hear shooting from next door.

'Leutnant Wagner,' Napier called out, throwing up the first German surname he could think of. 'We are under attack and I must get you to safety. Please come now.'

'Who sent you?'

'Oberstleutnant Dieter Bern sent me. Hurry up, we need to go now.'

Herr Dieter Bern had been his mathematics teacher at school, a man who made his dislike for young Frederick Balfour-Napier very apparent to all. Napier had no hesitation in throwing his name out there.

He didn't know the German Army ranks, but he knew an Oberstleutnant was equivalent to a Wing Commander, making him superior to Squadron Leader Jankowski, and therefore hopefully important enough to make the man come out. Napier had no desire to charge through the door into the unknown.

There was the sound of movement again and he heard the door handle rattle. The door cracked open and a pistol barrel appeared. Above it one eye was visible. Napier instinctively ducked his head, hoping the peak of the cap was enough to disguise him in the dark hallway.

The door opened further and he stepped forward, seeing Jankowski's face through the gap now. As they made eye contact, the Pole's face registered shock and he stepped back fast. The pistol cracked and Napier felt the rush of wind past his head, opening fire at the same time. Jankowski cried out and Napier barged into the room, shouldering the door open.

The Polish Squadron Leader was dressed in civilian trousers and shirt, the right sleeve of the white shirt now bloodied from the wounded hand he was cradling. He backed up to the wall, watching Napier as he stepped inside. His revolver lay on the floor.

The Browning was levelled at the Pole and Napier was breathing fast and shallow.

'So you have been sent to kill me, huh?' Jankowski said in heavily accented but flawless English. 'Is that what it has come to?'

'Exactly,' Napier snapped. 'And it's more than you deserve, you traitorous bastard.'

Jankowski gave a nonchalant shrug.

'So you say,' he said. 'There are many who would not agree. There are many who would call me a hero more than a traitor.'

'A hero?' Napier almost spat the words out. 'The hero who betrayed his fellow pilots and got them killed? Betrayed his family?'

Jankowski gave the shrug again.

'It is war...Balfour-Napier, isn't it? A member of the landed gentry, the great English upper-class?' He smirked. 'In war many bad things happen. For some, it is an opportunity.'

Napier's throat was tight as he stared at the traitor.

'An opportunity? To do what? Have innocent people killed?'

'There are no innocent people in war, you fool.' For the first time

Jankowski had some passion in his voice. 'There are just winners and losers.' He locked eyes with Napier. 'I decided I would be a winner... and here I am. A valued member of the Fuhrer's mighty Third Reich.'

'Feeding them intelligence against men who put their lives on the line for you,' Napier retorted hotly. 'Men who held you up as a hero, someone they would follow into battle.'

Again the nonchalant shrug.

'More fool them. I never asked to be put on a pedestal. I only ever wanted to survive, and the best way to do that was to look after myself. Nobody else would do it for me, that much was obvious. My country collapsed and the British let it happen. I fought...I fought hard, I took lives and nearly lost mine more times than I can remember. Yet when I am shot down, nobody comes for me.'

Napier scowled, his head aching, barely able to believe the self-righteous pity pouring from the man's mouth.

'Nobody came for any of us,' he snarled. 'That's not how it works, you ignorant bloody sod. You're on your own and you do what you can to get back to the lines and get up there to fight again. You don't sell out to the enemy!'

'But I didn't sell out.' Jankowski gave that smug smirk again, and Napier wanted desperately to wipe it off his face. 'I'm not a Nazi, nor am I a Communist. I am just me; one man on his own. As I said to you, I am doing what I need to do to survive.'

'So you're playing the Nazis as well?' Napier stared at him incredulously. 'Are you insane, man? You've had your family killed just to save your own skin.'

'It's the only skin I have,' Jankowski said coolly. 'If I don't save it, who will?'

Napier raised the Browning directly at his face.

'You bloody back-stabbing bastard,' he rasped. 'I can't believe I trusted you. Those poor buggers that fought with us...they trusted you with their lives.'

'I never asked them to.'

The revulsion in Napier's gut threatened to spill over. He wanted to be sick, to purge himself of the poison he was hearing. It astounded him that he'd been fooled by such a man.

'You can't kill me,' Jankowski said, full of confidence. 'I'm unarmed. You're an officer – a British gentleman. You can't execute an unarmed man.' He raised his hands, smirking. 'I surrender. I'm now your prisoner of war.'

Napier's gun hand was trembling ever so slightly, and his vision had narrowed down to a thin tunnel, Jankowski's face all he could see.

'I surrender,' Jankowski said, holding Napier's gaze. 'Take me back to jolly old England and I'll tell them all I know.' He inclined his head, a cocky tinge of superiority in his tone now. 'I'm a very valuable asset, you know.'

He eased his hands down and took a breath. Tilting his chin up, he gazed at Napier, his pursed lips betraying the slightest hint of a sneer.

The air seemed to have been sucked out of the room. A momentary image of young Leo going down flashed across Napier's vision. Brave Carla, the girl spy. Napier swallowed hard.

'Too late,' he said, and fired.

The bullet punched through Jankowski's forehead and there was a wet splat on the wall behind him. The bullet wound released a trickle of red down his forehead, and he slowly toppled forward.

Napier stepped aside and let the body crash to the floor. He stood over it, looking down at it. He felt nothing but the pounding of his own heart.

'This is for the blokes you betrayed,' he said quietly.

He fired again and the body jumped.

'Well that fucked him,' came a voice from the doorway.

59

Napier snapped the Browning up in surprise, lowering it immediately when he recognised Hastings.

'It's more than the traitorous bastard deserved,' he said. 'He should've hanged for what he did.'

'We need to go, there's Jerries everywhere,' Hastings said. He looked at Jankowski's body again, then back to Napier. 'That's definitely him?'

'Absolutely sure.' Napier gave a firm nod and holstered his Browning. 'That's the prick.'

'Good work. Let's go.'

They headed down the hall to the top of the stairs, but when they got there a squad of soldiers were pouring through the front door. A sergeant was at the door, waving troops in.

'*Achtung! Schnell!*' he bellowed, and they could hear more running boots outside.

He glanced up and saw the two men at the top of the stairs. His expression changed and he swung his MP35 up, shouting something else that Hastings didn't understand. The MP35 submachine gun opened up, raking the floor and balustrade in front of the two men, who leaped back down the hallway.

They reached Jankowski's room and Hastings slammed the door. He dragged the bed across it, flipping it up on its side for whatever protection it might afford. Napier glanced down at Jankowski's corpse then looked quickly away.

'The window,' Hastings said.

He threw it open, looking out onto a sloped tiled roof that dropped to a small courtyard. Behind the courtyard was a service lane, and he couldn't see any soldiers there yet. He was about to climb out when Napier grabbed his arm.

'Your coat,' he said, already shrugging out of his own greatcoat. 'Ditch it – that bloke was telling his men "The men in the greatcoats". We need to look like them.'

They quickly shed the heavy coats and Hastings led the way out the window. Already there was movement in the hallway beyond the door. He slid on his heels down the tiles and dropped over the lip, rolling when he hit the ground below. He looked up and gestured for Napier to hurry up.

The tiles were slippery and Napier's boots slid faster than he had hoped. He tumbled over the edge with all the grace of a new born colt and hit the ground with a thump. Hastings grabbed his arm and dragged him to his feet.

'Stop faffing about, nancy-boy.'

They hit the service lane and turned left, racing down it. There was a shout behind them and they spun, seeing a squad of soldiers entering the lane from the other end, maybe thirty yards away.

Napier didn't hesitate.

'Take the back door,' he shouted, gesturing towards the Commandant's house. 'We will circle around.'

'Yes sir.'

The NCO in charge led his men into the rear courtyard and the two intruders darted out of the service lane and went right into a side road. The siren was still wailing, but they couldn't hear any more shooting. Things had presumably calmed down, which wasn't good – it meant that a ground search would quickly start for the enemy who had killed their Commandant.

Slowing to a walk, Hastings took a deep breath and got his thoughts together.

'Job done,' he said, 'at least the first part. Now we need to find some wheels, find Carla, and get to the airfield so we can get the hell out of here.'

'I suppose there'll be Jerries all over the car,' Napier said. 'So we'll need to find something else.'

'And ditch these.' Hastings unslung his Sten. 'They make us look different.'

He took Napier's weapon as well and shoved them under a bush at the side of the road. It was a residential street and hopefully nobody would be doing any gardening in a hurry. He couldn't see any residents up and about yet.

'What've you got left?' Hastings checked his own kit – only one spare magazine for the MP40, the Welrod was almost empty and his Browning was half full and also had both spare magazines. He had no grenades left.

'I'm almost out,' Napier said. 'One spare magazine for this' – he tapped the MP40 – 'and I only fired a couple of shots from my pistol. Oh, and the grenades.'

He had four stick grenades, so Hastings took two of them and slipped them onto his belt.

'Come on,' Hastings said. 'You lead the way and we'll try and bluff our way out now – we don't have enough ammo to take on the whole garrison. But if it all goes tits-up we just go for gold, right?'

'Right.' Napier nodded, and Hastings stared at him for a moment.

The pilot seemed somehow calmer now, as if he'd crossed a hurdle. Hastings knew it was probably the fact of his first up-close and personal contact with the enemy. It changed a man in ways he could never describe.

'Hey.' Hastings paused a moment. 'You did good back there.'

Napier nodded, then gave a grin. 'Don't get all soft on me, nancy-boy,' he said.

Hastings grinned too. 'Come on, let's go.'

60

Reaching the road, they saw soldiers everywhere.

Split up into teams, they were searching properties and standing guard at all the junctions. Everyone was alert and orders were being shouted with typical urgent efficiency. A huddle of officers were standing by the Horch, deep in conversation. The Commandant's house was the focus of activity, with medics running in and out, while the SS house was billowing smoke from an upper window. They saw soldiers ferrying buckets of water into the house.

'Must've been all my grenades,' Hastings chuckled. 'Serve the bastards right.'

'This way,' Napier muttered.

He turned right, heading away from the scene of death. They walked purposefully to the next junction, where a fat young private stood watch. Napier returned his salute as they went past and the young private watched them as they crossed the road.

Taking the first turn, they reached a quiet side street, home to a clutch of business premises and houses, including the dormitory where Carla lived. The alleyway should be just past the dorm, but they saw immediately that they were never going to get to it.

Outside the dormitory building, fifty yards to their left, was a staff car and a pair of motorcycles with sidecars. A handful of black-clad SS men were standing on the footpath, watching as a girl was hustled out the door towards the car.

Another girl was also there, this one fat with mousy-brown hair in a bun, wearing sensible shoes and a maid's uniform. As they watched, the fat one spat at the dark one, who turned away. Beneath the long loose hair hanging over her face, they both recognised their contact.

'Carla,' Napier muttered, taking a step in that direction.

Hastings stopped him with a hand on his arm.

'We can't do anything for her,' he hissed. 'We need to get going.'

One of the SS men laughed and the fat girl laughed with him, looking from one to another as if seeking approval.

Carla was bundled into the car and the door was slammed behind her. She immediately pushed it open and one of the SS men stepped forward. He leaned into the car and punched her hard in the face.

'You filthy bastard,' Napier growled.

Before Hastings could stop him, he was striding down the footpath towards the huddle of black-shirts. He counted five enemy, possibly more inside. One behind the wheel of the car. One of the sidecars had a machine gun mounted on it – they needed to keep the SS men away from that.

'Oh, bollocks.' Hastings fell in behind him, flicking the safety off the MP40 as he did so.

Adopting his most pompous officer persona, Napier called out to the SS men, who turned to watch them approach.

'What is the meaning of this?' he demanded, gesturing towards the girl in the back of the car. 'Captain, what are you doing with this girl?'

The leader of the SS squad, a fox-faced *Hauptmann* with acne scars on his cheeks, squinted at the *Leutnant* coming towards him. He was the one who had punched Carla, and Napier locked onto him.

'It is none of your business what is going on here, *Leutnant*,' he sneered. 'And who do you think you are, addressing me like that?' He pulled himself up to his full height. 'Do you always speak to the Waffen-SS like this, or are you mentally challenged?'

That brought chuckles from his squad, who had begun to fan out behind him. They all carried the arrogant, superior demeanour that their division was famous for.

Napier finally reached them and fronted the Hauptmann from a few feet away.

'On the contrary, my dear sir,' Napier said coolly. 'It is not I who is mentally challenged. Allow me to introduce myself; I am Leutnant Eichmann.' He narrowed his gaze. 'Does this name mean anything to you, Hauptmann?'

The Captain hesitated. Of course he knew of Adolf Eichmann, one of the leaders of the feared Gestapo. But he also had his men with him, and he was not interested in being shown up by a young upstart subaltern.

'Your family name changes nothing for me,' he said carefully. 'This woman is an enemy spy and is being taken in for questioning.' His superior sneer returned and he stared down his nose at Napier. 'In fact, she is being taken personally by one of our finest officers.'

Napier hadn't expected that. Raising an eyebrow, he said, 'And who might that be?'

'Major Wolf.'

The driver's window of the staff car wound down, and Napier turned to meet the coldest eyes he'd ever seen. As pale blue as shards of ice, they bore straight through his skull, sending an involuntary chill straight down his spine.

Napier couldn't avoid a double-take. 'Major Wolf?'

'That is correct.' The Major's eyes narrowed and he ran his gaze up and down Napier again. 'You seem rather dishevelled, Leutnant. Where have you just come from?'

Hastings watched the other four SS blokes as Napier and the two officers spoke. They were watching him just as closely and weren't subtle about it. Whether it was the natural rivalry between different units or something else, he wasn't sure. Either way, they were bad news.

'We were at the Commandant's house when the attack happened just now,' Napier said, 'but I'd still like to know...'

The Captain sniffed, leaned closer, and sniffed again. It suddenly dawned on Napier that he and Hastings must reek of cordite, and there was no hiding it. He reflexively pulled back from the other officer, but it was too late.

Suspicion turned to realisation in the blink of an eye and the Captain opened his mouth to shout a warning, at the same time reaching for his holstered pistol.

The men behind him reacted fast, snatching at their own weapons, but Hastings was faster. He fired from the hip, pinning the trigger back and sweeping the barrel of the MP40 from left to right and back again.

All four men were hit in the initial long burst of fire, none of them even getting a weapon to bear before they were cut down. The chatter of the submachine gun echoed loudly off the buildings in the narrow street. One German managed to stay on his feet, struggling to draw a pistol, and Hastings hosed the MP40 back for a second burst, blasting him off his feet.

The Captain hurled himself at Napier, grabbing him by the throat with both hands. Napier staggered back and went down hard, the Nazi on top of him. He dug in with his thumbs and was choking the RAF pilot when suddenly he jerked upwards and went rigid. He let out a gasp and released Napier's throat, trying to turn and see what had happened.

Hastings stood over him, the Fairbairn-Sykes dagger buried up to the hilt in the man's side. Hastings hauled him off Napier and withdrew the knife, then stabbed him again, ramming the blade deep under the man's ribs.

An engine revved and tyres squealed and the staff car took off, peeling away from the scene. Hastings helped Napier to his feet, both men ducking instinctively as a shot sounded.

They spun to see the fat girl holding the pistol she'd taken from one of the dead SS men.

'You are the Englanders,' she spat, holding the pistol out in a trembling hand. 'You are the English spies.'

'You betrayed that girl,' Napier replied in German, staring at the wobbly barrel of the pistol. She was only a few yards away and probably wouldn't miss a second time.

61

'She betrayed us,' the fat girl retorted. 'She is a traitor to her country.'

Hastings threw himself to the side and fired from the hip as he went down. The last five rounds in the magazine chewed a line across the fat girl's torso and she dropped in a heap, the pistol clattering to the cobbles.

He rolled to his feet, automatically changing magazines.

'Last one,' he said, working the bolt to chamber a new round.

They both heard running feet, and reality came back with a rush.

'The girl's in that car,' Napier cried, 'let's go.'

Ignoring his natural reaction to just get on with the job, Hastings hurried over to the two motorbikes parked at the side of the road. He climbed aboard the nearest one, a dark green BMW RS750 and kick-started it, the engine roaring to life immediately. The sidecar mounted on the right of the machine had an MG34 secured to the bonnet.

'Get in,' he yelled, spotting troops racing around the corner straight ahead.

They hesitated, clearly unsure what they were seeing, and Napier took the opportunity to reach down and undo the belt kit of one of the SS men. He took it with him and jumped into the sidecar. One of the troops shouted a warning then fired a burst into the air, unsure if he had found the enemy agents or not.

'Shoot the bastards,' Hastings snarled, kicking the bike into gear and tearing after the disappearing Horch staff car.

Napier did as best he could with the bike bumping over the cobbles, and he unleashed a long volley of rounds from his MP40 as they sped past the startled troops. He saw a couple go down but whether they were hit or diving for cover, he wasn't sure. A second later it didn't matter as they were past them and racing up the next street, Hastings throwing the bike around like it was a toy.

Rounds whizzed past them but to no effect.

'Straight ahead,' Napier shouted, shoving the MP40 down into the footwell and turning his attention to the MG34. It had a belt of ammo attached and what felt like a full tin at his feet.

'That one up there?' Hastings shouted back sarcastically, zeroing in on the only car on the street.

The Horch had a good lead on them but the motorbike responded hungrily to Hastings' encouragement. The road surface was slippery from the melting snow and the BMW fishtailed when he opened the throttle, but he was used to handling a bike in all conditions. The cold wind made his eyes water.

They made quick progress and he heard Napier firing a few bursts behind them from his MP40. The staff car swung left at a junction.

'Where's he going?' Napier shouted, his words whipping away in the slipstream.

'That's north,' Hastings shouted back. 'Goes out of town...towards the airfield.'

It didn't make much sense to be heading that way unless the driver figured the town was being hit by a large force and was seeking protection. If so, that meant there was sufficient numbers at the airfield to fight back – it was intelligence they didn't have, but a big problem if it was true.

While Hastings focussed on staying upright and catching up to the car, Napier kept his head on a swivel, looking for threats.

'Oh, by the way,' Napier shouted over the slipstream, pointing towards the car they were chasing, 'that's Major Wolf driving.'

Hastings gave him a look of disbelief.

'Just thought you should know,' Napier shrugged.

Hastings shook his head. 'Typical,' he muttered, and hunched lower over the handlebars.

Reaching the corner that the Horch had taken, Hastings swung wide, steering into the tail slide to keep them on the road. A volley of shots flew close by as soon as they rounded the corner, and he saw a trio of soldiers thirty yards dead ahead, spread out across the road. Their machine pistols were spitting fire and he instinctively ducked. Bullets cracked all around him and he heard the MG34 beside him open up.

The machine gun snarled and immediately knocked down one of the soldiers. One other raced for cover but the third stayed where he was, feet planted in the middle of the road as he fired from the hip.

A bullet pinged off the sidecar and Hastings felt other impacts on the bodywork. The machine gun snarled again then they were on top of him, aiming to cut past. The soldier took several hits and staggered sideways, directly into their path. Hastings swerved but it was too late. The nose of the sidecar collected him across the knees and he collapsed across the machine gun.

Hastings accelerated again, carrying the dying soldier with them. More rounds followed them but they were too far away for any effect, and he threw the bike into a hard right after the disappearing staff car. The German soldier slid across the front of the sidecar and Napier grappled with him, trying to drag him out of the way.

Despite his wounds, the German bravely tried to fight back, clawing at Napier's face with one hand while trying to hold on with the other. His legs were kicking wildly in the air.

Napier punched him in the face and grabbed him by his tunic, yanking him sideways. Realising what he was trying to do, Hastings gave the bike a hard swerve to the left, giving his colleague enough leverage to throw the soldier off the sidecar. He hit the road and bounced across it while the BMW made good its escape.

Coming onto the road out of town, they could see the Horch staff car up ahead, going hell for leather. There was nobody else behind or in front of them and it was obvious now that they were heading towards the airfield. It meant they had only a few minutes at best to stop the car and rescue Carla, if that was even possible.

He knew from studying the map that there was a valley about a mile ahead, with a low bridge across a gorge. From there it was an easy run out to the airfield.

Hastings cranked the throttle harder and leaned into the chase.

62

The back of the car was cramped and Carla had been wedged on the floor behind the front seat, forced down by the car being thrown around corners.

Hauling herself up onto the rear seat, she could see they were out of town and motoring along a country road. She recognised enough of the countryside to guess they were heading for the airfield. They were approaching the narrow one-way bridge across the gorge.

Glancing out the back window she could see a motorbike and sidecar combo close behind them, two German soldiers aboard.

Her heart sank.

Major Wolf glared at her in the rear-view mirror.

'Get on the floor,' he growled.

Not moving, Carla tried to think. Her jaw throbbed where Captain Fischer had hit her, and her body ached.

Her eyes flicked to the rear-view mirror again, where the driver was still glaring at her.

'Get on the floor or I'll fucking shoot you,' he snarled.

Carla had no doubt at all that he would do just that. She also had no intention of being ordered about by this fascist thug. She'd had enough of that, and right now she was heading into captivity, which meant certain death. She would be tortured then executed and, in that instant, she decided she would not let that happen.

'I'd rather die,' she said, and lunged across the back of the seat at him.

With her grabbing at his face and head, the Nazi tried to hold onto the steering wheel with one hand and protect himself with the other. He hit the brakes and Carla was thrown forward, halfway into the front seat.

He threw an elbow into the side of her head and grabbed at her hair while she flailed at him with both hands. She managed to get a hand to his face and raked her nails across his cheek, causing him to shriek and stamp on the brakes again.

Carla was propelled headfirst into the dashboard, bright stars exploding across her vision. The car hit ice and slid, crashing into the brick siding at the start of the bridge. Lights popped and steel crumpled and they came to a jarring stop.

Trapped with her head down, Carla was unable to defend herself against the punches he threw. She raised an arm but it just exposed her ribs, allowing him to deliver a hefty blow that knocked the wind from her lungs.

There was a sudden flurry of activity, a shout and the driver was gone. The car stalled then started rolling forward again. Someone jumped into the seat beside her and Carla got a hand to the dashboard, pushing herself up. Seeing the grey German uniform beside her, she instinctively lashed out but her hand was caught tight.

'Easy, easy,' a soothing voice said.

She looked into the bright blue eyes of the gentleman Allied spy, and felt her heart surge.

'Thank God,' she panted, her ribs hurting with the effort. 'Thank you.'

'Here to help,' he grinned rakishly.

Glancing out the windscreen, Carla saw Major Wolf locked in a hand to hand battle with another man in German uniform. From his build and the fact he was punching the SS driver in the face, she guessed it was the other Allied agent, the rougher one who carried a knife.

63

The Nazi sagged with the last punch, and Hastings let him go to his knees on the roadway.

He stepped back, sucking in a breath, and watched as the other man tried to get to his feet. He caught a flash of silver and spotted the boot dagger in the man's hand at the last second.

The driver lunged and went for a strike to the gut, but Hastings twisted just in time and instead the blade ripped through the fabric at his hip. He felt the sting of a cut but blocked it out, focussing instead on the knife. The Nazi was on his feet now, his nose and lips streaming with blood but he wasn't out of the game.

He feinted with a jab and kicked at Hastings instead, catching him on the thigh. Hastings took it and staggered back, grabbing for the pistol on his hip. Wolf was on him before he could get it, snatching at his tunic and swiping with the short blade.

Hastings blocked the strike with his forearm and hooked the Nazi hard on the ear, knocking him sideways. He booted the man in the guts and grabbed at the dagger, getting his fingers on the hand holding it, but the major jerked his hand away.

The blade sliced across Hastings' fingers and he hissed with the pain. He drove his fist into the guy's throat, making him drop the dagger and forget everything but trying to breathe.

Hastings grabbed Wolf by the front of his tunic, smashed his forehead down onto the guy's nose, and swung him off his feet. Turning and using their combined momentum, Hastings backed into the bridge siding and heaved.

The man was off his feet and unable to stop himself. He was propelled over the top with his arms wind milling desperately. One hand snagged onto the bridge railing and for a long moment he was suspended in a bizarre mid-air handstand. He held there, his arctic blue eyes fixed on Hastings' face in a mix of terror and pure, unadulterated hatred. His legs dropped and swung down, the single hand still clinging on in desperation, and his body slammed against the side of the bridge.

Hastings stepped to the railing and looked down, seeing the rocky gorge far below. There was no way a man could survive that fall. He shifted his gaze to Major Wolf's face, breathing hard. The Nazi's teeth were gritted and he was scrabbling to get his other hand up for a grip. He managed to get it onto one of the steel poles that formed the side of the bridge, and a triumphant sneer broke across his sweaty, bloodied face.

'You can't...kill me...' he panted. His accent was strong but his English was clear.

'Yer reckon?' Hastings smashed his boot into the fingers of the hand clutching the lower stanchion, crushing the bones against the steel and bringing a scream of pain as Wolf let go.

Dangling from one hand, the four fingers locked on top of the railing now a bloodless white, Wolf squinted up at his tormentor.

'You are...a Jew?...filthy Jew.'

It was Hastings' turn to sneer, unable to hide his revulsion for the man. 'No, I'm a fuckin' Kiwi,' he snarled. 'And I like to kill fuckin' Nazis.'

Wolf gave an almost imperceptible nod, then turned his head to look down past his shoulder at the fate that inevitably awaited him.

He returned his gaze back to Hastings. Blood was leaking from a split lip, staining his lips and teeth red.

'A Kiwi…' he panted. 'Filthy…Jew-loving…scum.'

Hastings brought his right hand around and, slowly and deliberately, he drew the blade of the Fairbairn-Sykes dagger across the four white fingers clamped to the bridge railing. The wound opened up down to the bones, wide and vicious and bubbling red, and Wolf's eyes gaped wide with rage as he realised what was happening.

'Go to hell,' Hastings grated, locking eyes with him.

Unable to stop his natural reaction, a scream broke from Major Wolf's bloodied lips as his hand opened and he plunged into the gorge to his death.

Breathing hard, Hastings turned to see Napier and Carla watching from beside the car.

'Oh my God,' Carla breathed. 'You just killed him.'

Hastings sucked in a breath and spat contemptuously. 'Better than he deserved,' he panted. He touched at his side, his hand coming away bloodied.

'You're hurt,' Carla said, hurrying over to check his wound.

'I'm okay,' Hastings said, wiping his hand on his trousers. 'Just a scratch.'

'I can hear vehicles,' Napier said, looking back behind them.

Sure enough, the sound of approaching engines could be heard on the still, early morning air.

'We need to get moving,' Hastings said. He quickly checked the front of the Horch, but it was crumpled and one of the wheel guards was bent down onto the tyre. He turned to Napier. 'Can you drive a motorbike?'

'I've been known to dabble,' Napier grinned. 'I'll drive, you man the gun.'

'Let's go.'

They hurried over to the motorbike, and Napier paused beside it. 'Hang on a sec.' He stripped off his tunic and helped Carla put it on. 'Here, do that up or you'll freeze to death.'

She did as she was asked, giving him a shy smile of appreciation as she wrapped the oversized jacket around herself and did it up.

Hastings covered their backs while Carla climbed on behind Napier, wrapping her arms around his waist. They squeezed past the crashed staff car and Hastings undid the petrol cap of it before sliding into the sidecar as Napier began to accelerate. Hastings twisted in his seat and squeezed off two bursts at the car. The second one ignited the fuel tank, which went up with a low crump.

By the time they got to the other side of the bridge the car was well ablaze and providing an effective, if temporary, barrier behind them.

The countryside whistled past them and Napier handled the BMW well, keeping the speed up and steering smoothly through corners. With a few minutes to spare before they got to the airfield, Hastings got himself sorted. He was desperately short on ammunition so restocked his pouches from the kit that Napier had snaffled back in town.

That done, he turned his attention to the MG34. It was a good, reliable weapon that could throw out up to 900 rounds of 7.92mm Mauser a minute. There was a partially spent 50-round belt attached, and the box at his feet contained another four similar belts.

It was good, but he would have liked more. Nothing he could do about that just now though, so he set about linking the belts together to save time.

There was no spare barrel to change out, which he knew the weapon needed during sustained fire to avoid a jam. Another thing he had no control over, so he'd just need to control his firing as best he could. Seeing the perimeter fence of the airfield as they rounded a sweeping bend, Hastings touched Napier on the leg and signalled him to stop.

'What's the plan?' Napier asked, letting the BMW idle. Without his tunic or greatcoat on the wind was bitingly cold, and the adrenaline was only just holding it at bay.

'There'll be guards at the gate, and they'll probably be expecting us. With any luck though, they'll only be Luftwaffe, so shouldn't be much chop at shooting.' Hastings gave a cheeky grin. 'No offence.'

'None taken.'

'We've got two options; either we go head-on and push our way in, or we try and sneak in.'

Without hesitating, Napier interrupted. 'I say we go head-on. Sneaking in will take too long and we don't know how close behind us they are.'

Hastings gave an approving nod and a grin. 'I was hoping you'd say that. Go straight up to the gate and if we can bluff our way in, all well and good. We'll tell them the girl's a prisoner.'

Carla gave an indifferent shrug. She hadn't let go of Napier's waist yet.

'If there's any resistance, we take them out and just go for it. Head straight for the hangars and find the plane. I'll cover our arses, you fire 'er up and away we go. How's that sound?'

'Sounds pretty decent, old man.' Napier cocked his head and gave Hastings a curious look. 'Back there – I thought you said...you told him you liked to kill Nazis. You said Nazis, not Germans.'

Hastings flicked his eyebrows and tossed his head towards Carla. 'They're not all bad,' he said. 'Just Nazis.'

Napier gave a slow nod as he absorbed this. If he had a thought on it, he kept it to himself. He craned his neck to look at Carla over his shoulder. 'You alright there, love?'

She gave a scared smile. 'I am fine, thank you. Cold, but fine.'

'Alright, chocks away then.'

Napier engaged the gears and accelerated away.

64

The approach to the gates was half a mile long, and it was immediately apparent that they were expected.

Not only were the barriers down, but a truck had been parked across the road inside the gates. Guards were positioned behind the guardhouse and to either side of the road, with a machine gun positioned in the middle of the road in front of the truck.

Squinting against the cold wind, Hastings could see the MG was still being set up. Two soldiers were sorting out ammo belts and getting themselves into position. He needed to nullify that threat first otherwise they'd be shredded before they even got close.

Years of hunting had made him an expert with weapons from a young age. Three years of military service, most of it in combat, was complemented by intensive training in the SAS. Despite the superior numbers of enemy, Hastings was confident he had the edge over the gun crew he was facing. He got the butt of the MG34 into his shoulder and sighted down the long barrel, focussing on the two men now getting down behind their machine gum.

He fired a short burst, putting it too high. The next burst was lower, skewing off the road surface. They were three hundred yards away now and the enemy rifles were starting to crack. He didn't flinch

– too far away unless these guys were sharpshooters. No need to panic. He was closer with his third burst, then the gun crew opened fire.

A long burst sailed far overhead and he felt himself smile. It was hard to hit a moving target, especially when it was firing back at you and travelling at speed. He put a short burst off the road in front of the gun crew, close enough for the gunner to flinch and send his return burst into the sky. Holding his aim as steady as he could, Hastings stroked the trigger and saw impacts off the road surface as he walked a long burst onto his target.

The gunner's mate jerked as he was hit and Hastings shifted his aim slightly left, nailing the gunner with his next rounds.

They were only a hundred yards out now and the rifle fire was getting more accurate. He zeroed in on the guardhouse where he could see a cluster of grey uniforms, and pumped three good bursts into it. Glass shattered and pieces flew off the flimsy hut, and at least one man went down.

The motorbike was slowing down and Hastings swept his barrel right to left across the gates, blasting another gunman and sending others scurrying for cover. Someone doubled towards the stricken gun crew and a burst sent him tumbling.

'Go, go, go!' Hastings bellowed, seeing the enemy in disarray.

Napier revved the bike and they hurtled forward, the MG34 roaring and pouring rounds into the German positions. A submachine gun ripped up the air around them and bullets ricocheted off the front of the sidecar, close enough for Hastings to feel the rush of wind on his skin.

He pumped the trigger, bracing the ammo belt over his left arm so it didn't kink. The submachine gun went silent and he could hear frantic cries now as the troops panicked.

Napier braked hard as they got up to the gates and swerved the handlebars to get around the wooden barrier. It was too close for the machine gun, so Hastings took the opportunity to tug the cord on a grenade and toss it behind him as they cut around the barrier.

Turning in his seat, he awkwardly got to his knees with his MP40.

Troops were getting to their feet now the motorbike was past and he hosed them with rounds. The grenade exploded as the BMW raced away.

65

Straight ahead were structures that looked like admin buildings, with huts beyond that and then hangars adjacent to the small airstrip.

They could see fighters on the tarmac, and men rushing about. One plane was already taxiing down the runway.

'They're taking them up,' Napier shouted, 'trying to save them from attack.'

It made sense – the Jerries didn't know what type of attack they were under, but fighter planes were no use on the ground.

Napier aimed the BMW straight for the hangars, angling away from the troops they could see racing out of the huts, which he guessed were bunkhouses.

Some started firing and he heard the machine gun on the side car open up again. A second later the angle was no good for it and it was immediately replaced by the snarl of a submachine gun. He couldn't help but smile; this was classic Hastings. Any chance for a crack at the enemy was a chance worth taking.

He cut the bike to the left, away from the buildings and onto the tarmac towards the hangars. He counted roughly a dozen planes there, mostly Heinkell HeIII fighter-bombers.

There were also a couple of small civilian craft that he didn't recognise and a pair of the excellent Messerschmitt fe109 fighters. His heart dropped when he realised that the kite that had already got up was a 109, and another one was taxiing down the runway. He had clashed with them many times and knew the 109, although not as nimble as the almighty Spitfire, was a fast and deadly machine.

A handful of pilots and ground crew emerged from the closest hangar, pistols and rifles opening fire towards the speeding motorbike. The machine gun beside him roared again, a series of short bursts cutting into the enemy troops and sending the survivors scrambling back inside for cover.

Napier spotted the Mossie straight away and he could see a pilot running towards it. He raced after him. Obviously the kite was good to go; he just needed to make sure this pilot didn't get airborne. The pilot heard them coming and threw a desperate look over his shoulder at the BMW bearing down on him. He swerved, tripped and tumbled to the ground then they were past him.

Napier slewed the bike to a skidding stop and leaped off. He was racing towards the pilot while Napier was still clambering out of the sidecar. The pilot was almost on his feet when Napier got to him, and he looked up just in time to catch a boot under the chin. He went down on his back, out cold, and Napier started yanking his flight jacket off him.

'Not very gentlemanly,' he muttered, grabbing the flight helmet too. 'Sorry about that, old boy.' He took a second look at the helmet, recognising it as RAF-issue. 'Huh. At least I won't smell like a dirty old Hun.'

The Mossie normally had a crew of two, but today he'd have to both pilot and navigate. As he darted towards the kite, he heard the sidecar's machine gun hammering away. He spun to see Hastings sending bursts of fire into the remaining grounded aircraft, blasting off rotors and rudders and punching holes in the fuselages. One burst into flames then a few seconds later it exploded, scattering shrapnel far and wide and igniting the two planes closest to it.

'Watch our backs, old man,' Napier shouted as he went past. 'Don't let the buggers get us before we get up.'

Working as fast as he could, Napier ran a quick pre-operational check over the plane, making sure they could actually get off the ground. He cleared the chocks away and climbed into the cockpit. Powering it up, he checked that everything was functioning. Fuel, navigation, engines, armaments – all was in order.

It felt good to be in the hot seat again, even if it wasn't his favourite Spitfire.

'Freddie!'

'What, old man?' Napier leaned his head out of the cockpit to hear over the hammering of the guns.

'Do we go or blow?' Hastings' words were almost drowned out by his gunfire.

'What?'

'Do we go or blow?' Hastings paused to throw him a glare. 'Are we going or shall I blow the bastard up?'

'Stand by, old man. Give me one tick.'

'Huh.' Hastings grunted and did a fast magazine change on the MP40. 'Because I've got all the time in the world...'

Napier turned his attention back to the control panel, the training coming back in a rush. He took a breath and focussed. This was not the time to balls things up. He checked the wind sock for the wind direction and scanned the sky for the cloud cover. Within a few seconds he knew what he was doing.

The snarl of an MP40 from behind him let him know that Hastings was still holding off pursuers, but Napier was more concerned about the twin 109's that he could see. One was circling above while the second was now climbing.

'Bollocks to the lot of them,' he muttered to himself, and set about firing up the engines.

With the double Merlin 25s roaring, he shouted to Hastings to get aboard. Grinning, Hastings ran to the Mossie and helped Carla up into the bomb bay. Fortunately it was empty, but it would still be a cold and uncomfortable ride to England. He ripped off his own tunic and unceremoniously tossed it to her before slamming the hatch closed. He had no doubt he was going to be cold in the cockpit, but it would be a hell of a lot better than the bomb bay she was travelling in.

It took a few more seconds to get themselves seated and while Hastings was still buckling himself in, Napier manoeuvred onto the runway. The roar of the engines and the smell of aviation fuel was intoxicating and he felt the familiar buzz of impending battle.

Napier focussed back on the controls, knowing all the pressure was on him now. He got the nose straight into the light breeze and opened the throttles. The Mossie surged forward down the runway and he increased the speed, keeping one eye on the two 109s that he knew were waiting for them up there, circling like birds of prey.

Giving it full throttle, Napier lifted the nose smoothly and they were up, climbing as fast as the kite would allow – it seemed slower than the Spitfires he was used to, but he knew it was just his nerves. The Mossie was faster than the Spit, and this model was supposed to be the fastest yet.

'Enemy, three o'clock,' he called, spotting one of the 109s turning towards them. The fighter was maybe a thousand feet away and two thousand higher, and he knew the pilot would be confident in his ability to take down the heavier fighter-bomber. 'Jack! You see it, old man?'

'Got it,' came back the laconic reply. 'Go get the bastard, mate.'

66

N apier felt his lips settle into a grim line, and he focussed on gaining altitude as fast as he could.

Right now they were extremely vulnerable, and all he could do was get them in the air and avoid the enemy planes as best he could. If they got into a dogfight he was confident in his own abilities, but two on one was always a big ask, especially in an unfamiliar kite with faster, more nimble enemy.

He climbed as fast as he could, keeping his eyes on the two lurking 109s.

All of a sudden one of them wasn't lurking anymore. It dropped from his right and flashed towards him, the second standing off to watch. He had no doubt they had worked out a plan, and only wished he was privy to their radio comms. Even so, their plan was easy to anticipate – attack the Mossie while it was still climbing, stay away from its guns and rip it apart. Napier knew he would have done the same; it was a standard tactic.

But to combat it, he knew his defensive tactics had to be less than conventional. They had superiority of numbers and height, but there was one card he could play. The Alpenbad airfield was not far behind them, and he knew that any airman would be reluctant to put his own base and comrades at risk by engaging in a dogfight above them. If he had to he could use that as a fallback position.

Well, he hoped so, anyway.

The 109's guns had stayed silent so far, and Napier kept climbing. It could only be seconds now. He kept the throttle open, one eye on the approaching 109. The pilot really had some speed up and would be on them in a flash.

'Getting pretty close, mate,' Hastings commented from the rear. Napier was pleased to note that Hastings had figured how to use the R/T already.

'Hold on,' he breathed, still climbing. 'Hold on...'

The 109 closed and its guns opened fire with a test burst. Napier gave a slight jink but kept heading up, drawing the 109 in closer. 300 yards...another burst of fire, closer now...250...200...a solid burst of fire, tracer streaming past the cockpit.

'Now,' Napier snarled, and threw the Mossie into a hard right slip. Had he gone left, the wooden wonder would have been a sitting duck for the 109. Going right meant the 109 had to dive sharply to stay on target, and the pilot fired again, going well wide as the Mossie cut away beneath him.

Napier hauled the Mossie around sharply, banking in a tight right cutback. The 109 flashed past, the pilot's anticipation of an easy kill causing him to overshoot.

The 109 banked left to get away, realising the Mossie had swiftly turned the tables on him, but the Mossie wasn't quite around yet and the move threw the 109 across Napier's path.

He didn't hesitate.

The Hispano cannons roared and he blasted the tail off the 109 in one long burst of 20mm shells. The 109 dropped into a spin and Napier turned away, searching for the other fighter as he climbed again. The other pilot would be up there somewhere, angry now and armed with the knowledge that his opponent had some skills.

'Good shooting, mate,' came Hastings' voice over the radio. 'He's down in flames.'

'Keep your eye out for the other one,' Napier said, checking the control panel. All was well but he knew he needed to keep an eye on the fuel levels. Dogfighting burned a lot and there'd be no chance of topping up before heading for home.

'Got him, four o'clock,' Hastings called out. 'He's above us though.'

'Roger.' Napier twisted to see; sure enough the 109 was probably a thousand feet above them, tracking just below the cloud cover and preparing to strike. 'Keep your eye on him, let me know when he comes for us. I need to get some height.'

He increased the revs and kept the nose up, climbing steadily. It felt odd having a passenger with him, but he trusted Hastings to have his back, even if he wasn't an aviator. They were getting closer and closer to the cloud cover when he heard Hastings' voice.

'Here he comes.'

The 109 came in fast and flat, putting tracer across the Mossie's nose and causing Napier to quickly drop to avoid being hit. The 109 pressed on, closing fast and hosing rounds at them in a constant burst.

'Bastard.' Napier hadn't anticipated such an unusual move and it threw him.

He dropped the Mossie into a left banking move, sweeping easily to keep some distance and hoping the 109 pilot continued firing. He wasn't disappointed and had to jink quickly to avoid the tracer stream, but it told him something valuable; the other pilot was a rookie. Not only had he waited too long and let his enemy get close to the cloud cover instead of using his height advantage to strike, but he was expending too much ammunition on uncertain shots.

'Still behind us,' Hastings said, 'he's on your eight o'clock.'

'Roger.' Napier concentrated on keeping the sweeping turn nice and wide, drawing the 109 closer. He was conscious that he needed to lose this guy and get moving before any more enemy joined in, and time was ticking. There was every chance that flights would be deployed from other bases nearby.

'Getting closer, Freddie.'

Napier noted the use of his first name, and was sure he detected a touch of fear in Hastings' voice.

'Not a problem, old man,' he said with confidence, 'leave it to old Freddie. This is my game. You just sit back and enjoy the flight.'

'Uh-huh.' The Kiwi didn't sound convinced.

He spotted the 109 now, 300 out and closing. He knew that the 109 had a faster rate of climb than the Mossie, but was just slightly slower. In aerial combat the slightest difference could be the deciding factor, and he had been deliberately keeping the Mossie at a steady clip that was fast enough to keep the 109 pilot under pressure but still kept some in reserve.

The 109's cannons let rip again and he saw his chance. He opened the throttles wide, hurtling the Mossie into a tighter turn, angling back towards the 109 but pouring on the speed. The airframe trembled under the near-maximum thrust and Napier prayed it would all hold together.

The 109 pilot was caught out by the unexpected move and it was enough to give Napier the jump. By the time the German had stopped firing and started to turn, the Mossie was at his eight o'clock and the tables were about to turn.

Realising he was in trouble, the German dived into a steep left bank, aiming to slide underneath the Mosquito and shake his attacker. It was a logical move but he had underestimated two things about his opponent; his desperation to escape and his ruthlessness that came from battle experience.

The Mossie shuddered and Hastings was slammed against the side as the machine dived steeply sideways, dropping fast towards the 109. The engines were protesting and the wind was screaming past as they plummeted at an unnatural angle.

67

In the bomb bay beneath them, Carla was thrown bodily from side to side, crashing into walls and unseen parts of the fuselage she had no protection from. At least the two tunics around her afforded some padding, but they also restricted her arm movement and meant she was tossed about like a boat in a tsunami.

Slamming into one side, she could feel herself held there by an invisible hand as the plane dropped from the sky at a terrifying speed. Her stomach rolled at every nano-second and she was scared she was going to throw up. She tried to push off from the side but the invisible forces were too strong and she couldn't move.

In the darkness, she couldn't even tell which wall was the top and which was the bottom – all she could do was try and hold on and pray that it ended soon.

68

N apier heard a muttered curse from his passenger but he leaned into the dive, willing the Mossie to do what he wanted it to do. It was borderline madness to throw such a risky move and he knew there was a decent chance the Mossie could either stall or fall into a spin he couldn't control, but he had to get the 109 off their tail before they could get away.

Inch by inch the 109 crept into his view, all the while both planes were slipping at breakneck speed towards the earth below. Ten o'clock...eleven...a few inches more...Napier's forearms were trembling with the strain but his grip on the stick was rock solid, his trigger finger waiting for just the right moment.

Eleven thirty...a few more inches...the slipstream threatening to tear the plane apart and drop them all into space...a few more inches.

The 109's tail edged into his sights and Napier didn't hesitate.

The 20mm cannons and Browning .303s roared a song of death, ripping into the tail and blasting away the entire tail section. The 109 immediately twisted and began to fall, smoke trailing behind it. Napier instinctively began to ease back, knowing the plane was going down, but immediately an image of Jankowski flashed through his head.

The traitor who had sold out his own family and friends, his brothers in arms. The nation who had adopted him as one of their own. This pilot was one of those who would have played the death cards dealt by Jankowski and was just as responsible as the traitor himself.

His trigger finger tightened and he was about to finish the 109 off when a switch clicked and he eased off on the stick instead, changing direction to sweep away to the right. There was no need to slaughter the man in the air; to do so would be murder of the sort the Jerries had dealt to young Leo over the Channel. He was better than that.

Slicing away and letting the 109 go down in his wake, Napier realised they were almost on the airfield again. Burning aircraft on the tarmac were still pouring smoke into the sky. He could see the troops below letting loose with everything they had – rifles, machine guns, even one bloke down there with a pistol. They were so close he could practically see the whites of their eyes.

Adjusting his aim, Napier lined up the airfield and dived on it, strafing the troops and the sheds with several short bursts. He was over them in a flash and gone, climbing past for the cloud cover that would provide some cover.

'Jesus Christ,' Hastings said from behind him. 'That was something else.'

Napier let out a grim chuckle. 'That's the air war, my friend.'

'I nearly threw up on myself.' There was the hack of a throat being cleared. 'Any chance you could just get us home?'

'Hold onto your hat, old son, we're on our way.'

69

I t wasn't until they were near the French coast that they ran into trouble.

The last several hours had been a flat-out run for home, switching between hugging the treeline and hiding in the clouds. Napier had even thrown in a couple of switchbacks to confuse the Germans that he knew would have spotted them.

He kept their altitude deliberately low for one simple reason, despite knowing it made them easier to spot from the ground – the oxygen tanks were empty. Whoever had serviced the kite back in Alpenbad had overlooked the very simple task of ensuring there was sufficient oxygen that the pilot could breathe at altitude.

Even if there had been air for he and Hastings, he had to remember the unconventional passenger he carried in the bomb bay – not only was she probably knocked out cold from all the moves he'd thrown, but there was no oxygen mask down there for her.

There was no hiding where they were headed for, but so far he had managed to avoid any interceptors. At one stage as he crested a mountaintop he had seen an entire squadron of fighters taking off from an airfield below them and had climbed high, pinning his ears back and gaining distance.

But now, half an hour from home, trouble came calling.

They were hurtling along just above the cloud cover and he could almost smell the salt wind of the Channel, when he caught a glint in his peripheral vision.

A pair of 109s were belting in at his five o'clock, noses down, five hundred out.

'Bollocks.'

Napier dropped the Mossie straight down into the clouds, knowing that where there were two there would be more. He didn't have the fuel or ammo for a sustained fight.

Dropping out of the clouds, his eyes popped when he saw what was below him. A trio of Junkers Ju 88 bombers were heading towards the coast in a diamond formation. To their starboard a flight of 109s stood off as escorts and another flight were ahead and above.

'Oh pissing bloody bollocks.' Napier jerked the stick back up into the clouds, hoping against hope that the fighters hadn't seen them – although with the other two already onto them, it was a moot point.

He quickly relayed the situation to Hastings, getting a grunt in reply.

'Not really ideal is it?'

'Not really. The best I can do is try and avoid them, so hang onto your hat.'

'I hope the girl's okay down the back there,' Hastings commented.

'Either way, we'll know soon enough. Keep on with that radio, will you, old man?'

Hastings had been scanning through the radio channels that Napier could remember, hoping to pick up a friendly voice, but it had so far proved unfruitful. Every squadron operated on a different frequency to avoid overload, and it would be hit and miss as to whether they'd ever make contact.

The cloud ended and they burst into open space, a stream of tracer immediately flashing across the Mosquito's nose as the two 109s dived on them. Napier banked up and right, letting the rounds pass beneath them as he arced back towards the 109s.

One immediately broke away from him to the left but the other one was too slow. He dropped his nose to dive but in the split second that he crossed Napier's gun sights he took a burst through his right wing. Pieces of debris fell from the wing as he dived away, the dive quickly turning into a headlong drop towards the ground.

Napier cut back to the left and raced for the next bank of clouds, plunging into the murk that he knew would provide some temporary breathing space. They were so close now. He had to keep his nerve and think clearly or they'd fall at the last hurdle. They hadn't come this far to fail now.

Edging up above the cloud cover he saw the way was clear so he opened the engines up and gained height, angling away from the bombers and their escort but trying to keep on the bearing he'd set himself. Whether the bombers were trying a daylight raid or targeting shipping was a moot point for him – his problem was the 109s in the immediate area. They knew he was there, they would know he was alone and they'd be very eager to keep him away from their bombers.

Sure enough, seconds later two 109s popped out of the cloud cover behind him and zeroed in on his tail.

'Two behind us,' he told Hastings, 'keep an eye on them for me would you, old man?'

'No worries, mate. How far away are we?'

'Almost at the Channel, so we're almost there.'

'Uh-huh.' Hastings was silent for a moment, then added, 'Don't balls it up now then, eh?'

'I'll do my best...'

Napier climbed for height, the 109s still three hundred yards or so behind them and flying abreast. He could hear Hastings still coolly calling over the R/T in his ear, using Napier's name in the hopes of making contact with any outfits in the area.

The first burst came and Napier climbed harder, banking slightly and throwing a fast jink to avoid another burst of tracer rounds. He dipped suddenly and plunged into the cloud cover, levelled off fast and climbed again, cutting hard right as he emerged back into the light.

The 109s had dived into the clouds after him and by the time he was almost around on himself they were coming up again.

'Brace yourself my old son,' Napier muttered, focussing on the nearest one.

The pilot hadn't seen him yet and Napier hit home with a long burst through the side of his fuselage. The 109 immediately burst into flames and disappeared into the clouds again, the second 109 taking fast evasive action. Napier chased him hard, using his slight height advantage to get a better angle and put a burst past his cockpit before the plane disappeared into the clouds.

Knowing it wouldn't be long before the rest of the escort fighters joined the scrap, he poured on the speed and motored for home.

A long arc of tracer flickered through the sky past his canopy and he pulled the Mossie up sharply, twisting to see what he had behind him. Hastings beat him to it.

'Two of those one-oh-nines,' he said coolly. 'They're coming hard after us.'

'Well that's a bit of a bugger,' Napier said, continuing to climb. The sun was up and he was hoping to use it to his advantage. A thought occurred to him as he held the stick jammed into his gut. 'You know what a Messerschmitt 109 is?'

Hastings grunted. 'Of course. I'm not some dumb foot soldier, y'know.'

More tracer poured past them and Napier slipped to the right, off course but angling into the sun. He jerked the stick back hard and got almost vertical as he hurtled up. He fancied he heard a shout from the bowels of the machine and hoped Carla was okay down there. There wasn't much he could do about it just now, so he focussed on shaking the twin 109 fighters.

They were still on his tail, but his sudden climb had taken them by surprise and they were trying to make up ground. One let loose a burst of fire and both men felt impacts as bullets punched through the fuselage.

'Bloody hell,' Hastings grumbled, 'that was a bit close, mate.'

'Hold on,' Napier grated, 'it's about to get weird.'

He judged that he was about 400 yards or so ahead of the 109s when he pulled the Mosquito over into a backwards loop. The 109s were taken by surprise again and were too close to react. With Hastings' curses ringing in his ears, Napier hurtled the Mossie up and back in an Earth-turning flip. Cranking into line he blasted nose-down straight at the two Messerschmitt's. His guns roared and he hammered a hole through the nose of one of the fighters. It flipped sideways to try and escape the suicidal attack, but in doing so its left wing clipped the right wing of the other 109.

Both fighters veered off and disappeared from sight as Napier hauled on the stick, gradually pulling the Mossie out of the dive but not before he'd punched through the cloud cover. The two 109s were heading straight down, one completely engulfed in flames. No chance for the pilot in that one. The second one was going down too, but the pilot had already got out and was dropping under silk.

The attack formation was still below them, but he could see now that the two escort flights – or the four that remained – had broken away and were racing ahead of the Junkers bombers.

Looking that way, he could see Spitfires swarming towards them, maybe half a squadron of them. Guns were flashing already and he could see it was going to be a hell of a scrap. This close to the British coast there was no way the Jerries would want to turn tail and run, but the RAF lads were having none of it.

Almost immediately one of the Spitfires was hit and spiralled down towards the cold waters of the Channel far below them.

Gritting his teeth, Napier picked out the closest Ju 88 and dived for it. The 109s and Spitfires were into it, diving and wheeling and firing like a pack of angry dogs.

'Get amongst it, Freddie,' Hastings shouted from the rear. 'Give the bastards a taste.'

Napier needed no encouragement. He knew he should just pin his ears back and run for the coast, but his blood was up and he wanted to have a crack. Maybe Hastings was starting to rub off on him. Weaving away from the defensive fire from the Junkers' nearest gunner, he pumped short bursts at the lumbering beast. The gunner was getting close but Napier held his aim and got a good burst into the front of the fuselage before he was past the Junkers and swooping up from below.

A gunner on the next closest bomber spotted the Mosquito and poured fire at them, tracer streaking past them as Napier climbed fast and set his sights on the belly of the beast. He gave it a solid burst straight in the guts and saw the bomber lurch as he instinctively dropped away. The payload in the bowels of those machines were not to be sniffed at and he only hoped he hadn't pushed his luck by getting too close.

A second later his fears were justified when the bomber exploded in a fiery ball and disintegrated, flames and shrapnel and debris blasting out across the sky.

Napier dived, feeling the Mossie buffeted by the blast as he raced away. Hastings' voice cut through his headset as he saw a 109 falling in flames. The pilot managed to eject as he watched and a few moments later the parachute billowed open.

'Any units, this is Flight Lieutenant Balfour-Napier of Number 54 Squadron, does anyone read me, over?'

It had been the same message for the last half hour or so but suddenly, blessedly, they got a response. Napier felt a grin crack his face when he heard British voices through his headset.

'Green Leader, this is Green Two. I'm losing fuel, I may have to pull out, over.'

'Copy that Bill, stick with me for now. Green Leader to the Mosquito pilot, identify yourself.' The voice sounded remarkably familiar.

Someone else cut through. 'Watch your tail, Green Three, I'm coming to help.'

'I see it, Jimmy. If you wouldn't mind, there's a good man.'

Napier saw a Spitfire being chased hard by a 109, twisting and turning desperately to avoid the lead being thrown at him, while a second Spit dived down to help out his mate.

'Green Leader calls the chap who just cut in – identify yourself immediately, over.'

310 | ANGUS MCLEAN

Napier keyed the radio now. 'Green Leader, this is Flight Lieutenant Balfour-Napier of Number 54 Squadron, over.'

The diving Spit smashed the chasing 109 and sent it spinning down. Napier angled away to the edge of the scrap, knowing he was critically low on ammo now.

'Copy that Mr Balfour-Napier,' came the reply. 'Dickie Bird here, old man. We thought you might be turning up some time soon. Get yourself away and leave this to us, over.'

Napier grinned to himself. Good old Dickie – he knew he could rely on him.

'Roger, Dickie, see you in the mess.'

Napier dropped and banked, casting a glance behind him to make sure they were clear before levelling off and pointing his nose towards home. RAF Manston in Kent was not far now and he was increasingly aware of how tired he was. He forced himself to take a breath and relax. The kite was trembling and the controls were feeling looser than they should have, and he focussed on getting them home and down safely.

Glancing down, he noticed the oil pressure had plummeted. He tapped the dial just in case, but experience told him they had a problem.

Sure enough, the gods were in agreement.

The airframe trembled, the left engine coughed and sputtered, and he felt that familiar flutter in his gut. The next second the right engine stopped completely dead and the kite gave a shudder as if a cold chill had run down its spine.

'Oh bollocks,' Napier muttered, checking the left engine. It was lurching along but he knew it was only a matter of time.

'That doesn't sound good,' Hastings said. 'Need a mechanic?'

His effort at banter did nothing to lift Napier's spirits. They were still some miles out from land and with the controls feeling as slack as they did and only one emphysemic engine working, things weren't exactly going according to plan.

Napier eased back on the throttle to reduce the pressure on the engine, hoping he could nurse it along and glide in to the coast. Fingers crossed, they had enough height. He just needed the engine to last another couple of miles and he reckoned they'd be okay. He kept the speed at close to 120mph, knowing that he was in a dicey spot if the second engine cut out. Too fast and they would go into a spin he wouldn't be able to pull out of; too slow and they wouldn't have enough momentum to reach land.

Giving it his best guesstimate, Napier kept her steady at 120 and fired a quick telegram up to St Joseph of Cupertino. Any help just now would go down well.

In that moment, the left engine gave a last wheeze then a sputter, and the airscrew stopped turning. The only sound in the cockpit now was the wind whistling through the tiny gaps in the airframe.

'Well,' Hastings said. 'It's gone awfully quiet up here, Freddie.'

'Bloody bollocks,' Napier muttered, giving the control panel a thump with his fist. 'Come on you mongrel, don't let us down now.'

'How far to go?' Hastings asked, trepidation evident in his voice.

'Only a couple of miles,' Napier lied. 'Easy enough, we'll just glide in.'

He checked the dials again, hoping against hope for some miraculous recovery. The engines, or at least one of them, would spring to life and they'd be home free. Good old St Joe wouldn't let him down now, not so close to home. He'd had such a run of luck all day it couldn't turn now. As images of the day flashed through his mind, Napier realised how lucky they'd really been.

Getting to the airfield had been a miracle in itself, let alone getting airborne, but to fight their way clear and be on the home straight? He actually couldn't believe it himself. How many planes had he shot down? The two over Alpenbad, the four 109s just now plus the Junkers – seven definites. He'd got points on the board with the other Junkers too; hopefully he'd ripped up the cockpit.

Five confirmed kills qualified him as an ace, which he already had to his credit. Five in one go made him an "ace in a day", a much rarer feat. Despite the situation, Napier felt himself smiling.

'By Jove,' he muttered to himself, 'what'll Pa think of that, eh?'

'Think of what?' came Hastings from behind him.

'Oh, nothing. Just thinking out loud.'

'Be better if you just concentrated on getting us down, mate.'

'Righto, old man. Not to worry. We'll be home for tea and cakes before you know it.'

They glided on, the wind whistling through the cracks and the air currents buffeting them as they steadily lost altitude.

'I hope the girl's okay down there,' Napier commented.

'Uh-huh.'

They coasted for a few more minutes before Napier broke the silence again.

'Jack?'

'Yeah?'

'Thanks for looking after me down there, old man. I wouldn't have made it without you.' Napier paused to compose himself – his last effort at saying something heartfelt had fallen flat, and he didn't want to be embarrassed again. 'I'm glad you were there.'

There was a long pause and for a moment he wondered if Hastings had heard him.

'I guess so,' came the eventual reply. 'You did good, Freddie.'

Napier felt himself smile again.

'For a toffy-nosed RAF plonker, anyway.'

Napier grinned to himself. 'Piss off,' he replied. 'You filthy sheep-shagger.'

'I'm serious, mate.' There was an unmistakable sincerity in the voice coming through Napier's headset. 'I'm shitting bricks up here.'

'Really?' Napier couldn't hide his surprise – this was Black Jack Hastings, the fearless desert warrior of the SAS. Men like that didn't get scared.

'Bloody oath. All I want to do is get my hands on a weapon and shoot back. Plus, y'know...you drive this thing like a bloody drunk.'

Napier chuckled. 'Much more fun than tootling about on a motorbike, don't you think?'

'No,' Hastings said firmly. 'I don't.'

The coast came up on them quickly and so did the Spitfires, sweeping in from behind. A couple stayed high as top cover and Dickie Bird settled in to their right, level with their cockpit.

'Alright there, young Freddie?'

Napier threw him a thumbs-up. 'So far, so good,' he said. 'Don't know if we'll make it to Manston, but we're looking...'

At that moment the Mossie dropped like a stone, hitting an air pocket that gave the powerless machine no support.

Hastings swore and Napier instinctively tried to throw the plane into a side slip. The slight movement he managed did nothing to slow their fall and it was a gut-churning few seconds before they lurched again, buffeted and rocked by the air currents rising from below, the Mossie settling again.

Checking the altimeter, he saw they had lost close to a thousand feet. He swallowed hard and pushed the rising panic back down – no time for that now. He needed to get this kite on the ground in one piece, but he knew he had little power over it.

'Sorry about that, old chap,' he said. 'Nearly there.'

With Dickie Bird acting as a spotter, Napier lined up a farm that looked flat enough, maybe a mile or so inland.

'Keep talking me in, Dickie,' he said. 'You've got the height on me.'

'No problem,' came the reply. 'Just lift your nose a tad, Freddie. You're too steep.'

'I can't.' Napier pulled at the stick but it did nothing. 'The controls are too loose and obviously I've got no power.'

'You need to lift,' Dickie insisted. 'At this rate you'll hit the bloody cliffs, man.'

'Well I tell you I've got no control over it,' Napier snapped back, still trying to work the stick. 'It's as loose as a goose, old man.'

'Green Leader from Green Four, we've got company,' cut in another pilot. 'Two 109's dropping in on our six o'clock.'

'Copy that Green Four. Into them lads, follow my lead. Sorry Freddie, you're on your own for now.'

'Roger.' Napier hauled on the stick but it barely even flickered. 'No problem, we'll be fine.'

Sweat was trickling down his head into his collar. The controls were next to useless. He had no power. The only thing to do now was pray. With any luck St Joe was all over it.

Napier concentrated on trying to gauge their distance and angle. They were cruising in at fifty miles an hour now, the speed steadily decreasing as a headwind leaned on them. His eyes flicking between the control panel and the fields he had lined up, Napier mentally crossed his fingers. Barely three hundred feet up as they left the water behind them, he knew it was only seconds until they hit the deck.

'Brace yourself, Jack,' he said as calmly as he could manage. 'The controls are shot and we're in the lap of the gods. Could be a bumpy landing, old man.'

He heard Hastings give a grunt. 'Well the day was shit anyway,' he growled. 'Won't make much difference.'

Napier chuckled despite himself. 'Thanks for the support.'

'I trust you, Freddie,' Hastings said. 'Just do what you can.'

The green was rushing up now and they were rocking and rolling with the air currents. There was a wide farm track up ahead but Napier knew they would never make it. He checked the altimeter – fifty feet. Low rock wall dead ahead – bugger. He heaved on the stick and the Mossie gave the slightest twitch of a response. He trimmed the wings and leaned back as if it would help lift the nose.

Almost down now.

The rock wall was on them and he braced himself for the impact. There was a thump and a tearing screech as the wheels and props were ripped off then they were down, belly-flopping hard on the other side of the wall.

The Mossie bounced and rose another twenty feet in the air, dropping quickly back down with another bone-shuddering thump before plowing into the dirt and grass and lifting sharply at the tail. They skidded to a halt just short of the next stone wall and the tail dropped back down, throwing the two men around like skittles.

As dust and dirt billowed around them, Napier did a rapid self-check. He'd banged his head on impact but it felt like nothing was broken. Blood was tricking down his forehead and he felt like he'd been hit by a car, but he was alive.

The R/T was silent.

'Jack? Jack!'

Silence.

'Jack, you silly bastard! Are you alright?'

There came a groan from behind him, followed by a muttered curse.

'Bugger this for a game of soldiers,' Hastings muttered. 'I've flown twice with you, and both times it turned to shit.'

Napier laughed with relief and set about opening the hood. By the time he'd climbed out onto the wing, Hastings was struggling free of his own harness. He too was battered and bloodied, and he joined Napier on the wing.

'The girl,' Napier said suddenly, remembering their passenger. 'Christ.'

They both jumped down and hurried to the bomb hatch. The bottom of the kite was buckled and splintered from the landing and there were several bullet holes through the fuselage.

There was no way she could have survived. Meeting Hastings' gaze, Napier knew they were both thinking the same thing.

They called her name as they got busy gaining entry, but there was no response. Fear spurred them on and Hastings quickly lost patience. Pushing Napier aside, he lined up the area where a burst of shells had smashed through, weakening the fuselage.

He slammed the heel of his boot into the airframe again and again until it cracked and a small hole appeared. Getting his fingers into the gap, he ripped it open without a care for the damage he was causing to his hands. Making short work of it, he soon forced a gap big enough to see into.

'She's in there,' he panted. 'Not moving though.'

The first thing Carla saw as she came around was sunlight above her. The light framed the face of an angel, gleaming through golden locks as the angel peered anxiously down at her.

His soft blue eyes were filled with concern and she felt her spirit lift when she saw them. He was the handsomest angel she'd ever dreamed of seeing.

He smiled when he realised she was conscious, and she had the feeling she'd met him before. But that was impossible; you didn't meet angels until you had passed over to the afterlife. She could feel a strong hand under her head and soft grass beneath her.

Perhaps she wasn't dead, then. Her head throbbed and her ears were ringing and all she wanted to do was go to sleep. The light was too bright for her eyes to stand but, if she closed them, she was afraid she'd never see the angel with the beautiful eyes again.

She tried hard to stay awake but it was impossible. She closed her eyes and let go.

Saturday morning

'At least two weeks,' Jensen said, easing himself stiffly into the chair behind his desk. 'She's been horribly banged up, got a hell of a concussion apparently. Not that that's stopping the intel bods.'

'What about you, sir?' Napier inquired, plucking a Woodbine from a packet he'd scrounged earlier.

Jensen grunted. 'I'm fine,' he said. 'Nothing a good Scotch won't fix.' He fixed his two visitors with a steely gaze. 'That was a hell of a job you boys did over there, let me tell you.'

They both nodded wordlessly. Both men were dressed in fresh, clean uniforms and bore the scars of their operation – visible bruising and wound dressings, and they both moved gingerly. A night in hospital had meant medical attention, food and water, and a long sleep born of pure exhaustion.

'Of course the Mosquito's banged up to hell, but better that than the Jerries have it.' He crooked a grin. 'I have to say, I never thought you'd actually make it back. It's a bloody miracle.' He shook his grizzled head. 'Bloody miracle.'

'I rather thought it was all down to our talent, sir,' Napier said, coolly blowing a smoke ring.

Jensen eyed him across the desk. 'I'd normally say you were joking, Mr Balfour-Napier,' he said. 'But I'm inclined to agree. Sheer guts and will to succeed. You dared to win, and win you did.'

Hastings flicked his eyebrows but said nothing. He finished rolling a cigarette and fired it up.

'This mission has brought some pretty intense attention from upstairs,' Jensen continued. 'I've been told to tell you two things. Firstly, thank you. That's from the very highest of seats, I might add. The mission was a resounding success in every way.'

'Almost,' Napier muttered. 'Aside from our Lancaster crew, of course.'

Jensen gave a short nod of acknowledgement. 'That's true. We have word that four of them were captured and two are still missing. The others are dead.'

'God rest them,' Napier whispered.

'Indeed.' Jensen puckered his lips for a moment before continuing. 'As for your own actions, you should both be put forward for recognition. It would be a mere formality to have it approved. A Bar to the Distinguished Flying Cross for you, Mr Balfour-Napier. Ace in a day is no mean feat, but under the conditions you were in it's nothing short of spectacular.'

Hastings nodded and finally spoke. 'I second that,' he said.

Napier's cheeks flushed. 'Too kind,' he murmured. He glanced sideways to acknowledge his companion's support but Hastings ignored him, looking expectantly at the man facing them instead.

'And likely a Distinguished Conduct Medal for you, Sergeant Hastings. Without your guts, combat abilities and experience I'd be writing telegrams home to your parents right now.'

Napier grinned and clapped Hastings on the shoulder. 'Good old Jack, eh? Well done, old man.'

Hastings gave a brief nod and dragged on his smoke, a slight smile on his lips. He waited.

'Now I know that neither of you are in this for the glory,' he said.

'So you won't be disappointed to hear there won't be any medals dished out for this operation.'

Hastings' smile got bigger, and he glanced at his companion. Napier was doing his best to cover his surprise and disappointment, and not doing a very good job of it.

Jensen continued. 'This was a significant black eye for the enemy at a time when the country needs it. Not only did we steal back our own plane right from under their noses, but we sent the strongest of messages that treason will not be tolerated. Traitors will be hunted down and executed with extreme prejudice.'

He eyed Hastings through the swirling smoke. 'I imagine you won't have any objections, Sergeant Hastings.'

Hastings picked a flake of tobacco from his lip and flicked it away. He exhaled like a dragon.

'Sure,' he said. 'No complaints from me, sir.'

'Mr Balfour-Napier?' Jensen turned to the airman. 'You seem a little perturbed.'

'I...well, I mean...' Napier struggled to answer without sounding like a moaning ninny. 'It's just that...ace in a day is...you know...'

'Is secret, Flight-Lieutenant,' Jensen said firmly. 'That's how we operate. In the shadows, without fanfare. The more attention we get, the less effective we become.'

'Of course, sir, of course.' Napier's cheeks had gone a shiny pink. 'Totally understand, sir.'

'In the meantime,' Jensen said. 'Our friend Carla is being debriefed in great depth, and the intelligence she's giving is top-notch stuff.'

'What'll happen to her afterwards?' Napier asked.

'She'll be looked after,' Jensen said shortly. 'As for you two, you both need a day or two's rest, I'd dare say.'

The mention of rest made Napier stifle a yawn. 'I wouldn't say no,' he admitted. 'A few days with our feet up would do us good, eh Jack?'

Hastings gave a snort. 'I'm good to go,' he said. 'Sleep when you're dead, mate.'

'Two days,' Jensen said. 'Then you're off to Scotland.'

'I take it you're not sending us on holiday, sir?' Napier said hopefully.

'Anything but, Mr Balfour-Napier. You'll be completing SOE training from the start. Fieldwork, tradecraft, tactics, small arms, parachuting; the works.'

The two men glanced at each other then back at Captain Jensen. The Navy officer's face was blank as he watched their reaction.

'Yes, I realise some of these skills won't be new to you, and yes, I realise you have already completed a mission.'

'Unlike any other,' Napier murmured.

'You may think that, Freddie, but you'd be wrong,' Jensen said firmly. 'This is what we do. There is no room for ego and attitude. You'll start at the bottom like everyone else, and never forget your place. We have some outstandingly brave and brilliant people in our organisation, and as chuffed as you are feeling with yourselves right now, you are but two of them.'

Napier felt his cheeks flush and he smiled apologetically. 'Of course, sir. I didn't mean...'

Jensen pushed back his chair abruptly, the legs scraping loudly on the floor as he got stiffly to his feet. Napier and Hastings sharply followed suit. He thrust out his hand, firmly shaking each in turn.

'Enough talking,' he said. 'Time to crack on. Welcome to the SOE, gentlemen.'

THE END

For more information or other thrilling adventures, jump over to
www.writerangusmclean.com
or grab the latest from Amazon.

And if you enjoyed *Behind Enemy Lines*, please leave a review to let
me know.

AUTHOR'S NOTE

I have long had an ambition to write a thriller set in the Second World War, growing up as I did on a steady diet of Commando comics and Biggles books, Alistair MacLean novels and Boys Own-style tales of daring adventures.

Here is my tip of the hat to the WW2 generation, to the daring souls who fought for the freedoms we still enjoy. Long may those brave men and women be remembered and those freedoms enjoyed, and more fool us if we lose either.

The idea for Napier and Hastings came first, and the names stuck. The story came later, which is typical for me when writing a character-driven story. I liked the idea of a working-class Kiwi soldier paired with an upper-class British pilot, both experts in their own field and thrown into a deadly mission with nobody to rely on but each other.

This book has taken the longest to write of all my tales. Not just because I was held up by the Covid-19 pandemic last year, but also because I wanted to get it right. I wanted an entertaining yarn, one that would grab the reader and take them on the adventure, but I also felt it was very important to show some accurate detail and the true spirit of the men and women sent on these crazy missions.

The Second World War was a time of real ingenuity, and the SOE was home to true mavericks, those who maybe didn't fit in anywhere else but were ideal for the sorts of hare-brained missions they were tasked with.

In terms of research, I read three books in particular, which I highly recommend.

Tom Scott's *Searching for Charlie* is an in-depth piece on the legendary Captain Charles Upham, VC and Bar, the only combat soldier to ever win the highest gallantry medal twice. *Nine Lives* by Alan C Deere is the autobiography of a Spitfire ace who ended the war as New Zealand's second highest-scoring fighter ace.

The third is *SOE 1940-46* by the well-known historian M.R.D. Foot, a handy insight into the set-up and operations of this unit.

All three books were a great inspiration, and you will note that both Upham and Deere were Kiwis. I have taken the liberty of having Hastings originally posted to Upham's 20th Battalion and Napier to Deere's 54 Squadron, as a sly wink to these two legendary warriors.

"Legendary" is a term often misused, as is "brave". These two men, and so many others like them, are exactly that. In a time that idolises reality-TV stars, vacuous "social influencers" and any number of other so-called "legends", "idols" and "stars", it is important to remember those that came before. The real legends, idols and stars.

Long may their memories last, and their legends live on.

Angus McLean
  April 2021

www.ingramcontent.com/pod-product-compliance
Ingram Content Group UK Ltd.
Pitfield, Milton Keynes, MK11 3LW, UK
UKHW021507110325
456069UK00006B/487